Wolf in the Crosshairs

Also by Susan Klaus

The Christian Roberts Thrillers

Secretariat Reborn

Shark Fin Soup

Flight of the Golden Harpy Fantasies

Flight of the Golden Harpy

Flight of the Golden Harpy II, Waylaid

Flight of the Golden Harpy III, Sons of Shail

Wolf in the Crosshairs

A Christian Roberts Thriller

Susan Klaus

CLAY GULLEY Publishing

Myakka City, Florida

Cover by
Wolf Icon in chapter headings "image; Freepick.com"

First Edition hardcopy 2019 ISBN – 978-0-9979064-4-8

Ebook Edition 2019 ISBN – 978-0-9979064-5-5

Second Edition 2021 ISBN – 978-0-9979064-3-1

Clay Gulley Publishing, Myakka City, Fl.

Printed in the United States of America

Dedication

To my grandsons, Will and Christian,

with the hope wild wolves still exist in the future.

Acknowledgements

Chris Klaus for cover art, Jane Crick, cover design. Will Klaus and Scott Miles, computer security information. Sharon Burns, my sister and companion during my research throughout the northwestern US. Kari Klaus for the research in Playa Del Carmen, Mexico. Bobbie Christmas, my editor. Susan Gleason, my literary agent. Chris Hemsworth, actor, surfer, boxer, and ocean and wildlife lover who inspired the character, Christian Roberts. Niche, a gray wolf I once owned. Her beauty and gentleness encouraged me to write the novel about saving these majestic animals that are unfairly demonized.

PROLOGUE

The black wolf stood on a cliff and overlooked the wooded valley. His gold eyes searched the trees below for prey or danger. Tilting his head, he pricked his ears and listened. One ear tip was missing; a proud battle scar earned fighting for dominance in the pack. He heard a puppy whimper and looked behind him to the burrow under a ledge. A few days earlier his mate had given birth to a litter of four, a precious symbol of hope and renewal. The downside to the new additions was his female was confined to the den and couldn't help with the hunt.

He stepped to the lair and sniffed the chilled pup that had strayed to the open crevice and nosed it back to its siblings and their mother's gray fur. He nuzzled his mate's cheek, reconfirming their bond, and returned to his lookout.

His half-grown son approached and displayed the act of greeting and submission. With pinned ears and his wagging tail tucked under, he cowered at his father's feet and rolled on his back to expose his belly. The male growled low to acknowledge the only survivor of the previous year's litter and wondered if the teenager would reach adulthood in two more years.

Unlike their dog cousins, wolves matured slowly and bonded for life. Both parents raised and defended the pups. Further, only the alpha pair, the toughest and wisest in the pack, was allowed to breed and bear offspring. The strict regime ensured that pups inherited the best genes and also prevented overpopulation that might result in starvation during lean times.

The six-year-old male remembered a time of peace and plenty. He and his female had once been the alphas in a strong pack of ten, all blood related. Aunts, uncles, brothers, and sisters worked in unison to bring down moose, elk, buffalo, and deer. They reigned as top predators and were able to defend their meal, even from a grizzly. Death among their kind usually resulted from illness, injury, or old age.

Before the wolves arrived, large bands of coyotes dominated the terrain and devastated the smaller predators and prey, but with the wolf newcomers, most of the coyotes were killed or driven elsewhere. The male witnessed that with fewer coyotes, the wildlife population swelled. Animals long absent in the area returned and flourished. Beavers again built dams, and their ponds produced frogs, fish, and reptiles and attracted flocks of ducks and geese. The increase of mice and rabbits benefitted the fox, weasel and other small marauders, and their numbers grew. With more rodents and fish, bald eagles flew in and once again nested in the trees.

The male's wolf pack also stabilized the overpopulated elk and deer herds. They killed the weak, sick, and old, making the herds stronger, healthier, and less susceptible to winter malnourishment. Fear of wolves also changed the deer behavior. They stayed close to the forests, and stopped feeding in the open meadows. The previously overgrazed lands saw a burst of wildflowers that caused butterflies and humming birds to proliferate. Without deer, tree saplings took root on the eroded riverbanks. The rivers flowed with clear water and generated more trout. His ten wolves had transformed the landscape.

Humans, the strange, two-legged creatures, were not usually a concern, but the wolves instinctively avoided them. In recent years life changed, though. Man became a formidable threat who terrorized and slaughtered the male's pack. One by one his wolves were shot, poisoned, or snared until only two others beside him remained, his mate, and the grayish-tan pup.

The male's worst fears were realized last spring when he and his mate sought game along a riverbed. They heard a noisy flying machine rise over a hill. It hovered above as he and his mate raced for the tree cover. Panicked, they separated. He ducked into a hollow stump, while his frightened mate ran on. He heard a gunshot and dreaded the outcome; too many of his kind had met that fate. After the machine flew away, he left his hiding place and searched frantically for her, pausing only to howl, in the hope that she still lived and heard him. A miracle occurred: she answered to his call. He raced through the forest and found her in a meadow. While joyfully licking and nuzzling her, he noticed the leather strap around her neck and the human odor on her coat, but she appeared unharmed. They yipped, leaped, and charged through the flowers like youngsters.

The pursuit of hunters and fear of losing his family forced the male to abandon his home turf. He led his pregnant mate and their son several hundred miles south. The region seemed promising. He detected no human scent on the trails and saw no vehicles, campsites, or buildings.

The inexperienced pup was more a hindrance than help in a hunt, so the pair preyed on the smaller whitetail deer and sometimes antelope. They lacked the numbers to tackle thousand-pound game such as elk and moose, and moreover, they had become vulnerable. A bear or large pack of coyotes could drive them off a kill. Cougars regarded them as competition and exterminated lone wolves. Another wolf pack defending its territory could tear them to shreds.

The male gazed at the sun sinking behind the mountain ridge. Dusk provided shadow and cover so prey ventured out to feed and drink. He left the ledge and with his son trailing, he trotted toward the stream in the valley. They crept through the pine woods, and the male paused often to sniff the wind, hoping to scent quarry. They hadn't eaten in three days.

On the valley floor his son lapped up water from the gushing stream. The male started to join him, but his keen eyes spotted a quiver of brush along the woods on the opposite bank. He forded the stream and surprised a stag. The mule deer raced to the trees, and the chase was on. He and his son pursued their prey for several miles. The stag finally tired and turned to confront them, fending them off with his antlers as they circled him. His son managed to distract the deer, and his father saw an opening. He leaped and seized the deer's throat while his son stood back, too frightened to aid in the life-and-death struggle. Without the help of second wolf latching onto the deer's hind quarters, the male couldn't bring down an animal three times his weight. He clung to the neck while the mule deer flung him from side to side and used sharp hooves to gash his chest. When an antler stabbed his hip, he yelped and released his hold. Panting, he watched their meal disappear into the undergrowth.

The male had never been a solitary hunter. He would have to adopt a coyote's ways, watch for buzzards circling over a rotting corpse or rely on rabbits, raccoons, and other small game for food. He lay down and licked his bloody wound. His family would go hungry again. But soon all would be well. The new pups would have thick coats, and his female could leave the den and rejoin him in the hunt. He rose and limped toward home. His son jogged alongside, rubbing his head against his face.

CHAPTER ONE

"Jake, I ain't diggin' no hole, when the gator can take care of him."

Jake swatted a thumb-size mosquito off his ear. "Harold, use your dang head. Them gators are apt to leave body parts, and those Chinese boys want him completely disappeared."

Christian Roberts sat on the middle bench in a skiff with his hands bound and listened as his two captors discussed his demise. For the second time in his life, he had been abducted and was being held at gunpoint in the Florida sticks. Unlike before, when he'd been terrified and spiraling toward shock, he was composed and didn't fear the outcome, a testament to the fact that he had changed. He'd become a different man with different values, or the lack of them.

A few hours earlier, a breathtaking golden sunrise filled the sky when he'd stepped out of his double-wide trailer in Lakeport, a tiny town on the northwestern edge of Okeechobee, the largest lake within the US. Six months ago he had purchased the place as a getaway where he could relax without being recognized and spend time with his grandparents. He enjoyed fishing with his grandpa and feasting on his grandmother's southern home cooking. The best part about his grandparents was that they, unlike his mother, didn't pry into his illicit life. Every other weekend, he left his horse farm in Myakka City, and his grandparents departed from Sarasota. Traveling a hundred miles across the state, they rendezvoused at his fish camp. The folks were due in the late afternoon.

He had grabbed a bag of ice, a cane pole, pail of dirt with worms, and a mesh fish basket and strolled to the narrow canal in the backyard. At the end of the small dock, he hopped into his airboat and dumped the ice in a cooler and stowed the fishing gear. He climbed into the boat and settled onto the high seat in front of a large wire cage that protected the driver from the airplane propeller. Firing up the roaring engine, he adjusted the paddles and glided into the canal. The wind from the prop soon had the flat-bottom boat zipping toward the open lake.

The airboat skimmed the surface of a seemingly endless watery horizon as Christian looked down from the high deck and used nonglare sunglasses to search for tell-tale signs of nesting fish. Along the way, he spotted dozens of alligators and turtles plus hundreds of ducks and wading birds, but the most impressive creature was a huge water moccasin coiled in the cattails. The snake's girth was thicker than a man's arm.

After traveling a mile, he finally spotted the white sandy holes that blue gills, speckled perch, and shell-crackers dug out in the grassy bottom to lay and protect their eggs. He cut the engine a good distance away so as not to scare the fish off their nests, and dropped anchor. He took off his white T shirt, and using a cord like a necklace, he hung the worm pail chest-high to keep it dry and fastened the fish basket to a belt loop on his cutoffs. He retrieved the cane pole with its ten feet of line, small bobber, weight, and hook, and he slipped into the clear, hip-deep water. His plan was to catch a half-dozen pan fish for that night's dinner with his grandparents. He waded to the fish beds and flung the baited hook into one of more than twenty holes. Cane pole fishing was child's play, but tomorrow with his grandpa would be serious fishing that involved lures, spinning reels, and precise casting into the water lilies for largemouth bass.

It seemed like a perfect spring morning. The glorious orange and pink dawn mirrored the vast lake and lifted his spirits, and he was surrounded with the wildlife he loved. By nine o'clock, his basket held seven nice-sized shell-crackers, a fish that tasted similar to bass. He started back to his boat and noticed an eight-foot alligator trailing him underwater on the grass floor. The gator wasn't after him, but was obviously attracted to the basket of squirming fish at his side. "Go on; get your own," he said with a smile and poked the animal's leathery head with his pole. It fled, stirring up the translucent water with a cloud of sand.

He had just climbed aboard and placed the fish in the cooler when a banged-up johnboat motored up with two men in tattered shirts and stained jeans. Makeshift buoys of empty milk jugs and Clorox bottles attached to trot lines sat in buckets on the floorboards. The bare hooks conveyed that they had pulled their lines and were heading in. The guys were poor locals who scraped out a living from cat fishing. Not uncommon in Lakeport.

"How'd ya do?" asked the wiry long-haired man operating the rusted outboard. With a scraggly beard and weathered face, he appeared older than his years. His big partner up front was the opposite with a round, clean face and scant crew cut. His weight had the small boat resting several inches below the waterline.

"Caught enough for dinner. How about you?" Whether rich or poor, fishermen practiced a universal custom of chatting about their catch, so Christian was at ease with them.

"Piss-poor night," the man said, shutting down the rumbling motor. "The biggest dang thing on the line was a lousy mud fish."

"Sorry to hear," Christian said, "but those ugly suckers put up a hell of a fight. I've reeled them in believing a big bass was on the line. It's disappointing." He stepped to the front of the airboat to pull the anchor. "Hope you have better luck next time out."

"Our luck is fixin' to change," Jake had said as his big partner, Harold produced a shotgun from under a tarp and with a toothless grin aimed it at Christian.

Christian released the anchor rope and raised his hands. "What do you want, my boat? I don't have much cash on me."

"The only thing we want is you."

The men forced Christian into their boat at gunpoint, tied his wrists behind his back, and debated on what to do with him.

"I say shoot him and plant his body right over there." Jake pointed to an isolated forest on the edge of the lake.

"He's tied," said Harold. "We toss him overboard to drown. Them gators will do the rest."

Amateur hour with Jake and Harold, Christian thought, *Abduction in broad daylight with no plan to pull it off.* The hesitation to kill him immediately also suggested it was their first murder attempt. When stepping into their boat, he had considered fighting back. In a cramped fifteen-foot skiff, a hard, well-placed kick to Harold's face would likely disable him long enough to confiscate the weapon. Jake would be even less of an issue. Instead of resorting to violence and risk being shot, he decided to talk his way out. The good old boys weren't professionals, not terribly bright, and seemed more desperate than evil.

"Fellas, can I make some suggestions?" Christian asked. "I'm not going to drown in this shallow water, and gators favor rotten flesh. My body is likely to be discovered before the reptiles get the job done."

"See, Harold, I told ya so," Jake said.

"Shooting me also isn't feasible." Christian nodded at two bass boats half a mile away. "Sound travels across water, and those boats will hear a gunshot. And it's not duck season so they'll take an interest. That means witnesses."

Jake pulled a foot-long knife out from under the boat bench. "Maybe we'll stab you."

"You can try," Christian said with a lifted eyebrow, "but there's a better solution. Release me, and I'll double whatever the Chinese are paying."

Jake rubbed his scruffy beard. "We're talkin' a hundred grand, mister. Ya look too young to have that kinda dough."

"I've got the money. We can settle this right here and now. Do either of you have a bank account?"

"Got a checkbook in the back pocket," said Jake

Christian glanced toward his airboat. "The compartment next to the seat has my cell phone. I'll contact my bank and have the funds wired into your account. Before we part, you call your bank and make sure the money is there. Simple. You walk away with more money and don't have a death sentence hanging over your head. Another thing you oughta consider, the Chinese wouldn't chance you getting arrested and identifying them. More probable they'll kill you when you come to collect."

"So how do I know I can trust *you*? After we're done, you might call the cops."

"Whatever you've done, Jake, I've done worse, so I don't mess with cops. This is where the trust part comes in. I imagine those Chinese didn't mention why they want me dead."

"Nope," said Jake. "Just said you needed to be gone."

Christian sighed. "I killed dozens of people in China last year when they ate poisoned soup. Now that confession could end me. We have to count on one another to keep our mouths shut. Given my crimes, I have more to lose."

Jake took a long hard look at Christian, and his eyes grew wide in recognition. "Holy mackerel! You're that Florida boy, the terrorist who went on a rampage to save sharks. You were the talk in prison, and I saw you on the news. Harold, untie him. We're doin' things his way."

"That true? You really him?" Harold asked and loosened Christian's bonds.

"I'm him," Christian said with a weighty breath and rubbed his wrists. "I understand why the Chinese hired you. They'd stand out in Lakeport, and I and everyone else would see them coming, but I'm curious. How'd you get involved with them?"

"Ran into those two guys in Moore Haven when selling my fish," said Jake. "They seemed to know I just got paroled and my little girl was sick. I didn't have the money or insurance to help her. They handed me a thousand bucks and promised another forty-nine when I knocked you off. They said you was a tall, good-lookin' dude with blond hair. Told me about your comin's and goin's, and that ya should be on the lake this weekend in a fancy airboat, fishin' near Honey Pond. They also mentioned you might be a handful, and I should bring help. My cousin Harold here, volunteered."

"Sorry about your little girl. That's a tough predicament; my life or your kid's." Christian stepped out of the johnboat into his airboat and retrieved his cell phone from the compartment. Tapping the keys, he asked, "What's your checking account number?"

"No, no, you don't need to pay me."

Christian looked up from his phone and saw worry, not admiration, in Jake's eyes. He learned who Christian was and feared reprisal. Like having nabbed a rattlesnake, the man was trying to let go without getting bit. "A deal's a deal, Jake, and don't be concerned. I'm not interested in you, but for the money, I want information, the time and place of the payoff with these Chinese boys."

Harold grinned. "You plannin' to fuck 'em up?"

"Oh, yeah."

* * *

Christian guided the airboat down the canal toward his trailer, moving slower than when he had left. At the dock he climbed out and tied the boat to a cleat. For several long minutes he stood on the wooden planks with his hands on his hips and stared at the water, but wasn't seeing anything. The incident on the lake played over and over, and he smoldered.

He had completed the transaction with Jake and transferred a hundred grand from his Cayman account into Jake's checking. The only information Jake had on the Chinese was a phone number. To prove that Jake had fulfilled the hit, they staged Christian's murder. Christian smeared fish guts on his T shirt to resemble a gunshot wound and played dead as Jake took a cell phone picture. Jake sent the photo, along with a text asking the where and when of the payoff. In return, the Chinese told Jake to meet them at ten o'clock that night at a spot, outside of Miami.

Christian was familiar with the location, the Everglades Recreational Park on Highway 27, just north of I-75. The highway ran north to south through the center of the state, but the southern portion between South Bay and Miami was forty miles of sparse traffic in the sugarcane fields. Canals flanked both sides of the road, and there were no gas stations or buildings. The park offered a concession stand, a little zoo of Florida wildlife, and airboat rides, but was deserted at night. The desolate highway and park were perfect for snuffing someone out. The two Chinese men expected Jake, but they'd get Christian.

He shook his collar-length locks out of his eyes and breathed deeply. To pull his plan off, he needed to suppress his irritation. He wasn't upset with the Chinese. Although, he was not pleased they wanted him dead, he understood their motive for revenge and didn't take it personally. He was furious with himself. His complacency had put him in this situation. Jake said the Chinese knew his comings and goings. A genius level of intelligence wasn't required to know they'd tracked his movement with the GPS on his cell phone. Before leaving the lake, he removed his phone batteries.

Besides being careless, he also felt foolish. He had dreamed of returning to a normal life, but despite the longing to stay in a dream, eventually he opened his eyes to reality. The lake episode had been a wakeup call. He was Captain Nemo, the ecoterrorist. No getting away from his alias. He needed to get back on track and pick another wildlife cause. First, though, he had to send a message to the Chinese.

He put the cooler of fish on the dock next to a hose and rickety wooden table. He removed the fish heads, guts, and scales and placed them in a bag. In the trailer he set the fish in the refrigerator and took a shower. The soothing water calmed his riled mental state and made him focus. He dressed, checked his wallet for cash, and strolled up the dirt lane to the 7-Eleven a few blocks away on the main road. He purchased a Coke, sandwich, and disposable phone. Back at the trailer he munched on the sandwich and using the burner phone, he placed a call to his grandparents' home in Sarasota.

"Hey, Grandma," he said. "You all fixin' to leave soon?"

"Crissy, your grandfather just spent two hundred dollars at Walmart for a Penn reel. He's puttin' string on the darn thing now. As soon as he's done and the car is loaded, we're leaving, but I'm stopping in Arcadia for zipper peas and such. If they have key limes, I'll make your favorite pie."

"Can't wait for that pie. I left my farm early and am already in Lakeport, but some unexpected business came up. I won't be here when you arrive. The trailer will be unlocked, and fresh shell crackers are in the fridge for your supper. I should be back late tonight."

"Okay, Crissy. Your grandpa will be itching to go in the mornin' so he can use that stupid reel. I told him it won't help catch bigger fish or more.

"Not so sure, Grandma. Penn makes a pretty nice reel. Makes casting more accurate."

"Figured you'd agree with the old fool," she said and abruptly hung up.

He chuckled. His grandmother made no bones about speaking her mind. He considered making a second call to Sal, his middle-aged mob buddy. In New York Sal had nasty dealings in Chinatown and wouldn't hesitate to drive over and take out the Asians. Christian brushed off the notion and put the phone down. The situation was his problem.

From a bedroom closet he removed a box holding a nine-millimeter and pack of bullets. He had bought the weapon at an indoor gun range at Sal's insistence. Sal had said Christian's newly acquired trailer was in the heart of redneck country alongside a reservation of pissed-off Seminoles. He needed the added insurance. Christian went along and purchased the handgun for the trailer, but believed he'd never use it.

"Good ol' Sal," he mumbled when loading the clip. He heard a rap at the door and tucked the weapon into the back band of his jeans, covering it with his shirt. He opened the door to Jake's wide grin. In the front yard an old Chevy pickup was parked on the lane.

"Hey, ya, Mr. Roberts. Wow, you sure gotta a super nice trailer."

"Come in, Jake. Wanna drink?"

"Nah, I'm good. I'm here 'cause I got to thinkin' you might need help tonight. They see me and my truck, and they'll come out smilin'."

They sat down on the couch, and Christian turned to Jake. "Appreciate the offer, but I think I can handle it."

"Mr. Roberts, I ain't a smart man or even a good one, but I do have principles. That money you gave me will save my girl's life. I need to earn it."

The added backup couldn't hurt. "Okay, we'll do it."

At ten at night in the recreational park, Jake stood outside his truck, leaned against its banged-up door, and watched the occasional semi blow past on the highway. In the sugarcane fields and canal, the boisterous rhythm of clicking, croaking, and bellowing of the nocturnal creatures provided an Everglades rock concert. A few minutes later, a late-model sedan pulled into the parking lot and stopped thirty paces behind the old truck. Jake squinted in the bright headlights and grinned at the car occupants. He lifted a hand in greeting, but didn't budge. They'd have to get out and walk to him.

Two men in dark suits stepped from the car and started toward Jake. One held up a small black bag and said, "We have your money."

As they approached Jake, Christian emerged from the shadows with his handgun aimed at them. "Heard you wanted me dead."

Jaws dropped and their eyes grew big. The Chinese guy with the bag stuttered, "No, no, misunderstanding."

"Sometimes misunderstandings have consequences." Christian popped off two rounds, shooting both men in their foreheads, and they dropped at Jake's feet.

Jake jumped back, startled. "Holy shit! You don't fuck around!"

He ignored his excited new partner and picked up the two shell casings. He slipped into gloves to search the dead men.

Jake collected his wits and opened the small bag. "Paper, nothin' but damn cutup newspaper," he grumbled. "You were right. They weren't gonna pay me."

Christian removed two handguns from the men's shoulder holsters. "Yep, only would've gotten a bullet from these boys." He also confiscated the men's wallets, making the motive look like robbery along with their cell phones, so there'd be no trace of Jake's text. "Grab the bag. It has your prints. We'll dump my gun and their shit in the canal, twenty miles north. And Jake, avoid the blood when you back out. No sense in leaving tire tracks for the cops."

They climbed into the old pickup, leaving the car headlights shining on the corpses that rested on the bloody asphalt and slowly drove up the pitch-black highway.

CHAPTER TWO

The incident in South Florida had occurred four months earlier. So far the police had no suspects for the murder of the two Asian men. With the incident behind him, Christian stood alone on the pebbled bank alongside an aluminum canoe, contemplating the journey to his next crime. Traveling the river rapids at night would be a challenge. He leaned over, took off his leather glove, and dipped his hand into the clear water. *Wow, this sucker's cold,* he thought. If his canoe hit a boulder and tipped over, not only would he be miserable but it might end the mission.

He straightened his lanky frame and inhaled the cool dry air and pine scent. Bright yellow thickets lined the bank, and on the opposite shore, sheer cliffs streaked with grayish-green stone rose from the surging water. The setting sun highlighted the straw-like scrub that carpeted the surrounding hills, with occasional outcrops of black rock. Firs resembling Christmas trees grew in sparse forests in crevasses and basins. The terrain was so different from home that he felt like an alien.

He glanced at his watch, not having the leisure time of a tourist, and pulled a baseball cap from his back jean pocket to cover his blond hair. From his plaid flannel shirt he removed his Ray-Bans and pressed them against the bridge of his nose. Satisfied with his disguise as a visiting sportsman, he shoved the canoe into the water and climbed in. A few paddle strokes had him gliding with the swift current. Unlike most rivers that flowed south, the Salmon River flowed north in this part of Idaho.

He heard honking and looked up at a flock of Canada geese winging south. Around a bend he spotted a mule deer in the birch trees. The stag had an impressive rack and was huge compared to the tiny whitetails back in Florida. The animals, foliage, and weather confirmed the season. It was fall in the northwest. Christian reveled in the outdoors, but his enthusiasm faded when he realized why he was here.

With the onset of dusk, the colors became hazy and objects faded to shadows. Christian backstroked to briefly stop and dug into his duffle bag for the head lantern that was worn like a hat. He adjusted the light to shine on the river ahead and checked his GPS for distance to his target.

An hour later he paddled in darkness with only a full moon and his spotlight directing his path and preventing a calamity. As the wilderness gave way to civilization, he turned off the lantern and used the moonlight when skimming past the small houses and farms. The river flanked the highway, and through the trees he occasionally heard semi trucks shifting gears and groaning with their heavy loads. He drew closer to town, and the buildings became a muddle of homes and small businesses. Their outside lights resembled a strand of glowing Christmas bulbs lacing the shore. He saw the outline of two- and three-story buildings that made up the downtown.

At a fork in the river he veered to the right. A little further and he came upon a small park and then the bridge. The bridge supported Highway 93, one of the main arteries through the state. After the bridge, southbound traffic entered the heart of town, and the two-lane road became Main Street.

He beached the canoe under the bridge and slid it beneath the trusses to hide it. Removing his duffle bag of equipment, he used it as a pillow and stretched out on soft grass, waiting for the late hour when nothing moved on the roads, lights dimmed, and the town slept.

* * *

In a rustic two-story building, Fred sat on a stool, sipped his beer, and listened to his buddy, Ed, slur another over-told hunting tale to the barkeep. Behind the bar Bernie just smiled and washed a few glasses. Fred noticed that he and Ed were the last customers in the Salmon Lounge. Because it was a weekday, everyone else had gone home. He nudged Ed. "Let's go. Bernie wants to close up."

"Yeah, yeah," Ed grumbled and slid off his stool. He took the last swallow from his mug and wiped his gray-streaked beard with his sleeve. After tugging on his jacket, he staggered toward the exit. "The wife's gonna be pissed. I'll be sleeping on the couch."

"Won't be the first time," Fred said, following. At the door he nodded good night to Bernie.

The two men stepped out into the crisp air and stood on the empty sidewalk. "Sure is quiet tonight," said Ed as they gazed down the deserted street.

"What'd you expect in early September on a Wednesday night? But the out-of-state hunters will be here in no time." Fred clutched the top of his coat. "It's cold. Let's get." He climbed into his pickup as Ed got into the passenger seat.

"Drop me on the corner. Maybe she won't hear me come in."

"Good luck with that." Fred started the engine and turned on the headlights. "What the hell?" He nodded toward the sprayed graffiti on the brick wall. "Damn kids in this town, I better tell Bernie." He walked back into the bar and called. "Hey, Bernie, someone vandalized your building, sprayed it with paint."

Bernie hustled out from behind the bar and trailed Fred outside. The three men stared at the message that read 'Stop Killing the Wolves.' It was signed, 'Captain Nemo.'

"Who's Nemo?" Ed asked.

"Bet the son of a bitch is one of those lousy animal activists from last year," Bernie cursed. "I'd better call the police."

A large explosion echoed off the building. The men flinched and ducked, feeling the tremor through the pavement.

"Holy Christ," Ed exclaimed. "What the devil was that?"

To the west about a mile away, Fred saw the glow of fire rise above the dark buildings. "Over there." He pointed. "It looks like it's the carwash. Could be a gas tank blew up."

"More likely it's the restaurant next door," Bernie said and glanced at the graffiti. "The owner promotes wolf hunting."

* * *

At the Hammer Wheel Campgrounds in North Fort, Sal carefully lowered his large frame into a flimsy folding chair and smiled proudly at his accomplishment, a small pit fire that burned brightly at his campsite. From a good distance away, he heard a man chuckle outside his RV, but other than that, the place was quiet and nearly empty of guests. He gazed up at the moon and star-filled sky and thought it nice. Raised in the city, and in his mind there was only one city, he had never traveled much by car or camped. He had always been too busy working for Vince and the mob, but on reflection, he wished he had taken the time and gone camping with his kids. Too late now; they were grown, married, and gone, but Sal was still babysitting. He had promised Vince that he'd look after his adopted Florida boy.

Upon first meeting Christian, Sal couldn't stand him. He was too tall, too blond, and too pretty. In his late twenties, he swaggered with a cockiness that matched his smartass mouth. He also had issues, like a hair-trigger temper and a don't-give-a-shit-if-I-die attitude that made him unpredictable and dangerous. On occasion he'd slip into his dark place and become unbearably quiet. Vince had explained that Christian suffered from depression, feeling guilt over his wife's death, and he also showed signs of post-traumatic stress from killing people. Sal, however, lacked sympathy. Besides youth and good-looks, the kid was wealthy. He'd made millions in the horse racing business and then inherited Vince's vast fortune.

Sal's perspective of Christian changed after he brought down Vince's killer. Spending more time with the kid, Sal saw what the boss had seen and loved. Christian was smart, interesting, gutsy, and a straight shooter. He could be trusted. When committed to someone or something, he was fiercely loyal, putting his life on the line. Sal bought into Christian's bigger picture: making a difference in this world. Instead of retiring on a beach and blowing off his promise to Vince, Sal was here, helping the young guy break the law for his latest wildlife cause. Sal wasn't an animal lover, but he felt good doing something worthwhile. He also enjoyed the plotting and thrill. He'd committed crimes since he was old enough to run. Why get a conscience and go straight now?

He pulled out a cigar, held it to his nose, and savored the aroma of Cuban tobacco. With Christian in mind, he wondered how the kid had made out. Earlier, he and Christian had pulled off the highway at a clearing called the Eight Mile River Access. In the late afternoon on a weekday, no one was there. Christian slipped on gloves and removed the canoe from the top of the Dodge camper and carried it to the river. Sal brought along the duffle bag filled with an explosive on a timer, spray paint, and other gear. He handed the bag to Christian, wished him good luck, and drove north on Highway 93 through and out of the town of Salmon.

After thirteen miles, Sal stopped at North Fort and the campground. The place had a little grocery/gift shop, but more importantly, its campsites backed up to the Salmon River. In the office Sal signed in using a fake ID and the stolen license plate number off the Dodge. He paid forty dollars in cash for one night and mentioned to the owner he was there to fish and would be leaving before dawn.

He puffed on the cigar and checked his watch. Christian should be on his way after planting the small explosive at the restaurant.

"Wolves," he mumbled with a head shake, "Blood-thirsty varmints ain't much better than sharks."

* * *

Christian retrieved the canoe from under the bridge and shoved it into the water to continue his trek downriver. So far everything was going as planned. He had hiked through town using the shadowy side streets and alleys to avoid being seen or recorded by potential surveillance cameras mounted on store fronts.

On the outskirts of town he picked up the highway, and in less than a mile, he came to the Saw Blade Grill. He walked across the gravel parking lot to the small wooden restaurant with cream walls and secured the explosive at the back of the building near the kitchen propane tank. The timer was set to go off two hours later when he was on the river again and miles away.

The job would've been faster and easier if he had used the truck and driven into town, but doing so held more risk. A vehicle stealing through the streets late at night might be noticed. A single witness identifying the Dodge would make roadblocks a concern, especially in a river valley with few thoroughfares. Christian also considered his alias as Captain Nemo. The canoe was no *Nautilus* and the river no sea, but striking from the water was keeping with the hypothesis.

He had sprawled his warning on the nearby carwash wall. Hiking back through town, he decided to leave another message on an old brick building where no one would miss it. Back on the river, he used quick, strong thrusts to rapidly propel the canoe. The race was against time, distancing himself from town before the bomb went off. He also hoped to rendezvous with Sal at the campground before dawn to avoid being spotted.

To his left, he caught glimpses of the highway that ran parallel to the meandering river. He came upon another bridge, with the roadway moving to the right of the river. Several strenuous hours later, his arm muscles ached. He took a break to catch his breath and check his location on the GPS. The campground was less than a mile away.

He saw a heavily wooded area and pulled in to ditch the boat. He dragged the canoe a hundred feet from the river and shoved it under thick brush, confident no one would stumble upon it for some time. He flung the duffle bag over his shoulder and walked back to the river. Using a tiny strobe that gave off just enough ground light to prevent a misstep, he sprinted along the river, half the time splashing through the frigid water. At the late hour few cars traveled the road, and those that did could be seen and heard coming, giving Christian enough warning to extinguish his light.

He heard an eerie sound and froze in the ankle deep water. Tilting his head to the stars, he stood motionless and listened more carefully. Did he really hear it or was his mind playing tricks on him? Then it happened again. On a distant hill to south was the faint howl of a wolf. Christian gasped and his heart raced, not from running but excitement. The ghostly beautiful cry of a lone wolf brought moisture to his eyes. "I hear you, boy," he whispered. "Help is coming."

Not hearing the wolf again, Christian moved on. Eventually through the forest he spotted the outside lights of the campground building. He left the river and waded into head-high saw grass, following a dirt path that led into a small clearing of trees. He came upon the campsites and the white Dodge pickup with a camper. The dark grounds were silent, with everyone sleeping. In the east the vague gray light of dawn rose between the mountains and infringed on the black sky. He was cutting it close. He stepped inside the camper and turned his flashlight on Sal, snoring on the berth. His intermittent loud snorts could have attracted a wild boar.

"Sal," Christian said, shaking the big Italian's shoulder. "Wake up. It's time to go."

"What? What?" Sal said, startled. For a moment he stared in a daze and finally focused on Christian. "I see you didn't get caught."

"Not yet. I'll unhook the water and electric from the camper, and then we're outta here."

Sal scratched his curly black hair and sighed. "Okay."

"Hey, Sal, I actually heard a wolf. It was so damn cool."

"Yeah, yeah," Sal said unimpressed. "Glad *you* got off on it."

After disconnecting everything, Christian stepped back into the camper and remained as a precaution. He might have been seen or filmed in Salmon. As Sal climbed into the truck cab and drove north, Christian traded his wet clothing for a dry pair of jeans and long-sleeved shirt. He stretched out on the camper berth and shut his eyes. He should be tired, should rest, but he was too pumped up. Instead of sleep, he sat up and gazed out the window at the Bitterroot National Forest. The gorgeous landscape didn't distract him from his inner conflicts. Were his unscrupulous deeds worth it?

Blowing up an Idaho restaurant would not stop the ruthless slaughter of wolves with only the local press covering the story, but a terrorist attack from the notorious Captain Nemo would result in national coverage on wolf hunting and hopefully public outcry. The downside, he had picked an unpopular animal to save. Like sharks, the gray wolf population that was vital to the ecosystem was being decimated, but few people knew or cared. *Yeah, it's gonna be an uphill battle.*

After nearly a three-hour drive, Sal pulled into a gas station, climbed out, and tapped on the side of the camper. "Awake in there?"

Christian stuck his head out. "Where are we?"

"Missoula, Montana, and not far from the airport," Sal said while refueling the truck. "You can wait in the Lear while I deal with the rental. We should be on our way within the hour. For a spur-of-the-moment harebrained scheme, it came off without a hitch."

Christian lifted an eyebrow. "Let's hope so."

* * *

The explosion rattled the house and shook Charlie Tucker, Salmon's chief of police, from sound sleep. "Jesus, Mary, and Joseph," he said, stumbling out of bed.

His wife sat up. "What was that?"

"Sounded like a bomb." He had just pulled up his pants when one of his officers called. "What happened?"

"Chief, the back half of the Saw Blade Grill blew up," said the officer. "The rest of the place is on fire."

"Anybody hurt or killed?"

"I don't think so, but I just got here."

"All right, I'll be there in ten." He threw on a shirt and stepped into his boots that added height to his five-foot, eight-inch stature. In the foyer he yanked on his jacket and covered his balding gray hair with a cap. Outside, he hustled to his Jeep Cherokee. Through the buildings he heard sirens and glimpsed the flashing lights of a fire truck as it raced toward the restaurant on the outskirts of town.

He arrived at the restaurant lot and parked next to a fire truck. The Saw Blade Grill was engulfed in flames. Two fire crews fought the blaze, not to save the restaurant —it was gone, a bonfire of fiery rubble —but to keep the fire contained and spare nearby buildings.

He pushed through a dozen spectators and approached two of his officers standing by their cars. "Any ideas what caused it?"

"Chief," one responded, "The fire inspector says he won't know if it's accidental or arson until he searches the debris."

Another officer called from the adjacent carwash. "Chief, I got something."

Charlie hurried to the officer who stood in a carwash stall and stared at graffiti on the concrete wall. In black spray paint, it said 'Stop Killing the Wolves. Captain Nemo.'

Charlie removed his cap and ran his hand over his head. There was little doubt in his mind that the bomb and fire were intentional. "I warned those commissioners this would happen. Last year we received hundreds of angry emails about our wolf hunt. Now a damn fanatic has made good on the threat."

Charlie glanced at the onlookers. "Did you question them?"

"I asked if anyone saw something," said an officer. "They were all sleeping, and beforehand, they didn't notice anything out of the ordinary."

"I want roadblocks set up, in and out of town. With any luck the arsonist is still here, enjoying the mayhem. Stop every vehicle and get their plate number and name. If anyone acts suspicious, bring them in for questioning. I'll notify the state police to help out. Talk to the residents in the neighborhood near the grill. This town is too damn small for a stranger to slip in unnoticed. Okay, let's get snapping."

The officers hustled to their vehicles and drove off with lights flashing. Charlie walked back to his Jeep and radioed the police station. Besides requesting an assist from the state police, he ordered his off-duty officers to come in for the manhunt. But with no description of the guilty party, the odds of success weren't good. He learned from Dispatch that a second graffiti message had been scrawled on the brick wall of the Salmon Lounge.

Throughout the night Charlie remained on the scene and watched his forensic technician lift prints and took DNA swabs from the graffiti. The tech also photographed the carwash wall and made plaster casts of tire tracks and footprints in the parking lot. He then left to collect evidence at the Salmon Lounge. Charlie hoped for the best, but finding a good fingerprint on brick and rough concrete block wouldn't be easy. The arsonist also might've worn gloves.

The state police arrived and commandeered the roadblocks. Word of the fire spread to the media, and a camera crew from a local TV station arrived. They lost no time filming the blaze and interviewing Charlie. He told the reporter about Captain Nemo's graffiti, but until the investigation was further along, the fire could not be confirmed as arson. Sally, the young owner of Saw Blade

Grill, showed up and watched in tears as her business burned to ashes.

By sunrise the flames were extinguished. Despite the additional help of the state troopers, the roadblocks yielded no suspect. At midmorning, the fire inspector trudged through the smoldering ruins and searched for cause and clues. Near the rear of the building he picked up a few small items and called to Charlie. "I think I found something, Chief."

"What you got?"

In his gloved hand the inspector held a tiny melted battery and the face of a burnt wristwatch. "I believe this is what's left of the bomb. They used the watch as a timer. The minute hand has been removed, leaving the hour hand to trigger the bomb after the arsonist left. The transistor radio battery created spark to ignite the explosive. I'm guessing gelatin dynamite was used, very stable to handle, but won't know for sure about the bomb substance until the scrapings are tested. It's a homemade bomb but the work of a professional. At any rate, here's your proof, Chief, definitely an arson."

"Any chance of fingerprints?"

"You're kidding, right?" The fire inspector smirked while sealing the items in an evidence bag.

"Okay, I'll be at the station if you find anything else."

Charlie arrived at the police station north of town and turned on his computer. He immediately did an internet search on Captain Nemo. He was shocked to see the numerous articles. Some were from the big newspapers like *The Washington Post* and *New York Times*. He learned that Nemo was an infamous ecoterrorist known worldwide for his attacks on the shark fin trade to save the fish. The guy had not only bombed and burned buildings and boats in New York, Costa Rica, and the Bahamas, but had also killed nearly eighty people in China and Britain, when they ate poisoned shark fin soup. A Nemo message had coincided with each attack and warned to stop killing the sharks. The gist of the Salmon graffiti was the same except it pertained to wolves. The FBI investigation had yielded a possible suspect, Christian Roberts, in Florida, and a New York prosecutor charged him as a conspirator in the bombing of two grocery stores in Chinatown. The case never went to trial because the only witness disappeared. Nemo's campaign worked. He stopped finning and saved the sharks.

"Damn," Charlie whispered after reading the data. He leaned back in his office chair and stared at the photo of Roberts, a young guy with devilish blue eyes. He sat up, suddenly realizing his little town had been lucky. If Captain Nemo was in Salmon last night, it could've been worse than losing one restaurant. Someone might've been murdered. "Everyone, get in here," he called into the station. With most of his officers in the field, a young lieutenant and Helen, his middle-aged secretary, were the only ones there.

The two rushed in and the lieutenant said, "Yes, Chief?"

Charlie stood and pointed to the photo on his computer. "See this man? His name is Christian Roberts. He's suspected of being Captain Nemo. I want his photo and APB put out on him. This guy is a standout, six-two plus and a looker. People are apt to remember him if he bought a soda or gas in the area."

Helen held her cheek and zeroed in on the screen. "My word, I'd never forget him." She tilted her head. "With his gorgeous blue eyes and blond hair, he reminds me of Chris Hemsworth."

"You know you're right," the lieutenant said. "They're not only similar but tall and close in age. Hey, they're both Christians, have the same first name."

Charlie frowned. "Who the devil is Hemsworth?"

"He's an actor, Chief," said the lieutenant. "He plays Thor, one of the avengers in the Marvel movies."

Irritated, Charlie huffed. "I don't give a damn if Roberts resembles some actor. This boy is the real deal, an avenger that blew up a restaurant for wolves. Besides bombing and burning, he's a murderer, killed a lot of people for his causes. Add to the bulletin he's extremely dangerous and should be approached with caution. Now if you moviegoers are done, I'd like to get back to work."

After they left his office, Charlie returned to his chair and called the Idaho FBI. The local authorities would normally handle an arson case, but this was an act of terrorism and fell under federal jurisdiction. "This is Chief Tucker in Salmon," he said to an agent. "We got a serious problem here." He explained the fire, the bomb fragments, and Captain Nemo's graffiti threats left on two businesses. He also emphasized what he had learned about Christian Roberts on the Internet.

"Every agent in the country has heard of Captain Nemo," said the agent. "He's an ecoterrorist and well known for his worldwide attacks to save sharks."

"Apparently he's moved on to saving wolves."

"Apparently," said the agent. "We'll get right on it and should be in Salmon in a few hours. In the meantime, post officers at the arson and message sites so no one tampers with evidence. We'll go over it more thoroughly. Also tell your fire inspector and forensics officer not to mess with their findings. We'll send the evidence to the Quantico along with the photos of the graffiti. Our handwriting experts will analyze them. Christian Roberts is suspected of being the terrorist, but the evidence is circumstantial. Roberts lives mid-state in Florida so I'll call the FBI there and see if a Sarasota or Tampa agent can track him down at his home and see if he has an alibi."

"Besides what I learned about Roberts in the press, does the FBI have additional information that might help catch him?"

"According to Roberts's file the first Nemo attack occurred last year in the Bahamas so the Miami field office provided an assist. Agent Wheeler worked the case. He interviewed Roberts several times and probably knows him better than anyone. Here's his Miami number."

Charlie's next call was to Wheeler, but was told the agent was in the field. If it was an emergency, Wheeler would contact him or Charlie could leave a message.

Helen stuck her head in the door. "Chief, the governor is on line two. He saw the fire on the news."

Charlie held up a wait-a-minute finger and spoke into the phone. "I'll call Agent Wheeler later." He took the call from Governor Oran, no fan of wolves, told him what had happened, and that he'd requested an assist from the FBI. The governor said he'd notify the US Marshals to aid in the manhunt.

Charlie hung up and the phone rang again. The caller was a reporter with the Associated Press. He learned that Captain Nemo was back in action with a new cause, saving wolves and had targeted Salmon, Idaho.

Along with the arrival of the FBI, US Marshals, and press, roughly two dozen protestors showed up with signs supporting Captain Nemo and his cause for wolves. They demonstrated in front of the charred ruins of the restaurant. Their protest rally stirred up the locals, especially the hunters. A shouting match ensued between the two rivals, the wolf lovers and haters. The Salmon police were overwhelmed, trying to maintain order and prevent bloodshed.

Charlie stood on the sidelines with one of his officers as a network satellite van drove into the restaurant lot. "One man, just one, caused all this uproar," he grumbled. After a hectic day with little sleep the previous night, he left for home exhausted.

The following morning Charlie stood at his office desk and glanced at Agent Wheeler's phone number on the notepad. He called the Miami agent and told him that Captain Nemo had struck in Idaho and left his renowned calling card, along with a torched restaurant.

"So he's at it again," Wheeler said with a southern drawl. "I figured he'd retired after his shark campaign."

"You think this Christian Roberts is the terrorist?"

"I'm darn confident he is, but the boy is as slippery as a snake, doesn't leave any witnesses or evidence."

"We set up roadblocks and have questioned everyone in the area, but you're right, nothing so far."

"Given your town, Salmon, is named after a fish, I suspect there's water nearby, a lake, dam, or river."

"The Salmon River flows alongside town."

"Forget the roads, then. He came and went on the river. It's kinda his M.O. striking from the water like Captain Nemo and his *Nautilus* submarine. If there's any evidence to be found, it'll be there. I'd start checking boat ramps, boat rentals, campgrounds, anything connected to the river."

"That's a big job; would take days, maybe weeks. There's an access every few miles throughout Idaho."

"Wish I could be of more help."

"I spoke to the Idaho FBI, and they're having a Sarasota agent check out Roberts's alibi for Wednesday night."

"The agent might as well interrogate a corpse. Christian won't cooperate. He got a taste of jail and knows to clam up. He'll probably slam the door in the agent's face. I'll tell you what I'll do. I have his private cell number and will give him a call. He'll tell me his whereabouts on Wednesday."

"He trusts you?"

Wheeler chuckled. "Not enough to spill his guts, but I'll get some answers out of him. I'm curious, Chief Tucker. Why would Nemo target your town? I was under the impression wolves were protected under the Endangered Species Act."

"They were several years ago, but the president signed a bill delisting them and removed federal protection. Their fate is now in the hands of the states. Idaho caters to hunters and has deemed wolves as vermin that kill the deer and elk. The state has already eradicated over half of them. Salmon hosts a yearly predator hunt, so I'm not surprised that Captain Nemo came here and blew up the Saw Blade Grill. The restaurant owner sponsors the wolf derby."

CHAPTER THREE

In the small private jet, Christian sat in a plush, leather seat and leaned his head against the window as he watched the mountains of Montana vanish in the distance. Sal had leased the Lear under a dummy corporation to conceal their names in its flight plan.

Sal sat across from him reading a newspaper, but after a while, he dropped it on a side table. "All that traveling through Idaho, and I didn't see one damn potato farm."

"The Idaho potato was an advertising ploy," Christian mumbled, still focused on the scenery.

"Come on, Kid, snap out of it. Since we got on this plane, you haven't said two words. Instead of brooding, you should celebrate. Everything turned out good."

Here it comes. He wants to yap. Christian straightened, cleared his throat, and turned his attention to the big guy filling the seat. "I'm not brooding, Sal. I'm thinking that it's a damn shame I have to blow up some poor slob's business to bring attention to a cause."

"The slob will collect on the insurance and build a bigger and better joint. No harm done."

"I don't care about the damage." He gazed back out the window. "Wolves are being shot out there. I'm trying to figure a way to stop it and save them."

Sal leaned forward and grinned. "You have another target in mind?"

Christian smiled with Sal's eagerness. "Sorry, Sal, but I want to avoid future bombings. One Captain Nemo attack is enough to bring the press and shed light on wolf hunting. Besides, the world is a different place now. People are freaking out over the radical Islamic terrorists. I don't need to be in the same category with those sick bastards. Problem is I've picked an impossible task."

"So what are ya gonna do?"

"A lot of research and hopefully find a legit and normal approach to saving wolves."

"Hate to tell ya, but you ain't normal and don't have the patience for that approach." Sal twirled the ice cubes and bourbon in his rocks glass. "So why wolves? You jumped on this cause in a heartbeat."

Christian drew in a deep sigh. "Thousands of animals are facing extinction in the world, but I decided to start in my own backyard, the US. I learned about the wolf slaughter out West, and the restaurant sponsoring another hunt. So yeah, I jumped on it."

"You sure can pick 'em," Sal said, "sharks and now wolves. People don't give a shit if those bloodsuckers are gone."

"That attitude is why they need help. Sharks and wolves get a bad rap. In the US dogs kill over 300 people every year. Sharks kill one, and it's a headline. Wolves don't go after people. They're terrified of us. Only one person on record has died from a wolf attack and the animal was rabid, but the myths, fables, and even today's movies depict them as monsters. It's a damn lie."

"So Little Red Riding Hood is bullshit?" Sal chuckled.

"That's just one of many examples that portray wolves as man-killers, but in fact the research shows they're vital to the environment. Everything from plants to animals thrives when wolves are present. It's a shame. Wolves were finally making a slight comeback in the US after being exterminated a hundred years ago. I need to learn why they're being slaughtered again."

Sal set down his cocktail and scratched the back of his head. "Ya know, kid, you don't have to do these causes. You could quit and enjoy life. I understand your wife asked you to save sharks, and I was there when the lawyer read Vince's will giving you his dough so you could do this. But the boss and your girl are dead. You don't owe them shit."

"Allie and Vince were shot protecting me. That's pretty good incentive to honor their wishes. Besides, I want to save animals. What gives us the damn gall to snuff out a species? Animals have just as much right to this planet as we do, but some greedy, ignorant assholes are annihilating what little wildlife that's left. Sal, we're on the verge of another mass extinction, but this one is manmade. Pollution, climate change, loss of habitat, and hunting will wipe out a million species soon. It's fucking outrageous." He swallowed some Coke to calm down.

"I see you're pissed and committed, but you can't stop the inevitable. Why don't you focus on another cause, like starving children or some other crap? With your brains and money, you could make a difference, and those causes are legit. You won't go to prison."

"Plenty of people are dedicated to those charities. They don't need me, but wolves do."

"So where did this thing for animals come from?"

"Is this your attempt to keep me talking?"

"It's a long fucking plane ride, and I hate sharing it with a crash dummy."

"A dummy?" Christian responded with an icy glance.

Sal laughed. "Don't get your dandruff up, boy. It's just that usually our sit-downs revolve around crime; weapons, making a bomb, picking a lock, avoiding the law. You're a damn good student, probably know as much as me now. You refuse to talk about the juicy stuff like girls and sex. That leaves your thing for animals. Maybe I wanna know what makes you tick."

"Christ, I need a stiffer drink." Christian rose, filled a glass with ice and rum at a small bar, and returned to his seat. "So why animals?" he said, adding a splash of his Coke to the drink. He took a sip, reflecting. "I connected better with them. Always have preferred animals to people. It's probably my upbringing, being an only child, and raised on an isolated horse farm in the middle of Florida. My dog, the horses, and barn cats were my buddies, and I loved nature, wandering alone in the woods and seeing the deer, gators, snakes, or whatever. My thing for animals might also be inherited. My dad loved his horses more than me." He smiled to hide the hurt.

"That sucks."

"It doesn't matter now. He's dead. We did connect in the end. Dad gave me the race horse that made me wealthy and hooked me up with my wife."

"You must've had pals in school."

"I was rather withdrawn, especially after my parents divorced, and my mom and I moved from Ocala to Sarasota. I didn't have the same interests as other kids. But in high school I took up surfing and made some friends, and then there were the girls. They liked me. Mostly though, I was considered a loner. Still prefer it to socializing."

"I'd a thought with your build you'd go into sports like basketball, baseball."

"Nope, never felt the inclination to prove myself," Christian said. "I did take up boxing, but only out of necessity. Got tired of the jealous pricks beating my ass."

Sal chuckled. "I can see that." He drank some of his cocktail. "So back to these critters, I get why you like them, but there are millions of animal lovers. None take it to your extreme and put their neck on the line to save them."

Christian lifted his gaze to the big guy. "Come on, Sal. You know why. I'm fucked up. But when focused on a cause, I'm more grounded and have fewer dark spells, got a reason to climb out of bed. You could say that saving animals saves me. Without that..." He lowered his head. "Maybe someday I'll be okay."

Sal rubbed his jaw. "Jesus, Kid, you really do have issues."

"My shrink agrees."

* * *

In the middle of the night, Christian stared out the jet window at dark Gulf waters and the sparkling city lights of the Florida western coast. On the approach to the Sarasota-Bradenton airport, he recognized every river, bay, and channel along with the streets, buildings, and bridges that led from the mainland to the outer keys. Everything below was a part of him.

The jet landed at SRQ and taxied to Dolphin Aviation, a hub for private jets, helicopters, and planes. Christian grabbed his duffle bag and departed the Lear, but never entered the small airport building. To avoid witnesses, he walked straight to the chain-link gate and puddle-filled parking lot to Sal's Cadillac. While waiting for his partner in crime, he leaned against the Caddy, closed his eyes, and savored the warm, humid air, moist enough to drink. *God, it's good to be home.*

Sal strolled out of the building to his car and opened the trunk for their gear. "Looks like it rained a lot."

"It's September, height of the hurricane and wet season. Thunderstorms are the norm."

They loaded up the Cadillac, and Sal drove down US 41 toward the heart of Sarasota. Traffic was sparse at the late hour, and it was the off season. The tourists with children had left Florida with the start of school, and the heat and storms kept the snowbirds, the part-time residents, in their winter homes until late fall. Local business, especially restaurants and hotels, suffered from the lack of visitors, but Christian loved this precious month. For a brief time he and the locals enjoyed a peaceful town and uncluttered roadways.

Before the bayfront, Sal turned at the red light toward the beaches. "When you get home and settled, give me a call. We'll discuss this wolf business. Maybe I can come up with something."

"Thanks, Sal, but with Nemo back in the public eye, I'm expecting heat from the cops and press."

Sal laughed. "Yeah, you hit the hornet's nest with a stick, and there's bound to be buzzing."

They drove across the two bridges over Sarasota Bay and out to the keys. Sal veered right and crossed the bridge to Longboat Key. After several miles, they arrived at Vince's large bayside house that Christian had inherited. He rarely used the place but stored clothes, fishing gear, and coolers there. He was more content on his sailboat or in the country at his horse farm.

Sal pulled into the driveway, and Christian stepped from the car and retrieved his bag. He came alongside the driver's window. "Talk to you when things quiet down."

"Just be careful what you say to those assholes." Sal drove off, heading for his condo up the road.

Christian walked on the grass around the house to the backyard and dock. He dropped his bag into the dinghy and rowed a hundred yards in the choppy bay to his forty-seven-foot Catalina sloop moored offshore. He climbed aboard the sailboat that pitched in the strong breeze and gazed upward. A wave of fast-moving dark clouds rolled over black sky and stars. Another storm was blowing in, and he smiled.

The following morning Christian slept late on the sloop. Normally he rose at dawn, but the last few grueling days had wiped him out. He stirred in the berth when hearing his cell phone in the galley. He had purposely left the phone behind when visiting Idaho. He staggered through the companionway and picked up the phone. *Sure didn't take him long.* Agent Wheeler's name was on the caller ID. He yawned and hit the key. "Good morning, Dave." He heard Wheeler huff.

"Where are you?" he snapped.

"Umm, I'm sitting on my boat in Sarasota Bay, fixin' to make coffee. Had a fantastic storm last night that rocked me to sleep."

"Where were you Wednesday night?"

"What's this about?"

"Captain Nemo was in Idaho Wednesday and burned down a restaurant that was sponsoring a wolf hunt. He left two messages to stop killing wolves. But I suppose you don't know anything about it."

"Jesus, are we going down that path again? I'm not Nemo and have never been to Idaho. Although helping wolves sounds like a worthy cause."

"Christian, I need answers," Wheeler said crossly. "If you weren't in Idaho, where were you?"

"Here, I've been on Sarasota Bay for the last three days. Check my cell GPS."

"Just because your phone was there doesn't mean you were. Do you have any witnesses for an alibi?"

"That's not my job, Dave. You know the shit, innocent until you prove I'm guilty. But I'll help you out with some exculpatory evidence. Plenty of witnesses saw my boat moored off Longboat Key."

"Spoken like a lawyer's brat."

"My dad was a horse trainer. The stepfather is the lawyer. Are we done now?"

"Not quite. People might've seen your boat, but did they see you?"

"How the hell would I know? Get back to me when you have a case verifying I was out West destroying restaurants."

"Fine, Christian," Wheeler said with a weighty breath. "I'll submit your alibi that you were in Florida when the Idaho attack took place. Don't leave the country while this investigation is ongoing."

"Dave, if I wanted to be controlled, I would've come with a remote."

* * *

Trish sat in her cubicle at *The Washington Post* and studied the scribbles on her notepad. She turned back to the computer and the story she was writing. Frustrated, she shoved her lengthy hair out of her eyes and thought, *I'll never make deadline.* She clenched her teeth and reread the article for the umpteenth time.

"Problems?" asked a man's voice.

She swiveled in the chair and saw her editor, Larry James, standing there. "I'm not finding the right words."

"Drop it on my desk. Maybe I can soup it up. Right now I want you to concentrate on this." He handed her a printout from the Associated Press. "Your boyfriend has resurfaced with new objectives. Has he sent you any postcards that you failed to mention?"

Trish quickly read about the Idaho restaurant fire and Captain Nemo's messages and looked up at Larry. "No, I haven't heard from Captain Nemo or Christian. Actually, he's not my boyfriend anymore. We're still friends but stopped dating months ago. It got too complicated, and I sort of moved on."

"That's too bad. He sells papers and puts eyeballs on the site. See if you can nail him down about this new attack and get a story."

After Larry left, Trish reflected on how she'd met Christian. She had written a story on the evils of the shark fin trade. Afterwards, she learned about Captain Nemo's terrorist attacks in the Bahamas and Costa Rica and his warnings sprayed on boat hulls to stop shark finning.

She wrote a follow-up about Captain Nemo and his cause to save sharks and learned that the FBI considered Christian a person of interest. He must have read her story because prior to destroying two New York Chinese stores that sold fins, Captain Nemo sent her a postcard that said, "Stop killing the sharks." She flew to Florida and met the man suspected of being the lone-wolf ecoterrorist. Christian turned out to be every woman's dream: beautiful, interesting, and with loads of Southern charm. But he was also complex and hid his mysterious dark side. Despite the lack of proof, she believed that Christian and Captain Nemo were the same man.

Trish rummaged a drawer for her address book. Before dialing Christian's number, she took a deep breath and reminded herself that it was business; she had no future with him. She punched in his cell number and tapped her nails on the desktop.

"Hey, Trish," he said, obviously having seen her name on the caller ID.

Hearing his smoldering deep voice, she felt the fervent rise and fall of her insides. "Hi…hi, Christian," she stuttered. A moment of awkward silence followed.

"You okay?" he asked

Somewhat recovered, she said, "I swear you're the only man alive who turns me into a tongue-tied idiot."

"Should I apologize?"

She grinned. "Not at all. So how have you been?"

"I'm thinking you're not calling about my wellbeing. Agent Wheeler already phoned and asked if I was in Idaho last Wednesday, burning down restaurants. I assume you're interested in the same thing."

She sighed. "My editor told me to contact you."

"For the record, then, I wasn't out West, torching buildings, and I'm denying I'm Nemo, again. I was in Florida on my boat when the bullshit went down. That's all you're getting."

"I'm sorry, Christian, but it's my job."

"Call me when you're not on the job." He hung up.

* * *

Christian stood in the open cockpit of his sloop after his brief conversation with Trish. He placed his cell phone back into a cubbyhole under the steering column and reflected on her. After his brief stint in a New York jail, he began seeing her. The long-distance relationship was noncommittal. They just liked each other well enough to fly back and forth between Florida and DC. for a weekend rendezvous. She was great, had everything he wanted in a girlfriend, but with one problem. She was a reporter and naturally curious. He was a terrorist who pursued wildlife causes while avoiding arrest. Her probing and his concealment made the bond tricky. One slip of his tongue, and her loyalty would be tested between him and her job. Not wanting to put her in that unfair position, he ended the dating before they became too serious.

He gazed across the bay at Sarasota, overcast with dark clouds for its daily showers. Farther east, a lightning bolt crashed on the black horizon and rumbled across the water. *In for a storm,* he thought, but he wasn't referring to the weather. If Trish knew about Captain Nemo's hit in Idaho, so did the rest of the media. A deluge of reporters would soon flood his life.

He started the motor, pulled anchor, and turned the sloop into the breeze. After unfurling the mainsail, he cruised toward Marina Jack's near downtown Sarasota. He reached the mouth of the marina and the steady breeze had increased to gale gusts. On the rocking boat, he lowered the sail and motored into his dock slip. As soon as the boat was tied up and hatch locked, the clouds opened up, releasing buckets of rain. He jogged to his SUV in the parking lot and climbed in the cab soaking wet. Retrieving his cell phone from a pocket, he dried it off and called the manager of his horse farm, twenty-five miles east in Myakka City.

"Hey, Juan, just leaving my boat and should be home within the hour."

"Is everything all right, Mr. Roberts?"

"What's up?"

"Two FBI agents were here, looking for you. I told them you were sailing, but I didn't know where. I hope that was okay."

"That's fine, but go up and lock the gate," said Christian. "I'm expecting more unwanted company and don't want them on the farm."

"Sure thing, Mr. Roberts."

In torrential rain Christian drove through downtown Sarasota with the SUV headlights on, defroster blasting, and the wipers working at full capacity. He turned east toward Myakka, but a few miles from his Thoroughbred farm, the hard rain let up and became a sprinkle. Florida's tropical thunderstorms moved in and out quickly, but they could leave behind flooded streets, fried electronics and power outages from lightning strikes, and the gusts that occasionally reached hurricane strength could topple trees and damage buildings. While some people feared and cursed the September storms, Christian loved them. The thrill outweighed the drawbacks.

He pulled into his driveway and climbed out to unlock the gate. Starting back to the SUV, he noticed a van racing toward him and sighed, seeing its satellite disk and the Tampa TV station logo on a side panel.

The van slowed and stopped behind his SUV. Two men hopped out, one holding a camera and the other, a microphone. "Mr. Roberts, Mr. Roberts, can we get a statement about Captain Nemo's attack in Idaho?" the reporter asked, shoving the microphone toward him. A few feet away the cameraman focused his lens.

"Sorry, no comment," Christian said, and eased back into his SUV. He pulled onto the farm property and got out to relock the gate. The reporter followed, still firing questions. Christian ignored him and drove a hundred yards to his house.

Within an hour four more vehicles arrived. Through binoculars, Christian saw that three were from TV stations and the fourth from the Sarasota newspaper. The growing press parked along the roadside outside the board fence. Although annoyed, Christian anticipated the intrusion. The media, authorities, and public all believed he was Captain Nemo, but their opinions of him varied. Animal lovers and the ecology-minded saw him as a hero fighting to save wildlife. Others believed he belonged behind bars.

He turned away from the road view to clean up. By the time he'd showered, shaved, and dressed, the *Bradenton Herald* and

Tampa Tribune had joined the street party. The press invasion was not going away. In fact it'd only get worse. They'd camp at his farm until he gave them a statement.

He couldn't complain. He'd blown up a restaurant to get the press there, hoping their stories would expose the devastation of dying wolves. But the approach came at a cost. He hated the spotlight, harassment, and loss of privacy. *Might be worse,* he thought. *Instead of reporters, they could be cops with an arrest warrant.*

He swept back his hair and stepped outside. Beyond the horse barn, the eastern horizon was gold, orange, and shocking pink, a classic sunset after a thunderstorm. To his right a dozen reporters lined the front gate. They saw him and shouted his name. He strolled to them with his palms up for quiet.

"I'll tell y'all again," Christian said, "I'm not Captain Nemo. I wasn't in Idaho burning down a restaurant. I've been on my boat all week in Sarasota Bay. That's all I'm saying on the matter."

"Do you have a theory why Captain Nemo is trying to save wolves?"

"You people are supposedly good at research. Check it out. The federal government stopped protecting wolves, and the states opened up hunting season on them. In the last several years, half our wolves have been annihilated. That's sad."

"So Captain Nemo is against hunting?" asked another reporter.

"This has nothing to do with hunting. It's about exterminating a species. If some guy wants to bring home a deer and feed his family, I doubt Nemo has a problem with that. There's no shortage of deer, but there aren't many wolves. I believe that's why Nemo has taken on that cause."

"Will Captain Nemo continue his attacks for wolves?" asked another.

Christian scowled. "How in the devil would I know? I'm not him. I just wish the media would do your job. A dentist killed one lion in Africa after it was lured out of a national park. The press went crazy, and the story created public outrage. Millions of people were upset, including me. As far as that dentist goes, I hope the asshole eats shit and dies. It's tragic. There are only twenty thousand lions left in the wild, but most are protected. In the US, a couple of thousand wolves are struggling to survive out west. They're gunned down in our wildlife refuges, public lands, and national parks. We bitch about Third-World countries not doing enough to save their wild animals, yet here in the richest and most civilized country on Earth, we don't give a damn if one of our greatest predators is wiped out. Where's the outcry, gentlemen?" The subject triggered Christian's anger, and he decided to quit while ahead. "That's all I have to say." He turned toward the house.

A reporter called to him. "Mr. Roberts, do you *really* expect us to believe you're not Captain Nemo?"

Christian didn't respond and kept walking.

* * *

At daybreak Christian rolled from the bed and stepped to the window. Between the blinds, he stared at the empty road and tranquil countryside of misty pastures. The press had cleared out at nightfall. To avoid their calls, he had unplugged the phone, but the circus was far from over. Most likely another bunch would return today.

In the kitchen he started the coffee maker and taking a carton of eggs from the refrigerator, he noticed a package of uncooked chicken with an expired sell date. He smiled. *Bet the old boy is wondering, where is he?* He removed the chicken and walked out the back screen door to the small lake.

Standing on the lake edge, he called, "Al, come here, boy." In seconds a large alligator head surfaced and swam to him. Originally his wife's pet, the bull gator had lived on the farm for years. Florida law prohibited the feeding of alligators because they associated food with humans and lost their fear. Christian broke the law, a minor offense, compared to his other crimes, and gave Al his leftovers. He figured the gator wasn't in contact with the public and not a threat.

The ten-foot gator climbed up on the bank and lowered his head in front of Christian. "Here ya go," Christian said, and tossed the chicken pieces to Al who snapped them up. "Yeah, you missed me."

He returned to the house and thought, *Time to take the boring, lawful approach and spend some money.*

Although Christian lived in a small house on a forty-acre horse farm, drove a four-year-old SUV, and dressed casually, he was a millionaire who didn't flaunt his wealth. Horse racing had made him rich and put him in touch with Vince and his underworld. Upon Vince's death, Christian was shocked when learning he'd received the bulk of the gangster's estate. Including the house on Longboat Key and an apartment in New York, the fortune was valued at half a billion. Despite his worth, Christian's only extravagance had been the sailboat.

After breakfast and a second cup of coffee, he sat at the desk and called his accountant. "Hey, Brian, I want to donate to some conservation groups, say ten thousand each. Can you make that happen?" Given his wealth, he could've bestowed a larger sum to each, but he wanted to research the groups and learn if they were helping wolves.

"Of course, Mr. Roberts," said Brian. "Once I email you the information and get your signed approval, I'll wire the funds into their accounts."

"Sounds good." Christian read the names of several wildlife organizations.

They finished, and Brian asked, "Do these donations have to do with the story about you in today's paper?"

"Haven't seen the news, but I can imagine. They think I'm Captain Nemo blowing up things to save wolves."

"That's what they're saying."

"Make a note with the donations that the money goes for the defense of wolves. That'll give the press a little credibility. I'm not a terrorist, but as a concerned citizen, I want to help wolves."

He ended his call and walked to the front window. Sure enough, the reporters were back in greater numbers than the day before. This celebrity business not only made him a prisoner in his own home, but also the hounding media would hinder any future endeavors for his cause.

Since he was stuck inside, he decided to do a more in-depth study of wolves and their problems. He wandered into the spare bedroom and shoved a big trunk aside, giving him access to the floorboards. He removed a few planks and then a slab of concrete that masked a secret compartment for valuables. Burglars were not the issue. He had created the hideaway after the police raid on his home during the shark campaign. Everything in his stash was potential evidence that might send him to jail, but he wasn't worried. Only a hurricane destroying the house could uncover the material.

The compartment contained his fake driver's license and passport, documents on his Cayman bank account, a shark fin that was purchased in New York, his father's old .38, several disposable cell phones, and a small laptop that was registered under a fictitious name and address and was used to research his causes. He grabbed the computer, settled on the couch, and propped his bare feet on the coffee table.

He had learned about Idaho's resolve to eradicate wolves and the wolf derby in Salmon. Incensed, he'd flown out west to teach the bloodthirsty town a lesson Nemo-style. Although restaurant bombing created publicity, he needed to learn why after twenty years of protection and wolves gaining a slight foothold, they were being annihilated again.

On the Internet he read everything pertaining to wolves, starting with the US Fish and Wildlife's assessment to remove wolves from the Endangered Species list. Without federal protection, they were at the mercy of each state, and the states showed no mercy. Wolves were dying. What followed were a series of court battles. Fourteen conservation groups, including Defenders of Wildlife, Sierra Club, Humane Society, and Earth Justice, filed lawsuits against the federal and state government agencies and their politicians along with the gun and hunting clubs, claiming the defendants had violated the Endangered Species Act. Only 2,400 wolves existed in the Western US. A district court agreed and ruled in favor of the conservation groups, but in 2012 the president overrode the court decisions and signed a bill to remove wolves from E.S.A. In a few years over half of the wolves were killed. More lawsuits followed. A judge's ruling protected wolves in the Great Lakes region.

A record-breaking one million petitions were signed to save the wolves in the lower forty-eight states and fifty researchers and scientists claimed that wolves were endangered and needed protection. The politicians, however, ignored public demand and the studies. They allowed the wolf hunting to continue. The killing was especially copious in Idaho and Montana. The US Fish and Wildlife Service meant to protect wildlife, actually pushed for the reduction of the wolf population.

After hours of study, Christian learned that wolves weren't targeted because of their numbers or because they posed a danger. Preying on livestock was also not an issue. Wolves attacked a small number of sheep and cows, and the government reimbursed ranchers for their losses. Further, many wolves were shot on public land to defend the grazing livestock, yet the land had been set aside for nature, not cattle. The research further showed that when the alpha male and female in a pack were killed, the young wolves lacked the knowledge and numbers to bring down big game. Starving, many were forced to kill livestock to survive.

Christian concluded that the wolf extermination came down to greed. Ranchers played a part, wanting public land and national parks for their cattle, but the gun and hunting clubs deserved the most blame. They wanted the wolves exterminated to artificially inflate the elk and deer population for their hunters. With substantial bank accounts, these groups lobbied the politicians who took their money and disregarded ninety percent of the public demand to protect wolves.

Disgusted and furious, Christian shoved the laptop aside and stomped to his hideaway in the spare bedroom. He snatched up a burner phone and placed a call.

"Remember I said on the plane that I was going legitimate?" Christian said to Sal. "I've changed my mind."

CHAPTER FOUR

Felix furrowed his brow and stared at the computer screen. "What is this?" he mumbled and scanned the file. As an analyst and consultant, he had been hired by the secretary of state to review federal programs. He was on the fifth floor of one of many nondescript government buildings in the Foggy Bottom district of Washington, DC., and worked on the Department of Interior budget. He stared at the data, biting his bottom lip. The materials within the Endangered Species file CB10934.ESA were details of the Congressional budget of five million dollars slated for the study of wolves, except he had found a second file. It was identical in name, description, and funds, but the file number contained hyphens. It read CB1-0-934.ESA. A routine computer search matched only the numbers and would ignore the hyphens, making it virtually certain no one would catch that a second file existed. Whether a computer glitch or intentional, five million dollars had been allotted to each file.

He researched the second file and found that the funds had been transferred to a wildlife contractor with an offshore account. The trail ended. The five million in the first file had yet to be disbursed. With hundreds of budgets and billions of dollars, several million dollars wouldn't be missed, but he needed to report it. He walked to his supervisor's office.

Barbara Davis sat at her desk and leaned her head on a hand, reading a printout. Felix initially had designs on her. With narrow hazel eyes, pointy nose, and skimpy lips, she wasn't exactly attractive, but he liked the upright poise of her slender body. Upright and uptight, he quickly learned. She treated him like dirt and ran the office like a dictator.

Felix tapped on her open office door. "I have a problem, Miss Davis."

She looked up with a sneer. "What? I'm busy today."

"I found an apparent computer glitch involving one of the accounts." Felix explained the mysterious second file in the endangered species package and the missing money.

"What are you doing in endangered species?" she growled. "You're supposed to be reviewing the funds for windmills."

"I finished them. The president signed the bill that protected windmill companies from lawsuits for thirty years, so besides the budget, there weren't any additional funds going out."

She nervously straightened her desk, neatly stacked the papers, and arranged the pens. "Those petty lawsuits from Audubon had to be stopped. This administration is concerned with energy, not dead eagles. Now regarding this second file on wolf studies, ignore it."

"But it's clearly a misappropriation of funds and should be in my report."

Barbara glared. "Felix, you're giving me a damn headache. Go back to your computer and forget you saw it."

"Whatever you say." He walked back to his desk and stared at the computer file. *I'm not taking the heat if it's discovered.* He copied and pasted both files and sent them to his private email server.

At the end of the day Felix phoned Karen in Arlington. She wrote a blog for an environmental magazine and was a real estate agent who sold sustainable houses. Her husband, Steve, owned a successful computer company that installed security programs. Felix was friends with the couple whom he found motivated and interesting.

When Karen answered the phone, Felix asked, "Are we still on for dinner tonight?"

"Sure. Where are you working today?"

"Foggy Bottom, so I can be in Arlington by six."

"I feel like Indian. How about we meet at the Afghan place up the street from our house?"

"That works," he said. "I'm also forwarding an email to Steve. Ask him to take a look. I'd like to get his thoughts."

At five-thirty Felix left the District and drove over the Arlington Bridge. Several miles past the huge veteran cemetery, he pulled into the restaurant, parked alongside his friends' silver Prius, and entered the Afghan restaurant. Like some Chinese places, the tacky atmosphere gave him the creeps, but he loved the food.

He scanned the dining room of dusty, plastic flowers, hideous statues, and stained carpet and saw Karen and Steve waving him over to their table.

"You guys are punctual as usual," Felix said, and sat down across from Steve.

"I hate people who are always late," said Karen. "I hope it was okay, but we already ordered for you. I skipped lunch and I'm starving."

"No problem." Felix took a piece of flat bread and dipped it into the hummus. "Steve, any chance you looked at my email? I ran across those files today and couldn't believe it."

"I skimmed it, but that second file definitely looks suspicious," said Steve. "Are you going to report it?"

"I already did, but Miss Davis told me to ignore it. I got the feeling she wasn't happy I found it."

"She's the one you call The Bitch?" Karen smiled.

"That's her, Barbara, The Bitch," said Felix. "I really hate to piss her off and create flap, especially if it's just a computer glitch. Besides, the extra funds will show up in accounting at the end of the year. It's impossible to illegally transfer money out of those accounts."

"Nothing's impossible when it comes to computer fraud," Steve said and set down his wine glass. "If I get free this weekend, I'll dig closer into those wolf study files."

"A wolf study?" Karen said. "That's a coincidence. *The Post* ran an article recently about wolves because they're Captain Nemo's newest cause. He blew up an Idaho restaurant that was sponsoring a wolf hunt."

"Captain Nemo? Are we talking Jules Vern's antagonist?" Felix questioned as the waitress set a platter of green chicken curry on the table.

"No, Felix, this guy isn't fiction," Karen said. "If you weren't such a geek and paid attention to environmental issues, you'd know about Captain Nemo."

"He's an ecoterrorist, saved the sharks last year," Steve said, and spooned some rice onto his plate. "The FBI suspects some Florida guy, a hunk who has all the women drooling." He glanced at Karen and grinned.

"Excuse me, I don't drool, Steve," Karen said. "I only mentioned he had incredibly blue-blue eyes."

"I saw the picture," said Steve. "He uses colored contacts."

"Whatever," Karen said, rolling her eyes. She turned to Felix. "Changing the subject, I found the perfect girl for you. She's a real estate agent, really nice and pretty."

"Oh, please, no more matchmaking," Felix said. "I get my hopes up, and after one date, it's over."

"This time will be different. She's out of town now, but when she gets back, I'll set up a date. We'll do dinner and a movie, the four of us. Just don't bore her with work. I told her you're a science-fiction writer. Women are intrigued with authors."

"Karen, I don't even have a finished manuscript."

* * *

The employees had left the government building for the night, but Barbara remained, fretting in her office. She chewed the end of a pen and studied the second file on her computer that was part of the

Congressional budget for endangered species, primarily for wolf studies.

Felix was one of her best analysts, fast and thorough, but she was still astonished that the young man had stumbled across the file. Most analysts let their computers guide them through the system. Since a computer wouldn't pick up the error of hyphens between the numbers, an analyst also wouldn't see them or the duplicate file.

She crossed her arms with the dilemma. Would Felix ignore it or tell someone? If he did mention the fraudulent file to another employee or supervisor, the information could eventually end up with the FBI, which would investigate the misappropriation of funds and then turn their findings over to the attorney general. Her part in the cover-up could land her in prison.

She hit the computer key and deleted the second file from the system. Staring at the blank screen, she wondered if this would be the end of it. She grabbed her purse and coat and left her office. In the elevator she bypassed the parking garage and her car and got off at the street level. She strolled several blocks to her favorite lounge in need of a drink.

She arrived at Tonic, named because the old three-story brick building had once been Quigley's Pharmacy. The tavern was popular with the after-work crowd, mostly government employees. The place was packed, every bar stool and table occupied, so she took the staircase to the quieter third-floor bar and hoped the cute bartender was working.

She sat down at the small, cozy bar and stared at the fireplace and antique mantle.

The lean barkeep with high cheek bones and sparkling green eyes acknowledged her with a smile. "Hi, Barbara," he said, stepping to her, "Gin and tonic?"

Nodding with a smile, she thought, *Too bad he's gay, but that's the story of my life.* Felix was another example today. She couldn't catch a break. She gulped down the gin and tonic and ordered another. She dug into her purse for her mobile phone and tapped the number.

"What is it, Barbara?" asked a man's voice.

"We might have a problem."

CHAPTER FIVE

Christian made two more visits to the road, hoping to appease the reporters. Satisfied with his statement, some video, and pics, the mainstream media left his horse farm in Myakka City, but they'd been replaced with a different kind of press. The paparazzi cars now lined the gate. These guys were relentless and experts at waiting out a target. They worked around-the-clock shifts and had two-foot telephoto lenses on tripods focused on his house.

On the Internet Christian learned he'd become a tabloid celebrity. Most stories were flattering, portraying him as the handsome, lone-wolf terrorist who heroically fought for wildlife. He could deal with the limelight but was irritated that they barely mentioned the wolf massacre in America. Instead, they concentrated on his personal life. The articles disclosed everything about him; his age, height, the color of his eyes, his birthplace and passions, like sailing, surfing, and horses. They also interviewed people who knew him and might have earlier photographs of him. Annoyed, he refused to step outside and oblige the paparazzi for a new photo.

He had been dealing with the harassment and articles all right until a week earlier. One of the rags had published a story about the unsolved murder of his wife. The tabloid speculated that her death had unhinged the young widower and put him on the path of lawbreaking to help sharks. The information rang true to a degree, but rattled him so much that he wanted to pull out a gun and hunt down the reporter. Rather than resort to violence, he'd gotten drunk. The miserable hangover on the following day was a reminder. Drugs and excessive drinking ignited his temper and brought on suffocating despair. He had to remain stable for the sake of his cause.

As the days passed, he felt more and more like a caged animal, pacing past the windows. How long would the press stalk him? He grew bored of TV watching to pass the time. Researching the state of wolves in the claustrophobic house was also a mistake. A day earlier he had gotten so edgy and frustrated that he'd thrown a full drink against a wall. He gazed at the dripping wood and shattered glass, realizing he needed to lower his stress level. At that rate, he'd go on a rampage and destroy the place. Being an outdoors guy, he made a lousy shut-in.

He stepped to the bookshelf and looked at his collection of fantasy and science fiction novels. When owning a boat rental business, he had sat on the dock and devoured novels in between dealing with customers. He removed the first book in the *Game of Thrones* series and decided to reread it. The stories were lengthy, and he liked that George RR Martin portrayed wolves as noble characters. The author also supported a wolf sanctuary. *This is appropriate and should keep me busy.*

He closed the bedroom blinds and crawled into bed with the novel. He soon was transported into another world. After two days, he was halfway into the second book. He took a sandwich break and checked his computer. An eastern executive of the World Wildlife Fund had sent him an email, thanking him for his generous donation of ten thousand dollars and invited Christian to a private event in Atlanta for its supporters. The venue focused on WWF work with tigers and rhinos in India.

He nearly hit the Delete key and then reconsidered. He replied that he'd be happy to attend its event next month. Among wildlife supporters and enthusiasts he could discuss the wolf extermination. He closed the computer with a slight chuckle. *They obviously didn't put two and two together. Doubt I'd get an invite if they knew I'm the Christian Roberts suspected of being Captain Nemo.*

* * *

For two weeks the paparazzi staked out the farm gate, persistent to photograph and/or question Christian. At least the farm provided a good distance between them and his house door. Still, he'd grown beyond antsy with the home confinement and was losing his patience. He had finished the fantasy series but lacked the focus to start another book. His only visitor was Juan, who strolled up in the morning after feeding the horses. He gave Christian a brief report on the horses and filled any grocery requests.

During that time, a Sarasota FBI agent had called, obviously getting his cell number from Wheeler. The agent wanted an official interview on Christian's whereabouts during the terrorist bombing in Idaho. Christian said he'd already his alibi to the Miami agent, and unless an arrest warrant existed, he was done.

He also phoned to his mother, but only out of necessity. If he avoided her calls, she'd drive out to the farm and harp in his face. She expressed her concerns about the accusation in the news and his mental state. She begged him to schedule an appointment with his shrink. He assured her he was fine and was innocent of charges. Both were lies.

The alone time had him dwelling on his horrific past and symptoms of depression began. He knew the signs; nightmares, tiredness, a feeling of being worthless, and a desire to end it all. To combat those lows before, he'd worked outside until exhausted. Now, however, the activities of fence repair, mucking out stalls, working in the garden, or scrubbing down his boat were out of reach.

Adding to his growing gloom in the housebound hell, he questioned his role to help wolves. The shark cause had been a spontaneous reaction. His wife's death gave him the grieving rage and direction to abolish the fin trade. The wolf issues were more complicated; too many players in too many places, and Christian's motivating fury was gone. *Am I really up to this task?*

His only pleasant distraction was sneaking out at night to walk past the small lake and enter the barn. With the moderate weather, most of the horses, including Hunter, Christian's personal mount, resided in the pastures. Only the two stallions occupied the stalls. Stepping into the barn, Christian only had to say, "Hey, boys." Chris, his father's old bay stud, responded with a friendly, deep-throated nickering while Mystery, the fiery chestnut, whinnied excitedly. After grooming the boys and petting the barn cats, he returned to the house, feeling better. But every afternoon the thunderstorms rolled in and the overcast sky reflected his mood.

On the third week of confinement he had enough. His phones were probably tapped, so he picked up a disposable cell phone and called Sal. "I gotta get the hell out of here."

Sal chuckled. "Going a little stir crazy, are we?"

"Yeah, I'm miserable, ready to jump out of my skin."

"What about the press at your place? Not to mention the fucking cops are probably up the road doing surveillance. You leave, and they'll all just follow you."

Christian looked out the window at a car and van. "A few reporters still have a hard-on for me, but I haven't seen any unmarked cars. The closest food and toilet is seven miles away, and I've noticed they sometimes take off for an hour at night. That's when I'm making my break."

"Where ya goin'?"

"I'm taking Juan's old pickup and doing the back roads, going to Arcadia and doubling back on Clark Road to Sarasota and my boat. We need to hook up."

"Where?"

"O'Leary's on Island Park. It's down from the marina and my sloop. I'll meet you at noon tomorrow for lunch."

"Okay, but you're buying."

At midnight Christian saw the last car, a small compact, leave the road frontage to go north toward Sarasota. He hurriedly flung a duffle bag of clean clothes over his shoulder and picked up the computer case and a burner phone. He strolled down the dark drive past the barn to the back of the farm and Juan's house. In the bed of the old truck he placed his bag alongside a cooler full of groceries that Juan had left for him. He climbed into the cab and drove off the farm without headlights, using moonlight to guide him. After half a mile on the deserted road, he saw he wasn't being followed and turned on the truck lights. *What a pain,* he thought.

Nearly two hours later he pulled up to Marina Jack's and his docked sloop. The bayfront was empty except for a couple on a late-night stroll. After stowing the cooler and his gear, he collapsed on the topside bench in the open cockpit. The aromas of salt and seaweed drifted on the night breeze and seemed rehabilitating. He closed his eyes, and the torment of confinement diminished.

The following morning Christian woke in the cabin with no memory of a nightmare. Outside he heard the caws of gulls and the hum of an outboard motor zipping across the bay. He slipped into a pair of cutoffs and made coffee. With a mug in hand he left the galley and reclined on the outside deck. He gazed up at a cloudless turquoise heaven as the sun warmed his body and a light wind flicked at his hair. With the ambiance and freedom, he felt content and renewed. *Okay,* he thought, *let's save these wolves.*

At noon Christian dressed in a loose shirt and jeans and slipped on his sandals and sunglasses. He left his docked sloop and meandered down the boardwalk toward Island Park. When passing the large cabin cruisers that were sport fishing charters, he nodded a good morning to a few crewmen sitting on bait and ice coolers.

In five minutes he entered O'Leary's, a small tiki-style restaurant that hugged the shoreline, and he ordered sweet tea at the counter. With his cold drink he walked under the thatched-roof cabana with a panorama view of the bay and sat down at a picnic table. Two young women with basket lunches procured the adjacent table, facing him. One girl nudged the other and whispered, grinning at him. He reciprocated with his own smile, but worried if they'd seen his photo in a paper and recognized him. *This was stupid, parading around in the open as if I'm invisible.* Maybe he'd blown his location, or their interest might be merely physical attraction.

"Are you from around here or just visiting?" one asked.

Physical attraction, he thought with relief. "I'm a homeboy." Staying at the busy marina only a block from downtown was inviting the press to find him. After lunch with Sal, he'd move the sloop offshore.

He heard a deep Brooklyn accent behind him. "Okay, homeboy, let's take it to another table."

Christian glanced over his shoulder at a wall of loud floral on the huge guy. "Nice shirt, Sal."

They moved to the edge of the cabana, away from others. Sal placed his beer on the rough wooden table and straddled the picnic bench. "I hate these outdoor joints. I sweat like a pig and fight the damn flies for my food."

"But the view is great."

"I can enjoy the fucking view in air conditioning."

"Indulge me. I've been a shut-in for weeks and get bummed without sunlight."

"Kid, there ain't much sunshine in the slammer. Maybe you should consider a career change, quit while ahead."

Christian pushed his sunglasses up to his forehead, and his gaze penetrated Sal's. Somberly, he said, "I'll never go to prison."

Sal nodded, catching Christian's drift. "Ya know, Kid, takes a lot of guts to blow your brains out."

"I'm aware." *Well aware,* he thought. Twice his shaking hand had placed a gun to his head. However, fate, not a lack of guts, had interceded and stopped him.

"On a more cheerful note," Sal said cynically. "What's up?"

Over burgers and fries Christian explained how state and federal agencies had changed the laws and put wolves on the chopping block. "It's bad enough that hunters and ranchers are shooting wolves, but the US Forestry Service and the secretary of Agriculture have their own group of assassins. It's called Wildlife Services. These bastards used to be called Animal Damage Control, but the name was changed to fool the public. They're ruthless hunters and trappers who killed three and half million animals last year, everything from beavers to bears. That list included hundreds of wolves. Someone needs to send a message to those assholes."

"I'm assuming that someone is you."

"I gotta start somewhere."

"You want to target a federal agency?" Sal shook his black curls. "Let me enlighten ya. You're a newcomer to crime, but I've been at it since the Eighties, back in the mob's heyday, when we moved drugs from Miami to New York. It's no big deal to take out private enterprise, like a restaurant or knock off a competitor, but there's one rule we don't break; never fuck with the government. That means cops, politicians, or even agencies. They put you in their sights and don't stop until you're down and out. Kid, you don't want to go there."

"I can wreak havoc on the hunting clubs, ranchers, even a restaurant sponsoring a wolf hunt, but government is the root of the problem. I learned a thing or two with the shark cause. I wasted time and energy taking out fishing boats, exporters, and grocery stores that dealt with fins. Customer demand for shark fin soup was really the heart of the problem. Once I hit consumers, the shark slaughter stopped."

"There's gotta be another way."

"There isn't. The legal options have been tried. Conservation groups have filed lawsuits. The protests and petitions have failed. The government bastards have ignored everything, don't give a damn about what the public wants, and they definitely don't give a shit about wolves."

"Wildlife Services, huh?"

"Yeah, I just learned about a wolf pack in Washington State that killed a couple of cows on public land. Wildlife Services went in and exterminated the entire pack. There're hardly any wolves in the goddamn state, and the rancher could've collected government subsidies, and we're talking public land, paid for by taxpayers who want wolves protected. Those lousy cattle shouldn't have been there in the first place. It's bullshit."

"I see the boys in that agency really piss you off, but they're almost like cops. Kid, you need to rethink this."

"Sal, I'm going after them, with or without your help. I don't care if they work for the government, and I'm not concerned with consequences."

Sal poked a finger in his ear and stared at his mug. "Anyone ever say that you're a stubborn little fucker?"

"Haven't been called little in a while," Christian said, smiling. "Anyway, I've come up with a plan where no one gets hurt."

"Plan all you want, but shit happens. There're no guarantees that all goes smooth." Sal sipped his beer and sighed. "All right, first things first, you're too popular right now with the press and cops, so you can't be part it. You need an air-tight alibi when the shit goes down. I believe Vince taught you that."

Christian recalled when Vince arranged for him to hire a conspirator for the New York job. On the night of the bombing, Christian was in Miami, eating dinner with an FBI agent. It was a solid, almost laughable, alibi. Agent Wheeler, however, wasn't amused.

"If I'm out, who do you have in mind?" Christian asked.

"My boys won't touch it. They'd never risk pissing off the government." Sal looked up, contemplating and massaged his chin. "Ya know there is this guy, real professional but a brutal, cold-blooded killer. For the right price, he'd choke his grandmother and never lose sleep. I can hook you up, but I'm advising against it."

"I want him."

"Suit yourself, but you might regret it."

After lunch Christian followed the big Italian to his black Caddy in the parking lot. "When I get back to the marina, I'm moving the sloop offshore. Too many people here might recognize me." He pointed south along US 41 and the bayfront. "I'll anchor off Selby Gardens, not far from downtown for a hookup. When will you contact this bad dude?"

"I'll try this afternoon, but Vince asked me to look after you. Maybe I should handle the sit-down. Keep you out of the fray."

"Thanks, but no thanks. This is my gig, my ass if things go wrong."

"Okay," Sal said with a raised brow. "I should know something in a few days including how much this gig is gonna cost your ass. Just be careful. You tend to come off cocky, and it's irritating. You don't want to upset this guy."

Christian grinned. "I'll slap on a smile and kiss his butt."

"I'm serious, Christian," Sal said, and climbed into his car.

Watching the Cadillac drive out of the parking lot, he was struck that Sal had never called him Christian. He shrugged off the big guy's concern. Living with a death wish numbed most fears. He did, though, plan to be agreeable for the sake of his cause.

He wandered back to his sloop and started the diesel inboard. After casting off the dock lines, he backed out of the slip and motored to the fuel pumps behind Marina Jack's restaurant. Gas powered the engine that ran the generator. He wanted the boat prepared if the unexpected arose and forced a long stay on the water. When docking at the pumps, he noticed the thunder clouds in the east beyond the Sarasota high-rises making their rumbling march from Central Florida to the Gulf.

The sloop rocked in the strong gusts as Christian topped off the tank. He paid the dock attendant and said, "Looks like it's moving in fast."

"Yeah, gale warnings are up," the attendant said, looking at the threatening sky. "You need to tie up and wait until it passes."

Christian smiled. "I'm more a dance-in-the-rain kinda guy."

The attendant frowned and hurried inside for cover. Christian threw on a foul-weather jacket and fired up the engine just as the storm unleashed a downpour. In the heavy rain and thirty-knot winds, he guided the sloop out of the marina inlet and into the rough bay. The sloop heaved and rolled in the whitecaps. The trip was too short to bother with sails, so he motored through the anchored sailboats and past a large catamaran offshore of Island Park. Several hundred yards from the beach, he dropped anchor in front of Marie Selby Botanical Gardens, known for its research on exotic tropical plants.

He sat on the pitching deck and watched the lightning crackle and crisscross the gray sky. A loud boom followed a lightning bolt that struck the bay less than a mile away. Most people would hunker down in the cabin, but he thrived in these conditions; they made him feel alive.

After an hour the storm subsided and the bay calmed. In a steady drizzle, he stared across the water at Selby and recalled when he took Allie there. They had walked down the path inside the orchid solarium, and she instantly fell in love with the flowers. She'd grown up in central Florida which is prone to freezes that kill orchids. After walking the grounds, they entered the small gift shop, and he bought Allie her first of many orchids. The plants soon commandeered the back porch. After she died, he gave the orchids away. It was too hard. Every time one bloomed, it broke his heart.

For the next few days aboard, Christian kept busy while waiting for Sal's call. He used his laptop to investigate Wildlife Services and made mental notes on its operation and locations. He also worked on the sloop. Wearing a mask and fins, he jumped into the bay and scrubbed down the boat hull. The twice-a-year job kept the algae and barnacles from growing on the fiberglass. At sunset he fished for dinner, catching sugar and speckled trout with a small lure.

Sal called on the third evening. "Okay, he's flying in and will meet you tomorrow night, eleven o'clock at Monkey Business. It's a bar on Main."

"I know it. How do I find him?"

"He'll find you." Sal chuckled. "I described you as blond and the best-looking joker in there. He expects fifty grand upfront and another fifty when the job is done. You do have that kind of money on hand?"

"I have it."

"Okay, just remember. Behave."

The following morning, Christian woke with the dawn light filtering through the sloop portholes. He sat up in the queen-sized berth and rubbed the stubble on his jaw. Shaving wasn't a priority when alone on a boat, but for that night's visit to town, he'd clean up. *Need to make a good impression on my new employee.*

He slipped off the bed and stepped to a small closet. Like the secret floor compartment in his house, he had created a similar one on his sloop. He shoved the hangers of clothing aside and removed a wooden partition that hid a slot for valuables, such as his laptop and burner phone. The only difference was money. He had stashed several hundred thousand on board in case the authorities obtained an arrest warrant and came after him. His plan was to flee into the Gulf and disappear in the Caribbean. He took out a stack of bills, counted out fifty thousand dollars, and placed the money in a small duffle bag.

Toward evening he showered, shaved, and dressed in jeans and a dark blue shirt. Under cover of darkness, he flung the duffle bag over a shoulder and climbed down the aft ladder to the dinghy. The distance to shore involved a short paddle and didn't require the boat's ten-horse outboard. Besides being noisy, the expensive little outboard was a tempting target for a thief in a shadowy park. He rowed to O'Leary's, beached the small boat alongside several others, and strolled across the highway into downtown. He was tired of fish, so he stopped at Two Señoritas, a Mexican restaurant. At the bar he ordered a margarita and a taco platter. The place was quiet, but he kept his head down and didn't make eye contact, hoping to eat and slip out without notice. The ducking and hiding was getting aggravating, especially on his home turf. *Don't want to move but might have to.* Central America came to mind.

He finished his meal without detection. Not wishing to press his luck on the brightly lit and populated Main Street, he crossed the road and entered an alley. He walked in the shadows for several blocks and turned on Orange Avenue to reach the bar. Monkey Business was a lively place, but from the sidewalk, the dimly lit establishment appeared closed and resembled a small sandwich shop with a few tables and an unmanned back counter.

Christian opened the door, saw no one, and walked past the patched brick walls and empty tables. He stepped behind the counter, pushed aside a black curtain and proceeded down a bleak corridor that opened up to a brightly lit, crowded bar. He skipped the first lounge and shuffled through the patrons to the less-congested second bar. Beyond, a murky backroom contained with a few tables and a back door that opened to the alley. The place was an old-fashioned speakeasy and created the mood of stepping back to the 1920s during Prohibition.

He took up a stool at the end of the bar, lowered the duffle bag to the floor, and glanced at his watch. It was only 9:30. Sal's badass would not arrive for hours. The bartender asked Christian for his drink order. The place was known for its mixology and had a huge menu of original concoctions, but Christian wanted his wits about him and couldn't risk getting hammered on a strange drink. He normally was a rum and Coke drinker, but he'd started with tequila and figured he better stick with it. He didn't need to chance a hangover from mixing alcohol.

His margarita arrived, and he knocked off the excess salt on the rim before taking a sip.

A short slip of a man with greasy sparse hair sat down beside him and ordered a vodka and tonic. He turned to Christian and asked, "You come here often?"

"Once in a while."

"This place is great," the man said. "A guy at my hotel said I should check it. I needed a break from the old lady and kids, so I here I am. I plan to do some fishing when the family is at Disney." He leaned back to take Christian in. "You look like the outdoor type. Do you know much about fishing?"

"Some."

"Great, maybe you can tell where to go and what bait to use," the man said as the bartender placed his drink on the bar. "Hey, put his drink on my tab," he said to the bartender and with a grin, nodded toward Christian.

"No thanks, really. I'd rather buy my own." For the cost of a drink, he'd be stuck with the tourist yapping in his ear.

The guy shoved a twenty toward the barkeep. "No argument, I'm buying. My name's Bill."

"Chris," he said. Shaking Bill's hand, he got a good look at the mousey guy. Bill was flat-out ugly with not one redeeming quality. His eyes bulged and his big floppy lips held a smile of crooked teeth.

"Now let's talk fishing, Chris. I'm staying on Lido and thought I'd try Big Pass." He rambled on about his fishing experiences that consisted of the muddy lakes in Ohio, fishing for crappies.

Christian surmised that the poor guy was lonely and wanted a drinking buddy more so than fishing advice. Ordinarily it wouldn't be a problem. Christian didn't mind chatting with Yankees about fishing; however, he was there to talk business with a tough hit man and didn't need Bill interfering. Christian smiled politely but kept hoping Bill would go back to his hotel and family.

After an hour, Bill scowled. "You keep glancing at your watch. Are you expecting someone, a girl maybe?"

"No girl, but I am meeting someone."

"You don't need anyone else when I'm here." Bill leaned closer. "I'll take care of you, baby," he whispered and placed his hand on Christian's crotch and caressed his penis.

So shocked, Christian sprang backwards, stumbling while nearly overturning his stool. "Are you fucking crazy? I'm straight!" he growled with clenched fists and shuddered with the offensive assault. His outburst caused the other patrons to turn and look at him. He sucked in several deep breaths for control. He already had one battery arrest on his record for losing his temper and didn't need another, especially now.

"Sorry for the misunderstanding, but I doubt I'm the first gay man to come on to you."

"You're the first to grope me. Look, I'm not homophobic, but you crossed the line, buddy." Christian snatched the duffle bag off the floor, intending to find another seat away from Bill.

"Sit down, Christian." Bill's hokey voice took on an authoritative tone. "Your fat friend said you'd be the best-looking guy in the place. That wasn't an exaggeration. You're gorgeous."

Christian glanced at his watch, eleven o clock. "You're … you're the guy, Sal's guy?" He lowered the bag and slowly sat back down.

Bill grinned. "I also was told you're a hothead. In my line of work, I have to make sure the client isn't stupid or excitable enough to lose his head. You passed the test."

"And how many failed and knocked the crap out of you?"

"None, but then again, you're the only one to get that exam. I find you irresistible and nicely hung. I'd like to offer you a freebie. I'll do the job for nothing if you cater to my needs; an hour alone in my hotel room."

"Forget it."

"A hundred grand is a lot of money, and I promise you'll enjoy it. After I'm done, you'll be moaning for more. Are you sure about turning me down?"

"Dead sure, now do you want to discuss business or not?"

"I thought we were," Bill mumbled. "I suppose we should go into the alley so you can tell me what you want done."

Christian finished his drink and thought *I'm going to kill Sal. He set me up with this prick, knowing he'd hit on me.* He picked up the bag of cash and stood. "Let's go."

They walked into the dark back room, and Bill said, "Last chance, baby. Drop your jeans and keep your money."

"Bill, if that's your real name, I've got money so you can't bribe me, but even destitute, I wouldn't be tempted."

"That's a shame but consider I'm willing to do things for you that no one else would."

Christian shook his head. Within a few hours, Bill had become obsessed and his hounding Christian for sex would be ongoing. *Time to end this bullshit.*

In the doorway Christian hesitated and looked down at Bill who stood chest high. "Let *me* explain things. I've known a lot of homosexuals, especially when I owned a boat rental business and had a following of gay customers. Some approached me, but it didn't bother me. I just brushed off their advance with a polite no thanks. Many of those guys became good drinking buddies. But you're obnoxious pestering is pissing me off." He looked out into the alley. "We step out there, and the only ass you need worry about is your own 'cause I'm close to kicking it."

"But you won't. You have bigger fish to fry."

CHAPTER SIX

On the Salmon River south of North Fort, Idaho, Teri sat in the front of the canoe and gazed at the forest lining the bank. Halfheartedly she'd paddled, preferring to be just a sightseer. Melvin, her boyfriend of a few months, was in the back doing most the work and used his paddle like a rudder to guide the boat in the swift current.

"Mel, I have to go," she said, and glanced back at his frown.

"Jesus, Teri, you just went. At this rate we'll never catch up. The others will be done with lunch and gone by the time we reach the picnic area. Can't you wait?"

"No," she said and leaned back to remove another canned drink from the cooler. "I was a good sport to go on this little canoe trip of yours, but I have needs."

"If you stopped guzzling Cokes, you wouldn't have to pee so often."

"I'm thirsty. Now pull over, before I wet my pants."

"Jesus," Melvin grumbled and maneuvered the canoe onto the bank. Head down with disgust, he stared at the idle paddle that rested across his knees.

Teri clumsily climbed out of the canoe and stood on the shoreline, scanning the tree line that was several yards from the river. "Do you think bears are in there?"

"No."

She took a few steps toward the brush and stopped. "What about snakes? Maybe you should go with me."

"Jesus, it's too cold for snakes. Will you please get on with it?"

"Fine," she said with a huff and stomped into the bushes and trees. A good distance from the river, she unfastened her jeans and squatted. "I'm done with this jerk," she muttered and then noticed a shiny object that mirrored sunlight from the underbrush. She pulled up her pants and stepped toward it to investigate. A few minutes later she emerged back on the river by the canoe. "Melvin, you're not going to believe what I found."

* * *

In the town of Salmon, Charlie Tucker, the chief of police, leaned back in his office chair and propped his cowboy boots on the desk. A tabloid rested in his lap as he read the story on page eight. The caption said, "Captain Nemo Suspect Refuses to Cooperate with Authorities." Above the article was a photo of Christian Roberts. "Son of a bitch, making a mockery of this case," he cursed and tossed the magazine into the trashcan.

As the Miami FBI agent predicted, no evidence or witness had been found to tie Roberts to the restaurant bombing, even with the help of the feds and US Marshals. A crime unpunished in his town didn't sit well with Charlie. Desperate for a clue, he had his secretary gather every scrap of news on Captain Nemo and Roberts. Most of the articles in the mainstream press appeared within a week of the terrorist attack, but the public grew fascinated with Roberts, and the tabloids put him in their sights. Rather than condemn Roberts for his possible crimes, the magazines glorified him as a charismatic anti-hero committed to protecting wildlife.

Helen entered his office and placed a magazine on Charlie's desk. "Here's another one, Chief. There's nothing new, but it has a nice photo of him on his horse farm. He's a pretty boy."

"Helen, try and remember he's a felon, and stop swooning over him." He plopped his boots on the floor and stood. Looking down at the new photo, he grumbled, "If this young whippersnapper thinks he can get away with blowing up a business in *my* town, he's got another thing coming."

"Maybe he's innocent."

"Horse shit." The phone on Charlie's desk rang, and he snatched it up. "Yeah, what is it?"

"Chief, you'd better come up to Wagon Wheel in the North Fort," said one of his officers. "A young couple traveling downriver discovered a canoe. It was hidden deep in the bushes about a mile south of the campground. The kids pulled it out and towed it here. Millie called us in, thinking it might belong to that terrorist."

"I'll be right there. Keep those kids there, and don't let anyone touch the canoe." He hung up and looked at Helen. "Call that FBI agent in the Idaho office and tell him we have an abandoned canoe at the Wagon Wheel in North Fort. It could be Captain Nemo's. Then call Roy and have him bring the river skiff to the campground."

"Will do, Chief," Helen said as Charlie grabbed his hat and jacket off the coat rack. He hustled outside to his Jeep.

Charlie arrived at the Wagon Wheel, but instead of stopping at the office, he drove through the campsites and parked next to his officer's car. He crossed a small bridge over a stream and took a path through a sparse forest. He saw his officer and several others standing around a canoe. A second canoe, an outpost rental, was beached on the riverbank.

"Anything in it?" Charlie called when approaching the group.

"Nothing but a paddle and leaves, Chief," answered the officer. "The manufacturer's metal plate and number has even been removed. No telling who owned it."

Charlie glanced into the canoe and then focused on the bystanders, Millie and her husband, Harold, who owned the place; a couple of men in camouflage hunting jackets, obviously campers; and a young couple. "Are you the two who found it?" he asked the couple.

"Yes, sir," answered the guy, "found it about a mile upriver. I went through the trouble of dragging it through heavy brush and towing it downriver. I planned to come back for it with my truck. Now this officer says I can't have it."

"That's right," said Charlie. "It might be evidence in a crime. After we're finished with it, it's yours."

"Wait a minute," said the girl. "I found the canoe. It's mine."

"Jesus, you don't even like canoeing," said the young guy, "and I did all the work getting it here."

Charlie broke into the couple's argument and said to young guy, "You said you found the canoe in heavy brush. About how far was it from the river?"

"At least a hundred feet," answered the guy. "It was a ways."

Charlie scratched the back of his head and looked at the leaves in the boat hull. "Did you remove any debris from the boat?"

"No, sir, Chief, I was in a hurry, and figured I'd clean it up at home."

Charlie held his chin in thought. The small amount of leaves in the canoe confirmed it had been there only a month or so. River flooding occurred in the spring, so it hadn't floated into the trees. Someone stashed it there around the same time as the bombing. "You kids stay here until our police boat and FBI arrive. They'll take you upriver, and you can show us exactly where you found this canoe." Charlie turned to Millie and Harold. "While we're waiting, I'd like to see your guest registry for the night the restaurant was bombed."

"Of course," Millie said. She, Harold, and Charlie started up the path to the office. "You know I already showed it to an officer, a few days after the bombing."

"Your campground is the closest place to the ditched canoe and road access. Good chance the terrorist left from here."

"Your officer showed me the photo of a young blond man and said he might be Captain Nemo," said Millie. "He never was here and I'd remember. You don't come across many with his looks."

Just like Helen, Charlie thought. *Women are taken with this guy.* They entered the office, and Millie placed the registry on the counter and flipped to the day in question. The sheet contained the camper names, make and model of their vehicles, and the license plate numbers. "Looks like you had only two campsites rented that night. Do you remember the people?"

"Chief, that was nearly a month ago," said Millie. "I don't recall the visitors from last week."

Harold stepped forward. "I remember one of them, a great big guy, looked Italian and came from the East, had a New York accent." He pointed to a name on the registry. "That's him, George Smith. He was alone and paid cash for the site. His truck was a rental. You see enough of them, you know."

"So why do you remember him?" asked Charlie.

Harold grinned. "The guy struck me odd. He said he was here to fish, but he didn't know the difference between fly fishing and using a reel. Then it took forever for him to figure out the electric and water hookups to the truck, and it was pretty funny watching him try to make a pit fire. He wasn't much of a camper."

Millie scowled at her husband. "Why didn't you say something about him sooner?"

Harold shrugged. "I was out back when the police were here, and you said they were after a blond guy."

Charlie took out his radio and called the station. "Helen, run a plate check, and let me know as soon as you have it." He read off the license number and hung up. "I'd like to take this sheet and have it checked for fingerprints and DNA."

"You won't find anything, Chief," Harold said. "That was another strange thing. It wasn't cold, but the guy wore leather gloves when he signed in."

"I want the sheet anyway for a handwriting comparison," said Charlie. "Harold, I'd like you to describe that man to a police artist."

Millie's eyes grew big. "You think he's connected to the blond?"

"Could be."

* * *

Steve sat in his home office in Arlington, Virginia, and worked on the computer, installing a security program for an Arizona company. His wife, Karen, walked in with a scowl on her face. "Steve, I just did laundry. There's change all over the bottom of the washer. I wish you'd remember to empty your pockets."

"Sorry," Steve mumbled while tapping the keys on his computer. "By the way did you get a hold of Felix about tonight?"

"No, and I've called him all day. He's not answering his cell or home phone and hasn't responded to my texts. He was excited about his blind date tonight, but he hasn't bothered to find out where or when we're going."

Steve looked up from the computer screen. "That's not like Felix. He sleeps with his cell phone. Maybe the battery went dead or he's in an area out of range."

"Even so, he'd find a way to call us."

He glanced at the time. "If you don't hear from him by this afternoon, I'll go to his condo."

When Felix failed to contact them, Steve climbed in the car and headed for DC. He turned off the highway onto Corcoran Street in the quiet neighborhood. The road was lined with shade trees, bumper-to-bumper parked cars, and connecting three-story apartments and condos. Steve slowed at Felix's red brick building and saw his silver Honda parallel parked out front. He had to be home.

With no available parking space, Steve drove to the end of the block and left his car. He walked down the uneven sidewalk back to Felix's bottom-floor condo. He pressed the doorbell, but no one responded. Growing impatient, he banged on the door and yelled through the open window. "Felix, are you in there? It's Steve. Get up and answer the door."

He thought about leaving. Perhaps Felix was out with a friend in their car, or he might have walked to the nearby highway and was in a restaurant or coffee house. Those were the reasonable explanations for his absences, but a nagging feeling kept Steve on the doorstep. Felix was too reliable. He would never forget or blow off a dinner date without calling.

Steve took out his phone and called Felix's cell. He heard the *Star Wars* theme of Felix's cell phone ringing inside the condo. The music played and stopped, followed by the recording to leave a message. Steve's annoyance shifted to worry. Felix would never leave without his cell phone. Steve turned the door handle and was surprised to find it unlocked. He pushed the door open and stepped inside the small living room. "Felix, Felix," he called. "Are you in the bathroom?" After checking the kitchen, he entered the bedroom. "Oh, my god," he gasped and covered his mouth.

Felix lay on the bed fully clothed, his open brown eyes staring at the ceiling. Steve stepped closer and touched his friend's shoulder. His body was stiff and cold. He jumped back in shock. "Jesus, what happened?" He then noticed the syringe in Felix's arm.

Steve backed out of the room and fumbled for his phone. "I just found my friend in his condo. He's dead," he said excitedly to the 911 operator.

"Calm down, sir," said the operator. "Are you sure he's dead?"

"Yes, he's as hard as stone."

He gave the dispatcher the address, and she said to wait outside for the police. On the sidewalk he leaned against a huge elm tree and fought the growing moisture in his eyes.

A police car with flashing lights arrived in minutes. Steve explained to the two officers that he was a friend of the deceased and had come to Felix's condo when unable to contact him. Steve led them into the bedroom as two more squad cars and an ambulance arrived. One of the officers took his name and information for his report and told him to stick around. A detective would take his statement. Steve returned to the sidewalk and called Karen with the devastating news.

"A syringe?" she questioned with a sniffle. "Felix didn't do drugs."

"I know." He saw an unmarked car pull up and two men stepped out wearing suits. One was a big white guy with light cropped hair, and the other a medium-built black man. "Karen, I've got to go. I think the detectives are here."

The two detectives walked into the condo. A forensics van soon joined the line of law enforcement vehicles. After a while the black detective came outside and stepped up to Steve. "I'm Detective Graham. I was told you discovered the body."

"Close to an hour ago," Steve said, looking at his watch. He explained that he and his wife had dinner plans with Felix that evening, but grew concerned when they couldn't reach him.

"What can you tell us about your friend?" asked Graham.

"He is or was thirty-five and single, lived alone. He worked as a computer consultant for the government. He was originally from New York, and I believe his brother and parents still live there."

"We found his address book and will contact the parents about his death," said Graham. "Have you ever known him to do drugs?"

"No, he didn't even smoke cigarettes. At his government job they do random drug tests. He wouldn't risk being fired."

"Your friend doesn't appear to be a user. No track marks on his arms, but heroin was found inside the bathroom vanity. Maybe he was trying it for the first time and miscalculated the dose."

"No way," Steve said, shaking his head. "Felix never miscalculated anything. None of this makes sense."

"We'll know more when our investigation is further along," said Graham. "Forensics is dusting for prints, and we'll question the neighbors, but there's no sign of foul play or a break-in. Nothing disturbed, and his wallet with cash and credit cards is on the dresser and his laptop is on the desk. In the next few days I'll need you to come to the station and sign a statement." He handed Steve his card.

Head down, Steve walked down the street to his car. He stopped and looked up as the coroner van drove past.

A few days later Steve went to the police station and met Detective Graham. He was introduced to Graham's partner, Detective O'Conner. Steve read his typed statement as Graham waited for his signature.

"Yeah, that's about it," Steve said and scribbled his name on the paper. "Did you find out anything new on Felix's death?"

"The autopsy confirmed that Felix Alveras died from a heroin overdose, but you were right," said Graham. "It wasn't accidental. We found a one-line note in the printer tray that basically said that he couldn't handle the pressure. We've ruled his death as a suicide."

"I don't buy that," Steve said adamantly. "Felix was happy. He wouldn't kill himself. He was looking forward to his date that night and told me he planned to buy a new car."

O'Conner added to the conversation. "Some people hide their depression, even from family and friends. We interviewed his supervisor, Barbara Davis, and she concurred, saying your friend seemed down and was moody in the workplace."

"Felix might've been moody with Davis. He didn't like her, and if he was down about his job, he would've quit. With his qualifications, he could work anywhere. Another thing. A one-line note doesn't sound like him. His emails were page-long."

"Maybe he was in a hurry," said O'Connor. "Who knows what goes through a person's mind?"

Steve looked at the two detectives. "I knew this guy, saw him nearly every week. There's more to his death."

Graham placed his hand on Steve's shoulder. "I'm sorry for your loss, but we have to go where the evidence takes us. We're releasing his body and closing the case."

A week later, Steve and Karen flew to New York for Felix's funeral. After the service, they introduced themselves to his distraught family outside the small Catholic church. Gill, Felix's brother, took them aside. "My brother mentioned you two," he said. "It seemed you were always part of his weekend plans."

"He was our best friend," Karen said and dabbed a tissue to her tears.

"I wasn't close to my brother in the last few years," Gill said, "but heroin and suicide? I still can't believe it."

"Don't," said Steve. "We saw him enough to know if he had issues. Something stinks. The case was wrapped up too fast and neat. I'd love to see Felix's laptop, go through his emails and documents. Maybe there's a clue that the police missed."

Karen said, "Steve installs computer security for companies, and he's as good as it gets when it comes to hacking."

"I'd appreciate it if you checked it out. My parents are overwrought, so I'm handling Felix's affairs. Next week I'm taking off work and coming to DC. to box up my brother's belongings and meet with a real estate agent to list the condo. I also have to swing by the police station and pick up Felix's wallet and laptop. When I have them, I'll call. We can figure out a day to get together."

On Sunday afternoon Steve sat at his desk and tapped the keys on Felix's laptop. Gill sat next to him, and Karen stood behind Steve's chair. They all intently stared at the screen.

Steve leaned back in the chair after hours of scrutiny. "Nothing, just typical emails," he said with a sigh. "Some are to coworkers about the job. Here's one to an author, asking if she'd look at the first chapter of his manuscript. He was writing a science fiction novel. Another one to his supervisor, requesting his vacation dates. I've scanned all his files and gone through several months of emails, downloads, and documents. His most recent search was for sports cars." He looked up at Gill. "He said he was buying a new one next month. Who kills himself when they're about to get a new ride?"

"It's the one-line suicide note that bothers me. That's not Felix," said Karen. "If he planned to kill himself, his explanation would have been a lot longer."

"I mentioned that to the detective," said Steve.

Gill stood and circled the room. "If he wasn't using drugs and didn't commit suicide, what happened?"

With an elbow on the desk, Steve held his chin. "Maybe he was murdered. Someone held him down and shot him up with drugs."

"But who, why?" asked Gill.

"Unfortunately his laptop is a blank, no mention of any problems."

"Wait a minute, Steve." Karen leaned over and stared at the laptop screen. "Maybe it's not what's on his computer, but what isn't. Where's the email about the wolf study and the mysterious second file that he sent to his private server from work?"

Steve tapped the keys and scanned the old, sent, deleted, and spam emails again. "It's not there, not even in the archives. Whoever deleted it also bleached it, so it could never be recovered. They knew what they were doing."

"Felix didn't do it," said Karen. "He wanted that file for insurance, in case the misappropriated funds were discovered and it meant his job."

"What are you talking about?" asked Gill.

"Felix was working on the Congressional budget for endangered species," said Steve. "He came across a file for the funds slated for a wolf study, but an identical second file had been created, and the money, several million, appeared to flow into an unknown account. Felix and I dismissed it as a computer glitch, but possibly the person responsible for the second file was covering his tracks. He kills Felix, deletes the file, and then prints out a fake suicide note."

"My god, it sounds like something out of a movie," said Gill.

Karen gripped Steve's shoulder. "Felix forwarded that file to us, and that email is also missing. The killer knows we're involved."

CHAPTER SEVEN

"I got her signal. Move to the left," Gary ordered the helicopter pilot. "She's up ahead."

The pilot adjusted course as they flew over the vast Idaho landscapes of snowy forests and mountains. No dwellings or vehicles had been spotted for miles. "Are you sure we're supposed to be here, Gary? Congress designated this Boulder-White area as a protected wilderness. Hunting is prohibited. People can't even camp or hike here."

"We're Wildlife Services, and go where we want," Gary said and looked down at the radar screen in his lap. "Slow down; we should be able to spot her." He put the tracking device aside and picked up his rifle. He stared out the window and pointed. "There, there she is, and another one is with her. Get on top of them." He took aim, putting the grayish-tan wolf in the crosshairs of the scope and fired. When the wolf collapsed in the snow, he felt the rush of accomplishment, like winning a gold trophy. "Got one!" he shouted and quickly pushed another shell into the firing chamber. The second gray wolf ran toward the valley. "Go after her."

"Isn't one enough?"

Gary glanced up from the rifle at his new pilot. Jason's lame attitude was spoiling the fun and glory of the sport. "Shut up and get on it, boy."

The helicopter followed the wolf down the mountainside into a valley. Gary set his sights on her and mumbled, "Run your heart out, bitch. You're not going anywhere." He fired again. The wolf toppled head over heels. When the tumbling stopped, she sat up, yipping, and circled, dragging her crippled hind legs. Another shot and she was still. "Put it down."

Jason landed the helicopter near a half-frozen stream but didn't get out. Before the blades stopped rotating, Gary slid his big frame out of the passenger seat, still holding his weapon, and walked to the lifeless wolf. He poked her ribs with the rifle barrel to make sure she was dead. He heard growling and looked to the trees. A large black male had emerged from the forest. The wolf's back hairs were raised, and from his graying muzzle, he bared his teeth and snarled.

"Aren't you brave?" Gary grinned, slowly raised his rifle, and took aim. He shot the wolf in the chest, but it didn't immediately die. The male crumpled and clawed at the snowy ground to escape. Gary strolled within close range and delivered the fatal shot.

Jason left the chopper and opened the storage compartment as Gary picked up the black wolf and flung him over a shoulder. He ambled through the white drifts toward the helicopter.

"This big fella is heavy and has some age on him," Gary called, experiencing the same joy when a youth after shooting his first songbird with a BB gun. A day like today made him appreciate his profession, a year-round quest for wildlife. At the chopper he heaved the dead wolf on a canvas in the compartment and ran his hands over the plush black coat. "I'll be charging more than a couple hundred for his hide."

Jason touched the wolf's head and sighed. "I can't believe he came out of the woods and faced you."

"No doubt he was an alpha defending his female. Better go get her." After retrieving the gray female, he placed her body alongside the male. "It's been years since I brought down three in one afternoon. Heck of a hunting day."

Jason gazed at the female's collar. "Not sure I'd call it hunting. This radio collar led us right to her. It's supposed to be for research, but it's a death sentence. These poor wolves didn't stand a chance against a rifle and chopper."

Gary frowned at the pilot. "You're starting to irritate me, boy. You were hired because you're a veteran, accustomed to missions and bloodshed."

"I did two tours in Afghanistan and never had a problem shooting at someone who shot back, but slaughtering defenseless wolves is different. I thought the Wildlife Service was supposed to help animals."

"You thought wrong. We're paid to wipe out animals. Now let's go pick up the other one."

Jason started to close the compartment. "Gary, this female had pups." He pointed to the gray wolf's underbelly and the milk-filled mammary glands.

"I noticed. Damn shame her pups will probably die in the den. That'll mean fewer pelts for me. Let's get going. I'm hungry."

On the mountainside they landed on a shelf to collect the third wolf. Gary plodded through the deep snow to the grayish-tan wolf. Upon closer inspection of the animal, he was disappointed. The male was a half-grown youngster with a slender body and shabby coat. He grabbed the pup, observing it weighed half as much as its father, and returned to the chopper. He tossed the flimsy body on top of its parents, and he and Jason headed back in.

They flew to Hailey, Idaho, and the Wildlife Service helicopter landed at the Friedman Memorial Airport. Gary grabbed his rifle and climbed out. He opened the compartment and gazed at the three wolves on the bloody canvas. Jason joined him after the chopper blades stopped and the engine was silent.

"No sense lugging them to my pickup. I'll drive over. You can lock up after."

"Whatever you say," Jason grumbled with a lowered head.

Gary was getting fed up with his sullen partner. "Boy, you'd better get with the program. We work for the US Forestry Service and have the blessings of the secretary of Agriculture and the Interior. Last year we removed close to four hundred wolves and millions of other critters. If you don't have the stomach for this work, you need to move on. I'll get someone else."

"No, I need the job. My wife is expecting our first baby."

"All right," he said and marched across the tarmac to his blue Ford pickup that was parked next to a hangar for small planes. He drove alongside the helicopter, got out, and loaded the wolf carcasses into the truck bed. He turned to Jason, who was securing the chopper. "Come Monday, we'll head back to Boulder-White for more aerial hunting. While there I'll set out some foot-hold traps and cyanide bombs. Nothing escapes those babies."

"What about other animals that might die?"

"Bobcat, cougar, coyote, or a bear; it's all good; one less vermin to contend with."

Jason gave him a weary glance and walked to his car.

Shaking his head, Gary climbed into the pickup. He'd have to tell his supervisor that his new pilot was too soft, wasn't working out. Unfortunately he'd have to make do until Jason's replacement was found. *Goddamn bleeding-hearts. Animal lovers got no place with Wildlife Services.*

He drove down the highway and out of town until he came to a dusty road that led up into the hills. He arrived at his manufactured home and parked in front of a small warehouse where he performed taxidermy in his spare time. With hunting season in full swing, he was behind. Several deer heads and a cougar sat in a chest freezer and needed to be mounted for customers. He was also expected in Oregon that weekend. He placed the three wolves in a second freezer, figuring he would skin and tan their hides later.

The following morning, Gary bundled up two wolf and ten coyote pelts and put them in his pickup. He drove across the Idaho border into Oregon and arrived in the small town. On the one main street, he parked in front of Betty's shop that sold jewelry, Indian and Western stuff, and rustic furniture. He walked inside and heard Betty's elevated voice at the back counter as she argued with a customer. Not wanting to get involved, he stayed at the front of the store and pretended an interest in the junk.

"Wolves multiply like rabbits and kill people," Betty thundered, her round cheeks flushed with anger. Her large frame was pressed against the register, and her hard stare was focused on a blond woman who stood by a display of hanging pelts. "The sooner they're gone, the better."

The woman smiled. "There are less than eighty wolves in Oregon, so they're hardly multiplying like rabbits. As far as dangerous, wolves have killed only one person in the last hundred years. You should get your facts straight."

"And what makes you an authority?"

"I've done the research. I'm an author and am writing a novel about the wolf massacre out here." The woman turned to leave but paused. "By the way, you and your shop have made it into the book."

The woman left the shop, and Gary meandered to Betty, who still cursed under her breath. "Trouble?" he asked.

"These damn environmentalists and animal fanatics, they come in all smiles until they see the wolf fur. Then they start howling." She slammed the cash register shut. "So what do you have for me?"

"Two wolf and ten coyote pelts," said Gary.

"Just two wolves?" she said. "I'll have to order more from Canada."

Gary glanced toward the empty door. "That woman had a point. Wolves don't multiply fast, and their numbers are down."

"I get five hundred a pelt. Maybe I should raise the price."

* * *

Christian returned to his sloop at one in the morning after his meeting with Bill in downtown Sarasota. Along with the payment and instructions on the next Captain Nemo attack, he gave Bill an envelope containing a postcard addressed to Trish Stevenson at *The*

Washington Post. Several days before the terrorist attack, Bill would mail the Nemo warning.

In the cabin Christian plopped down on the small couch and grabbed the cell phone.

"What's up?" Sal asked groggily.

"You son of a bitch, I should tear you a new one. I just left Bill."

"What, did he come on to you?"

"You knew he would. The fucking prick not only hit on me, but grabbed my jeans and groped me."

"Holy shit!" Sal said and began laughing so hard that he coughed and choked. He managed to collect himself. "Sorry about that, Kid. I kinda figured he'd find you mouth-watering, but didn't know he'd go that far."

"You could've warned me he was gay."

Sal launched into another hysterical laughing fit. "Sorry, sorry, but I'm just picturing your face when that homo went for your dick. You're still breathing, so I take it you didn't deck him."

"I considered it but was more pissed off at you."

"Hey, I offered to handle the sit-down, but nooo. You wanted to be the big shot and do it. I, at least, warned you to keep your cool. That little fag don't look like much, but he's lethal, the best in the business."

"Whatever, I'm done," Christian said. "You can deal with him from now on." He decided to stop ranting about the humiliating incident when Sal was only enjoying it. He changed the subject. "Tomorrow morning I'm moving the sloop and mooring it off Vince's old place. It's easier to come and go. Next week I'll be in Atlanta for a wildlife event."

"Maybe I'll stop by before you go. We'll have a drink poolside."

"Sal, you can take that drink and shove it where the sun doesn't shine."

"Aw, the poor Kid," Sal said in a sappy tone, "still feeling mortified. When you're over the bruised ego, give me a call."

The following day Christian sailed the sloop under the John Ringling Bridge and into north Sarasota Bay, dropping anchor off Longboat Key and Vince's home. He still referred to the place as Vince's, even though Christian owned it. Over the next few days he spent most of his time on the boat except when he didn't feel like cooking. He then motored the dinghy with its small outboard to the waterfront restaurants for takeout.

The World Wildlife Fund party for wealthy donors fell on a Wednesday night, the next week. After emailing his RSVP, he had researched the conservation group that seemed focused on saving rhinos, elephants, and tigers, but recently, it had taken an interest in helping the American bison. Buffalo outnumbered wolves twenty to one, but wolves had an unpopular reputation. He hoped to change that misconception. The trip to Atlanta would be different than the one to Idaho; no secrecy involved. He didn't care who saw him there and planned to use his regular cell phone and leave a paper trail of credit card statements for gas and hotel bills, all to prove his location. It was his alibi.

Monday morning he took the dinghy to the house and tied it to the dock, planning to leave the following morning for Atlanta. He walked up the sidewalk past the manicured lawn and sparkling pool to the back door. He'd hired a real estate agent to employ services and maintain the property. So far, she was doing a good job. He had mulled over selling the place, but he and Vince had good times there, and Christian wasn't hurting for money. He considered also that someday he might get his head on straight, have friends over, and enjoy the luxurious waterfront home. The someday was wishful thinking.

He retrieved the key from his pocket, unlocked the door, and walked across the marble floors to the master bedroom. He had donated Vince's clothing to charity, so the nearly empty walk-in closet appeared massive. Some of his own clothes hung on hangers in case he spent the night. After thumbing through the shirts, he realized his suits and good clothes were at his mother's house and the farm. He wasn't about to drive out there and retrieve them. WWF expected a rich guy, and he decided to give them one. People listened better when impressed. He plopped down on the bed and mumbled, "God, I hate shopping."

He stood and looked in the mirror at his stained white T-shirt, tattered cutoffs, and sandals. The days living on the boat had him looking like a vagrant. He rubbed the stubble on his face and thought about shaving and changing into better clothes. "Screw it."

He had given Vince's cars to Sal to disperse them among his men, and since Christian arrived by boat, his first buy would be transportation. He pressed the Uber app on his cell and was informed a car would arrive in ten minutes. He walked to the kitchen, snatched a Coke from the sparse fridge, and stepped out the front door to wait for his ride. A tan SUV drove up to the curb, and Christian climbed in.

The driver said, "So we're going to the Porsche dealership on the South Trail?"

"Yeah, need some wheels."

The driver looked at his grubby clothing and chuckled. "Whatever you say, Buddy."

The previous year Christian had nearly purchased a Ferrari in Miami, but life and his causes got in the way. The Ferrari's maintenance might also be a problem, with no dealership in Sarasota. Kate, an ex-girlfriend before Allie, owned a Porsche that he had driven. Kate was a psycho bitch, but her car was really nice.

With light traffic he was at the Porsche dealership in half an hour and was meandering through the showroom of shiny new sports cars. The 911 Carrera S Cab was the most expensive at $190,000, but Christian was drawn to a sleek little black number, a convertible Boxster S that was half the price. In their glass offices, a few salesmen sat at their desks and glanced at him, but with his shabby appearance, they never left their seats. Christian smiled inwardly. The cliché "Never judge a book by its cover" came to mind.

A salesman entered the showroom from the back door and walked to him with a grin. He looked like a typical white guy until he spoke. "Hi, I'm Warren," he said with a South African accent. "Can I help you?"

Christian nodded toward the Boxster. "I want this one."

Warren smiled. "Son, you do realize that this car is ninety thousand."

"I can read a sticker." He removed his driver's license and the black American Express from his wallet and handed them to Warren. "Write it up."

With a glance at the card with unlimited credit, Warren's demeanor changed. "Mr. Roberts, I'm so sorry, but we don't accept credit cards anymore."

"All right, I'll wire the money from my bank."

"That will be fine, sir, but don't you want to test drive it?"

"I know how it handles, and I'm kinda in a hurry." When he purchased his SUV, he went through the buying-a-new-car hassle. Back then he was a struggling small business owner and was counting pennies. The renegotiating of the price with the back-and-forth game playing among the salesman, manager and him and then the car loan, credit check, and mile-long paperwork had taken all afternoon. He wasn't going through it again.

"While you're wiring the money and signing the papers on your car, I'll have the Boxster removed from the showroom and re-cleaned. I should have you out of here within the hour."

"That works."

They walked to an office, and Warren chuckled. "I've never made a sale so fast."

An hour later, Christian sat in the Porsche and was zipping around the slow-moving traffic on the highway. He glanced at the speedometer and saw he was going ninety in forty-five mph speed zone. "Whoa," he said, easing off the gas. "This baby is really smooth and fast." He grinned. "And fun."

He drove toward the University Mall for new duds, realizing if he gave up his causes, he could kick back and enjoy his wealth. Happiness might not elude him. He shook his head. *A year tops, and I'd be bored silly.*

He entered the mall, and after several hours of shopping, he concluded that buying the car was painless in comparison. Finding, trying on, and purchasing decent clothing was drudgery. He spent another six grand on a black Armani suit, a couple of linen shirts, a pair of shoes, tie, some casual wear of jeans, and a leather jacket. He trudged into the parking lot and loaded the packages in the Porsche's front trunk. Opening the car door, he thought, *I don't get women. This shit is exhausting, but at least I'm now good to go for a casket.*

On his way through town, he stopped at his regular hair salon for a quick trim, preferring not to have his collar-length mop butchered in a barber shop.

Pam greeted him with a smile. "Hi, Christian. We've been following you in the news."

He glanced at three doting beauticians who were twice his age. "Ladies, don't believe everything you read in the media. Pam, you got time for a touchup?"

"For you, always."

Pam had been his hairdresser for three years, starting when his wife took him to Pam's Myakka City shop. She styled and layered his hair so it hung naturally and never looked hacked. When she relocated to Sarasota, he remained her customer.

He left the salon and picked up a McDonald's hamburger and fries for dinner before heading back to Longboat Key. At the house he parked the Porsche in the three-car garage, and rather than return to his boat, he decided to crash in the home. He wanted an early start for the long drive, and this would save some time.

The next day he cruised up I-75 with the convertible top down and reached northern Florida, the halfway point in the eight-hour drive. With new wheels and rags, he felt good, optimistic, but knew the feelings wouldn't last. Depression was like scaling a mountain range, with highs and lows and sheer cliffs that beckoned an end. A few years before, he was a normal, easy-going guy. He was angry he couldn't regain stability, but a lot had happened in those years.

He arrived in Atlanta in the late afternoon and checked into the downtown Hilton. The next day was the World Wildlife Fund party, but he had his own party in mind.

* * *

Steve sat on a kitchen stool and gazed at the papers on the granite countertop. The printouts contained the second government file that Felix had discovered. Karen walked into the kitchen after walking Coconut, their little poodle.

Steve looked up at his wife. "Karen, I can't take these to the police."

"Why not? They're proof that someone misappropriated funds from the wolf study, and Felix was killed to cover it up."

"That's a theory, not proof." He wearily ran his fingers through his hair. "Let me walk you through this. If I take the printouts to the police station and hand them to Detective Graham, this is what will happen. In the first place, there's no proof that the funds were misappropriated. It might be a computer glitch, like Felix and I had thought. Secondly, there's no proof someone else deleted the file on Felix's computer. The cops will probably assume Felix did it. There goes the motive. And thirdly, these papers are evidence that Felix committed cyber fraud and stole government documents when he copied and emailed them to his computer and me. That makes me an accomplice. Not only could I go to jail, but the backlash will also destroy my security company. Now do you understand?"

"Grrrrrr," she said and held her head. "Some asshole murdered our friend, and I'm not about to let it go. If we can't talk to the police, what about the press? We can hand the file to a reporter and explain what happened."

Steve chuckled. "So we end up like Snowden, leaking government documents to the media and hiding out in Russia. No thanks. Besides, even a reporter needs proof to run a story."

"With today's news, I'm not sure those ethics apply anymore." She covered her mouth with fingers and gazed upward in thought. "Maybe it takes a criminal to expose a criminal." She retrieved her cell phone from a nearby counter and tapped the keys.

"Who are you calling?"

"I'm doing a search," she said. After a minute she showed Steve the screen. "This is who we need."

Steve looked at the month-old *Washington Post* article about Captain Nemo and his terrorist attack on an Idaho restaurant. "Captain Nemo?" he questioned. "Why would he be interested in Felix's death?"

"Wolves, Steve," she said. "Felix discovered that funds slated for a wolf study were being stolen, and Nemo's newest cause is saving the wolves. There's the connection."

"Okay, that's a stretch." He chuckled. "But how do you plan to contact the guy?"

Using her fingers on the phone screen, she enlarged the print to read the byline. "Trish Stevenson. She's the journalist for *The Washington Post* who wrote the article. She interviewed him and probably has his phone number."

* * *

Karen left Arlington and drove over the bridge into DC to meet Trish Stevenson. She called Trish the day before and only had to mention misappropriation of government funds, murder, and wolves, to spark the reporter's interest. Steve was concerned about getting involved and arrested for Felix's cyber fraud. He suggested that their meeting shouldn't take places at the *Post* with scores of witnesses. She and Trish decided to link up at the Albert Einstein Monument across the road from the Vietnam Memorial.

Karen parked on a side street and walked a block in the brisk weather to the monument. She entered a circular courtyard on a hill that overlooked the street and gazed up at the massive bronze statue of Einstein sitting on two steps with a book on one knee. Sitting down on a bench across from the statue, she checked her watch. She was early. Her thoughts drifted to Felix who had always poked fun at her punctuality. She missed him.

A taxi cab pulled up to the street curb, and a slender woman with shoulder-length chestnut hair stepped out. Karen recognized the journalist from her newspaper photo and waved to her. Trish bundled up her coat and strolled over. They introduced themselves with a handshake and sat down on the bench.

"My husband isn't crazy about me talking to you," said Karen. "The evidence concerning my friend's murder was obtained illegally. That is why I'm speaking to you instead of the police."

"Anything you tell me is confidential."

With that reassurance, Karen told her everything pertaining to Felix's death. When she finished, she asked, "What do you think?"

"It's a fascinating story, but unfortunately there's no solid evidence that proves your friend was murdered or that there was a misappropriation of government funds. I don't think my editor will let me print it. I'm sorry."

"My husband predicted you'd say that," said Karen. "There is one thing. Someone stole money from the wolf fund, and the government removed protection from wolves to wipe them out. I think there's a correlation. Captain Nemo is trying to save the wolves. I'd like to talk to him."

"I know Christian Roberts," Trish said with a nervous laugh. "We even dated for a time. He's the prime suspect in the Captain Nemo terrorist attacks, but Christian has always denied it. That last attack in Idaho has the media bombarding him. I'm told he's become a recluse. He's hiding out on his Florida horse farm and refuses to speak to anyone. I doubt he'd talk to you."

"I've seen his picture in the paper. He's very handsome."

Trish smiled. "Yes, he is, even more so in person." She lowered her head. "But he's also a really nice guy. I feel bad for him."

Karen glanced at Trish. She obviously had deep feelings for Christian Roberts. "I loved my friend Felix too. If you contact Mr. Roberts, please tell him what I've told you."

CHAPTER EIGHT

Christian woke at dawn out of habit and untangled his nude body from the sheets in the king-size bed. He crossed the hotel room to the window and pushed the curtains aside for a spectacular view of Atlanta. Through the high rises he glimpsed a golden sunrise. He'd stayed at this Hilton before, but it seemed like a lifetime ago, when he was fresh-faced and viewed the world with wonder. He and some buddies had come to Atlanta for Dragon Con, a huge fantasy and science fiction blowout. In this hotel he fondly recalled meeting and shaking hands with William Shatner, the *Star Trek* captain of the *Enterprise.* He turned away from the view and put aside the memory. He needed to focus on the present.

That night's party started at six o'clock in Buckhead, an affluent district on Atlanta's northside. He had no plans for the day except to make his presence known. He stepped to the desk and thumbed through literature on the local attractions. A pamphlet for the Atlanta Aquarium caught his attention. *This works, gotta reputation for loving fish.*

He showered, dressed casually, and sipped coffee brewed in the room. Before heading out, he decided to call his farm. "Hey, Juan, everything going okay?"

"Yes, Mr. Roberts, the horses are fine. A Mr. Magee called and asked if I could train his two fillies. I was going to call today and ask if that was okay."

"It's fine by me. Glad you're making a few extra bucks on the side. By the way, I'm not on the boat. I'm in Atlanta, but I should be back in a few days."

"Okay, Mr. Roberts. You will be happy to know the reporters left the gate."

"I guarantee they'll be back. Tell them that I'm in Georgia. I almost forgot. I bought a Porsche, so you can pick up your truck at the marina. I won't be needing it."

"You finally got the sports car. I am so glad. You deserve to put some joy back in your life."

After the call, Christian took the elevator down to the hotel restaurant called Southern Elements. Unlike his previous visit, the dining room was half empty. The hostess seated him, and he glanced through the options on the breakfast menu. He found it strange that a place called Southern Elements didn't serve Southern staples. A waitress came to the table.

"There's no grits on the menu," he said with a smile. "Isn't that a crime in Georgia?" As she fumbled with an explanation and apology, he stopped her. "It's okay. I'll live."

His breakfast arrived, and as he ate his sunny-side-up eggs, sausage with red-eye gravy, and sweet tea, he noticed four waitresses clustered at a coffee station were staring at him and giggling.

His waitress came to his table. "Would you like more iced tea?"

"No, I'm good. Just the check," he said.

She stepped away and returned with the bill. When he handed her his credit card, she studied it and looked up. "Mr. Roberts, we thought it was you. One of the waitresses saw your picture in a magazine. It's so great you're helping those poor wolves."

He lifted his eyebrows. "Yes, they do need help," he agreed, sick of denying he was Captain Nemo and responsible for the cause.

She bit her lip. "Would you mind if I got your autograph?"

"Sure." He took her pen and paper and scribbled his name. He glanced at the other grinning waitresses. "I suppose they want one too?"

"Oh, yes."

His table was soon surrounded by admiring staff. He cordially signed autographs, smiled for their smart phone photos, and even kissed the cheek of a gray-haired maid who had wandered in from housekeeping. He thought it odd that they saw him as a celebrity rather than a terrorist. It didn't matter. They were witnesses, more valuable than fans.

In the cool fall weather he slipped into his jacket and left the hotel. A short taxi ride later, he was at the downtown aquarium. Staring at the fish tanks, he realized how much he missed scuba diving. His fascination turned to grief when recalling his last dive in the Bahamas. The next day his wife was murdered. *Allie, Allie, Allie, you're always on my mind.*

After the aquarium, he stopped at a small bar for a cocktail and spoke to a few guys about the upcoming Georgia Tech game, though he wasn't a football fan. Rather than use cash, he paid for the drink with a credit card, confirming his presence in Atlanta on Wednesday.

He returned to his hotel room and took his time cleaning up and dressing. With a close shave, blow-dried hair, and wearing the expensive black suit, he looked sophisticated, easily fitting in with the well-to-doers. The last accessory was a new silver tie. Beginning to knot it in a Windsor, he grumbled, "What the hell am I doing?" He ripped off the tie and unfastened the first two shirt buttons. He intended to make an impact, but not at the expense of comfort. The printout for his invitation to the event rested on the desk, and he reread the material. Next to its panda logo was their motto, Be the Voice for Those Who Have No Voice. *Time for me to howl.*

At 5:30 he traveled north on I-75 but got stuck in the after-hours traffic. Inching along on the bumper-to-bumper interstate, he finally got off the Paces Ferry exit to Buckhead. He drove though the curvy roads of forest-covered hills and passed one lavish estate after another. Sarasota had some big, beautiful homes, but the Buckhead mansions were mind-boggling. He arrived at the house that was hosting the World Wildlife Fund event and parked on the car-lined street. He rang the doorbell, and a woman admitted him. In the foyer a huge, art glass chandelier moved up and down, and he recognized Chihuly as the artist. As the woman led him through the house, he became overwhelmed with the artwork. More giant pieces of Chihuly glass occupied the rooms, along with original works by Dali, Picasso, Chagall, Warhol, and others. He grew up in the culture mecca of Sarasota with its notable Ringling Museum, and where celebrated artists and authors walked the streets. As a result he was knowledgeable and appreciated fine art, but the private collection in Buckhead was a jaw-dropper.

The party room contained about thirty people, and he was introduced to Jake Sole, the World Wildlife Fund rep who had emailed him the invitation.

Shaking Jake's hand, he said, "Christian Roberts."

"Christian, I'm so glad you could make it." Jake looked to the left of the room. "There's wine at the bar, and help yourself to the hors d'oeuvres. Our program starts in fifteen minutes."

Christian ordered a glass of Chardonnay from the bartender and popped a cheese cube into his mouth. He sat down on a couch next to a thin silver-haired woman and introduced himself as Christian. When she asked where he was from and what he did for a living, he kept it brief, saying he had a horse farm in Florida.

"Horses. You must be a true animal lover. I'm here to save the animals for my grandkids"

He smiled and thought, *Screw the kids, these animals have their own right to be here.*

A pretty woman from India picked up the microphone and began the program with a talk about the WWF's work, illustrated by slides of Indian rhinos and tigers. She ended her talk on a high note, saying tiger numbers had climbed for the first time in decades. She then took questions from the audience.

After a few questions and answers, Christian raised his hand and stood. "Your work saving these animals is great, but I'm wondering why aren't you helping the wolves in this country?

They're American icons, like grizzlies and bald eagles, but they're being slaughtered in the Western states. Fewer than two thousand remain. I recently read that the packs protected in Wyoming, the Great Lakes area, and Alaska might soon come under fire." He looked to the Indian girl for an answer.

Jake stepped forward. "Yes, the WWF is aware that the wolf population has been cut in half in the lower 48 states. It's very sad, Mr. Roberts."

"What are you going to do about it?"

The silver-haired woman rose from the couch, ogling him. "Mr. Roberts? My god, I...I knew you looked familiar," she exclaimed and moved away from him. She turned to the audience. "He's Christian Roberts from Florida, Captain Nemo, the one that the newspapers are saying is an eco terrorist."

Stunned silence permeated the room. The people close by became fearful and retreated out of his reach.

"Mr. Roberts, is that true?" Jake asked.

Christian awkwardly smiled. "Partly true, I've been accused of being Nemo, but there's no proof I'm him. The term lone-wolf terrorist is kind of a paradox, since wolves don't terrorize or harm people." The shocked group seemed beyond understanding or caring. "Guess about now you'd like me to go?"

"I'm afraid so," said Jake. "Our organization does not condone violence, and we can't associate with you or your reputation that you might be Captain Nemo. I'm sorry."

"Didn't mean to disrupt your fancy get-together, but was hoping you'd put wolves on your agenda." Not about to rush out like a criminal, he took his time, swallowed the last of his wine, and set the glass on the coffee table. "It's been great meeting y'all." He walked out amid the flashes of cell phone cameras. On the street he strolled to his car and heard a woman calling his name. A young woman in a short dress jogged in high heels to him.

She tossed back her long, dark hair, exposing big brown eyes and plump lips. "Hi," she said, a little out of breath. "I was wondering where you're going, darlin'," she asked with syrupy Southern accent.

"Back to my hotel, I guess."

"Want some company?"

He slowly smiled. "Sure, why not," he said, and opened the passenger door.

* * *

In Idaho, Gary sat at his kitchen table and drank coffee while he watched the weather report on the news. The prediction was clear skies and minimal winds, ideal for aerial hunting. For the last three days, he and his chopper pilot, Jason, had scoured the Boulder-White area in search of wolves but left empty-handed. A coyote and two raccoons had been found strangled in his snares, but their pelts were hardly worth his time. He hoped today's hunt would be better, and he'd bring back wolves.

His phone rang and he saw Jason on the caller ID. "What's going on, Jason?"

"Gary, the chopper caught fire last night. I'm at the airport looking at it, and it's a total loss."

"Shit! How did that happen?"

"No one knows yet. One of the maintenance guys saw the chopper burning around midnight and called it in. Right now the fire department thinks it's accidental, possibly a spark from the battery set fire to the gas tank, or a smoker got careless with a cigarette, but the cops want to talk everyone connected to the chopper. I just got here."

"I'll be right there." He hung up, grabbed his coat, and hustled outside. A white sedan drove up, stirring up the dust from road, and pulled in behind his pickup. A small man with bug eyes stepped out of the car. He reminded Gary of the funny-looking, little kidnapper in *Fargo,* one of his favorite movies.

"Howdy," the man said, grinning wide. "Someone said you did taxidermy. I hit a fox, a real beauty, and would like it mounted. It's going to be a gift for a friend."

"I'm in a hurry. Come back later."

"It's a long drive here. Can't I just leave it with you? You can call me when it's ready."

"All right, but let's make this quick." Gary walked to the man and his car.

"It's in the trunk. By the way, my name's Bill." He fiddled with his car keys to open the trunk. "I heard you're a darned good hunter, have killed a lot of wolves."

"I've killed my fair share."

"Good. Wanted to make sure I had the right guy," Bill said with a grin and popped the trunk.

Gary frowned, seeing it was empty. "Where's the damn fox?" He then saw the Taser in Bill's hand. "What the hell?"

"Actually you're the gift for my friend," Bill said solemnly and fired the high-voltage stun gun at Gary's chest.

* * *

Jason and a few men who worked on planes at the airport stood on the tarmac and watched the firemen poke around the smoldering rubble that had once been the Wildlife Service helicopter. The police had questioned them, but everyone had been at home when the fire started. The surveillance camera attached to the hangar roof had malfunctioned and was blank.

Jason looked at his watch and said to the men, "I wonder where Gary is. I called him two hours ago."

An officer stood outside his car and talked on his car radio. He walked to the men. "I just spoke to the FBI, and they want everyone to remain for questioning. They're interested if you saw any strangers hanging around here. It's looking like this wasn't an accident."

"What makes them think that?" asked one of the men.

"Two more helicopters that belonged to Wildlife Service were torched last night at other airports in the state. This might be the work of Captain Nemo."

"Jesus," one man mumbled. The officer started back toward his car.

"Wait a minute, Officer," said Jason. "Gary, the man I work with in the chopper should have been here an hour ago. I'm getting concerned."

"I hope he doesn't drive a blue Ford pickup."

"He does. He lives in the hills west of town."

"It just came over from Dispatch," said the officer. "A blue pickup was discovered burning in that area. It appears the driver lost control, taking a curve too fast on the dirt road, and plummeted into a ravine. If that's your friend, I'm afraid he's dead."

* * *

Thursday morning Trish sat in *The Washington Post* newsroom and read the notes she'd taken during her interview with Karen. She could protect her source, but the story lacked reliable evidence and credibility. Still, she wondered if she should show it to her editor and let him decide. The misappropriation of government funds and murder made juicy reading.

Andy, the mail-delivery boy, stopped at her cubicle. "Hey, Miss Stevenson," he said bashfully while sorting through his basket of correspondence.

"Hi, Andy, you have something for me today?"

Andy's freckled cheeks blushed as red as his hair whenever she acknowledged him. The poor kid obviously had a crush on her. "You got a postcard, Miss Stevenson."

The word *postcard* bolted her upright in her seat. The front of the card had a picture of a gray wolf with a mountain backdrop and "Idaho" written on one corner. She turned it over and read the message. "The government must stop killing our wolves, Captain Nemo." The postmark was dated three days earlier from Idaho. She covered her mouth, and through her fingers, she muttered, "Damn him."

"Bad news?" Andy asked.

"You might say that." For a moment she felt paralyzed. Should she race into her editor's office and show him the card or call the FBI herself? Instead, she tapped the keyboard and did a hasty Internet search on Captain Nemo. The Associated Press had run a small story about three Wildlife Service helicopters that had been destroyed Wednesday night in as many airports in Idaho. No one was hurt, but the details remained sketchy. The FBI stated it could be a Captain Nemo attack. Trish called Christian.

His phone rang three times before a woman answered. "Hello?" she said with a sleepy voice.

"I'm sorry. I must have the wrong number."

"Honey, are you looking for Chris?"

"Yes," she said slowly. "Who are you?"

The woman chuckled. "That's none of your business, sweetheart."

"Well, where is Christian?"

"The shower's running, so I'm guessing he's in it."

"I mean, where is he? Is this Idaho?" Trish asked.

"Idaho? This is the Hilton in Atlanta," she said with a Georgia twang. "Wait a minute, the water stopped." She then called into the room. "Chris, there's a woman on your phone."

Trish heard Christian's muffled voice in the background. "I don't know who she is," said the woman, "but she sounds insistent, like a girlfriend or wife."

"I don't have either," he said and took over the call. "Hello."

"It's me, Trish. I didn't mean to interrupt you, but it's important."

"Okay, what's going on, Trish?"

"I received a postcard from Captain Nemo, saying the government must stop killing our wolves. And I just learned from the AP that three government helicopters belonging to Wildlife Services were destroyed in Idaho last night. This postcard ties Captain Nemo to the attack on those helicopters."

"So what does that have to do with me? I'm in Georgia, been here a couple of days."

"I have to turn the postcard over to the FBI."

"Do it. I didn't mail it, and I've got plenty of witnesses confirming I wasn't in Idaho."

"Is that including the woman in your bed?" She shuddered, instantly regretting the personal question.

There was a pause. "Anything else, Trish?"

"I'm sorry. Your life is none of my business. There is one other thing, probably nothing, but I interviewed a woman, and she asked me to relate her story to you. Her friend, a computer analyst, discovered a government file that showed federal funds going to a wolf study were missing. Soon after, her friend died from an overdose. She insists he was murdered because he discovered the file, but the police here ruled his death a suicide. Because it concerned wolves, she wanted you to know." Trish expected him to disregard the account.

"She lives in DC.?"

"Close by, Arlington," Trish said. "Do you think there's something to it?"

"Tell her I'll be in Washington tomorrow and want to talk to her."

CHAPTER NINE

On Thursday morning, James Sanders dressed impeccably in a linen suit that matched his graying hair. The sky-blue tie harmonized with his hawkish eyes. With a winning smile of perfect teeth, he was born for politics. He picked up his briefcase and climbed into his white Mercedes parked before his stately home in north DC. As he navigated through the congested traffic on his way to the White House, his private cell phone rang. "Yes?"

"Mr. Secretary, I need to update you on the issue concerning the wolf file."

"Okay, Vern, but I'm busy all morning. It'll have to wait until noon."

"Yes, sir. I'll be at our usual place."

Sanders nervously ran his fingers through his hair. Vern called only when important. The tall, strapping man was ex-military and had been an undercover operative for the CIA. Now he had a security agency and worked in the private sector. He and his team did contract jobs, legal or not. Sanders had met him through his association with the gun lobby.

At his office Sanders went through the motions. He had a staff meeting at nine. Afterwards, he reviewed a Congressional bill before convening in the Oval Office. As secretary of the Interior, he had the ear of the president, who was more fixated on his golf game than on concerns with the environment. The press loved this president and rarely gave him grief, even when he gave the drilling rights in the Gulf of Mexico and Arctic to oil companies. The minority party was too worried about the bad economy to focus on anything else. Under trouble-free conditions, Sanders made decisions that lined his pocket.

At noon Sanders broke for lunch and walked to his car with wolves in mind. Several years earlier, the hunting and gun clubs had lobbied to kill wolves, since they affected the deer and elk populations. For a payoff, he had the US Fish and Game remove wolves from the Endangered Species list, even though their small numbers qualified, and wolves had proven to balance nature and benefit the environment. The decision created outrage with the conservation groups who raised a stink with petitions and lawsuits. When a judge agreed with researchers to protect wolves, Sanders urged the president to sign a bill that would delist wolves and override the lawsuits.

Sanders drove to a small park and left his car on the street. Strolling down the sidewalk, he spotted the buzzed white hair as Vern waited like a linebacker on a bench. He sat down beside him. "What is so important, Vern?"

"It's the couple in Arlington, sir. We wire tapped their house and phones and learned they're not ignoring the wolf study file that the analyst uncovered and emailed to them. And they're not buying their friend's suicide. They think he was murdered because of the file."

"Have they gone to the police?"

"They can't without putting themselves in jeopardy. They've aware the file was obtained illegally, but there are concerns. The wife contacted a journalist, Trish Stevenson at *The Washington Post*. We used the ACISS to track the wife's car with her GPS."

"ACI...what?

"ACISS stands for Augmented Criminal Investigation Support System. It uses cell tower sites to locate a GPS. Anyway, the wife met Stevenson at the Einstein Memorial, and we recorded their conversation. Stevenson said she couldn't run the story because of a lack of evidence."

"So what's the problem?"

"Captain Nemo, sir," said Vern.

"The terrorist who saved sharks? What does he have to do with this?"

"His new cause is wolves, and he recently blew up an Idaho restaurant that was sponsoring a predator hunt. Christian Roberts is suspected of being Captain Nemo, and he's acquainted with Stevenson, *The Post* journalist. The wife asked the reporter to connect them, under the belief that Roberts might be interested in the missing funds for wolves. You see how this is spreading."

"Great," Sanders said with disgust. He ran his hand through his hair. "I thought the matter would go away, and we wouldn't have to deal with the couple. Now a reporter and this fanatic might get involved."

"I suggest a wiretap on the reporter, but one on Roberts could be tricky. A source told me the FBI is watching him. His phone and house are probably already wired. It's not wise to cross paths with the feds."

"Do you think Roberts is Captain Nemo?"

"If I had to guess, yes. I did a workup on him. All the evidence points to him, but there isn't enough for an arrest." Vern pulled some papers from his inside coat pocket and handed Sanders a photo. "This is Roberts."

"I doubt this boy has difficulty with the ladies."

"Probably not, sir," Vern said and read his report. "He's in his late twenties, six-two plus, a hundred and eighty-five pounds. He was born in Florida and lives near Sarasota, staying either on his horse farm or sailboat. His record is pretty clean, never been convicted of a crime, but he was arrested twice, once for assault in Miami. The charges were dropped, and last year he was detained for conspiracy in the bombing of two Chinese grocery stores that sold shark fins. He spent a few weeks in the New York jail, but his case never went to trial. The star witness disappeared. No surprise, since Roberts has mob ties."

"Mob ties? He doesn't look Italian."

"He got connected through horse racing." Vern put the papers down and looked at Sanders, "Sir, Roberts might be young, but he's no dummy. On his boat, he's out of reach of surveillance, and rarely uses the Internet or phone, at least those registered in his name, and he removed the GPS in his SUV. Meaning, he's hard to track down. Roberts is also wealthy, made millions with the horses. One final thing. If he is Captain Nemo, he's not only talented but a serious threat. He's murdered a lot of people and never been charged."

"I can't believe he's still walking the streets."

"Like I said, he's no dummy, has the FBI spinning its wheels. So what do you want me to do?"

"Go ahead with the wiretap on the reporter. Hopefully it'll reveal Roberts's whereabouts and intentions. We'll do a wait-and-see. But if there's a risk of exposure, you'll have to step in." Sanders breathed deeply. "I thought this ended with the analyst."

* * *

After her call to Christian, Trish picked up the postcard from Captain Nemo and the printout of AP story on the destruction of three Wildlife Service helicopters. She walked down the aisle to her editor's office and placed the items on his desk.

Larry looked up for an explanation.

"He contacted me."

Larry scrutinized the postcard and article and smiled. "So he's still using you to spread his messages. Get to work on the story. I'll contact the FBI."

Three FBI agents arrived shortly. With gloved hands, one placed the postcard in evidence for handwriting analysis and fingerprint check. Two other agents interviewed Trish. She'd grown used to the drill, making a statement every time Nemo wrote to her. Upon receiving the postcard, she admitted her call to Christian Roberts, suspected of being the terrorist. He said he was in Atlanta on Wednesday and had witnesses to prove it. Trish didn't mention the latter half of her call—that she had told Christian about her interview with Karen, and he was coming to DC.

She spent several hours with the FBI, rehashing her ties to Captain Nemo and Christian Roberts. Her story about the shark slaughter for Chinese shark fin soup was the start. Her follow-up story concerned Captain Nemo's terrorist attacks in the Bahamas and Costa Rica to save the fish. Nemo must have read her articles, because soon after, she got his postcards. A phone conversation with a Bahamian officer led her to Christian Roberts, at the time an FBI person of interest. She interviewed Roberts in Florida, and they became friends. When speaking to the agents, she left out their intimate affair and her feelings for him.

Once the questioning was over, she knocked out a story for the morning paper about Captain Nemo's latest postcard threat that coincided with the terrorist attacks on the helicopters. She added a statement from the Idaho FBI agent who said he could not confirm this early in the investigation that Captain Nemo was responsible for the attack.

She left the *Post* after a hectic day, but feeling ecstatic. After months she'd see the man who dwelled in her dreams. On her way to her car, she called Karen with the good news. Christian was coming to Washington tomorrow and wished to talk to her about the mysterious file and the analyst's death.

Driving home, Trish stopped at a few stores along the way and picked up rum, Coke, sweet tea, cheese appetizers, eggs, grits, and ham—Christian's favorites—along with roses for the table. She returned to her apartment and went into a cleaning frenzy, scrubbing floors, doing laundry, and washing dishes. At midnight the place was immaculate. As she put fresh sheets on the bed, she thought, *we're not together anymore, but he has to sleep somewhere.*

The following day her story appeared in *The Washington Post.* Nemo's postcard and Trish were the buzz. Her cell and office phones rang constantly as reporters from other media outlets inundated her with questions. By late afternoon she had grown irritable with the onslaught. She snapped at a late caller. "Trish Stevenson, what is it?"

"Having a bad day?" asked a man with a soft, deep voice.

She instantly recognized him. "Christian, it's been crazy here since I got your postcard."

"Not my postcard."

"Whatever. Where are you?"

"Outside in the park."

"You're here already? I didn't expect you until tonight. I'll be right out." She grabbed her purse and coat and hurried to the elevator. On the ride down she managed to apply lipstick and brush her hair. She sucked in a deep breath to get calm, not wanting to appear eager. She left the lobby and casually stepped out on the sidewalk to scan the park across the street. He was easy to spot, his collar-length blond hair offsetting a black jacket. He squatted under a leafless tree and tossed chips from a bag to the surrounding flock of pigeons. He noticed her and rose with a smile materializing in his five o'clock shadow.

God, he's gorgeous, she thought while waiting for a break in the traffic to cross the busy street. "Only tourists feed pigeons," she called, walking to him.

"Don't mind being a tourist. It's too friggin' cold to live here." Pushing his sunglasses up to rest on his blond locks, he cupped her cheek and kissed her, not a quick peck on the lips but a swooping, devouring kiss that left her dizzy. He stepped back, and through long lashes, his sapphire eyes gazed into hers. "Good seeing ya, Trish."

She cleared her throat, trying but failing to brush off his effect. To lighten the mood, she jokingly asked, "Who taught you to kiss like that?"

"It wasn't my mother." He chuckled and crumpled up the chip bag. Glancing toward the vending trucks that lined the park curb, he said, "Drove all night on Coke and stale Doritos, so I'm kinda hungry. You wanna grab a bite?"

"Sure," she said. They walked to the food trucks, and he bought a cup of tomato soup and a grilled cheese sandwich, and she settled for a yogurt. They sat on a bench to eat with a view of *The Washington Post*.

"Haven't had tomater soup in a while," he said, his twang revealing his Southern roots. He dipped the sandwich in the soup and took a bite. "Nice building," he commented, gazing at the red brick high-rise. "The *Post* must sell a few papers."

"It's new. We moved in last year. So what are your plans?"

"Foremost, I want to talk to this Karen and her husband about the file."

"I meant where are you staying?"

"Where should I stay?"

"With me," she said and felt a blush.

"Okay."

He followed her home in his new black Porsche, the perfect car for a bad boy. He was acquainted with her apartment, having spent the night when they dated.

She told him to make himself at home while she fixed drinks and snacks. He dropped his travel bag on the floor and took off his jacket and shoes. Sitting down on the couch, he picked up the TV remote. From the kitchenette she heard the newscast as she arranged the cheese, crackers, and olives on a plate and poured rum and Cokes into glasses of ice, topped off with a lime slice.

His kiss in the park had ignited flames of desire, and she couldn't wait to crawl all over him, but in the living room, she found him asleep with his lean frame curled up catlike on the couch.

She sighed and set the tray of food and drinks on the coffee table. He probably had little sleep Wednesday night, entertaining that woman in Atlanta, and then he drove straight through on Thursday. No wonder he was wiped out. He stirred slightly and clutched a cushion when she covered him with a blanket. She sat down in a chair, and her insides ached, watching him doze.

She had kidded herself into believing that their relationship was over, but now in his presence, she couldn't deny her true feelings. *I'm in trouble. I love this guy.*

* * *

Christian woke at dawn and sat up on the couch. "Shit," he mumbled. He'd fallen asleep on Trish. He ambled into the kitchen, opened the refrigerator, and saw the eggs and ham. He could at least make her breakfast. He started the coffee brewer, but decided to clean up before cooking. He grabbed the shaving kit from his bag and quietly tiptoed down the hallway to the bathroom. After a shower and shave, he wrapped a towel around his waist and stepped out to retrieve a change of clothes, but found Trish waiting in a silk robe.

"Sorry, didn't mean to wake you," he said.

"I'm usually up this early."

He gnawed his lip. "Guess I owe you another apology. Pretty lame, nodding off last night."

She tugged at his towel and it fell at his feet. "I'm sure you'll make up for it."

"Yes, ma'am."

After Trish had left for work, Christian drove out of the District and headed toward Arlington. He'd used Trish's phone and called Karen. Her husband Steve answered, and they decided to meet at a small diner near an out-of-the-way subdivision. Trish had wanted to come with him, but he put the nix on it. Better that she not be involved in his causes, for obvious reasons.

He arrived at the roadside diner and pulled into a bumpy dirt lot with a few cars, but red flags went up when seeing a white van with tinted windows, bearing the name of an electric company. He parked near the front door and entered. The only couple sat midway down the room in a window booth, and he assumed it was Karen and

Steve. Steve was lean with the clean-cut look of a professional, and Karen was an attractive, long-haired blond. She acknowledged Christian with a smile.

He removed his sunglasses and started toward their table, but noticed two men dressed like electricians who occupied the next booth. One looked up at him but quickly refocused on his menu. Steve and Karen already had their coffee, so the men had come in after and sat close enough to overhear their conversation.

Christian stepped to the couple's table but didn't sit down. "Pay up. I'll meet you outside," he said quietly and returned to his car.

When the couple joined him outside, Karen asked. "What's the matter?"

"Follow me." Christian climbed into his Porsche and drove off with the couple trailing in their Prius. After driving a mile through a sleepy neighborhood, he pulled over next to an empty lot. Steve parked behind him, and they got out.

"Are you going to tell us what's going on?" asked Karen.

Christian leaned against his car door. "I didn't like the looks of the men behind you. Blue-collar workers seldom have manicures."

"You've got to be kidding. We left because some guy had trimmed fingernails?" Karen sniped. "You're awfully paranoid, Captain Nemo."

"Call me, Christian, please," he said with same insolent tone. "If your friend was murdered, and the murderer deleted the file from his computer, he saw that the file was forwarded to you."

"We realized that," said Steve. "We shut down our email address and erased everything as a precaution."

"Obviously not fast enough," said Christian. "Or else those boys wouldn't have followed you to the diner." He crossed his arms and addressed Karen. "And yes, my dear, I'm paranoid. It's kept me out of prison and alive. You know the old saying, 'Expect the worse and hope for the best.' Can I see the file now?"

Steve handed him the printout. "So you're going to help us prove Felix was murdered and maybe expose his killer?"

Christian lowered the papers. "We have different agendas. You want to avenge your friend's death. I want to save wolves. This file might accomplish both. First, we need to find out where the money in the second file went, find it, and find the bad guy." He turned to Steve. "Trish mentioned you work with computer security. I assume you can hack a system."

"I can, and I even have Felix's laptop, but it's a dead end. The file was bleached, gone."

Christian pushed the hair out of his eyes and took a moment to consider. "Besides you, who else knew Felix uncovered the file?"

"Felix reported it to his supervisor, a Barbara Davis," said Karen. "She works for the secretary of state, reviewing Congressional budgets."

"So she's probably the connection who got your friend killed," Christian said. "I imagine the information we need is on her computer."

"I'm sure it is," said Steve. "But her computer is in a secure government building and unreachable."

"Suppose I got it."

"Given that impossibility, you don't want to steal her computer," said Steve. "That would set off alarms, and she'd dump her files from another computer. If you managed to get access to her computer, you could install a RAT into its USB port to the hard drive."

"A rat?" Christian frowned.

"RAT stands for remote administrative tool. It's not considered malware, so it wouldn't be blocked by security software. I'd have the password to access it remotely, and everything on her computer would show up on mine. The beauty of a RAT is there's no indication a computer has been infected. Actually, I probably have one in my desk."

"This is all fascinating, boys," Karen said sarcastically, "but how do you plan to get at her computer, *Christian*?"

"Let me worry about that," said Christian. "Just do your part and get that RAT to me this afternoon. I'd like to wrap it up this weekend."

"You're rather arrogant, ordering us around like employees," said Karen.

"Karen, be nice," Steve grumbled. "We need his help."

Christian chuckled. "She's a trip, but that's all right, Steve. I'm not a fan of sappy suck-ups. My wife gave me plenty of grief, but I loved her for it." He glanced down the road. "I might seem pushy, but it's for your own good." He grabbed a scrap of paper and pen from his car, jotted down a number, and handed it to Steve. "Here's the number of my burner phone. Buy your own throwaway to reach me. You'll also need a new computer with a fake address and ID for this RAT. In the meantime, I'll hit a library computer and get the lowdown on Davis. Call me when you're set up."

"Ridiculous," Karen said with a headshake. "You don't know for sure we were followed. Now we're supposed to buy another computer and phone because of your suspicious delusions?"

Christian couldn't afford distrust from his new partners in crime. He clutched Karen's shoulders and turned her to face the end of the street. "See the white van that just pulled up down there? It's no delusion, sweetheart. It's the same van that was at the diner and belongs to those phony electricians with manicures. They knew about our breakfast meeting this morning. That means your house and phones are bugged. They found us here, using the GPS in your cell phone or car. Right now they're probably hoping to get close enough to record our conversation. This is the real shit that can get you killed like your friend, Felix. You need to be cautious."

Karen gasped and with a startled expression looked to her husband.

"Christian, are you sure it's the same van?" Steve asked.

"Dead sure, but I'll prove it. Just watch them." He opened his car door. "They know about you, so they're more interested in me, the new guy."

He hopped into his car and floored the gas. At the crossroads he drove through a stop sign. In the rearview mirror he watched the van pull away and speed past Karen and Steve. It also blew through the stop sign in pursuit. As the van grew closer, he downshifted and put the sports car through its paces. He flew down the back roads and hugged corners at speeds that might flip or spinout an average car, confident that a van couldn't keep up with a Porsche.

Zipping around in the flashy car to lose bad guys reminded him of Vince who had called him Mr. Bond, even in his will. "Doing the thing, Vince," he murmured. He lost sight of the van and returned to the beltway back to DC. He whipped around traffic and was doing ninety over the Arlington Memorial Bridge. A speeding ticket was more of a concern than his pursuers.

In the District he slowed to the limit, certain he'd eluded the van. His head spun, no longer thinking about a car chase. Someone high up in government had access to the wolf study file and misappropriated millions. *And these were serious suckers.* Some poor analyst was killed over the cover-up. Steve and Karen's attempt to expose their friend's murder had made them part of the deadly game. The connection with them turned him and Trish into players. He needed to defuse the situation for everyone's safety.

He drove into a bank parking lot, took out his regular cell phone, and called the couple's home number. "Hey, Steve, it's Christian. I've thought about all you and Karen told me, and I don't want any part of it. I suggest you also forget it."

"But what you said…" Steve sputtered.

"Yeah, about that. Take my advice. I'm heading back to Florida. It was nice meetin' ya." He hung up, hoping Steve read between the lines and would purchase a disposable phone to stay in touch. He next called Trish at work. Her phones might also be compromised. "Hey, Trish, want me to swing by and catch lunch? Somehow, I keep missing breakfast."

"Lunch sounds great. I'll be out of front in an hour. How did your meeting go with Karen and her husband?"

"Nothing but smoke and mirrors. I didn't find them or the file credible. I'd forget about their claims." Besides lying for the sake of those who could be listening in, he'd decided to keep Trish out of the fray. He might have to become Captain Nemo and break some laws.

"You didn't find Karen believable? I thought she was."

"Hell, she said I was arrogant. You believing that?" He chuckled.

"Absolutely. You can be egotistical and condescending."

"Jeez, and I thought I was perfect," he joked. "But getting back to these government files, I also figured it wasn't smart to get involved. The law already thinks I'm Nemo, and with his current cause, I'd only face more heat, sticking my nose into a wolf study."

"Christian, give me a break. You're all over the media, standing up for wolves. You and your picture are even in today's Atlanta paper."

"What does it say?"

"That you showed up at a World Wildlife Fund event and ranted about wolves. The picture's nice. You look great in that black suit."

"First off, I didn't just show up; I was invited. And I didn't rant. I explained that wolves were in trouble. Since I'm accused of being Nemo, I thought I should check out his newest cause. Sure enough, wolves are getting screwed. I went to Atlanta like any other caring citizen to find out if the organization could help them."

"Are you're practicing your alibi, Captain Nemo?"

"Can we get off the Nemo inquest? It'd be nice to just enjoy each other. This morning was a great start."

"This morning was good."

"Just good? In my defense, I had less than an hour."

"See, Karen is right about you," she teased.

Christian sighed. "Can't win. I'll pick you up at noon."

He ended the call but kept thinking about Trish. She was trying to play it cool, jokingly harassing him and acting aloof. They were supposedly only friends, but he saw through her masquerade. She cared for him. The problem was he also had feelings for her. He had ended their relationship the previous year, convinced that a bond between a reporter and terrorist was a disaster waiting to blow up. It was only partly the reason. They were growing serious. When he let her go, it hurt.

Now he was reviving his fondness for her. This morning wasn't casual sex; he made love to Trish. Why? He realized he wasn't the same man when they had met and dated. Back then he had been recently widowed and was still angrily grieving his loss. On this visit, the door to his heart was slowly opening to let another in, and Trish was everything he wanted. Trying to bottle up his feelings was causing him torment. He fired up the Porsche. *I can't let us dangle in the wind. I have to decide. Either I pursue this relationship or move on.*

* * *

Steve stood at the kitchen counter and slowly hung up the phone, baffled. He stared intently at it, consumed in thought. Was Roberts really blowing them off? He heard Karen's footsteps as she came down from the bedrooms.

"Who was on the phone?" she asked, placing an empty dog bowl in the sink.

"Christian," he muttered. He looked up at her. "He says he gave it some thought and doesn't want any part of us or the file. He's driving back to Florida."

"Good. I don't want any part of him. He's a paranoid, conceited nutcase. Thinks he's hot shit and can order us around."

"But, Karen…"

"I don't want to discuss him, Steve." She snatched up her purse and the car keys. "We're out of dog food and need to go to the store." She dangled the keys in front of his face. "I'd like you to go with me."

"All right." He sighed, putting on his jacket. "I don't think Christian was so bad. He seems rather smart. I can't understand your attitude toward him."

"He acts like a self-indulgent rock star. You might be a fan, but I find the jerk repulsive. And like I said, I don't want to talk about him anymore." As they walked outside, she said, "Let's go to Costco. The printer is nearly out of ink."

Ten minutes later they walked across the Costco parking lot. Karen giggled. "So you think Christian and I fooled them?"

Steve stopped short and stared at her. "Fooled me. I thought you hated him, and he was leaving town."

"Honey, you're extremely bright with computers, but sometimes you take things too literally. When you said he was going back to Florida, it was an obvious ploy to throw off the listeners on the phone tap. I played along in case the house is also bugged."

He shook his head and continued walking. "You two belong in movies, with your acting. Do we need anything else besides dog food and ink?"

She frowned. "Steve, we have plenty of dog food. We're here to buy the computer. You think Costco also carries disposable phones?"

After buying the phone and a small laptop, they returned home. In his home office Steve set up the new computer with a fake ID and then rummaged through his desk drawers for a RAT.

Karen came into the office with their little white poodle on her heels. "Are you finished?"

He nodded and held up the small device. "I thought I had one of these."

She handed him the disposable phone, indicating he should call Christian. He retrieved the scrap of paper from his pocket and called the number, but when Christian didn't answer, Steven texted him the message. "All set."

* * *

Christian drove to *The Post* and picked up Trish for lunch. She directed him to a small Chinese restaurant in the downtown area. "I hope it's okay, captain," she said. "They've never served shark fin soup."

"Will you ever quit insinuating that I'm Nemo?" He stopped the car and looked over his shoulder to parallel park.

"I'm sorry, but when you deny you're Nemo, I think you don't trust me. That bothers me." She opened the door and stepped to the sidewalk.

He walked to her as she stared at her shoes, clearly troubled. He gently lifted her chin so she focused on him. "Trish, I wouldn't be here if I didn't trust you, but think about it. Say I admit I'm Nemo. It's not *if*, but *when* I'm arrested and you're called to testify at my trial. You'll either have to lie for me or tell the truth. Say they have proof you lied; you could be charged with perjury, obstruction, and possibly a conspiracy of terrorism. This has nothing to do with distrust or fear that you'll betray me. I deny I'm Nemo to protect you. You get it?"

"I get it." She wrapped her arms around his neck and pulled him close. "I promise I won't insinuate or harass you anymore concerning the captain, but you should know I'd take the risk and lie for you." She stood on her toes and kissed him.

His disposable phone buzzed, and he read the short text message from Steve. He returned the phone to a pocket and noticed her curious expression. "It's just business."

In the restaurant they ordered a combination of Chinese dishes. Their conversation was light. They talked about the cold weather and the fine restaurants and current Washington events, which led her to ask about their plans for the evening.

He set aside his chopsticks. "I'm sorry, but I'm busy tonight. In fact I'm not sure I'll make it back to your apartment."

"Busy doing what? Does it have to do with that text message?"

He pursed his lips, eyeballing her, and didn't answer.

"Right," she said and flung back her lengthy hair. "No pestering about the alias and your other life."

After lunch Christian dropped Trish off at *The Post* and found a nearby library. He sat down at a computer, and before logging on, texted Steve with his location. He did an online search on Barbara Davis, Felix's supervisor. Her status as a government employee, of public record, was easy to find.

A half hour later, Steve tapped him on the shoulder. "Learn anything?"

Christian looked up. "Enough," he said, tucking his notes into a pocket. He logged off and rose. "Come on."

Steve followed him down an empty aisle between the bookshelves.

"You have it?"

"Yeah, and lucky I do," Steve said and slipped him the tiny device. "You can't just go to a store and buy one. I would've had to order it online from Rubber Ducky. Being it's nearing the weekend, I'd be surprised if it came tomorrow, even with overnight shipping."

Christian examined the thumb drive. "So I just plug it in?"

"That's it. The RAT will download the files in seconds."

"Okay. Leave first, in case you were followed."

Steve chuckled with a shrug. "I'm not sure I'm any good at this spy stuff."

"Get good. This is serious."

CHAPTER TEN

Barbara Davis glanced at the wall clock and sighed. It was five pm, the start of a long, lonely weekend. She shut down the computer on her desk and listened to the employees outside her door discussing their plans. Barbara considered her options as a single woman approaching forty who hadn't dated in months. Dining out with boring women friends didn't appeal to her, and the newly released movies on cable were garbage, not worth renting, even for a laidback night on the couch. She rose, condemned to a joyless two days of cleaning her apartment, buying groceries, and doing laundry.

Claudine, a suck-up seeking advancement, stuck her head into Barbara's office. "Good night, Miss Davis. I hope you have a nice weekend."

Fuck you, bitch, Barbara felt like saying but responded with a nod. Soon the staff cleared out and quiet reigned. With her coat and purse in arm, she strolled past the empty desks toward the elevator. She hesitated at one desk and bit her lip. Felix had been a good analyst, smart, fast, and efficient. She recalled being flattered when the young man had initially flirted with her before she put on the brakes. An office romance with a subordinate was unwise.

She ran her hand across his desk. *Shame that he'd overdosed on drugs.* She refused to accept that she might have had a hand in his death. She rode the elevator down to the lobby. With Felix in mind, she longed for a drink, and it was, after all, Friday. Instead of going to the garage for her car, she decided to walk to her favorite bar, where she could slurp cocktails and nurse delusions about the cute bartender, ignoring that he was gay.

She clutched her coat and stepped outside into the brisk breeze. She froze, not from the cold weather, but from the stunning creature capable of stopping most women in their tracks. He leaned against a lamp post, his sunglasses resting on his blond locks, while he studied a map.

He glanced up. "Ma'am, I'm hopin' you could help me out with some information."

Barbara looked around, making sure he had addressed her. "Of course," she said and did a quick take. His accent confirmed his Southern origin, and his boyish looks suggested he was in his twenties, still starry-eyed and unlike the men her age, losers or cynical divorcees who she normally dated.

When he drew his lanky frame from the post and stepped to her, she noticed his height. Even in high heels, she had to look up and was then struck by his hypnotic blue eyes. He was so distracting that she had a hard time concentrating.

"I'm a dumbbell when it comes to maps and big cities." He chuckled at himself.

Beautiful and modest; that's refreshing, she thought. "What do you want to know?"

"I've been sightseeing all day and freezing. I was lookin' for a drinking hole to warm up with an Irish coffee. Unfortunately a GPS and this city map don't specify. Figured it'd be better to pull over and ask a local."

"Actually I'm going to a lounge right now. It's a charming, historical place and within walking distance."

He shivered in his jacket. "I had my fill of walkin' today, especially in this weather. Us Floridians ain't used to cold. I'll drive. Just point me in the right direction."

She pointed down the street. "It's called Tonic. Go two blocks and take a left. It's several more blocks on the right."

"Ma'am, I'd be happy to give you a lift. Then for sure I won't get lost."

Normally she'd never dream of getting into a stranger's car, but he seemed genuine. "It is a bit chilly. A ride would be nice. I'm Barbara."

"Christian. It's good meeting ya." He stepped to a lavish sports car at the curb, and when he opened the passenger door, she noticed his Rolex watch. She climbed in, thinking, *He's no slouch. Has money.*

He got in and started the engine. "Thanks for coming. I hate drinking alone."

Fishing for more information, she commented, "Perhaps you should have brought your girlfriend or wife on this sightseeing trip."

"Don't have a girl."

"That's too bad," she said a little glumly, but was cheering inside. The boy was running off the charts on the dating scoreboard.

They arrived at Tonic and entered together. She usually ducked in and slipped upstairs, embarrassed at having no companion, but she showed off her newfound heartbreaker through the crowd of patrons, savoring the gawking women.

She turned to Christian. "All the seats are taken, but there's always an empty table on the third floor." She led him upstairs, and they sat down at a table near the fireplace.

"This place is very cool, really rustic."

"It used to be a pharmacy," she said.

Rather than a cocktail waitress taking their order, the bartender came over. "Hi, Barbara, who's your friend?" he asked, eyeing Christian.

"He's a lost Floridian I picked up on the street. I'll have the usual, and I believe he'd like an Irish coffee."

"One gin and tonic and Irish coffee coming up." With a smirk, he asked, "Sir, do you take whipped cream?"

"Straight coffee," Christian communicated. After the bartender left, he smiled. "Believe your barkeep was hitting on me."

She suddenly grasped that Christian was so stunning that he might be a homosexual. "Are you interested in him?" she blurted. She then realized her question might offend a straight man.

"No, Barb." He laughed, not the least bit insulted. "The boys like me, but I've never felt the inclination to go there. I prefer ladies."

Another plus, she thought. *He's not insecure.*

Their drinks arrived and the chitchat of the newly acquainted ensued. Christian briefly explained he was an environmental advocate and had come to DC. on conservation business. He decided to stay the weekend and see the capital for the first time.

"So what's your story, Barb?" he asked.

She hated being called Barb, but with him, the nickname was more than okay. She told him about her short bad marriage and her devotion to her job, working as a supervisor in the State Department and overseeing the Congressional budget. She found that Christian was a great listener, rarely talking about himself, but he proved to be intelligent and well-read. He was capable of commenting on any subject she brought up. With an easy-going manner and a good sense of humor, he seemed perfect, the ideal man, especially after a few hours of drinking.

Christian swallowed the last of an Irish coffee and scowled. "I'm sick of these. Are you game to switch it up?"

"Sure," she said. "I'm having a great time."

He motioned to the bartender. "We'd like two shots of your best mescal with lemon and salt."

"Mescal?" she questioned.

"It's similar to tequila, but has a smoky flavor, and it's made from a different variation of cactus. It also has a worm in the bottle. If you can stomach gin, you'll like this, especially the slight hallucinogenic high that brings you up instead of down."

The shots arrived at their table along with a napkin holding lemon wedges and a salt shaker. Christian said, "Here's how to drink it." Making a fist, he licked an area between his thumb and wrist and the sprinkled salt on the wet spot. He licked the salt off, downed a mescal shot in one gulp, and bit into a lemon slice. After a slight shudder, he grinned. "Great stuff."

By the second round, Barbara mastered the technique except for downing a shot in one swallow. It took her several sips. At midnight she felt the room swaying. "Christian, I think I'm getting drunk."

"You seem a little wasted. Let's get outta here." He helped her down the stairs and out to his car. He drove back to her office building and parked on the quiet street. "Guess this is goodbye." He leaned over and gave her long, slow kiss that sucked out all of her resistance. The kiss evolved to fondling. As she caressed his lean body, her craving grew. She wanted him in the worst way, but not on the street in a tiny car.

"There's a couch in my office," she said between heavy breaths.

"That'll work."

"We'll go in through the parking garage so I don't have to explain you to the guard in the lobby." They walked past the building front doors and down the street to the parking garage entrance. After stepping around the barriers, they passed rows of parking spaces and came to the elevator. She dug in her purse for her security fob and swiped it across a front panel. The elevator door opened, and they rode it up to the fifth floor. In her office she frantically removed his clothing, feeling like a kid opening a fabulous package. Stepping back to take in his seemingly mile-long tan abs and the rest of his nude body, she mumbled unconsciously, "Oh, my god."

With her reaction, he smiled slightly, took her into his arms, and softly kissed her. His approach was smoother and more seductive than hers. Although young, he proved to be worldly wise in the lovemaking department. They retired on the couch, and she let him work his magic.

* * *

At two in the morning Christian gazed down at Barbara, half dressed and passed out on her office couch. He had played the role of the lost Southern boy in the big, cold city, embellishing his accent and pouring on the charm, and a vulnerable guy asking for help attracts more women than a braggart or macho man. After one drink, he sensed her snobbery and switched gears, proving he had brains. Add alcohol, and the manipulation was a breeze.

He picked up his jeans from the floor and removed the RAT from a pocket. He turned on her desk computer and plugged the thumb drive into a portal. He dressed as the device infected the computer files. He removed the device and careful wiped the computer keys of his prints. At the door he glanced one last time at her. He'd normally feel guilt for blatantly seducing a sad, lonely woman, but her crimes were worse and included the analyst's death.

He lifted the collar on his jacket, kept his head down to prevent a good photo of his face from surveillance cameras in the building, and left her office. He had done the same when arriving.

A security pass was necessary to get into the building, but not leaving. If stopped by a guard, he wasn't concerned. Sleeping with an office worker wasn't against the law. He took the elevator down and exited the parking garage without notice.

In his car he drove out of the Foggy Bottom district and past the Lincoln Memorial, continuing southward over the bridge into Arlington. The traffic was sparse, making a tail easy to spot. Even in this late hour, he wanted to get the RAT to Steve so he could immediately download it, not chancing that the file might be erased from Davis's computer. Plus the sooner he knew who he was up against, the better.

A few miles past the Arlington Cemetery, he pulled off the highway into a strip mall that contained an open convenience store and parked in the farthest dark corner of the lot. He called Steve's burner phone.

After four rings, Steve answered. "Christian, it's three in the morning."

"I got it, and I'm in Arlington." He told Steve the name of the street and store.

"That's only four or five blocks from my house."

"Good, sneak out and walk here. On foot you're less likely to be followed."

"Geez, you are paranoid. All right, let me get dressed. I should be there within a half hour."

While waiting for Steve, Christian walked into the store. He was still a little high from the earlier cocktails. Food might help bring him down. He grabbed a Coke, a bag of chips, and some beef jerky. Paying at the counter, he realized his junk food diet was becoming a habit. He returned to his car and munched on the food, deciding to start eating healthier when home.

Steve walked up to his car window. "I can't believe you got it so quick. How did you get at her computer?"

"Gotta few things going for me. Hop in."

Steve climbed into the passenger seat and shivered. "Damn cold out there. Next time we meet, I'm driving."

Christian dug into his jean pocket and produced the thumb drive. "How long will it take for you to download it and get the info?"

"No time at all to download, but digging through those files might take some time."

"Okay, but don't put this off and screw around. We need to find out who we're up against." Christian grabbed the paper bag from the store, tore off a piece, and jotted down his email address. "Here's where you can send the information. My laptop is also untraceable. After you're finished, find a good place to hide your computer and disposable phone. These guys had no problem breaking into your friend's home. If they get into your house and find the computer, you could end up like him."

"That's reassuring."

"I'm heading back to Florida, probably on Sunday and this time for real. I doubt we'll have another face to face, but you know how to reach me. Once you have the file information, we'll get our ducks in a row and go from there."

Steve gazed at the thumb drive in his hand. "If this reveals that someone misappropriated funds, it proves there was a cover-up, and it was the motive for Felix's murder. Maybe then we should notify the police."

"I don't do police. You contacted me, aware that my methods aren't legal. You want justice for your friend? I'll give it to you. Steve, this whole thing stinks of government corruption. Don't make the mistake of trusting cops when they could be working for the killer."

"You have a point."

"Gotta go. Good luck," Christian said and offered his hand.

"You too." Steve shook his hand and stepped out of the car.

With a nod Christian sped off into the night.

* * *

Trish had fallen asleep on the couch, waiting and hoping that Christian would return to her apartment. She had dozed off around midnight while watching a late-night talk show. A tap on the door woke her, and she squinted to focus on her watch. At four-thirty in the morning, it had to be him. She jumped up and hurried to the door. "Who is it?"

"It's me," he said.

She opened the door and gazed at his tousled hair and unshaven face, and his weary look of a rough night. He stepped inside, and she fought the urge to ask where he'd been and with who. She had agreed at lunch to end the reporter probing. Those were the terms if she wanted to keep him. And she did.

Without a word he passionately kissed her and then swept her up into his arms.

"I'm glad you're here," she whispered into his ear as he carried her into the bedroom and placed her on the sheets. He stripped out of his clothing and climbed on top of her.

She grasped his silky locks behind his head as he penetrated her. Tears of ecstasy filled her eyes, and for the first time, she came clean about her feelings. "I love you, Christian."

* * *

Christian was roused by bright sunlight filling the bedroom and the smell of brewed coffee. For several minutes he gazed at the ceiling, his mind on Steve, the information on the RAT, and his next move. The clang of a pot conveyed that Trish was in the kitchen, cooking. His thoughts shifted to her and her declaration of love that he had not reciprocated.

He sat up and felt beat, but the cause wasn't from a long night of drinking, little sleep, and the efforts to satisfy two women. He suffered from mental anxiety, similar to being in a car race. He was gripping the wheel, speeding ahead, encountering bumps and treacherous curves. One false move spelled disaster, and usually the lines blurred between winning and surviving. Should he really invite a passenger on this ride? That decision resided in the other room.

He slipped into his jeans and ambled into the kitchen. "Mornin'," he said and kissed Trish's cheek.

"It's almost noon." She smiled. "Are you hungry?"

"I am. No dinner. I seem to skip meals here." He sat down at the small table as Trish poured him a cup of coffee and set a plate of sunny-side-up eggs, ham, grits, and buttered toast before him. "Damn, this looks good. Girl, you know what I like. Makes leaving hard."

"When are you leaving, if you don't mind my asking?" she said and joined him at the table.

"Tomorrow," he said and took a sip of coffee.

She nodded. "So, we have one more night."

It was more question than statement. "I'm totally yours for the next twenty-four hours." Despite her smile, he saw the uncertainty in her eyes. "Yeah, we need to talk."

After breakfast, he took a needed shower and then found Trish cleaning the kitchen. He took her hand and led her to the couch. She was quiet, letting him start the conversation. Telling a woman, "We need to talk." often meant bad news.

"I want to be honest, Trish, and that's something I usually avoid. I have feelings for you. I do. If I could have a relationship, it would be with you. I realized it last year when we split up, and I missed you."

"I was afraid it was one-sided. You know, out of sight, out of mind."

"No, more like absence makes the heart grow fonder. But how is this going to work? I'm a guy with no future, looking at prison or a nut ward. Dragging you into my mess would ruin your life."

"You could quit. Give up your causes."

"Seems like a no-brainer, choose the girl, family, and a normal life, but I can't abandon wildlife and my beliefs. And going legit and doing charity work is like spinning my wheels. It doesn't get the job done. I must have purpose and am driven to do this. It's hard to explain, but without these goals, I shrivel. Even if I retired and became a law-abiding citizen, the damage is already done. My past deeds will eventually catch up to me, and where would that leave us?"

"Christian, there are no guarantees in life. Everyone who enters a relationship hopes for the best, but there's always the chance things will end badly. When I first heard about Captain Nemo, I fell a little in love with that daring anti-hero risking his life for sharks. Then I saw you on that red horse, racing down a lane of trees. My god, I was breathless. You captured my heart even though I knew who you were and what you'd done."

He stood and gazed out the window. "You don't know me. I'm not a hero or a cool guy who spends time with you. I have issues.

You've never seen my temper. When pushed, I lose it. I'm also screwed up in the head." He turned to her. "When you saw me on that horse, I was suicidal, hoping to fall off and die. I have lows, get real moody and quiet. It feels like I've fallen into a pit and can't climb out. My shrink says I suffer from depression and possibly PTSD." He returned to the couch and took her hand. "I put on a good show, but inside I'm damaged goods, broken. You deserve a decent, stable guy. That's not me."

She sighed. "From the start, I knew you had problems. Our first night together on your boat, you tossed with nightmares and then curled up and sobbed in your sleep. I guessed you suffered from depression. And to take on these causes, you'd have to be little crazy, maybe even suicidal. Christian, I didn't fall in love with the cool guy. I fell for you."

"All right, Trish," he grumbled. "Aside from my fucked-up head and I'll probably end up in prison, consider it's dangerous to be with me. People want to kill me. I've already lost my wife and my best friend. They were killed protecting me. We hook up, and you might be next."

"If you're hoping to scare me off, it's not working. I'm willing to risk everything to be with you. Christian, I love you."

"Goddamn it!" He sprang up and paced the room. He stopped and looked at her. "What am I supposed to do here? Be a selfish son of a bitch and keep you in my life? Or opt for the right thing and end us before you're hurt?"

"I'll gamble with the son of a bitch. We can make this work."

* * *

Barbara woke on the couch with her head pounding from too many shots of mescal. Looking around, she saw her handsome lover was gone. "What a night," she mumbled, seeing it was nearly four in the morning. She retrieved her panties from the floor and buttoned her blouse. After straightening her skirt, she searched for a note, business card, or phone number from him but knew the hunt was in vain. Her night with Christian had been a one-time fling, and he hadn't promised anything more. Instead of pining, she felt lucky. He was a dreamboat in a sea of men. She'd never meet another one like him.

God, I need to forget him. He's unattainable, so get over it. She reapplied her makeup and fixed her hair, in the off chance she ran into someone working the weekend. When home, she planned to focus on priorities; drink a lot of water and take painkillers to combat the hangover, followed by a long, hot bath and reclining on the sofa with a tub of ice cream. Pathetic, but anything more plausible required effort.

She picked up her purse, preparing to leave her office, when she heard the pinging of the elevator stopping at her floor. *He came back!* She pushed the bounce back in her hair and leaned against her desk, waiting for him to walk in.

She smiled as the door eased open, but it wasn't Christian. A tall, muscular man with buzzed white hair stood in the doorway.

"Miss Davis, I work for Secretary Sanders," he said. "I need to ask you a few questions."

She blinked away the smile and straightened. "Oh, of course, anything for the secretary," she said. "You certainly work odd hours."

"Yes," he said sternly and stepped inside. From under his suit jacket he removed a vanilla envelope and pulled out several eight-by-ten photos. "What do you know about this man?" he asked and showed her the first picture.

She gawked at the photo of her and Christian in front the building as she stared up into his eyes. "He was asking for directions. I don't know him."

The man showed her a second picture with her getting into Christian's Porsche. "Do you make a habit of going with men you don't know?"

She chuckled nervously. "You're getting the wrong idea. I mentioned I was going to a lounge, and he offered to give me a ride. He was very sweet."

"Sweet enough to seduce you inside this government building," he said and produced another photo.

She covered her mouth, staring at the photo of her and Christian slipping into the parking garage. Worry and embarrassment turned to anger. "Fine, I brought him here and slept with him." She fumed. "That's not a crime. I want to know why the secretary is having me followed and photographed. My personal life is none of his business."

"The secretary doesn't care about you, but he is concerned about this man. I tracked him using the GPS in his car, and it led to you. His name is Christian Roberts, but his alias is Captain Nemo. You might've heard of him. He's suspected of bombings, arsons, and murders."

"He's…he's Captain Nemo?" she muttered, recognizing the name in the news. She slumped into a chair. "Christian said he was an environmental advocate."

"That's putting it mildly, considering he's a notorious eco-terrorist. Did he say anything else significant, like his plans? Did he mention friends, any names?"

She shook her head. "No, he hardly talked about himself."

"All right," he said. "Do you know if he gained access to your computer?"

"It's possible. I fell asleep. When I woke up, he was gone." She looked up teary-eyed. "Will I lose my job over this?"

"I wouldn't worry about it, Miss Davis."

CHAPTER ELEVEN

At the Miami field office, Agent Dave Wheeler held his jaw and read an autopsy report of a bank clerk shot the previous week during a heist in Broward County. A surveillance camera had identified the killer, a local with an extensive rap sheet of drug-dealing, mugging, and knocking over convenience and liquor stores. He'd been recently released from prison, but the murder had placed him in the big leagues. Bank robbery was a federal crime that brought in the FBI, and the case had fallen into Dave's lap. The police were doing the heavy lifting with the manhunt. They raided the killer's possible hideouts and questioned his friends and family. Dave simply steered the investigation and officers in the right direction, anticipating a quick capture. The guy was a loser.

The phone rang, and seeing the caller ID, he rolled his eyes, thinking Idaho must be low on crime. "Agent Wheeler," he dryly answered.

"Chief Tucker here in Salmon. I got the report back about the canoe. Your people found nothing, no prints or DNA. They learned the boat's manufacturer, but with the ID plate chiseled off, there's no telling what store sold it. A sales clerk might've identified Roberts as the buyer and tied him to the restaurant bombing."

"Chief, I've told you this boy isn't a dummy. He'd never walk into a store and expose himself to cameras and witnesses to buy a canoe to use in a crime."

"Yeah, yeah, slippery as a snake, but Wheeler, I've killed my share of snakes."

"So what can I do for you?"

"Just keeping you updated. Besides the canoe, I checked out the big Italian who rented a campsite downriver from Salmon. Turns out he used a fictitious name and had a stolen plate on his truck when he checked in, so it's a good bet he was working with Roberts. I had a police artist do a sketch from the campground owner's description."

"You should send it to the Idaho FBI."

"I did, but those guys have their thumbs up their asses and don't do squat. They ignore me like I'm a small-town hick, but you're different. Plus, you know Roberts and know how he thinks. You steered me in the right direction, saying he struck from the river. And you just saved me some leg work, hitting every outfitter store with Roberts's mug shot."

"I didn't say you shouldn't check out the stores. You might get lucky." Wheeler gazed upwards, wanting to come up with a polite way of get Tucker off his back. "Look, Chief, I'm glad I've been some help, but Captain Nemo is no longer my concern, unless he commits a crime in South Florida, which is unlikely. There are no wolves here."

"But Roberts lives in your state."

"He lives mid-state, out of my jurisdiction. The Tampa and Sarasota FBI are keeping track of him. I'll be happy to give you their numbers."

"For Christ's sakes, he just blew up three government helicopters. Every damn agent in the country should be after that boy. Has anyone even bothered to interrogate him?"

"The Sarasota agents tried, but he declined an interview. I phoned him and asked about his alibi on the night of the restaurant bombing. He claimed he was aboard his sailboat on Sarasota Bay. The local agents confirmed it, found several bay residents who spotted him on his boat. I also checked the cell towers, and he spoke to me from Sarasota."

"That's another reason you should be involved. He won't talk to anyone else, but he obviously trusts you. I've left him dozens of messages, and the little jerk won't return my calls. Wheeler, you can get close to this boy and bring him down. You belong on this case."

"No thanks. I'm done with Captain Nemo and Christian Roberts. I have plenty of bad people in Miami who keep me busy."

"We'll see about that."

Several days later Dave received a call from the assistant director of the FBI in Quantico, informing him that he had been reassigned to handle one case, Captain Nemo's, and was the lead agent heading the task force. Apparently, a senator, congressman, or governor had requested his transfer. No mystery about which state they represented. With that kind of pressure, he took the case. The only other choice was to quit or be fired.

He hung up the phone, cursing Chief Tucker. "Asshole," he growled, and kicked the trash can. He slumped in his chair, distressed with the new assignment. Christian was a criminal and deserved to be punished, but Dave didn't want to be the one to put him away.

He reflected on his first interview with Christian in Nassau. The Bahamian authorities had an unsolved murder at sea and requested an FBI assist. Christian was the prime suspect. Over the following months, Dave enjoyed the cat-and-mouse game with the cocky young man who proved to be bright, unpredictable, and tough; more than a worthy adversary. He was obviously Captain Nemo; there just wasn't enough proof. Then one night on Miami Beach, their relationship changed. The agent and outlaw became friends. Bringing down Christian was like wrestling with thorns.

He scratched the back of his head and turned to the desk computer. Instead of doing a search on Christian Roberts, he typed in Charlie Tucker, police chief in Salmon, Idaho. How did a chief in a little town influence Washington elites and the heads in the FBI? Dave read several profiles pertaining to Tucker and the answer became clear. Tucker was described as a hard-nosed, decent, and highly respected lawman. With his flawless record of arrests, his reputation was indisputable. No criminal escaped Charlie's scrutiny.

Citizens admired him, and the Idaho senators, congressmen, and governors sought his endorsement. One article said Tucker could've climbed the political ladder with his rough, no-nonsense approach and been successful in any position, but he declined, saying politics was too shady and he preferred the quiet life as a small town chief.

Dave crossed his arms and stared at a picture of his caller. Tucker wasn't impressive, actually a short, scrawny, middle-aged man with crow's feet around his brown eyes and a balding head surrounded by short gray hair.

* * *

On Sunday evening Christian drove south on I-95 toward Florida. The problem with a monotonous long trip was having too much time to think. During the weekend, he and Trish had talked about dining out, seeing a play, and visiting a museum, but in the end, they never left the apartment. Lovemaking took priority. In the late afternoon, he tore himself away from her and started for home.

She wanted him in her life, and he'd walked out of her door, reluctantly agreeing. On the road for several hours, he was in headshaking mode. What had he been thinking? It wasn't Trish. She was great. He cared for her and she made him happy, an emotion that often eluded him. But given his circumstances and who he was, he could only offer heartbreak or worse. He should have had the balls to walk away, but instead he'd got swept up in the passion and delusion that he could have it all.

He wondered if missing his wife had played a part in his decision. Trish and Allie were similar; beautiful, intelligent, confident, and they weren't inclined to see him with glazed-over eyes. They were strong women who stood their ground. He liked that.

"Goddamn it," he cursed. Trish was perfect for him, but he was far from it. His longing for love and his weakness had put him in a commitment that was wrong. With a thousand other worries, he'd just added another. She could pay a dear price for being with him.

His cell rang; it was Agent Wheeler. *Thank God! Get my mind off this fuck-up.* He swiped the Answer on the phone. "Hey, Dave."

"I see you finally got the new car, but a Porsche instead of the Ferrari."

"How'd you—Dave, are you on my tail again? Thought that job belonged to the Tampa and Sarasota FBI?"

"They're still keeping tabs on you, but I was reassigned. I'm in charge of the Captain Nemo investigation."

"Wow, congrats...I think," Christian said. "So is this a heads-up call?"

"Somewhat. Christian, I didn't ask for this assignment, but now that I have it, I'm calling to learn why you were in Washington."

"I was visiting a girl. Curious, did you track me using the GPS on my phone or car?"

"Both," said Wheeler. "I see you also spent a few days in Atlanta. You want to tell me about that visit?"

"I'll tell you that when I get home, the GPS is coming out of this Boxster. It's an option I don't need."

"What about Atlanta?"

"Come on, Dave. You already know why I was there. It was in the Atlanta paper that I attended at a wildlife event. Witnesses and my credit card statements will also prove I stayed at the Hilton."

"So that's your alibi while Nemo was blowing up choppers out West?"

"Pretty solid, isn't it?" Christian chuckled. "For the record I didn't blow up any choppers. Damn, I've missed the game playing with you."

"Yeah, but the game ends with your arrest."

"Always the optimist, but it happens, I prefer you nail me than some career dipshit. Speaking of, how's the partner?"

"Ralph meet a girl and transferred to Washington to be with her," said Wheeler. "So you won't get your kicks provoking him, but you have riled up a police chief in Idaho. He's not happy you destroyed that restaurant in his town."

"Didn't know anything about the restaurant, but I am getting familiar with Chief Tucker. He keeps ringing the farm and leaving messages. The last one had me in stitches. Said if I didn't return his calls, he'd come to my house and shake a confession out of me. I gotta admire the guy's commitment."

"Commitment isn't the word. He's more like a dog and you're the bone. I checked him out. He's has a heck of a reputation and an arrest record. He's not going to quit and forget you. Anyway, I plan to come to Sarasota and get an official statement regarding your whereabouts during those Nemo attacks. I imagine you'll bring a lawyer."

"Naw, no lawyer, but I'm not spending a day in some shitty interrogation room, even for you. I'll give you a statement, but only aboard my sloop. Let's make this fun. We'll cruise the Gulf, toss down a few, and grill some steaks. Life's too short."

"All right, as long as you don't feed me to the fish."

"Dave, that hurts. Heck, you're one of the few people I respect and like."

"I like you, too, Christian. I just wish you'd…"

"Don't go there. We have different priorities. That'll never change. About this sailing trip, let's aim for this Saturday. I'll be at the marina."

"That should work for me."

Christian disconnected, looking forward to seeing Wheeler. They were friends but with limited expectations. Unburdening his heart to this pal had serious consequences. With Wheeler back on the case, Christian would have to be extra cautious. He glanced at the time, still early enough to call his horse farm.

"Hey, Juan, letting you know I'll be back tomorrow."

"Oh, good, Mr. Roberts. Are you coming here or staying on your boat?"

"Why?"

"After chores on Tuesday, I planned to leave for Miami so I can breeze the two fillies at Gulfstream Wednesday morning. My mother is also coming to visit her sister. I'll have Gigi feed the horses while I am gone."

"Don't bother Gigi. I can take care of them. I'm ready for some alone time with my kids. Is the press still camped out front?"

"No, they left last Thursday. When I opened the gate to let the Stockyard Feed truck in, a reporter asked when you were returning from Atlanta. I told him I didn't know."

"Glad they're gone. I'll see you soon."

Christian eased back in the seat, preparing to reach Sarasota without stopping. Sunday night meant less traffic on the roads, compared to the Monday daytime congestion. If he got tired, he could catch a few winks at a rest stop. He mapped out his week: get back and recuperate Monday, move the sloop and retrieve his laptop Tuesday, and be back on the farm and feed horses Wednesday while Juan was away. For the weekend, he'd hook up with Wheeler at the marina.

His thought drifted to Steve and what he had uncovered with the RAT thumb drive. He was itching to know but not enough to risk a call. Even a brief conversion could be overheard by other means, and the exchange was dangerous.

Boredom set in with the tedious, flat highway, and he couldn't stomach reading another billboard. He dug under the car seat for his disposable phone for an untraceable call rather than use the car's Bluetooth for his regular cell phone. He hit the keys and Sal answered.

"It's me."

"Shit, Kid," Sal muttered. "It's fucking midnight. What's wrong?"

"Nothing. Just driving back from DC. Since you're a night owl, I figured you wouldn't mind."

"DC? Saw a cold front moved through up there. I bet you were one miserable cracker."

"Yeah, froze my ass off."

"Wait a damn minute. Don't tell you were there to see the reporter?"

"I went for business but did stay with her. But yeah, we're kinda together again."

"You don't fucking listen. Vince and I warned you to stay away from that bitch. She gets you between the sheets so you'll run your mouth. Before your pants are back on, you're a headline."

"Trish wouldn't betray me, and Sal, I missed her."

"Bullshit! You missed the tension, the rush of being with a woman who could destroy you. It's called fatal attraction. You got the looks and charm to have any chick. Rather than dating a busybody, get a girl that turns a blind eye and won't hurt you. You're thinking with your pecker instead of your brain."

"Enough with the lecture," Christian said. "I'm already conflicted, but my concern is for Trish. She's strapping herself to a time bomb."

"Fine. I'll shut up. I'm wastin' my breath anyway on a guy, willing to hang himself."

"Naw, that takes too long. Harakiri is an option if I find myself without a gun."

"That might be funny if you were joking. On another matter, our little friend phoned. He says you owe him the last half for that job. I offered to pay, but Bill wants to collect from you and specified a face to face. I believe he's in love." Sal laughed. "It seems you have all kinds wantin' your ass."

"As if I don't have enough headaches," Christian said with a sigh. "Tell him I'll get with him Friday. Speaking of wanting my ass, Wheeler's coming to Sarasota, and I'm taking him out on my boat Saturday."

"Wheeler? The FBI guy?" said Sal. "Jesus, you're meetin' with a fed and hit man on the same weekend. You are *nuts*."

"I wanna get all this shit behind me so I can focus on my cause for wolves. I'm expecting information that might be useful for my next move. Over lunch maybe you can give me advice on how to tackle it."

"Here's some advice now, Kiddo," Sal said. "Cancel the boat ride with Wheeler. He's one tricky dick, and you shouldn't talk to him without a lawyer. And if he's takin' an interest, you might wanna postpone your next move. Lastly, dump the girl. She's turned your mind to mush, and you're fixin' to be fucked in a bad way."

"Appreciate the warning, but I can handle it."

"Famous last words. I'll see you around, maybe."

* * *

In Salmon, Idaho, Charlie Tucker arrived at the police station with a folder in hand and a smile on his face. Earlier he had convinced his political connections that Agent Wheeler should head the FBI investigation for Captain Nemo. The governor and a senator had agreed and used their pull to make it happen. With Wheeler running roughshod over the case, Charlie was finally getting results. He had faxed Wheeler the sketch of the large Italian who stayed at the campground the night the restaurant blew up and who was possibly a Nemo conspirator.

Within minutes Wheeler phoned back, saying he had a good idea of the man's identity. He'd have the Idaho FBI hold a photo lineup to campground owners, but Charlie convinced him that he could do it better and faster.

Charlie had just returned from North Fort campground, where the owners positively identified the big Italian. He stopped at Helen's desk, opened the folder, and tapped his finger on one of the six photos. "This guy," he told her. "His name is Sal Lamotte. I want his picture sent to every law enforcement agency in Idaho. He's a person of interest in the Captain Nemo attack."

"Sure thing, Chief," said Helen.

He walked into his office, sat down at the desk, and called Wheeler. "You were right again," he said.

"So they identified Lamotte?" asked Wheeler.

"Yes, sir, and I'm sending out his photo statewide. With any luck, we'll tie him to the canoe purchase or something else, and he'll give Roberts up."

"Chief, I know you're in a hurry to wrap up the case, but there are procedures to be followed. Number one, Lamotte should be questioned about his alibi."

"Baloney," Charlie said and jumped out of his seat. "I got two damn witnesses who say he was here."

"Granted, but there's no hard evidence that connects him to Roberts and the bombing. His credit cards statements, plane fares, the truck rental, gas and motel bills all need to be checked to prove he was in Idaho. Eyewitness accounts aren't reliable. Then the search begins for evidence that puts him with Roberts out there. And there's still no proof that Roberts is guilty. It takes time to build a case and make it stick."

"You're not talking to some damn amateur here. I've put a lot of felons behind bars."

"I realize that, but terrorism is a federal crime. If this goes to trial, the case won't be heard in a country court with a small-time judge who can pass the buck."

"Christ," Charlie grumbled. "We can cut through the crap if we bring this Lamotte character in and threaten him with prison until he admits to helping Roberts."

"Sal Lamotte wouldn't rat out anyone. He's a career criminal and was a captain in the New York mob. Those guys live by a code."

"How'd you know it was Lamotte after seeing only a rough sketch?"

"I recognized him. For years I tried to bust Sal and his boss, Vince Florio, for drug smuggling, even some murders in Miami, and with no success. When they moved their operation to Sarasota, they met Roberts through horse racing and became friendly."

"So that's the connection. But a fifty-six-year-old New York mobster and your outdoorsy Florida kid are an unlikely pair. I understand mob loyalty, especially when it's suicide to squeal to cops, but I don't see Lamotte protecting Roberts, if it means his own skin."

"I've seen the police reports and studied their profiles. Sal and Christian have an interesting history together. They were drawn together out of loyalty to Vince. It's public record that Christian saved Vince from drowning during a boat accident, and later Vince took a bullet for Christian and died. Given those events and that Sal is as devoted as a dog, he'd never turn on the young guy."

"Where's that leave this investigation?"

"I'm visiting Sarasota next week to interview Christian. He's agreed as long as we talk while sailing on his boat."

"Wait, you're getting on a boat with a terrorist?"

Wheeler chuckled. "Christian is more a vigilante than a terrorist, and he's too smart to harm an FBI agent."

"Okay, Wheeler. Let me know how it goes."

After hanging up, Charlie gazed at the ceiling. His conversation with the agent didn't sit well. He'd pulled strings so Wheeler would head the FBI investigation into Christian Roberts, alias Captain Nemo, but he was now having doubts. Was Wheeler the right man for the job? Whether intentional or not, the agent revealed his association with Roberts was beyond familiar, more like chummy. He referred to Roberts by his first name and was going boating with him, and several times had called Roberts *smart*, almost like he admired him. Also why hadn't Wheeler wanted the case in the first place? Roberts apparently had a mobster in his pocket. Adding up little details and doubts had Charlie's radar up. *Something's going on between those two. I need to get to the bottom of it.*

* * *

Late Monday afternoon, Christian pulled into the driveway of his horse farm and climbed out to unlock the gate. He took a moment to gaze at the brilliant blue sky and savor the moist breeze bearing smells of citric and tropical flowers. Like Dorothy clicking the heels of her ruby red shoes, he said, "There's no place like home." No matter where he'd been or what he'd done, coming back to Florida was always the same, always comforting.

After relocking the gate, he drove up the lane to the house. Foremost on his mind after an exhausting haul and rough weekend was sleep. He dropped his bag in the bedroom, took off his shoes, and called the caretaker's house at the back of the property. "I'm home, Juan, but whipped after that drive. Unless there's something pressing, I'll talk to you tomorrow over coffee."

"Okay, Mr. Roberts," said Juan. "I'm glad you're back."

Christian thought about taking a shower and then searching the kitchen for a bite to eat. Instead the bed won out. Still dressed, he collapsed on the quilt and fell asleep.

At six in the morning the phone rang. He groped for it on the dark nightstand, still half asleep. Pressing the receiver to his ear, he muttered groggily, "Yeah?"

Juan's alarmed voice said, "Mr. Roberts, Chris is down in his paddock and can't get up."

Christian's eyes popped open, and he jerked upright. "What do you mean he's down? Is he colicky or injured?"

"He's not showing signs of colic, not nipping his sides or rolling, but I don't see any injuries, either. I've already called the vet. Could you open the gate for her? I don't want to leave him."

"Of course I'll be down in a few minutes." He leaped off the bed, put his shoes on, and flew out the door. The faint light of dawn broke the horizon as he ran to the gate in the cold morning dew. After opening the gate, he raced to the barn. On the other side of the fence in the pasture, the horses seemed to sense his panic. They whinnied and galloped alongside, following him to the barn. He didn't give them a second glance, focused only on his father's old bay stallion.

His eyes watered at the silence of the barn. The stallion had faithfully always greeted Christian with his low nickering. He took a breath, not from running, but from a feeling of being punched in the stomach. He hustled down the lit barn aisle, stepped into the bedding of wood shavings in the last stall, and stared out the doorway into Chris's small paddock. Juan held a flashlight and stood over the dark-brown horse lying on the grass. It didn't look good. Hesitating for a moment, Christian sniffled up his resolve and with his sleeve wiped away the growing moisture in his eyes before hurrying to them.

Juan clasped a lead that was attached to Chris's halter and looked up at Christian. "I'm sorry, Mr. Roberts. I have tried to pull him up, but he can't."

Christian squatted over Chris and stroked his head. Christian had grown up with this horse and was extremely attached. "Don't give up on me, boy," he said, and glanced up at Juan. "Maybe he's sick."

"His eyes and nose are clear of fluid, and no coughing. Yesterday he ran around like a colt and ate all his food. It's unlikely he'd go down this fast with an illness. If he cannot stand…"

"Let me try." Christian stood and took the lead from Juan. "Come on, boy. Let's go," he said and tugged on the lead. Chris lifted his head and straightened his front legs. He struggled to a sitting position, but couldn't get his back legs under him and rise. His front legs trembled, and after a minute, he collapsed with a thud and groaned.

"Oh, God," Christian cried and dropped beside him. He rubbed the horse's neck, saying "It's okay. It's okay, boy."

The stallion had gathered all his courage and strength and put aside his pain to rise for Christian. The display of devotion broke Christian's heart. Uncontrollable tears streamed down his face and he gasped between breaths. "What do you think is wrong with him, Juan?"

Juan drew in a deep sigh. "I believe he hurt himself. This spot near the oak is where he likes to roll in the dirt and sleep. He either laid down too hard or rolled over and injured his spine or a hip. His shaking front legs are an indication." He stepped to Christian and clasped his shoulder. "Mr. Roberts, he's lived a good long life, twenty-nine years, but it's his time."

Christian covered his mouth and nodded. Chris wasn't the average old horse. He had had the speed and heart to win many races and had passed those genes onto his offspring, but his good manners and gentle nature made him exceptional, especially for a stud.

"The cats will miss him," he said, recalling that the two barn cats and Chris were buddies. Starting as kittens, they crawled on top of the fence posts and played with him, and Chris nuzzled and nosed them around. Allie had found it comical that a stallion would befriend cats. Christian remembered how much his dead wife and father had also loved this special horse.

"Goddamn it, Chris," Christian muttered. "For the first time in your life, you're letting me down."

A half hour later the vet, a young woman, and her assistant arrived. They examined Chris and administered fluids, painkillers, and antibiotics in case he was ill. When he didn't respond, they agreed with Juan. Chris had injured himself. Juan had known the end result before the vets arrived and tried to prepare Christian. It's a death sentence if a horse can't stand.

Christian sat on the grass holding Chris's head in his lap as the vet pushed aside the black mane and administered a lethal dose in his long brown neck, a neck that Christian once stroked on their peaceful rides through the woods. They had moved as one, and only a horse lover could relate to the bond. The stallion closed his eyes and quietly went to sleep. The vet removed the syringe after the stallion stopped breathing.

Juan called Paul, Chris's farrier, and asked him to come over with his backhoe to dig a grave for Chris. Juan's eyes watered when he returned his cell phone to a pocket. "Paul said he had never worked on a gentler stallion, and he will miss Chris. He will be here within the hour."

Christian removed Chris's halter. Clutching it like a cherished memory, he rose. "I'm sorry, Juan, but I can't stay here," he said and swallowed the lump in his gullet. "I don't want to see him buried."

"I understand, Mr. Roberts. I'll handle everything, pay the vet and Paul. We will put Chris right here under his favorite tree, and I'll cancel my trip to Miami. You shouldn't have to do chores tomorrow when you're upset."

Christian cleared his throat. "No, you go. I need something to do. Otherwise I'll just mope around the house." For the last time he patted the horse's body, so different in death than in life. Christian was trying to control his emotions but failing miserably. He trudged into the barn and stopped at Mystery's stall. He stroked the young red stallion's white blaze and said, "You're in charge now."

A big black barn cat rubbed against Christian's legs for attention. He reached down and petted the cat. "Blackie, your good buddy is gone." Speaking those words opened the flood gates of grief. He crumpled to the floor, hugged his knees, and openly wept.

He had intended to drive to Vince's house, retrieve his untraceable laptop, and leave his Porsche in Vince's garage, out of the weather. He'd then sail his sloop moored off the backyard to the marina and hose it down for the weekend with Wheeler. Juan could pick him up and bring him back to the farm before going to Miami. With the laptop he could open Steve's email and learn what he'd uncovered in the files. The full day of activities were scratched, however. He'd lost the gumption to accomplish anything.

He ambled back to the house and curled up on the couch, mentally devastated. His stomach churned between his bouts of sobs. The sorrow was magnified because it triggered his depression.

The result was he lacked the concentration and energy to function. The loss of the horse affected Christian like when he'd lost Allie.

He realized he needed to snap out of his pathetic state and put the grief behind him if he planned to help the wolves. *I'm totally devastated over an animal. I can't understand people who have fun killing them.*

CHAPTER TWELVE

After the horse's death, Christian remained in seclusion, lacking the motivation to rise from the couch, but he heard the comings and goings on the farm. First the vet's SUV left, and soon after Paul's noisy diesel truck came in, towing the rattling trailer holding a tractor. Beyond the barn a tractor fired up, and then came the reverberating echo of its backhoe digging Chris's grave. Forty-five minutes later, the deed was done, and Paul left.

In the late afternoon, Juan called and said the horses were fed, and he would soon load the fillies and leave for Miami. "Are you sure you want me to go?" Juan asked.

"Yes, go. I'll be okay." Embarrassed, he forced a chuckle. "I don't know why I'm taking this so hard."

"You and Chris were the same age and grew up together. Your father even blessed you both with the same name. It's understandable why you are taking it hard."

"I suppose. Hate to admit it, but I cared more about that horse than I do about most people."

"If you're not up to it in the morning, Gigi will be happy to do the morning chores."

"I'll manage. You and your mom have a safe trip, and I hope the two fillies have decent times."

After Juan's call, Christian thought about ringing Trish, but what could he say? That he was suffering a terrible stint of depression because an old horse had died? *She thinks I'm a badass, but if I break down and cry on the call, she'll realize I'm a pitiful, sick asshole.* The thought had him questioning his new relationship.

Trish was supposedly the woman in his life, but he was uncomfortable opening up to her. With Allie, he never hesitated to pour his heart out, but back then, he wasn't as screwed up. *Another example of why I should be single. I don't trust anyone with my issues and feelings.*

He considered reaching out to Mary Jane, his shrink, to get him over this hump, but quickly changed his mind. He knew her drill, endless office visits and a pocketful of prescriptions. Call it stupid or stubborn, but he didn't want to go there. If cured of depression, would he lose the suicidal drive to save wildlife?

He wandered into the kitchen. Food might help him feel better. He opened a can of soup, and as it warmed on the stove, he saw Juan's truck and horse trailer drive out, stopping briefly at the road to relock the gate. He set the soup bowl on the coffee table and grumbled, "I've got too much to do and gotta snap out of it." He turned on the TV, slid the *Guardians of the Galaxy* disc into the DVD, and sipped soup, hoping the humorous sci-fi would lift his spirits and get him back on track.

Christian woke in the dark to the alarmed honking from the pair of sandhill cranes in the front yard. The house was pitch black, since the TV tuned out after four-hours. He sat up, confused about the time. With the birds calling at night, he assumed it was either an hour past sunset or predawn. A glance at digital clock that said midnight had him rise with concern. Only a predator disturbing the nesting cranes would cause them to sound off at that hour.

He stepped through the shadowy living room, keeping the lights out to better see the outside. At the window he expected to gaze upon the usual intruders: coyotes, stray dogs, or the bear that rambled in through the back of the property from Myakka State Park. He scanned the moonlit grounds of silver and grays. His grogginess vanished and his eyes widened when he spotted a black car parked on the driveway between the road and house. For it to be there, the chain on the gate had to have been cut. The distressed cranes honked again and drew his attention to the crouched figure of a man creeping through a stand of maple trees toward the house. Movement drew Christian's attention to two more, one approaching on the driveway and the other in a field on the far left. The three were spread out to cut off his escape to the road.

He noticed they held handguns and stepped back from the window. With sneaky tactics, they were not likely to be cops, and they obviously planned to harm him. He did not have time to retrieve his own weapon in its bedroom hideaway or hop in his car and blow past them. His only option was to slip out the back door and edge his way around the lake to the barn. On a horse he could cover the ground faster than on foot, travel over the vast back pasture, and disappear into the thick pine forest.

He quietly opened the screen door and stepped outside, when it occurred to him that the only horse in the barn was Mystery. Christian had never attempted to ride him, lacking the experience to handle the spirited racehorse. *Take on three armed men or kill myself on Mystery? Not fearing death and wanting it were two different things.*

He hunkered low to the grass and crept to the lake. Behind him he heard the bang and crash of the wooden front door and glass shattering inside the house. He made his way along the edge of the lake to the northern end and the stand of cypress trees. If he made it there, the cover would get him to the barn unseen. As he approached the trees, a man growled out from the dark.

"Hold it right there or I'll shoot."

Christian froze. There were four men, not three. He straightened and turned to a man who stepped out from behind an orange tree. "Who are you?"

"Hands up," the man said and stepped to him.

Christian raised his hands and sized up the burly man. "What do you want?"

"Shut up and turn around," he said while pulling a pair of handcuffs from his pocket.

Christian turned and faced the lake, inches from his feet. As soon as the man grabbed his wrist to apply the cuffs, he whipped around and slugged him in his jaw. The man dropped the gun in the water and staggered backwards. In the fight for his life, Christian attacked with all his speed and strength. He hit him hard in the stomach and face as they staggered into foot-deep water. The guy was tough. He wouldn't go down, but his reaction time was slow. Christian hammered him like a punching bag as the guy blindly swung back. With only seconds to take out his adversary and get away clean, he kicked the guy's balls. The man collapsed in the water but came up holding his gun. On his knees he pointed the weapon at Christian and cursed, "You're a dead fucker now."

Christian swallowed and took a step back. The man started to rise, but suddenly jerked around and released a blood-curdling scream. He turned the weapon toward the water and aimlessly fired. Kicking and wailing, he cried out to Christian, "Something's got my leg. For God's sake, help me."

In the moonlight Christian then saw Al's broad back and swishing tail surface. The splashing and fist fight had attracted the ten-foot alligator that had latched onto the man's calf to drag him into deeper water where the gator would go into a death roll and drown his victim.

The gunfire and man's yelling alerted his buddies. The screen door slammed and a man's voice hollered, "What's going on?"

Christian ran through the cypress trees and into the barn. He grabbed a bridle from the tack room and entered Mystery's stall. "Okay, fella, be good for me," he said, placing the bit in the horse's mouth. He climbed onto the big chestnut's bare back and grabbed a clump of red mane. "Okay, let's go."

Mystery shot out of the stall as if bursting out of a race starting gate, and the pair left the barn at a full gallop. Christian hung on and guided him to the back of the farm. They raced past a lane of trees, and he saw the shadowy board fence ahead. Christian pulled back on the reins to stop Mystery, planning to hop off and open the gate, but the horse only accelerated. Too late he realized a racehorse was trained differently from other breeds; a tight rein meant go and a loose rein meant slow to a halt. "Whoa, boy," he said, but with no effect. Mystery wasn't stopping. Grabbing the horse's mane with both hands, he was unsure if the Thoroughbred would jump the four-foot fence or plow through its wooden boards. Christian gritted his teeth and clamped with his legs when Mystery sailed over the top board. Coming down hard left Christian tilted slightly off balance on the horse's back, but he managed to right his seat and stay on. Mystery didn't miss a beat and flew across the open pasture in less than a minute. "Damn, you're one hell of a horse," he said into the horse's ear.

They reached the pine forest, and Christian slackened the reins. "Whoa, boy, whoa." This time Mystery came to a stop, but his hooves danced in place, wanting more. "Easy, easy, boy," he said and patted the horse's shoulder to calm him. He stared across the field to see if they were followed. Several minutes later the probing car lights moved down the driveway and stopped at the barn.

Sound travels a good distance in the open countryside so Christian heard the car doors slam and the men's voices. One man shouted, but his words were garbled. Their flashlights flickered in and around the stable. They must have heard Mystery's galloping hooves, but probably assumed a horse was running in a pasture. The open tack room and stall door, along with the fresh horse tracks in the lane likely confirmed he had escaped on horseback. They loaded into the car and followed the torn-up grass created by fleeing hooves.

The men apparently planned to pursue Christian, so he guided Mystery deeper into the woods. He was confident they'd never catch him. A vehicle couldn't penetrate the pines, and on foot they didn't have a prayer. Still, headlights and even a flashlight could cause an animal's eyes to reflect the light, and an unwanted horse whinny could pinpoint his location. Mystery might be the fastest horse on the planet, but he couldn't outrun bullets. Christian wasn't taking any chances.

He slunk low over his horse's shoulder so the branches wouldn't smack his face as they slowly weaved deeper into the forest. The only sounds were a hooting owl, the distant utterance of a cow, and Mystery's hooves crunching pine needles. If they continued west, they would eventually enter Myakka State Park, where he could find a ranger or camper who could call for help.

They had traveled a half-mile when the pop-pop of distant gunfire rang out at the farm. Christian brought the horse to a standstill and listened. His imagination ran wild. There was nothing to shoot at except his horses. Four more shots erupted. Worried, Christian turned Mystery back toward home.

They arrived at the open pasture, and Christian saw from far-off the two sets of car lights near his house. The red taillights signaled a car leaving the property, and the other was the headlights of a car that had entered from the road. More gunfire erupted. The car occupants were apparently shooting at each other. The second car had to belong either to the police or a concerned neighbor who had heard the commotion.

With a slight kick to Mystery's ribs, the horse leaped into a full-out run. The intruders had left the gate open so Mystery never broke stride rounding it and raced up the driveway to the house. Up ahead Christian saw the black car leave the property and speed down the road. A white compact car was parked on the driveway next to the house. He urged Mystery forward and stopped him at the car, bullet holes peppered its doors. Behind the open driver side door, a crouched balding man slowly rose with his .45 revolver aimed at Christian. He eyed Christian for a second, chuckled, and lowered the weapon. "Christian Roberts, I assume. You're just the man I was looking for." He glanced at his bullet-riddled car. "Son, you certainly live dangerously and don't disappoint."

Christian swept the hair from his eyes while gripping the reins on the prancing horse. "Who the hell are you?"

"Charlie Tucker, chief of police in Salmon, Idaho."

* * *

Steve strolled down the dark sidewalk in Arlington, heading home after meeting Christian at a convenience store. The guy was so overly cautious they had driven several blocks into a quiet neighborhood before Christian handed over the RAT. It was now official. Steve had accepted government files stolen from Barbara Davis's computer and was an accomplice in a crime.

He shuffled along and clasped the tiny thumb drive in his pants pocket. If busted with the RAT, his life would be destroyed. He had always been a law-abiding citizen, only committing minor offenses such as smoking a little weed and illegally downloading new movies. His security company was also based on honesty. His clients trusted him to protect their business computers from hackers and viruses. He was now guilty of hacking, theft of government documents, and conspiring with a terrorist that could result in a prison sentence. He thought about Christian, the guy who put him on this path.

Prior to meeting Christian, Steve had questioned the wisdom of seeking him out. After all, he was supposedly Captain Nemo, a deadly terrorist with a deranged agenda. Karen had argued he was a threat only to people obliterating wildlife, and she and Steve needed Christian to prove Felix's murder. The police were no help. Christian's current cause was saving wolves, so the mysterious government file funding a wolf study might interest him. Plus, she possessed the determination of a dozen women, when her mind was set. It turned out Christian did want to meet them, so Steve thought, okay, let's at least check him out.

On their first encounter, Karen pegged Christian as paranoid and arrogant. Initially, Steve was also not impressed. The guy looked like a surfer straight off a beach, with a lanky tan body and tousled sun-bleached hair. His Southern manner and accent were also disarming. He hardly seemed smart or dangerous. It was a ruse. After their meeting, Steve found Christian to be witty, well informed, and ballsy. He was also down to earth with good instincts, and used common sense to make decisions. Steve liked him.

But still, Steve was conflicted about getting involved. He wanted to do right by his friend and expose his killer and was convinced the Floridian would come through. It was a gamble, though. Despite Christian's objection, Steve flirted with going to the police with the evidence that showed the motive for Felix's murder.

He arrived home and stepped into the foyer. Their little poodle greeted him, jumping up and down at his feet. As he petted Coconut, Karen asked from the bedroom staircase, "Did you get it?"

He nodded and removed his jacket. He stepped to the linen closet and rifled through a stack of blankets for the hidden laptop with the fictitious registered name. Karen followed him into the office where he sat down at his desk. He plugged the RAT into the computer and typed in the password. Hundreds of files appeared on the screen. "Wow, this is going to take some digging."

"Are you sending it to him?" The *him* was Christian.

"Not yet. He'd never find what we need. He won't be back in Florida until Monday, so I have the weekend to narrow it down."

Karen stood behind him and watched, but a while later, went back to bed.

Steve kept at his mission until his vision blurred and birds chirped outside with dawn. He unplugged the RAT, stuffed it back into his pocket, and re-hid the laptop. Upstairs he slipped into bed next to Karen, hoping to catch some sleep.

He woke late Saturday and worked on the files for the rest of the day and into the night. Felix's supervisor or someone had deleted the duplicate second file containing the Congressional budget slated for the wolf study. Once he recovered it, he followed the funds to a bank on Mauritius, an island off the African coast. The Cayman Islands and Panama banks were well-known places for money laundering and untraceable accounts to hide wealth, but

Mauritius was growing in popularity. The account holder of the wolf-study funds could not be verified, and the name must have been falsified. The real name would take more time to uncover. He checked out the source of other deposits made into the account. Some money came from different government wildlife studies, and significant amounts were from companies with suspicious names. Further probing revealed they were gun and hunting organizations. At midnight he called it quits, but was closing in on the account holder's bona fide name. Tomorrow he should have it, and Christian would be back in Florida Monday to get his email with the information.

* * *

On Saturday in the Foggy Bottom district in DC. at five in the evening, Tyrone and his three-man cleaning crew drove into the parking garage of the government building. After checking in with the guard and swiping his security pass at the elevator, they and their equipment rode to the top floor to work their way down.

They encountered several government employees toiling through the weekend to meet deadlines. Sitting at their desks, they focused on their computer screens, oblivious to the cleaning crew. Tyrone's men hit each floor, and all seemed normal until they reached the fifth floor.

One man ran the vacuum over the carpet. A second man hit the restroom with a mop, bucket, and cleansers. Darrel, the new kid with dreadlocks, emptied the trash cans and dusted blinds and desks. Tyrone's job was easy, supervising and seeing that the work was done right.

Darrel entered a separate office space, but rushed out shouting, "Mr. Tyrone, Mr. Tyrone, you need to come quick!"

"What is it?" Tyrone asked, hurrying across the room.

Darrel pointed into the office. "There's a woman on the floor in there. I think she's dead."

* * *

On Sunday morning Steve rose with a groan. "Back to the grind," he said to Karen.

Karen looked up from the sheets. "Take a break. You've been working day and night. I'll cook us a nice burrito breakfast, and then we'll take Coconut to the park."

"A walk and fresh air might clear my head, and I do have until Monday to get it done." He showered and dressed while in the kitchen Karen fixed burritos stuffed with scrambled eggs, sausage, peppers, and onions, topped with salsa. The breakfast had become their favorite after living in Mexico for a few years.

Steve walked downstairs with his mouth watering from the aromas. He stepped outside to fetch the Sunday paper off the lawn. The overcast sky and the bitter windy weather made him shiver. The neighborhood of small, well-groomed houses seemed deserted. No cars moved or people strolled on that freezing morning. He hustled back inside with a brr. "Karen, it's really cold out there," he said and walked into the kitchen. "We'll be the only ones crazy enough to walk a dog. The neighbors have the good sense to stay in bed." He placed the newspaper on the counter and sat down on a stool as Karen placed his breakfast before him.

"Coconut could pee in the backyard, but I need the exercise." She joined him at the counter with her plate. "You don't have to go with me if you don't want to."

"No, I'll go," he said and opened the paper to the local section.

"I don't know why you're still reading the paper, when all that information is available on the Internet. Plus some tree died for that paper."

"Spare me. I look at computers screens constantly. I like holding a newspaper."

"Whatever," she said and turned on her iPad to check her emails and Facebook page.

Steve read through the police briefs, but after two few bites of food, he dropped his fork. It clattered on the plate. "Holy shit," he said, staring at a short article.

"What's the matter?"

"Barbara Davis. Isn't that Felix's supervisor?"

"What about her?"

"A cleaning crew discovered her body last night in her office. She was strangled and possibly raped. The time of death was between two and four am. It says she was a supervisor and worked for the secretary of state." He looked at Karen, shocked. "That's her, right?"

Karen grabbed the paper and quickly skimmed the article. She looked up at him and shook her head. "No, Steve. I know what you're thinking. He wouldn't do that."

"How do you know?" He pushed his plate aside and stood. "You met Christian once, one damn time. The time of death puts him with her when he downloaded the files off her computer." He paced in front of the counter. "Christ, I've been worried about being charged with hacking and receiving stolen government documents. Now I could be arrested as an accomplice to murder."

Karen stared dismally at her food. "I don't believe he did it. The way he talked about his wife, he's not the type to hurt a woman."

"Female intuition doesn't hold up to hard facts. You know I asked him how he got to her computer. The smug son of a bitch said he had a few things going for him. I didn't realize those things involved killing a woman. We need to call the police right now. If we give them the RAT, tell them everything we know, we might get off the hook, with our testimony and the help of a good lawyer."

"You're jumping to conclusions. You're not even giving him a chance to explain."

"Asking him to explain suggests we think he did it. If he gets that idea in his crazy head, we might be his next victims. And we wouldn't be the first. I read he was arrested for terrorism, but the case never went to trial because the star witness disappeared. Karen, we're playing with fire."

"I thought you liked him."

"I like him when he's on my side, but I sure don't want him for an enemy."

"So you call the police, and everything is blown. We never find out who holds the account and murdered Felix. Give it a few days, and we'll call him when he's back in Florida, a long ways from us. We'll feel him out and then decide what to do. Someone else could've murdered her."

"That's pretty damn slim."

"I'm telling you. I don't think he did it. Please, Steve, let's just wait."

He held his forehead and breathed deeply. "All right, I'll call tomorrow night and tell him we learned about the woman's murder. See what he says. But I swear to God, if he gets incensed or I get a strange vibe, my next call is to the cops."

"Fair enough," she said and glanced at her breakfast. "I've lost my appetite. I'm going up to get dressed and take Coconut to the park."

Shortly afterwards Karen came downstairs and ruffled the dog's topknot. "Coconut, you want to go for a walk?" The poodle happily barked and wagged her tail before racing to the front door where her leash was hanging. Karen clipped on the leash and turned to Steve. "You'll see I'm right about Christian."

"Yeah, yeah," he grumbled.

They walked outside and turned toward the park, only two blocks away.

"Wow, it is cold. I think I'll jog." She and Coconut sprinted ahead.

Steve followed at a brisk walk, but Karen was soon two houses in front of him. He stared down at the sidewalk cracks as he passed the houses and parked cars lining the street. His mind was not on his surroundings, but on the decision not to notify the police right away.

He was upset with Karen for talking him into it and upset with himself for caving in. No doubt Christian had killed the woman. What were the chances of him and some other murderer being at the same place at the same time? When he and Karen reached the park, they'd have a serious talk and reassess the situation and their choices.

Behind him, a block away, he heard a car engine start. He didn't give it a second thought. It was probably a devoted churchgoer braving the bitter weather. Tires squealed on the asphalt so he looked over his shoulder and saw a window-tinted white van barreling in his direction. He fumed at the idiot for going this fast in a neighborhood. His anger turned to fright when the van veered into a driveway and drove down the sidewalk, racing toward him. He leaped behind a large tree a moment before the van blew past, missing him by only a few feet. He saw his wife and the dog up ahead. They were stepping off the curb to cross the street. He screamed, "Karen, watch out!"

CHAPTER THIRTEEN

Charlie Tucker stood by his rental car. The headlights lit up the horse and its bareback rider. Helen, his secretary, had said Roberts resembled some actor, and indeed, Charlie felt like he was in a movie. First there was a hairy shootout with thugs, and now this bare-chested, bare-footed loony charged up on a fiery red stallion.

"What are you doing here, Chief?" Roberts asked as the horse snorted and tossed its mane.

"Apparently saving your life."

The horse reared, and Roberts reined him down. "You're a little late. Already had some help, but appreciate your running those pricks off." He slid off the horse and patted its neck.

"Who were they?" Charlie asked, trying to collect his wits and gain calm. The adrenaline from the gunfight left him shaken and wobbly.

"No idea. I've pissed off more than a few people." Roberts smiled when Charlie's trembling hand holstered his weapon. "Sit down and take a break, Chief. I'll be back in a bit." Holding the bridle, he started to lead the horse toward the back of the property.

"Where are you going?"

"To put my horse up," he said with a backward glance. "We'll talk when I'm done."

"Don't you think you should first call the police?"

"Why? You're a cop, aren't you?" Roberts and the horse soon disappeared into the dark. A cool breeze blew across the pasture, and Charlie compared the Florida winter to an Idaho summer.

He leaned against the white rental car, still traumatized from his brush with death, but Roberts had seemed unfazed, as if assassins regularly showed up to kill him. Given his terrorist occupation, maybe it was the norm.

He looked up at the stars and muttered, "This was a wasted trip." He had come to Florida to scare a confession out of Roberts for bombing the Salmon restaurant. It wasn't going to happen. Agent Wheeler had warned him that Roberts was as cool as a cucumber, never rattled under pressure. Charlie was learning firsthand that intimidation from a small town police chief was a joke. Perhaps incensing him might work.

Forty-five minutes later, Roberts strolled toward Charlie and the house. "C'mon in, Chief," he said, opening the door. When the inside lights came on, he cursed, "Sons of bitches."

Charlie kicked aside the broken dishes and stepped inside. "They sure made a mess," he said, staring at the overturned furniture and the floors littered with papers, glass, and kitchen items.

Roberts gave him an incredulous look. "Ya think?" He up-righted the kitchen chairs and placed them around the small table. "I need a drink. Care for one?" He retrieved a Bacardi rum bottle and a can of Coke from a cabinet.

"I could use something to steady my nerves, but you seem to take this whole affair in stride."

Roberts chuckled as he fixed the cocktails. "Hey, I was freaking, especially when one of those boys got the drop on me. Luckily my gator grabbed him so I could get away." He handed Charlie his glass. "Have a seat."

"Really, you have an alligator?"

"Everyone here has a gator," Roberts said, joining Charlie at the table.

"What happened to the guy?"

"Hell if I know. I wasn't about to hang around and find out. He could be floating in the lake outback, but more likely he was let go. Gators rarely prey on humans."

"Suppose those men come back?"

"Doubt it. They've lost the element of surprise. They might try and take me out again, but it won't be here.'

"I really think we should call the police."

Robert sipped his drink and leaned back in the chair, his cold blue eyes staring into Charlie's. "Can you identify them, Chief? Get their plate number?"

"Well, no, I was too busy ducking, but you should file a police report."

"No thanks. The cops would rather jail me than arrest those assholes. That brings me to you. What did you hope to gain by coming to my home?"

Charlie took a gulp of his drink and breathed deeply. "I hoped you'd confess to destroying the restaurant in my town."

Roberts smiled. "You made a long trip for nothing."

"At least I'm talking to you. That's more than the rest of law enforcement has done about this Nemo bombing."

"But I'm not Nemo. Besides, I've already spoken to Agent Wheeler and given him my whereabouts when it happened. We're meeting next week for an official statement."

"Meeting on your boat," Charlie said. "You two seem pretty tight, and he obviously doesn't want to apprehend you. That has me wondering if you're paying him off or have something on him."

Roberts flung the blond locks from his eyes, revealing a hard stare, and crossed his arms, telltale signs he was irritated. "Chief Tucker, no amount of money can buy Dave, and he'd expose a blackmail scam in a heartbeat. He's a smart, honest lawman. We fall on opposite sides of the fence, but we have mutual respect for each other. But if he had the goods, he'd arrest me. Dave isn't corrupted, so you need to stop wondering and get off the witch hunt."

Charlie massaged his chin, studying Roberts. He came off with an air of arrogance, like dirt couldn't stick to him, but his edgy tone was a hint of his smoldering temper. Charlie decided to push it. "Your praise of Wheeler only arouses my suspicions. Something happened to create this friendship between you two, and respect has nothing to do with it."

Roberts's eyes narrowed and he sucked in an aggravated breath. "I'm wasting my time on you," he said. Swallowing the last of his drink, he rose from the table. "Sorry about your restaurant, but I had nothing to do with it. However, I will pay for your damaged rental car. Just send me the bill. Least I can do for helping me out here." He opened the kitchen door. "Other than that, our little talk is over. You need to go, Chief."

* * *

Christian stood in the doorway and watched the taillights from the compact car slowly disappear on the empty country road. Chief Tucker might be a small-time cop, but he had powerful connections. With Tucker's influence, the FBI had promoted and reassigned Dave. He was now Special Agent Wheeler in charge of the Captain Nemo case. *No ignoring this ol' boy.*

He closed the door and his mind to Chief Tucker, and turned his attention to the earlier brush with the bad guys. "Fucking Chinese assholes," he mumbled. They had hired locals six months earlier to kill him. With tonight's second attempt, they apparently hadn't given up. He retrieved a large flashlight and walked to the lake, worried about Al. Had the gator been shot when biting the man? There was also the other concern. He might have to depose of a corpse. Al had never been a threat, at least until now, but feeding the gator had given him the courage to the attack the stranger, and that had saved Christian's life.

He shined the light across the small lake and called, "Al, come here." The flashlight lit up a pair of white eyes that moved across the surface toward Christian. Al knew his name and came when called. "You okay, buddy? Come here. Get up on the bank so I get a look at you." Al climbed out of the water and lowered his head. Christian used the flashlight to inspect him for bullet wounds. "You look all right. Now what did ya do with that guy?" Scanning the lake for a body or clothing, he smiled. "Guess he wasn't to your liking."

He strolled back to the house, relieved he wouldn't have to dig a grave. As he straightened the furniture and cleaned up the mess, he noticed that his regular computer and answering machine were not on the desk. The cleaning mode ended, and he searched the house for other missing items. In the bedroom, his wallet with cash was still on a dresser, but his cell phone was gone. He raced into the spare bedroom and moved the trunk that hid his stash of disposable phones and fake IDs. Comforted that nothing else had been taken, he sat down on the bed to reconsider the assassins and their motives.

The Chinese wanted revenge and his death. If theft was also their motive, why leave a wallet full of cash? The intruders were interested in his business. The computer, phone, and answering machine would reveal his contacts and what he had learned. He thought about the dead analyst in DC. who was murdered for the information on his computer. He reconsidered the man who accosted him in the backyard. Why didn't he just shoot Christian? Instead the man attempted to cuff him. Maybe the men planned to stage his death like the analyst's. An overdose, accident, or suicide would prevent a drawn-out murder investigation.

His thoughts jumped to Steve and Karen, also potential targets. He snatched up a phone and called the number of their burner phone. No answer. Rushing to his bedroom, he removed a slip of paper from his wallet that contained their regular cell and home numbers. The hectic calls only yielded voice mail. He looked at his watch. Four in the morning. "They gotta be home."

His thoughts turned to Trish. She had met Karen to discuss the mysterious government file, but never ran a story on it. She also put him in touch with the Arlington couple. Beyond that, she knew nothing about their cloak-and-dagger activity in DC. Still, he worried. Had her small involvement placed her in danger?

He made a second drink and then called her.

Three rings, and finally a soft groggy voice answered. "Hello?"

"It's Christian."

"I didn't recognize this number."

"It's temporary. Lost my cell. Sorry it's so late, but you were on my mind, and I wanted to check on you."

"I'm glad you phoned. After you left I was afraid I'd pressured you into a commitment you didn't want. When I didn't hear from you, I thought I'd scared you off and it was over."

"Honestly, Trish, I don't know what I want right now. Let's play this out and see how we end up. I nearly called you the other day. My stallion had to be put down, and I was pretty bummed."

"Oh, Christian, I'm so sorry. Are you okay?"

"I'm good. Nothing else new going on. Listen, I just wanted to hear your voice. Go back to sleep. We'll talk later."

He hung up less anxious, but pondered whether he should have asked if she could check on Steve and Karen. Probably better if she wasn't further involved, especially since her phone might be tapped.

Too restless for sleep, he reclined on the couch and waited for dawn. A few hours later he was in the barn, loading buckets of grain into the golf cart to feed the horses. After rushing through the farm chores, he jumped into his car and headed for Longboat Key. His sloop was moored off of Vince's house and it held his anonymous laptop that might have an email from Steve. On the hour drive, he tried to reach the couple again. With no response, he worriedly pushed the Porsche's speed gauge to a hundred on Fruitville Road, the long stretch into Sarasota. In town the car whipped through the congested tourist traffic that worsened on the roads and bridges to the keys.

He finally reached Vince's place, and after parking in the three-car garage, he ran to the backyard and down the dock to his dinghy. As he rowed rapidly to his sloop anchored offshore, panic grew in his gut. To cover up the file of misappropriated funds, the killers who came after him last night, the ones who murdered the analyst, would logically eliminate Karen and Steve too. He hopped aboard the sailboat and hurried to the forward berth for his hidden laptop.

In the galley booth, he powered up the computer. Nothing, no email from Steve about the information contained in the RAT. Even if Steve was still researching or had failed, he would've contacted Christian. Something was terribly wrong. More disheartening, there was no explanation of their whereabouts. Were Steve and Karen still alive?

He swept back his hair and stared upward, tormented with unanswered questions. He closed his eyes and recalled Sal's warning, "Never fuck with the government."

* * *

Outside the Tampa hospital, Vern stood on the dark sidewalk under a cluster of swaying palm trees and pressed the phone against his ear and white hair. "Sorry, sir, for the late call," he said, "but we've had a string of bad luck in Florida. The mark got away and is still a problem."

"He's one guy. How'd he manage to outmaneuver you and your men?"

"He had help. The mission was obstructed by animal problems. First, some noisy birds blew our cover and woke him. Then an alligator attacked one of my men when he held the mark at gunpoint. The distraction allowed him to escape on a horse."

"Alligators, birds, horses, what is he, Crocodile Dundee?"

"No, but he is Captain Nemo, a successful terrorist who knows how to get out of tight situations, and he lives with animals. I just wasn't expecting those creatures to help him."

"So, what now?"

"Currently I'm outside aTampa hospital, waiting for the results on my injured man. His ankle is broken and the laceration required stitches, but the concern is the reptile bite. Apparently, an alligator's mouth is full of deadly bacteria that require strong antibiotics, even a hospital stay. I should be back in DC. tomorrow, and I'll start work on another plan to get this Nemo character."

"Did you at least get the files?"

"We ransacked the house looking for anything related to the files and confiscated his laptop, cell phone, and answering machine. I've already checked his cell. It showed no contact with Arlington. Several calls were made to and from *The Washington Post* reporter, but that was expected. He's had an on-and-off relationship with her and stayed last weekend in her apartment. Once I'm back, I'll give the computer to my expert, and he'll check it for the files."

"Is there any more news on the couple in Arlington?"

"No sir," said Vern. "The woman's condition is critical, so she might not survive. The police are calling it an accidental hit-and-run, and no mention of a vehicular homicide attempt. The husband is still at the hospital, so it's hard to get at him. When he returns home, we'll take care of him."

"Vern, I'm a little disappointed. I'm not surprised the terrorist was a problem, but this couple, a computer geek and real estate agent…they should be history."

"Sir, I agree, but enacting an accident is tricky and doesn't always produce the desired results. A hit-and-run can leave injuries instead of corpses. And in Florida, we planned to hang Roberts. No one would question his suicide, because he'd got PTSD and sees a physiatrist. Believe me, sir, they'd all be dead now if I could shoot them, but that opens the door to a homicide investigation, with the authorities digging into their affairs. We'd like to avoid that."

"I only know they've avoided you and are still around to cause me grief. Handle it, Vern."

* * *

Detective Tom Graham sat at his desk in the DC. precinct and stared at the photo of the murdered woman lying on her office floor. Her white blouse was partially unbuttoned, revealing the dark red throttle marks on her neck, and her face displayed terror during her last moments. Tom's partner strolled in. "How was the vacation, Jordon?"

Jordan dropped into the chair at the neighboring desk. "Lousy. Long, hot lines with screaming kids, sore feet from walking miles, and I spent a fortune. No more Disney. Next year it's a quiet hotel and sitting by a pool with a cooler of beer."

"I'm sure your family had a good time."

"They'd better have. So what did I miss?"

Tom handed him the case photo and said, "Barbara Davis, a thirty-seven-year-old divorcee and a State Department supervisor. She was strangled in her office between two and four Saturday morning in the Foggy Bottom District. A cleaning crew found the body. Do you recognize her?"

Jordon studied the photo. "Should I?"

"We interviewed her about a month ago. One of her analysts overdosed, and we did a follow-up. When I entered the crime scene, I realized I'd been in her office before."

"Where are you now?"

"I already have a suspect. The surveillance photos off the street cameras show Davis leaving the building after work with a tall blond man." He handed the eight-by-ten pictures to Jordon. "The next photo was taken at midnight when they came back and entered the building. The last pic is candy. The blond comes out alone at two am, time of the murder, gets in his car, and drives off."

"Nice ride," said Jordan.

It's a Porsche Boxster S, the latest model. Trouble is the picture of the car's back bumper was taken at night, and the tag light was out or had been removed. I couldn't make out the plate numbers and state."

"That's suspicious."

"I thought so too. I just got the autopsy report back. She was intoxicated, way over the limit, and had sex before she died. There was live sperm in her that helps narrow down the time of death."

Jordon grinned. "That means we got his DNA."

"Yeah, forensics also pulled a blond hair off the couch. The vic had slight vaginal bruising from rough sex, but the coroner doesn't think it was rape."

Jordan massaged his chin and gazed at the suspect's photo. "It wasn't rape. Look at this boy. He doesn't need to rape or get women drunk to score. My guess, they had one too many and were having kinky sex. He choked her to climax and went too far. Manslaughter."

"Or she pissed him off. Then we're looking at second-degree murder."

"Any luck with prints?"

"Nothing matching any felons, but witnesses might help," said Tom. "I've already talked to the security guards in the building. They never saw the woman or guy and said he must've come and gone in the parking garage elevator. A guard checked the in-house cameras, but funny thing, the tape for that night was blank. Guard claimed probably a technical screw up. No one had access to the monitoring room to erase it."

"It doesn't sound like you need the footage." Jordon said. "There's already enough evidence for an arrest."

"Yeah, but first, we need to learn who he is, and a DNA test can take too long. He also might not be in the system yet." Tom rose, grabbed his suit jacket off the back of the chair, and slipped it on. "The woman's co-workers might know him and a possible motive. They were gone on the weekend, so I'm heading over now to question them." He picked out the clearest photo of the suspect.

Jordon stood. "Let's do it."

Tom and Jordan arrived at the government building, and after checking in at the desk, they rode the elevator to the fifth floor. Tom stepped into the bustling room of employees seated at their desks or milling around. The setting was different from the weekend when the guards, cleaning crew, and police spoke quietly around a corpse.

Jordon took charge and brought the room to silence. "Excuse me," he shouted with his booming voice. "I'm Detective O'Conner, and this is Detective Graham. We're investigating Ms. Davis's murder and need your cooperation. If any of you saw her Friday after work, we'd like to speak to you."

A slight woman stepped to them. "My name is Claudine Fisher, and I saw Barbara after work. She came into Tonic, a lounge a few blocks from here."

"Was she alone?" asked Tom.

"Oh, no, she was with a young man."

"Can you describe him?"

"He was tall, possibly six-three, had longish blond hair, and was very attractive. Barbara was beaming, paraded him around like a trophy. He was far too young for her, maybe in his mid-or-late twenties. It's sometimes hard to judge a man's age. Some like Brad Pitt keep their boyish looks into their forties."

"Have you ever seen him with her before?" Jordan asked.

"Never," she said with a grin. "And he was unforgettable."

Tom showed a photo to Claudine. "Is this the guy?"

"That's him." Her grin faded, and she looked up uneasily. "Do you think he might've killed Miss Davis?"

"It's too early in the investigation to make that call," said Tom. "We're trying to track Miss Davis's movement and who came in contact with her. So they walked into the bar together and then what?"

"The bottom floor was crowded, so they went upstairs. Tonic has second and third floor bars. I left an hour later and didn't see them again."

"Thank, Ms. Fisher." Jordon gave her his card and said she might also be called in to identify him in a line up.

They drove to Tonic and asked around about the bartenders who worked the upstairs on Friday night. Luckily the third-floor bartender was on duty. They walked upstairs and took up stools at his bar. Tom flashed his badge. "We investigating the Barbara Davis murder and was wondering if you waited on her Friday night."

The bartender, a good-looking guy in his mid-thirties, nodded. "I saw Barbara Friday. I heard she was killed. Damn shame. She was a nice lady and generous tipper. I'll miss her."

"Did you notice if she was with anyone?"

The bartender smiled. "Detective, everyone noticed. She strolled in with a stunning creature from the South. He was something."

"Did they seem to be getting along?" asked Jordon.

"I'd say so. He hung on her every word, and she loved it. They drank mescal and had a great time. That's the sad part. Barbara always drank alone, and I felt sorry for her. Friday was the first time I ever heard her laugh." He pointed to a table near the fireplace. "They sat over there and left around midnight."

"You said he was from the South." Tom said. "How did you know?"

"His accent and he had a great tan," said the bartender. "Barbara confirmed it, said he was from Florida."

Tom produced the photo. "Is this him?"

"That's the man." The bartender breathed a sigh when gazing at the picture. "Too bad he was straight."

"Thanks; we'll be in touch."

The bartender stepped away to serve another customer.

Tom turned to Jordon. "A Floridian with a brand-new black Porsche: that helps narrow it down. We might not need the DNA test to make an arrest."

"Let me see that photo again." Jordon studied the picture of the man and Davis on the street. "I don't remember her, but him…." He tapped the photo. "He looks familiar. I've seen his face before. It'll come to me."

CHAPTER FOURTEEN

At the Arlington, Virginia hospital, Steve sat at his wife's bedside in the Intensive Care ward and held her limp hand. After four days, he had grown accustomed to the hum, beep, and blinking lights of the surrounding machines that monitored her condition. Karen had a pneumothorax from her fractured ribs and was recovering from surgery on her ruptured spleen. The doctors had intubated her and induced a chemical coma. Now Wednesday, she was finally stable.

Every time he closed his eyes, he relived the accident; him screaming before the van struck Karen and threw her ten feet into a yard and then crushed their little poodle. What followed were flashes out of a nightmare. He vaguely remembered holding her bloody body and telling her to hang on as a man, presumably the house owner, stood behind him and called 911. He remembered shaking and stuttering when the paramedics pushed him aside to work on her, and when his next-door neighbor gripped his shoulder and said he'd take care of the dog. The ambulance ride, the blaring siren, and the rush into the ER were hazy.

He looked up at his mother-in-law who had flown in two days earlier. "She'll be okay," he said, uncertain if he was reassuring her or himself.

"Karen is the strongest person I know," she said. "If anyone can pull through, she will. Steve, you look exhausted. Why don't you go home, clean up, and get some rest? I'll call if anything changes....I mean when."

He rubbed the bristles on his jaw. "I could use a shower and shave and change of clothes, but mainly I'd like to go home and get my cell phone. My employees know what happened, but they can't reach me." He bent over, kissed Karen's forehead, and rose. "Okay, but I'll be back in a few hours." He hugged Karen's mother and walked out.

At the nurse's station, he called for a taxi and stepped outside. A half hour later he was home. On the front door was a note from the neighbor that said, "I buried Coconut in the backyard under the Japanese maple. I hope that was okay. We're praying for you and Karen." He stuffed the paper in his pocket and unlocked the door.

Once inside, he was struck by the stillness. No yap from the dog while she bounced up and down at his feet, and no voice greeting him. Time had stopped. The Sunday paper still lay open on the counter, and the breakfast dishes were stacked in the sink. He walked outside and trudged across the backyard to a barren little tree and slight mound of fresh dirt.

Since Sunday he had suppressed his tears, but standing over the dog's grave with its little white cross, he broke down. He fell on his knees in the moist grass and openly wept for his girls, Karen and Coconut.

After a while, he collected himself and returned to the house. He methodically washed the dishes, took out the garbage, and went upstairs. After he cleaned up and dressed, he packed Karen's makeup, toothbrush, deodorant, and her robe in a travel bag. She'd want them when she felt better, he thought. He skipped the nap and went downstairs to his office and played the messages on the answering machine. Most were from friends and relatives who learned of the accident and offered their sympathy and help. A few calls were from a number with no caller ID and message. "Christian," Steve grumbled, recognizing the Florida area code. He found more of the same calls on his cell phone that was plugged into a kitchen outlet.

Screw him, Steve thought. *I'm not calling the jerk back.* He snatched up his car keys and Karen's bag, locked the house, and climbed into the Prius for the trip to the hospital. He fastened his seatbelt and pressed the starter button, but the car made a clicking sound and wouldn't turn over. His cell phone chimed, and he saw the same anonymous number on the call ID. "Christ," he snarled and took the call. "What do you want, Christian?"

"I've been calling you. Where are you?"

"I'm sitting in my car, trying to get the damn thing started so I can get to the hospital and see my wife. I don't have time for your shit. As far as I'm concerned, we're done. I don't know you, never met you."

"What happened to Karen?"

"A van jumped the curb and hit her while we were walking to the park Sunday. It nearly got me."

"Steve, I'm so sorry. How is she?"

"Still in critical condition, but the doctors say the outlook is good."

"Do you know who did it?"

"Kids, according to the police," said Steve. "The van was reported stolen, and someone saw them joyriding in our neighborhood, driving through the lawns."

"But they haven't caught those kids yet, have they? I also doubt the caller who reported them left his name."

"I don't know who called it in, and as of this morning, the police haven't caught the kids, but they assure me they will."

"They won't, because the kids don't exist. This wasn't an accident. That van was meant to kill you and Karen."

"How do you know, unless you're behind it? Good chance you arranged the hit-and-run to shut us up because we know you murdered her."

"Murder, what murder?"

"I guess it's hard for you to remember all your victims. I'm talking about Barbara Davis, Felix's boss. You strangled her to gain access to her computer."

"Shit, I didn't even know she was dead. When did that happen?"

"Around two in the morning Saturday, in her office," said Steve. "You were there, same time and place, when you used the RAT and downloaded the files. We met right after, at three-thirty, remember? Heck, I could be charged as your accomplice. I should've never gotten involved with you."

"Steve, I didn't kill her. We got drunk at some bar, went back to her office and screwed around. After she passed out on a couch, I took the files. I swear. When I left, she was alive."

"Tell that crap to the police. Maybe they'll buy it."

"Don't get a fucking attitude with me," Christian growled. "I'm the last person you wanna piss off."

Hearing the outrage in Christian's voice, Steve backed off. The guy was over a thousand miles away, but the terrorist could still intimidate. Not wise to irritate him. "Okay, okay, you didn't kill her. I believe you, Christian."

"Never lie to a liar, Steve. We know bullshit. I realize it looks bad, especially with my reputation and all, but I can prove I'm innocent."

"I'm listening."

"Did you recover the files and learn who took the money?"

"I got most of the data. The file had been deleted, but I was able to retrieve it. The funds were transferred to a bank off the coast of Africa, but the account holder's name proved to be anonymous. A little more digging and I'd have it, but at this point, what does it matter?"

"It matters because the guilty party who stole the funds also killed your analyst friend and now Barbara and also targeted you and Karen."

"How can you be so sure?"

"Do you have the laptop?"

Steve tapped his fingers on the steering wheel. Christian might be telling the truth. "It's hidden inside. Hold on. I'll get it." He climbed out of the car and returned to the house. He set the phone down, dug through the blankets in the linen closet, and pulled out the laptop and the throw-away phone. "It and the burner phone are right where I left them."

"But are the files still on the computer?"

"I'm sure they are. Nothing's been disturbed in the house."

"Check the files, Steve."

He huffed with annoyance. "Give me a darn minute to bring them up." He set the laptop on the kitchen counter, turned it on, and searched for the files. He caught his breath and anxiously looked around while he fumbled for his cell phone. "They're gone, Christian!" he voiced. "The whole computer has been wiped clean."

"So we're screwed. We'll never find out who's behind the killings."

"Probably not," Steve said. "Wait a minute. The RAT! I forgot to take it out of my pants pocket. It should be in the hamper." He raced upstairs with his cell phone and pulled the tiny thumb drive from the dirty clothes. "I got it."

"That's good."

"Yeah, Karen always bitches at me for not emptying my pockets when she does laundry. Thank God for bad habits. Christian, how did you know all this?"

"Because the same assholes that came after you came for me Tuesday night," Christian said. "I got away, but they stole my laptop. That's when I put it together. Those suckers are knocking off anyone who knows anything about the stolen funds in those files."

"Karen. I have to get to the hospital and protect her," Steve said and scrambled down the stairs.

"Hold up. You said your car wouldn't start. Is that normal?"

Steve stopped at the front door. "No, it usually fires right up."

"Someone might've messed with the electrical and rigged an explosive. Don't use your car."

"Are you certain?"

"No, but if I wanted you dead, that would be my next move."

Guess it takes a killer to know one. "All right, I'll call for a ride." He stepped to the front door and stared out. "Christian, I know you don't want to involve the police, but maybe it's time I called them."

"And what are you going to say? You have no solid proof, can't even point a finger and give them a name. The cops listed your friend's death as suicide and think the attempt on you and Karen was an accidental hit-and-run. Try explaining that you hacked into government files, and you'll be charged. Also the guy we're after is obviously high-up in government, and whoever you talk to might be on his payroll. Don't count on the cops."

"So what am I supposed to do?"

"Go back to Karen, but pick up a new disposable phone and text me its number. The other one is probably compromised. Y'all should be safe at the hospital, but don't go outside or any place alone. I'll send some guys there tomorrow. They'll act as bodyguards. You gotta trust me now."

"Who are the guys?"

"They'll be Italian. And Steve, take the laptop and work on the files. Without a name, I'm swinging at shadows."

* * *

"Son of a bitch," Christian cursed after ending his call with Steve. Two women, one murdered, one maimed because of his dabbling into the government files to help wolves. On the open deck of his sloop, he slowly sat down in the cockpit and held his head.

Poor Barb, he thought. She was insecure and desperate for a man but chose the wrong one. He had used her and tossed her away. He felt even worse about Karen, more his type. She was confident, with plenty of attitude. She'd known the risk going in, but placed her faith in Christian, and he'd failed her.

He covered his mouth and felt the sickly pangs of guilt, a far too familiar sensation. His wife had died because of his stupid determination and actions. Now he had the blood of two more women on his hands. He closed his eyes and lifted his face to the noon sun. *Don't go there, damn it. Don't get bogged down,* he told himself. *Shit happens, so get your fucking act together and put the blame where it belongs. You didn't hurt Karen or kill Barbara. I got too much to do and need to put this out of my mind.*

His thoughts shifted to all his screwups with Barbara. The bar crowd had seen them drinking together, and the street cameras had them entering the building and him leaving alone, not to mention the additional surveillance inside. Even more damning, he slept with her and left his DNA. At the time he wasn't worried. Seducing a woman wasn't a crime, and Steve had assured him that the RAT was untraceable. No one would know that Christian downloaded the files. Considering it all now, though, he didn't even have a decent alibi when Barbara was strangled. He was alone in his car and met Steve and then Trish afterwards.

Christian also realized his picture had been plastered in the media as the man suspected of being Captain Nemo, and he hadn't bothered with a disguise. Someone was likely to recognize him. Even if he got lucky and no one IDed him, his DNA would seal his fate. The cops were putting their case together, using forensics. He figured he had a couple of weeks, at best a few months, before the law learned who he was and came after him. His many mistakes had his head spinning, and he saw no way out. He started out to save wolves, but he'd soon be hunted and doomed like them.

He breathed deeply and savored the sea aromas while really appreciating the open blue sky and green bay waters, like seeing it for the last time. *No sense fretting,* he thought. He'd chosen his existence, dangling on the edge, and knew his days were numbered. With his cell phone, he called Sal. "Hey, it's me. I need to hire a couple of your boys for a job in DC."

"When do you want them?" asked Sal.

"Four days ago." He sighed. "But tomorrow is good. I'm on my boat off Vince's. I'll meet you at the pool."

"Okay, I'll make some calls. Kid, you sound a bit down."

"Sal, if you only knew," Christian said. "See you in a bit."

He hung up and stepped below into the cabin to change clothes. Up north people bundled up to combat the cold, but the Florida weather was a mild seventy-five degrees. He stripped out of his jeans and shirt and put on cutoffs and a flimsy T-shirt before rowing the dinghy to Vince's stately house.

Sal lived in a condo a few miles up the road, and he already sat on a stool at the pool bar when Christian tied up at the dock and walked into the backyard. "All that dough and you still dress like surfer trash," Sal said.

"You're sounding like my mother." Christian tossed the house keys to Sal. "Fix yourself a drink. I need a minute to cool off."

"By the way, I spoke to your boyfriend," Sal said, rising. "Friday night works for him. He'll meet you at the Ritz at ten o'clock. Give him his fifty grand and get that dick off your ass."

"Yeah, and you're not figuratively speaking," Christian said, removing his T-shirt.

Sal laughed. "Ain't that the truth. He'd love to get a hold of your ass."

Christian shuddered with the thought and dove into the pool. He swam several laps while Sal was inside.

Sal returned to the pool cabana with two cocktails. "Rum and Coke, right?" he said and set Christian's drink on the bar. "I got the feeling you needed one."

"Probably more than one." Christian climbed out of the pool, shook water droplets from his hair, and stepped to the bar. He normally sipped a cocktail, but inhaled half of the drink in one gulp.

Sal must have noticed. "Wow, you really are in trouble. All right, what have you done, and what can I do, besides loaning out my two guys?"

Christian grinned at the big man, appreciating the gesture. He had believed when Vince died, he'd lost his one true friend, a father figure who was always there for him, but here was Sal, the replacement, the new confidant, ready and willing to help him. "You remind me of the guy who used to live here."

"I miss Vince, too." He eyeballed Christian. "So let's hear it. What's up?"

Christian told him about his hookup with Karen and Steve and learning about the fishy government file. He then talked about his theft of the files and the attempt on his life at the farm. Several drinks later, he wrapped up with the news he'd heard that day. Steve and his wife had also been targeted and Barbara's murder. "Normally I'm damn careful, but how could I know that someone would come in and kill her right after I left?"

"You are fucked." Sal pulled out a cigar from his shirt pocket and lit it. "All right, first things first, concerning your couple. Frankie and a guy named Mitch are booked on an evening flight from Kennedy to Reagan."

"I remember Frankie," Christian said. He was a huge guy, bigger than Sal, and he worked down here for Vince. When Vince died, Frankie moved back to his home in New York.

"Frankie tends to be unforgettable. Anyway, when the guys set down in Washington, they'll call ya for the low down on this couple."

"Thanks, Sal."

"Now about those pricks who tried to off you at your farm. They can be handled, but that chick's murder, that's a toughie. I heard DC. has ten thousand street cameras, so besides your DNA and the witnesses, they got your picture, coming and going."

"I know. I know. I'm screwed."

Sal took a puff on the cigar and released the smoke with a weighty sigh. "Kid, I don't see a fix, short of nuking the fucking capital to get rid of the witnesses and evidence. Seriously, though, my advice is to run, take off before you're arrested. Don't fool with lawyers or trying to manipulate your way out of this mess. Forget the animal causes, kiss your folks goodbye, and dig out the fake passport. You got the smarts and means to disappear. Find a little out-of-the-way place and settle down with a hot babe who will fuck your brains out. It's either that or prison."

Christian swirled the ice in his glass. "Sal, I killed a lot of people, but I'll probably go down for a murder I didn't commit. Guess that's ironic justice."

* * *

Agent Wheeler sat at his desk with his index finger pressed against his temple as he read the handwriting expert's report; nothing surprising or useful. Last year's Nemo threats concerning sharks that were scrawled on boat hulls or on postcards, were identical to the new ones about wolves. Two warnings had been spray painted on outside walls in Salmon, Idaho, and the last one, a postcard, was sent to the reporter at *The Washington Post*. Each message coincided with a terrorist attack. The report stated that the same person wrote all the samples. Unfortunately, Christian was wise enough to use block letters and disguise his writing. The evidence was worthless in court.

The clerk staffing the front desk approached. "Agent Wheeler, I received a message for you," he said, and handed him a folded slip. "I'm sorry, but the caller wouldn't leave his name."

The note said, "Sailing, twelve noon Saturday at Marina Jack's in Sarasota." Wheeler looked up at the clerk. "It's all right. I know who sent it."

After the clerk left, Wheeler grinned. The meeting with Christian was FBI business, getting the guy's official statement and whereabouts for when the restaurant and three helicopters were destroyed in Idaho. Wheeler, however, considered the get-together a mini vacation. He'd been on Christian's sailboat but only when it was docked, once in the Bahamas when he investigated the murder of Christian's wife, and again at a Key West marina with a search warrant after Christian was arrested and shipped to New York. The sloop was luxurious and had the capability to circle the globe. This weekend he'd be enjoying a leisurely cruise instead of searching for evidence.

He also looked forward to seeing Christian, although he wondered which Christian would show up. The young man was complex, with multiple personalities. Sometimes he was the raggedy sailor with an in-your-face attitude that would make a nun curse. After the first interrogation, Wheeler wanted to pop the smartass. He'd also seen the quiet, moody Christian, quick to anger, with signs of suicidal depression. And then there was Christian the Southern gentleman, groomed to perfection in an expensive suit and displaying lighthearted, sophisticated intelligence. Wheeler had been so impressed with Christian's transformation that he nicknamed him the Chameleon.

Wheeler believed Christian had once been a nice guy, but that was before the tragic loss of his wife, before guilt and bitterness turned him into an unhinged, dangerous criminal.

The desk phone rang, and Wheeler sighed, seeing the caller. "What is it, Chief Tucker?"

"Oh, you know it's me."

"Ever heard of caller ID?"

"My secretary screens my calls. Anyway, I talked to our suspect, Christian Roberts, since nobody else in law enforcement has bothered."

"I told you I'm scheduled to get his statement, meeting him this Saturday. But he took your call? That's astonishing."

Tucker scoffed. "Hell, no, he hasn't answered my calls, I had to fly clear across the country and catch him at night on his horse farm."

Wheeler chuckled with the image of the obstinate little chief banging on Christian's door. "I bet you surprised him. So did you learn anything that might help your arson case?" he asked, but he already knew the answer.

"I didn't learn squat from that tight-lipped punk."

"Sorry to hear, but I did warn you. The only thing Christian dishes out is frustration."

"Yeah, he's a pain in the ass, but I did learn that young tomcat has some serious enemies. I pulled in his driveway, and a carload of guys fired at me. They were apparently after Roberts. They shot up my rental car before leaving the place. It was pretty hairy."

"Was Christian hurt?"

"Not a scratch. Did you know he's got a pet alligator? The damn thing attacked one of those men and allowed Roberts to get away on a horse. That boy has wildlife on his side. Proves he's Nemo."

Dave chuckled. "I doubt that evidence would hold up. So these men, did Christian know who they were?"

"He claimed he didn't, but I think he had a pretty good idea. That's the strange thing. I'm in his trashed house, shaking in my boots, but Roberts took it all in stride, like attempts on his life occurred every day. He refused to file a police report. At any rate, I'm reporting it to you."

"Thanks. When I see him, I'll ask. Maybe he'll tell me who's after him."

"Good luck with that."

CHAPTER FIFTEEN

Steve returned to the hospital and was grateful to see Karen's faint smile. He expressed his concern about her condition, but she managed to say, "Coconut?" His eyes watered and he bit his lip and shook his head. With tears, she turned her head away from him.

After a few hours, Karen's mother left for her hotel to clean up and rest. Only then did Steve disclose to Karen what he'd learned at home.

"I knew Christian didn't kill her."

"You and your female intuition," Steve said. "I was sure he was guilty, but when I discovered those deleted files, that clinched it. Whoever broke into our house also tried to kill us, and they murdered Felix and Barbara Davis. It's all connected to those files."

"These killers are probably still after us."

"Christian is sending us some bodyguards."

"He's a good guy," she said and closed her eyes. "I don't care what anyone says."

When Karen drifted back to sleep, Steve plugged in his laptop and worked to reestablish the file with the RAT. Late at night, he took a break and dozed in the chair. He woke to the buzz of his new disposable phone. "Yes?" he answered, expecting Christian.

"This Steve Mills?" asked a gruff man's voice.

"Who's this?"

"Roberts sent me. I'm downstairs in the emergency waiting room."

Steve forced his eyes open, still half asleep and disorientated. "Christian sent you?"

"Yeah, yeah, the Florida boy," he responded. "He says you need protection."

"Okay, I'll be down in a minute." He hung up and considered contacting Christian to verify the caller, but realized only Christian had his number. The man had to be on the level. Further, he should be safe in a room full of people.

He entered the waiting room with rows of connecting chairs. On one side sat a black couple with two young children. Two women, one young, one old, occupied the center chairs, and off in the corner were two dark-haired men in suits who looked Italian. One, a lean man, read a magazine, while his robust partner sipped from a Styrofoam cup.

The big guy looked at Steve and nudged his buddy. They rose and ambled to him. "Steve, right?" He extended a hand. "I'm Frankie, and this is my associate, Mitch."

Steve shook their hands. "You're friends of Christian's?"

"Let's say we're friends of a friend," said Frankie. "I heard there're some scumbags after you and your wife, so this is how it'll work. One of us will be outside her hospital room at all times. Come mornin', Mitch will go to your house and check out the car. You want anything from your place, make a list and he'll get it. And, Steve, this is important. Don't go anywhere without one of us. If someone wants you dead, they can take you out even in an elevator. You got it?"

"I understand. How long do you plan to stay with us?"

"That depends on Roberts. The sooner he smokes these dudes, the sooner we all go home."

Steve nodded, realizing the urgency of hacking the file. He had to give Christian a name.

* * *

On Friday evening Christian left Longboat Key and traveled up US 41. He turned into the long boulevard to the Ritz Carlton that sat on a small inlet off the bay, just west of downtown. At the hotel front doors, he handed his car keys to the valet who didn't give his Porsche a second glance. Expensive sport cars were as common as Chevys in Sarasota, one of the wealthiest cities in the country.

Christian strolled through the lobby to the back lounge that overlooked the marina of yachts. At 9:30 on a Friday night, the place was busy. He found a seat at the bar and ordered a drink while waiting for Bill.

According to Sal, the odd-looking little guy was the deadliest hit man in the business, but this didn't bother Christian. He'd dealt with plenty of depraved characters. He was, however, concerned that Bill still had designs on him. At their last meeting in a bar, Bill had groped him, and Christian had put on all his brakes to stop from knocking him off the stool. Christian now sat in another lounge and chewed his thumbnail, wondering how their second sit-down would go. With his elbow on the counter, he held his head and stirred his drink with the straw. *I got enough problems. Don't need any more from that cocksucker.* He jerked to attention when hearing Bill's voice behind him.

"Do you have a headache, sweetheart?"

"Yeah, you're giving me one. Sal offered to pay. Why didn't you take his money?"

Bill chuckled and sat down next to him. "Isn't it obvious? I wanted to see you again after you've had time to reconsider my offer." His lecherous eyes scrutinized Christian's body. "Five minutes upstairs in my room and I'd be yours. I'll do anything for you, Christian."

"Forget it," Christian snapped. Nothing had changed. Bill was relentless. He started to launch into a tongue lashing, but the bartender interceded and asked Bill for his drink order.

"Vodka and tonic, and give my friend here a refill." After the bartender left, Bill said, "Are you sure I can't change your mind?"

Incensed, Christian clenched and ground his teeth. He suddenly realized that the situation was laughable. Why was he letting the little bastard get to him? He relaxed and chuckled. "Bill, dealing with you has become a learning lesson." He leaned back and crossed his arms. "I now know how a woman feels when a pig sexually harasses her."

Bill grimaced. "You're calling me a pig?"

"Yeah," Christian said, smiling. "I realize you're a dangerous little prick, and you frighten people because they care about living. I don't. You should also know I have a temper, and I'm losing it. If you don't back off and stop bugging me for sex, one of us will die."

"You don't mince words."

"Nope."

"All right, Christian," Bill said exhaling deeply. "I don't want you feeling like a victimized woman. I just really like you. I hope we can at least be friends. Despite what you think of me, I can help you."

"You have. I appreciate the job in Idaho," Christian said as the bartender delivered their drinks.

Bill paid for them. "Let's step outside. It's too crowded in here to talk about business."

They picked up their drinks and found an isolated table on the open balcony overlooking the inlet of docked boats. "Your money is in the trunk of my car," said Christian. "Three choppers down with nobody hurt."

"That's not exactly true. One of those wildlife officers had a little accident."

"By accident, you mean he's dead?"

"He drove off a cliff but consider it a freebee."

"Damn it, Bill," Christian said and rubbed his forehead. "I didn't ask you to do that. My conscience is already on overload. "

"The guy was a monster. He held the record for killing the most wolves in Idaho. Do you want to save your wild canines or protect cunts like him?"

"Okay, but no more killing, at least on my behalf."

"Anything you say, sweetie."

Christian glared at him.

"Sorry," Bill said. "I promise I'll tone it down." He lowered his head and muttered. "I have no one, Christian. I love no one and no one loves me, but since we met, you've made life worth living."

Christian realized Bill wasn't an annoying, obsessed stalker looking for ass, but had truly fallen in love with him. "Oh, man, you're wasting your time, pinning your hopes on the impossible."

"I know. I know. But it's my time, my hopes. Just because you'll never have feelings for me doesn't mean I can't care about you."

Christian placed two fingers over his mouth and held his chin. He felt sorry for the guy, but the circumstances were awkward. He'd never been in such an uncomfortable position. "Let's talk about something else."

"Yes, yes." Bill grinned "Tell me how your wolf cause is going."

"It's not going. In fact the situation with the wolves is getting worse. Congress passed a bill allowing the state of Alaska to run its wildlife refuges. The state has opened hunting on bear and wolves to inflate the caribou herds for hunters. Politicians don't care about wildlife, ecosystems, or what the public wants. They cater to wealthy hunting and gun lobbies."

"Sounds like a real problem, but Captain Nemo's attacks are making a difference. They put the issue in the public's eye."

"That's what I'd hoped for. I'm switching gears from terrorist attacks to working the inside track on a corrupt politician. Trouble is I've hit some snags. Not sure how it will play out."

"You do whatever, but I believe that keeping Captain Nemo in the news helps your cause."

They talked for several hours, and Christian explained why he wanted to save the wolves. "Google a short video called How Wolves Changed Rivers. It's about the fourteen wolves that were introduced into Yellowstone twenty-years-ago after they had been killed off in the US. It'll make you a believer on why wolves are vital to the environment."

"How Wolves Changed Rivers," said Bill. "I'll watch it."

"Ya know wolves kill coyotes, but when wolves were exterminated a hundred years ago, the coyote population exploded. They moved east and are now found in nearly every state, wiping out the fox, skunks, rabbits, even cats and dogs. People complain about them, but it's our own damn fault, screwing with the balance in nature."

"I heard coyotes have been spotted outside of Chicago."

"Hell, they're in Atlanta, New York and have taking over Florida. Seen them on my farm." Christian glanced at his watch. It was going on midnight. He swallowed the last of his drink and rose. "I'd like to hang out and discuss this more, but I got a busy day tomorrow. You ready to collect your money?"

"Do you have a quiet place for the handoff? Parking lots have too much surveillance."

"I know where, and it's just up the road."

They walked to the front of the hotel, and the valet produced Christian's car. They climbed in, and Christian drove toward Bird Key, but before John Ringling Bridge, he took the turnoff that led to the city fishing pier on the northern bay. The road continued under the bridge to a bait shop on the south side. He pulled over under the dark bridge pilings, and they climbed out. Christian noticed two fishermen farther down on the seawall, but they were focused on casting their lines toward the outgoing tide and paid them no heed.

The night wind blew off the water and Christian's tousled hair whipped at his face as he popped the car trunk and handed a satchel of money to Bill. "So where're you off to next?"

"Maybe Alaska," Bill said. "I heard some interesting things are happening there."

* * *

Early Saturday morning Agent Wheeler placed a small overnight bag and his gun in his car trunk and left Miami for Sarasota. His normal attire when questioning a suspect was a suit and tie. Today, however, he wore casual slacks and a cotton pullover shirt for his noon rendezvous with Christian on his sailboat. His pocket held brief notes concerning the times and dates of the terrorist attacks in Idaho and a small tape recorder for Christian's interview. The large file box on Captain Nemo remained in his office.

He had learned that locking Christian in an interrogation room for hours was a time waster. Instead of a confession, Wheeler got sarcasm. A social meeting and friendly chat, however, was more productive, and the young guy tended to opened up. Even on the boat, Wheeler doubted Christian would reveal anything useful for the case.

Three hours later, Wheeler pulled into Marina Jack's and parked. He walked down the concrete pier full of docked boats, recalling when he and his partner, Ralph, had raced down the pier last year with a warrant for Christian's arrest. *Slippery as a snake,* he thought. The guy had slithered away and was still as free as a bird.

As Wheeler approached the sloop slip, he saw Christian on his hands and knees washing the deck near the forward hatch. Wearing only cutoff jeans and sunglasses, he looked like a sunny boat dweller, not a terrorist. "Cleaning it up for me?"

Christian looked up, smiling. He dropped the rag in a bucket and stood. "Having a boat is a love-hate relationship. Going out on the water is great, but maintenance is a bitch." He stepped to the railing and offered his hand. "Glad you could make it, Dave."

"Me too," Wheeler said, reaching up to shake Christian's hand. He had never seen Christian bare-chested in shorts. His lanky tan frame with six-pack abs would ignite envy in most men. "You certainly are in shape. Do you work out?"

"Yeah, running from the law keeps me fit." Christian laughed and picked up the bucket. With agility he skirted the railing, treaded over lines, and ducked wires holding the mast, and hopped into the cockpit. "Come on aboard. Like to get underway before someone spots me and my boat and calls the press."

Wheeler stepped into the boat. "You don't keep your sailboat at this marina anymore?"

He gave a mocking glance. "No, I moor it off a Longboat Key house. You want the address?" He detected the difference between an innocent question and a lawman's probing.

"Sorry, it's part of the job."

"Dave, if you stopped fishing, I'd worry you were losing it." Christian started the motor and let it rumble in idle. He pointed to the back of the sloop. "Could you release that aft line?"

As Wheeler unhooked the rope from the dock, Christian scampered to the bow to pull up the fender and free the front line. With a foot he shoved the sloop away from the dock, and in a flash, he was behind the wheel, backing the sailboat out of the slip.

Wheeler sat down beside him and gazed up at the clear blue sky. "Looks like a great day for boating."

"Once we're in the bay, I'll cut the engine and raise the sails. Now I need to ask. Do you get seasick?"

"I don't know. I've never been sailing."

"We'll play it safe and stay in the bay. The Gulf is pretty choppy today."

The sloop motored out of the harbor inlet into the bay channel. After it cleared the nearby bridge and entered the north Sarasota Bay, Christian unfurled the mainsail, set the jib, and shut down the motor. The sloop heeled to one side, and the only sound was the slush of small waves hitting the hull as the bow plunged forward through the serene green water.

"This is peaceful," Wheeler said. "I understand why you love sailing."

"If you're not in a hurry, it's the only way to go. You should get yourself a sailboat."

"I'm afraid I'm too old to jump around a deck like you. Besides, I don't know anything about sailing."

"Age is no excuse. You get the boat, and I'll teach you to sail. That is if you haven't put me behind bars," Christian said with a chuckle.

"Speaking of jail, let's get this interview over so I can enjoy myself."

Christian agreed and Wheeler retrieved the small recorder from his pocket. He questioned Christian for a half hour about his whereabouts during the Idaho terrorist attacks. Christian answered briefly, to the point, and didn't change a word from his earlier statements on the phone.

With FBI business done, Christian turned the boat over to Wheeler. "First lesson, keep her on a straight heading toward that channel marker. Any hard turns, and you'll screw up the sails. I'll go below and fix us some snacks and drinks I picked up this morning. You still drink Scotch rocks?"

"You have a good memory. Scotch is fine," Wheeler said, clasping the wheel.

Christian disappeared into the cabin but soon returned with their drinks and a few trays of appetizers that included shrimp cocktail, crab legs, cold-cuts and cheese with a variety of olives.

"You want to take over?" Wheeler asked.

"Naw, you're doin' good."

Wheeler kicked back on the open deck and steered the boat while he munched on the food and sipped extra smooth Scotch that probably cost more than a hundred dollars a bottle. "This is the life," he commented. "You sure know how to entertain."

"I usually do this only to charm the ladies." He smiled. "But in your case, I'm trying to avoid a fucking." His expression turned serious. "Speaking of being fucked, you could have a problem. Chief Tucker showed up at my farm in the middle of the night and is under the impression I'm paying you off or have something on you. I stuck up for you, told him he was wrong, that our association is based on respect. He wasn't buying it."

Wheeler sat up. "He actually said you might be bribing or blackmailing me?"

"In so many words. That crusty old sucker flew across county and that proves, he's damn eager for an arrest. If he can't have me, he might settle for you. You'd better watch your back, Dave."

"Great," Wheeler said and took a gulp of Scotch. "I checked him out, and he's one determined lawman with some influential backers. I already told him you agreed to talk to me on your boat. Guess he took it wrong. I'll straighten him out when I get back." He looked at Christian. "But let's talk about that night on your place. Tucker wasn't your only visitor. You want to tell me about it?"

"Not really." He nodded up ahead. "We'll drop anchor off that mangrove shoal. I'm grilling steaks for dinner."

Wheeler wasn't about to let him drop it. "If someone is trying to kill you, Christian, I might be able to stop it."

Christian chuckled. "No one can stop a murder if someone really wants you dead."

"It can be prevented if the intended victim cooperates with law enforcement."

"Dave, you know I'm not the cooperating type." His cheery mood died away as his focus veered from Dave to the watery horizon. "There is something I'd like to discuss on another matter," he said quietly. "It's kinda serious, but we'll talk after dinner. No sense in ruining my appetite and wasting a good steak." In seconds his dark mood passed, and he grinned. "Can I get you another drink?"

An hour later, they sat on the deck watching the sunset and dined on tender porterhouses and baked potatoes. "I hope you're not driving back to Miami tonight."

"Definitely not after this many drinks," said Dave. "My bag is in the car and I'll find a motel in Sarasota."

"If you don't mind sleeping on the boat, the aft cabin has a decent queen-sized bed. You're welcome to it, and you'd also be doing me a favor. Won't have to look for channel markers in the dark going back to the marina. We can stay put."

"I've never slept on a boat. It should be interesting."

Christian smiled. "She'll rock you to sleep like a baby." He rose and took Wheeler's empty plate, stacking it on top of his own. "There're new toothbrushes and razors under the sink in the head. Help yourself." The sun had disappeared into the horizon, so he flipped on the cabin lights and stepped below.

Wheeler followed him down and saw him washing the dishes in the galley sink. "Can I help?"

"Nope, but you could refresh our drinks." As Christian put the dishes away, he said, "I was just thinking. The last time I cooked for a man in this galley, it was for Vince."

"That guy," Wheeler grumbled, fixing the cocktails. "Guilty of everything, and we couldn't even give the jerk a parking ticket. He obviously taught you how to elude the law." Setting their drinks on the table, he reclined in the booth.

"Yeah, he taught me a few things." Christian settled on the cushion across from him and sipped his drink.

"Sorry, I know you and Vince were close and he died saving your life, in New York. He apparently had some good in him."

Christian raised his glass in a toast. "To Vince, then."

"To the SOB that got away," Wheeler said, lifting his drink. After a swallow, he centered his attention on Christian. "You said you wanted to discuss another matter."

"Speaking of Vince, about now he'd kill me for talking to you," he said with a chuckle. "I'd like this off the record."

"I can't promise that."

Christian muttered, more to himself than to Wheeler, "At this stage in the game, it doesn't matter." He looked up. "Okay, here it is. Before long I'll be arrested for murder. The evidence is overwhelming, puts me there during the crime. But don't get your hopes up. This murder has nothing to do with your Nemo case. I realize plenty of times I've claimed I'm not guilty, but I swear to God I didn't kill the person."

"Who's the victim? Where did it happen?"

"Give me a break, Dave." He smiled. "I'm giving you a heads up, not serving myself up on a platter."

"So why the tease?"

"Because you're the only guy in law enforcement who gets me," Christian said. "You know I'm not stupid or careless enough to leave DNA, surveillance photos, and witnesses, especially in a murder. The victim was killed right after I left. It looks like a slam-dunk case, but I'm asking you to keep an open mind. All the evidence against me is proof I'm innocent."

"So you're not guilty because you're an efficient, smart criminal and would never get sloppy when committing a felony? Christian, I don't think that defense would play well in court."

"No shit, but you know it's true."

CHAPTER SIXTEEN

James Sanders, the secretary of the Interior, sat at his mahogany desk in his home office, mulling over the papers for the president's newest agenda. Wiping out wolves was one thing, but turning the national parks and wildlife refuges into oil fields was another. Despite the president's popularity, there might be serious opposition, and not from just the conservation groups.

Sanders shrugged and took a gulp of brandy. When the president gave away the leases in the Gulf and Arctic to the oil companies, the press turned a blind eye. The result was no protests and little public outcry. Liberals believed the president could do no wrong, and the conservative working class was concerned only with the loss of jobs and homes. This new proposal might slip through without a peep.

He heard the click click of high heels on the staircase and lowered his pen when Amber, his wife of five years, walked in. She still took his breath away. She was younger, close in age to his oldest son, and not terribly bright, but her flawless face and body more than compensated.

He had met her on the campaign trail in an Illinois diner when she served him lunch. For the waitress, he'd ended a perfectly good marriage to a loving wife who gave him two children and used her family wealth to bankroll his rise in politics. He now had his trophy wife, but no money of his own. To keep up appearances and finance their lifestyle, he resorted to payoffs and fraud. Of late his crimes had escalated to contracting murders. He smiled at his wife and thought, *All for Amber*.

"What do you think of my new dress, Jimmy?" she asked dropping her full-length fox coat over a chair. She swirled around on the oriental rug to show off the low-cut gown that hugged her slender waist and hips.

"Radiant. You're absolutely radiant," he said, not mentioning that the women at that night's event might disapprove of her tits spilling out of the dress.

She sauntered behind his chair and hugged him. "I wish you were going with me," she cooed in his ear. "Those old bags ignore me when you're not there."

"I'm sorry, dear, but I have to work. If you're not happy at these gatherings, you shouldn't go."

She stepped back, looking disconcerted. "I have to. We're raising money to save a little bird in the Florida marshes. I can't remember its name, but it's very pretty. I'll need twenty thousand for the donation tonight."

"Twenty thousand?" he said and swallowed. "How many of these birds are there?"

"Not many. That's why it's important. I've already promised the money."

"All right," he said, taking the checkbook out of a desk drawer, "but Amber, don't make any more promises unless you ask me first. These donations are adding up." He wrote the check, thinking the funds had come full circle. He had stolen money meant to help wildlife, and his wife was returning it. He handed her the check and sighed.

"Thanks, Jimmy. I should be home by ten." She kissed his check, put on her coat, and hurried outside to the waiting driver.

He looked out the window as the town car drove away. He punched the numbers on his cell phone. "She just left."

Ten minutes later a black SUV pulled up to the house. Sanders walked to the foyer and opened the front door to let Vern in. "I'm not crazy about us meeting here, but it's too damn dark and cold in that park," he said, strolling back to his office. "Have a seat, Vern. Care for something to drink?"

"No, sir," Vern said, and his hulking frame filled a wing chair opposite the desk.

Sanders returned to his desk. "So, where are we?"

"My expert examined Roberts's laptop and found no files or emails from the Arlington couple, though that's not surprising. A terrorist can't afford to leave an incriminating trail. He likely uses burner phones and a separate laptop with an anonymous name when he sends his emails through a VP network on the dark web. That way they'll bounce around countries and can't be traced."

"Spare me the tech lingo. Bottom line, he might have the files. Before long, that son of a bitch will know who I am, and I'll have to worry if he'll blow up my car. What are you going to do about him?"

"Two of my men are watching him. He's on his sailboat and would be an easy target. A high-powered rifle could take him out tomorrow, but as we've discussed, a murder investigation would have the police scrutinizing his affairs. They might come across his laptop and discover the files. We also have to consider his notoriety as Captain Nemo. His murder would bring nationwide press."

"He's that famous?"

"He's an antihero with a pretty face. The media loves him but that might soon end and result in another option for us. He slept with the Davis woman right before she died. My informants in the DC. precinct say the detectives have witnesses, photos, and DNA that all point to Roberts as the murderer, but as yet, they haven't identified their suspect. It's only a matter of time. He'll soon be charged, and we won't have to deal with him."

Sanders stood and moseyed around the room. He stopped short in front of Vern. "That's not going to work, Vern. When he's arrested he'll spill his guts and say he was in her office to download the files. It will all come back to me. He has to be dead before the police find him."

"I've implemented a second plan that will appear like an accidental death. Next week we'll follow through."

"It better work." Sanders returned to his desk. "What's happening with the computer geek and his wife?"

"Steve Mills is not the average geek. He's at the top of his field when it comes to security. When my man found his hidden laptop, Mills had already hacked into the files and was close to learning your name. He should've died in a car explosion, but he didn't use his car. I've since learned that two men from New York with mob ties are protecting Mills and his wife at the hospital. Roberts is connected, so this is his doing. Getting at the couple in the hospital was hard, but with those bodyguards, it's nearly impossible. We'll have to wait until they're home. I'm thinking gas leak and house fire."

"What a mess," Sanders said and held his forehead. He looked up. "Just get Roberts. He's the key. He dies, and the couple will run for cover and forget about the file. If this second attempt fails, shoot the bastard. I'll take my chances with a murder investigation and the press."

Vern left, and Sanders wandered to a small wet bar. After this meeting, he needed a drink. He fixed a martini but found the olives hadn't been replenished. He cursed and threw the cocktail shaker into the sink. Ice hit the counter and floor. Missing olives weren't the source of his irritation. A lifetime of work might go down the toilet because of some Florida eco jerk. He also wasn't happy with Vern. The guy was an ex-Seal, ex-CIA operative, and supposedly an expert in undercover work and eliminating enemies. But he'd been outmaneuvered by this Nemo character, a kid, really, still in his twenties. Vern claimed it was bad luck, but Sanders saw it as incompetent bullshit. He was further annoyed that Vern thought Roberts's arrest would solve the problem. "Idiot," he rasped. "I'm dealing with a damn idiot who can't see down the road." The last thing he wanted was Roberts talking to the authorities. The prosecutor would accept his guilty plea for the secretary of the Interior's head.

He returned to his desk, downed more of the martini, and placed a call to Texas.

"Jim, nice to hear from you." said Russ Manning, the behind-the-scenes head of the NGA, the National Gun Association. "How are things going?"

"Not good," said Sanders. "I'm rather disappointed in the man you sent."

"Vern? My god, he's highly qualified. You won't find anyone better to handle the situation."

"He's not handling it, and the shit storm is on the verge of blowing up in my face."

"I warned you that stealing funds from the wildlife studies was risky. You should've been content with our generous donations. Instead you got greedy."

"You're calling me greedy?" Sanders fumed. "You and your hunters got greedy, wanting all the deer, so I instigated bills to wipe out the wolves. Hell, I just manipulated Alaska for your hunters. The state now has open season on bears and wolves in the wildlife refuge, so there's more moose and caribou to kill. Given there's no livestock loss up there, even the US Fish and Game fought the bill."

"All right, you don't need to ramble on. So what's your problem?"

"Have you heard of Captain Nemo?"

"Of course. He saved the sharks, and I read about his latest attacks in Idaho, stirring up trouble to save wolves. He's a minor thorn in our side."

"That thorn is zeroing in on me. Christian Roberts is supposedly Nemo, and he got wind of the computer files that show the misappropriated funds. The file leads to my bank account with your large donations. People fund your organization because they're afraid of losing their guns. If Roberts exposes your payoffs and the public learns your plan to wipe out the predators, I wonder how they'd feel. Surveys show that ninety percent of voters want wolves protected. You see how this thorn might stick the NGA?"

"Vern can't take care of him?"

"He tried and failed. He also couldn't take out a computer nerd helping Roberts. Vern said the job should be done by next week, but I'm losing faith. I thought I should give you the lowdown."

"If Vern doesn't eliminate Roberts, I'll send in somebody else, but this guy will cost you."

"I don't care how much as long as he's gone."

Russ chuckled. "Don't worry, Jim. That lone-wolf terrorist is biting off more than he can chew. He messes with the NGA, and we'll bury him."

* * *

On Monday Christian sat on his rocking boat deck and huddled in a foul-weather jacket as he drank coffee and watched the dawn peek through the Sarasota high-rises. Last night's wind and heavy rain had blown in a hard cold front. The sky had cleared, but the blustery wind turned the bay a choppy gray. Florida was like a faucet that quickly ran hot and cold. Don't like the weather, just wait a minute.

Small-craft warnings had kept the fishing and pleasure boats at dock. Only Christian and a pod of bottle-nosed dolphins were at ease on the white-capped swells. In the frigid air he clutched the mug to warm his hands and listened to the whistling wind, the clang of the halyard against the mast, and the distant cries of gulls.

He normally relished the peace and isolation on the water, but the previous week's torrid events occupied his mind. The rollercoaster had started with grief from the death of his beloved stallion and soon turned into an adrenaline rush with his escape from the assassins who had invaded his farm. The visit from the pigheaded Idaho police chief was also unexpected. He then learned from Steve about Barbara Davis's murder, a huge problem since all the evidence made him the prime suspect. Afterwards he discussed the crises with Sal who advised him to run for his life. Friday involved paying off Bill, the infatuated little hitman. Christian was still unsure how to deal with him. The rest of the weekend he spent on his boat with Agent Wheeler. He told Wheeler about his probable arrest for murder without going into specifics. It was straw grasping, hoping the agent could help him. Wheeler recommended turning himself in. Neither Wheeler's advice nor Sal's sat well with Christian. There had to be another way out of the murder rap.

Christian had dropped the agent off at the marina late Sunday morning. Although Wheeler's agenda was to jail him, Christian enjoyed the man's company. Their friendship was like a chess game, players on the opposite side of a board, trying to outsmart each other. During the shark campaign, Christian won the game. This go-round with wolves might have a different result. The pieces were closing in, and he was running out of moves.

He heard his cell chime in the cabin. At such an early hour, he figured Juan was calling with an update on the farm and horses. Few others had his temporary phone number. He stepped below and realized he needed to replace his stolen phone, mainly to avoid his mother's nagging when she couldn't contact him. Even a telemarketer was less annoying than her. They had once been close, but after his wife's death, Mom couldn't deal with his sulking, and his New York arrest as suspected terrorist bomber fractured their relationship. Out of politeness he spoke to her, but no longer divulged his feelings or plans. He grabbed the phone off the counter. "Yeah?"

"It's Steve. I know I'm supposed to email you the file information, but this couldn't wait. I got the name, and you're not going to believe who's behind the fraud and murders. It's James Sanders, the secretary of the Interior."

"You're sure?" he asked and slowly sat down in the booth.

"It took some doing. He moved the funds out of the African account to one in the Cayman Islands, all under anonymous names, but all the data leads to him. It's mind-boggling."

Indeed, Christian had difficulty absorbing the far-fetched revelation. He'd expected a top aide or a government supervisor to be the guilty party, but not a member of the president's cabinet. It did add up, though. Who else had the power to manipulate and steal funds and could get killers at his beck and call? "Okay, y'all are in real danger, even at the hospital with two bodyguards. When will Karen be released?"

"Her doctor says Sunday."

"As soon as she's out, leave town. In fact get out of the country. Don't go home. Head straight for Reagan airport. I'll have a chartered jet waiting. When you and the guys are aboard, tell the pilot where you want to go. Private jets can submit a flight plan at the last minute."

"God, Christian, you really think that's necessary? What about our house, my business?"

"I live by the old adage, 'It's better to be safe than sorry.' Have someone handle your business and close up the house, but don't leave a paper and internet trail or tell anyone except me of your new location. In the meantime, Frankie can get you fake passports."

"I'll do as you say, but I'll tell you now we'll probably go to Playa del Carmen in Mexico. It's a modern little town about forty miles south of Cancun. Karen and I lived there a few years ago in a gated community, very secure with guards. She loved it. In high school she was a foreign-exchange student in Spain and speaks the language."

"Sounds good," said Christian. "Email me when you get settled and have an address. I'll wire money to take care of your expenses."

"That's nice of you, given we dragged you into this mess of finding Felix's killer."

"No one drags me into anything."

"That's probably true." Steve chuckled. "By the way, I sent the files. They should be on your laptop. What about you? You're in just as much danger as we are."

"I'm a fisherman, Steve. You need the right bait to catch the big ones. I'm staying put to lure these fuckers in."

* * *

In his DC. apartment, Vern sucked in an irritated breath and placed meticulously folded clothes in a carryon bag for his second trip to Florida. His weapons and other lethal items that might cause problems with airport security were already there. Two of his men had driven the gear down prior to the farm raid, and they stayed to maintain surveillance on the target.

The target was a punk with no military or law enforcement training and no criminal record, but he'd managed to outfox Vern and galloped away on a horse. Vern took it personally, being played for a sucker. Adding to the insult, he had to listen to the sleazy politician's griping.

He made a call before departing for the airport. "Is he still on the sailboat?"

"Yes, sir, Mr. Vern," answered Brian, his man in Florida. "The weather was dicey on Monday, so we had to abandon the launch and watch him from a seawall. So far he hasn't left his boat."

"Call if the situation changes. I'll be in Sarasota at eight tonight."

"Sir, I'll be there to pick you up. The bay is calm, and the motorboat is loaded and ready."

"Very good," Vern said. He had no sooner pocketed his mobile phone than it buzzed with a call. Russ Manning's name was on the caller ID. "Hello, sir."

"How's it going, Vern?"

"I was just leaving for a flight to Florida."

"Business, not pleasure, I take it. That's why I'm calling. I talked to Sanders, and he wasn't too pleased that things hadn't been wrapped up."

"Yes sir; there have been some missteps, but I tried to explain to the secretary that staged accidents don't always come off as planned."

"How do you plan to handle this boy?"

"Drowning, sir," Vern said. "He lives on a sailboat, and no one would question if he slipped on the deck, hit his head, and fell overboard. The following week, we'll deal with his accomplices, an Arlington couple."

"Sounds like you have everything under control, but you should know. If Sanders is indicted, it could have a ripple effect and cause trouble for our organization."

"Sir, I promise that *boy* will be gone, if I have to throttle him myself."

Russ chuckled. "You've never let me down."

Vern hung up and grumbled, "Damn right, I've never let him down." Prior to cleaning up Sanders's mess of witnesses, the job had been removing a circuit court judge who was set to rule against the NGA in a lawsuit worth millions. With a dose of succinylcholine, the judge conveniently appeared to die from a heart attack. That was Vern's specialty, eliminating the problematic without drawing attention. He zipped up his carryon, picturing Roberts's body bag, and headed out.

* * *

At midnight Christian was curled up in a blanket, dozing in the cabin of his anchored sloop. The open hatch above him allowed starlight, sea fragrance, and a cool breeze to invade the forward berth. The lone hum of an outboard motor resonated in the distance; it wasn't uncommon for boats to zip across the bay at that hour. When the reverberation neared and the motor throttled down to just above an idle, he instinctively woke. He didn't move but listened for the reassurance of boisterous men coming home after a night of fishing. He heard no voices and then the motor went silent about thirty yards behind his sloop. Most boaters were considerate and wouldn't encroach on another's space. The invasion aroused Christian's suspicions.

More concerning, the boat approached from behind, so no one in the cabin could look out the side portals and see it. He slipped into his cutoffs to investigate. The boaters could be thieves after the small outboard on the dinghy tied to the aft ladder, or worse, they might be the same men who came gunning for him on his farm. Stepping to his dresser, he retrieved his father's old .38. He felt the slight tilt of the sloop from the weight of someone stepping over the starboard railing onto the deck. They were on his sloop. To travel so silently and fast, they must have used a battery-powered trolling motor to close the distance between the boats.

Here we go. He flipped the safety off on the revolver and hoisted himself out of the open hatch near the bow. Laying low on the deck in the dark, he peeked over the cabin. In the dim light, the silhouettes of two men stood in his cockpit. A third man remained in a twenty-foot launch alongside the sloop, holding the railing to prevent the boats from bumping and alerting Christian.

Christian stuffed the handgun into his back waistband, scuttled on his belly to the bow, and quietly eased down the anchor line into the water, careful not to create a ripple. To go unseen, he swam underwater the length of the sloop to their boat. He emerged at the rear of the motorboat near the outboard well and saw the two men had gone into the cabin, obviously searching for him. The other guy was still in their launch, gripping a weapon and keeping the boats apart. Focused on the sailboat invasion, he didn't notice when Christian slinked aboard and crept up behind him.

Christian wrapped one arm around the man's neck in a sleeper hold and pressed the gun barrel against his temple. "Drop the weapon," he whispered into an ear. The man immediately complied, and his gun fell into the bay. "Very good, now quietly, let's step aboard my sloop." As they climbed onto the sailboat deck, Christian overheard the men in the cabin.

"Where the hell is he?" one barked.

"Sir, I don't know. I saw him here, and he never left. His dinghy is still tied to the sailboat."

"So he either swam to shore or someone picked him up, maybe when you left for dinner."

"No, sir, we never took our eyes off this boat. He's got to be in here somewhere."

"Jesus Christ, first the farm and now the boat," he grumbled. "Is this damn kid Houdini? Go do another sweep and recheck the engine area. He could be hiding under some gear."

Christian poked his weapon into his hostage's ribs and whispered, "Tell them you got a problem and to come up."

"Sir, Mr. Vern," the hostage called into the cabin, "I have a problem and need you."

Christian moved away, but kept his gun trained on the man. In two back-stepped strides, he was on top of the cabin, crouching over the hatch.

A huge, white-haired dude pointing a weapon ascended the three steps. The guy was a monster, twice Christian's mass. Seeing only his accomplice on the deck, the man lowered his handgun and snarled. "What is it?"

Christian grabbed the overhead mast boom and swung it hard against the big guy's head, dropping him on the deck. Springing off the cabin, he snatched up the man's weapon.

The large guy looked up, frowning, and held his head. "Where the fuck did you come from?"

"Been waiting for ya, Mr. Vern," Christian said. "Now call out your other boy."

Vern gathered his limbs and sat up. "Brian, get up here."

Brian raced up the steps to his parked boss with bloodied hair. "What happened?" He then spotted Christian, who held them at gunpoint.

Christian put out his hand. "I'll take that, Brian." Brian hesitated, unwilling to give up his 9 mm. "You don't want to go there."

Brian sighed and gave up his weapon.

"Now go stand with your buddy," Christian said. "You too, Vern, get over there with your boys."

Vern rose with a groan and joined his two men.

"When ya'll tried to ambush me on my farm, you should've learned that attacking a guy on his home turf lowers your odds of success," Christian said, smiling as he swapped out guns, stuffing the .38 into the waistband and used the 9 mm to hold the three at bay. If there was any shooting, ballistics would lead to Brian's weapon.

"All right, you little shit," said Vern. "What are you going to do with us?"

Christian calmly pushed his wet hair out of his eyes. "Well, Vern, I'm not too happy with you. To cover up the misappropriation of funds in the government files, you killed that poor analyst in DC., made it look like an overdose. You then used a van to mow down my friend Karen when she and her husband got wind of the files. And now you've come after me twice. What I don't understand is why you strangled Barbara Davis. She told you the analyst had discovered the file and that got him killed. The woman was on your side."

"She fucked you, compromised her side and couldn't be trusted anymore. She was also careless, letting you get access to her computer. But what I did to her and the others is nothing compared to my plans for you."

Christian lifted an eyebrow. "Realize you're angry and not thinking rationally with the head bump and all, but try and remember who's holding the gun here. Given your plan for me, I should just blow y'all away."

"You'd never get away with it," said Vern.

Christian chuckled. "If you only knew how many times I've heard that. But you could be right if we were in another state, but this is Florida, and we've got some quirky laws. Ever heard of Stand Your Ground? It created quite a controversy in the Trevon Martin case. I believe it applies here. You invaded my boat to kill me. That gives me the right to shoot you in self-defense."

"You're Captain Nemo. No one would believe a terrorist."

"Um, I'm suspected of being Captain Nemo. Besides, I have proof of your murder attempts. You recall the shootout with the little white car when you fled my farm? You were shooting at a chief of police. I believe he'd make a damn fine witness and be willing to testify."

"I'm tired of your yapping," said Vern. "If you're going to kill us, do it."

"Very brave," said Christian, "Shame you're not too bright. I'm thinking if I do you in, Sanders will just send replacements, and I'll have to figure out who they are."

Vern looked up with surprise at the mention of Sanders's name.

"Yeah," Christian said. "I know the secretary of the Interior is behind all this shit, trying to save his butt from fraud with these murders."

"So you've learned who's after you. What now?"

Christian scratched his head. "Given your boys call you sir, I'm guessing you're ex-military."

"We served in Desert Storm," said Vern.

"I like veterans, respect what they've done for our country. I'll tell you what, Vern. I'm gonna let you and your boys go, but tell Sanders any more attacks on me or my friends, and the files go public. I die, they go public."

"Is that it?"

"No, I want Sanders to push the president into passing a bill that says no politician has the right to manipulate the Endangered Species Act and end protection for a species. Researchers and scientists should make those decisions. Also our national parks, refuges, and public land are set aside for wildlife. They're not private shooting galleries for hunters or some rancher's cattle. That needs to change. If Sanders doesn't come through, the files go public."

"That's blackmail," said Vern.

Christian chuckled. "Been accused of worse. Speaking of which...." He turned serious. "Tell that fucking secretary that if the wolf killing continues, I'll destroy him and you."

Vern looked intently into Christian's eyes. "I believe you."

CHAPTER SEVENTEEN

In Alaska on a remote snowy mountainside covered with pine forests, Bill leaned against a trunk of an Englemann spruce that grew in moist landscapes and stared below through his binoculars at the hunting lodge on a half-frozen lake. The two-story log building had a long dock, and at its end a helicopter rested on a landing pad. A caretaker and his wife maintained the hunting camp with the chopper pilot, and four men the current guests.

Prior to arriving, Bill had done his homework. Hacking into the state's database on hunting licenses, he learned the four occupants had purchased bear and wolf tags. Hunting season for deer, moose, and caribou was over, so only Alaska's iconic predators could legally be taken. Once Bill knew the men's names, he followed their movement online. Credit card statements revealed flight bookings and lodge reservation. He then studied the camp layout, its staff, and how to reach the place from Anchorage without being noticed. The proof of the men's intentions hung outside the lodge. Two wolf pelts and a bear skin were suspended and stretched on posts. Game changer: the hunters had become the prey.

He set the binoculars on the snow bluff and took in the view. Most visitors would be awed by the vast wilderness and majestic mountains, but he was a city guy, noticing only there were a hell of a lot of trees and no bars. He preferred civilization.

"Fucking cold," he lamented and stuffed his gloved hands under his armpits to warm his numb fingers. Glancing at his semi-automatic rifle with its large scope that rested against a branch, he wondered if he'd stop shivering long enough to steady the weapon and pull the trigger. After several days of driving through monotonous woods on a gravel back road, he sat here, freezing, cursing, and questioning his sanity. He'd receive no compensation for the expensive venture and his misery. Avenging wolves wasn't a motivation. He didn't care if the howling beasts were exterminated, but Christian did. Bill was here for him.

Bill reflected on the young man, seductively hot like Satan and just as devious. During their initial meeting in the downtown Sarasota bar, Bill experienced love at first sight. The boy was flawless. After listening to Christian's sultry voice and getting a dose of his attitude, Bill's heart was racing for the first time. At their second encounter in the Ritz, Christian revealed his passion for wolves, their importance to the ecosystem and the trouble they faced with survival. Bill found Christian's commitment for wildlife endearing.

Bill's circumstance probably also fueled the obsession for the young man. He was an assassin and a homosexual. Socializing was difficult and unwise. Visiting gay bars, he had to lie about his murderous profession, and his appearance hindered a relationship. With a short, skinny body and a face that didn't require a Halloween mask, he wasn't fighting men off. In his mid-forties, he looked back at his life as a series of one-night stands with male prostitutes. They met a physical need but not the emotional.

But Christian changed everything. Bill was as giddy as a school girl in love. Life was suddenly worth living. Bill also liked that he could be open with Christian. They were both killers with the smarts not to get caught, although they had different objectives. Bill executed people for money, and as a psychopath, he felt no remorse. Christian struggled with his conscience, and his motive wasn't personal gain. Digging into his shrink's records, Bill learned the young guy suffered from guilt and depression, but it hadn't stopped him. He was willing to risk his life and soul for wildlife.

Bill sat on a frigid mountain, aware that a sexual liaison between him and Christian would never occur. Christian had been adamant about that. Still, Bill was content with being in his life, a partner of sorts. To accomplish that goal, he took up the boy's noble cause and used his own talent to stop the wolf slaughter.

"Come on, come on," he groused, becoming impatient with the late risers. He and those men hunted, but their prey diverged from the two-legged to the four. He puzzled over their gratification. With little risk and skill, they shot ignorant, innocent creatures from a mile away. It was hardly sporting or worthy of bragging rights. Hunting was also expensive. He had seen how much the four men shelled out for a flight to Alaska, their lodging, and the rented helicopter for aerial hunting. *I'm supposedly twisted. But these bastards kill for a lousy head and hide. In my book that's sick.* He huffed.

He leaned forward, finally noticing movement at the lodge. The door opened, and five men strolled out. He picked up his rifle and trained the sights on the four who had guns slung over their shoulders. The unarmed fifth man would be the chopper pilot. Their jovial voices echoed in the valley with their eagerness for the coming hunt.

"Hate to ruin your fun, boys." Bill murmured, and waited until the men were halfway down the long dock between the lodge and the helicopter. With little cover, the pickings would be easy. When they reached the point of no return, he purposely targeted their legs. He wanted them to know how a scared, injured animal felt. Four shots later, they were down, screaming from their wounds. Two began to crawl on their bellies toward the safety of the building. The pilot had jumped off the dock onto the frozen lake and hid behind the dock pilings for protection.

Bill tilted his rifle upward and sighed. If it were up to him, he'd finish them off along with everyone else in the place, but Christian didn't want people killed. He was interested only in messages to stop the wolf slaughter. He wasn't pleased to learn that Bill had wasted the callous Wildlife Service guy in Idaho.

Bill reconsidered. At significant cost, time, and bloody-cold agony, he'd driven to the lodge and deserved more satisfaction than putting several men in a hospital. *Fuck it.* He took aim at the helicopter gas tank and emptied the magazine. The chopper exploded into a fiery ball of flames, and he grinned. "Now there's a message."

* * *

The enjoyable weekend of sailing, drinking, and spending time with Christian in Sarasota was over, and Wheeler was back at work in Miami. Sitting at his desk, he looked over Christian's statement that had been transcribed off the recorder. It had some holes. During the restaurant bombing in Idaho, Christian claimed to be on his boat in Sarasota. To confirm his whereabouts, the local FBI agents talked to the neighbors who lived near Vince Florio's former home. They saw Christian's SUV in the driveway and his sailboat moored off the house, but no one actually saw him on the boat until two days after the bombing.

Sal Lamotto had been spotted in Idaho, but there wasn't any evidence that linked him to Christian and the attack. Being a career criminal, Sal refused an interview with the agents, and their hands were tied without a warrant. During the three helicopter bombings, Christian had plenty of proof he was in Atlanta and then DC., not in Idaho when the attack took place.

Wheeler set aside the Captain Nemo case and thought about the murder that Christian had discussed on his boat. He'd said the evidence was overwhelming, making him the prime suspect, but he alleged he wasn't guilty. Normally when denying a crime he'd joke and lie through his cocky smile, and Wheeler would brush off his claims of innocence. This time Christian was believable, sincere, and worried, and he had a persuasive defense. He wasn't stupid and would never leave incriminating evidence in the commission of a crime. Not in a hurry to be arrested for the crime, he refused to divulge who was killed and where.

When driving home from Sarasota, Wheeler had been conflicted about Christian's predicament. Should he stay out of the murder case and let due process take its course? Even if innocent of the murder, Christian was guilty of other felonies and deserved prison. Then again, he didn't ask for any favors. He only hoped that Wheeler would keep an open mind.

The curiosity won out, and Wheeler looked into the murder, starting with unsolved homicides in Sarasota that took place over the last several months. In all, none listed a blond male as a possible suspect. He next looked at Christian's whereabouts in his statement. Perhaps the murder had occurred in Atlanta or Washington. He took a deep breath. Given the numerous homicides in those cities, his investigation would take days to research.

His phone rang, and he saw that Ralph, his ex-partner, was calling. "How's the fiancée and new job treating you?"

"Ginger, her name's Ginger and we're fine and the job is good," said Ralph. "I don't regret the transfer, but I sure miss the Miami weather. It's damn cold in DC."

"I assume you're calling because you missed me."

"No, just the weather." Ralph chuckled. "But seriously, I got a call that I thought you should be aware of. A police chief in Idaho apparently found out that last year we were partners when investigating the Captain Nemo case. He asked me all kinds of questions about your relationship with Christian Roberts."

"Chief Tucker," said Wheeler. "The man is becoming a pain in the butt. He's under the impression that Christian is blackmailing or bribing me, and that's why I haven't arrested him."

"Yeah, that pretty much sums up his call," said Ralph. "How'd you know?"

"Christian told me. Tucker went to his farm and brought up the same crap."

"Where'd Tuck come up with such an idea?"

"I mentioned I was questioning Christian about the recent Nemo attacks while we were sailing on his sloop. You know how Christian is. He clams up in an interrogation room. But in his comfort zone, he tends to opens up. Tucker must've taken it wrong."

"I can see that happening. Rather unorthodox for an agent to question a suspect on his boat. Anyway, I backed you. Told Tucker you were an honest agent and no amount of money or leverage would change that."

"It's the damn truth."

"Is it? I'm talking about your night on the beach with Christian. Before then, you couldn't wait to put Roberts away, but after that night, you and that dipshit became buddies."

"We still are, but it doesn't mean that if I find the evidence I won't arrest him."

"Whatever you say, Dave."

Wheeler slammed down the receiver without saying goodbye. He was highly irritated that Ralph questioned his integrity and methods. To catch a bee like Christian required honey or a pleasant voyage. Pin him under a net of a police station and his stinger came out. No amount of intimidation or manipulation worked. If Ralph had any brains, he'd know it by now.

Wheeler was even more aggravated with the meddling Chief Tucker. On a hunch, Tucker was making false accusations and reading more into his relationship with Christian. Sure, the young guy was a refreshing break from the mundane, and Wheeler liked him. Ralph had brought up the night on Miami Beach. It was true. After that evening, Wheeler's perception of Christian changed. Not only did they become friends, but Wheeler also owed Christian a debt of gratitude that could never be repaid.

He picked up the phone, intending to call Tucker and straighten him out so he'd end unfounded probing. "Screw him, it's none of his goddamn business," he grumbled and slammed the phone down. He hadn't broken any laws or compromised his job with the Nemo investigation. Further, Christian never had or would hold the events of that night over Wheeler's head. The young guy might be a vigilante, but he wasn't a back-stabbing sleaze ball.

Wheeler slumped back into his chair and rubbed his forehead. *I don't need this turmoil. Maybe it's time to retire.*

An agent at a nearby desk had his phone pressed to an ear, but heard Wheeler's swearing. "Everything okay, Dave?"

"Some days it rains clowns."

The agent appeared baffled but nodded his understanding. "Hold on," he said into the receiver and turned to Wheeler. "Um, you might want to take over this call, line four. It's an agent in Alaska and has to do with Captain Nemo. Four hunters were wounded by gunfire at a lodge and their helicopter was destroyed."

"Why does he think it's Nemo?"

"The men were hunting wolves, and right after the shooting, the Anchorage newspaper got an anonymous text message that said, "Stop killing the wolves—Captain Nemo."

Wheeler sighed and reached for his phone

* * *

"Jordon, we got him," said Detective Tom Graham, staring at his computer in the DC. precinct. "The DNA test came back with a hit on the Barbara Davis murder."

"So the CODIS forensics came through?" responded Jordon at the adjacent desk.

Graham grinned. "A felon can't blow his nose without it showing up on the FBI's international database." He rapidly tapped the kcys for information on the suspect.

"So who is he?"

"Goes by Christian Roberts and the biogeographic testing was dead on, Caucasian, blond, blue eyes. Strange, his rap sheet shows he was arrested twice, an assault in Florida and conspiracy in New York, but no convictions." He suddenly stopped scrolling the data and stared intently at the screen. "Jezzz, this is unbelievable."

"What?" Jordon asked, rising. He stepped behind Graham to view his computer screen.

"This guy has an alias." Graham looked up at Jordon. "Suspected of being Captain Nemo. You know, the domestic terrorist famous for murdering and blowing up things to save sharks. His latest thing is protecting wolves."

"Damn, I knew that guy seemed familiar. With his looks, I thought he was an actor. I wasted time searching movies and TV shows."

"He is a celebrity, just not the Hollywood type. The bartender at Tonic was right about his origin. He was born in Florida, and his last known address shows he lives near Sarasota."

Jordon put his hand on Graham's shoulder and smiled. "Tom, you know what this means? We've made the big time. When we bring this guy down, we should get a promotion."

"Hold on. Says we're supposed to notify the FBI if Roberts is suspected of a crime."

"Bullshit! We do all the leg work, compile the evidence, and then hand this guy over in a neat package so the FBI gets all the credit? This is our murder case, an affair that went bad. It's has nothing to do with a terrorist attack."

"I'm not screwing this up so you can blow your horn. I'm calling the Bureau."

"Fine, but wait until the afternoon. That should give us time to see a prosecutor and have him get a bench warrant from a judge. Then the case is legally ours."

"A few hours shouldn't matter."

They had met with a prosecutor, and for more incentive Jordon promised an easy conviction. The prosecutor thumbed through the police report, looked at the crime-scene photos of the dead woman, and briefly read the witness statements. He moved to the street surveillance photos of the victim and suspect, and Roberts leaving the scene. When the prosecutor came upon the DNA results confirming that Roberts's semen was found in the woman, he nodded and smiled. "You're making my job easy."

Jordon also had an ear-to-ear grin. "We aim to please."

Graham shifted uneasily from foot to foot. "How long before we get the warrant for this guy?"

The prosecutor looked at his watch. "Judge Baker is breaking for lunch soon. I should be able to catch him in his office, show him the evidence, and have him issue an arrest warrant. I'd say you'll have it within a few hours. Baker is a no-nonsense judge; loves to put people away."

"Great," said Jordon. "Let us know."

As they left the building, Jordon gave Graham an elbow nudge. "Don't be so worried. Think of this, we fly to Florida and have the locals help us arrest Roberts. Once he's in custody, the US Marshals can take over and ship him north while we celebrate with a cocktail on the beach. It's a mini vacation with no kids."

"I'll be happy when I've contacted the FBI."

CHAPTER EIGHTEEN

On the dark Sarasota Bay Christian stood in the speeding motorboat beside the driver and kept the revolver trained on Vern and the other man at the stern. Without boat lights, they reached the center of the three-mile-wide waterway and he said, "This is far enough. Pull up." The man drew back on the throttle until the boat idled in the slight chop. "Join your buddies." The man moved to the back of the boat and sat down on the outboard well between Vern and Brian.

"Change your mind, boy?" Vern called. "You decide to take us out."

"Nope, but you are going for a swim." Christian waved the weapon toward the water. "Time to get off, gentlemen."

Vern glared at him, and his two henchmen looked fretfully at the cold, black waves and the distant city lights. "That's a long ways to shore," one muttered.

Christian thought, *I can't believe these dicks*. Even though, they had tried to kill him, he was giving them a break and letting them go. His goodwill was gone. "You're leaving now, dead or alive," he said coldly. The two men scrambled overboard and floundered nearby in the water.

Vern slowly rose. "You and me aren't done."

"Didn't figure we were, Vern. Now get the fuck out before I reconsider and blow you to hell."

Vern stepped up on the boat side and dove in.

Christian reached into the bow storage and retrieved three life preservers. "So you don't drown," he said, and tossed the life jackets to the men. "But bull sharks are in these waters, and can't guarantee you won't get eaten." He smiled at the men's enormous startled eyes. He had to have some fun. The chance of a bull shark attack was probably one in a million.

Stepping behind the steering wheel, Christian shoved the throttle forward, and the boat dug in and planed off, leaving the three men in its wake. He raced across the bay toward Longboat Key and pulled up alongside to his moored sailboat. So far, his luck was holding; everything was going as planned.

Days earlier he had decided to take Sal's advice. The law and his enemies were closing in, and he needed to get away while the getting was good. With surveillance photos and his DNA, the DC. police would soon learn who and where he was. His arrest for the Barbara Davis murder was assured. The FBI and Agent Wheeler also nipped at his heels for the Captain Nemo crimes. Eventually they'd catch a break, finding evidence for charges and his conviction.

Then there were Christian's other adversaries. The Chinese probably still sought revenge for the murders in their country. Even more pressing was Secretary Sanders. Anyone who knew about the government file on misappropriation of funds had become a target and died. Christian was on that hit list. Tonight, Christian added another pursuer. Vern was pissed. Twice Christian had foiled the contract killing and slipped away. The man now had his own agenda.

Out of time and options, Christian had prepared for an extensive trip. The sloop was fueled and its water tank full. During the rainy squalls on Monday, he went ashore and bought enough provisions for several weeks. He purchased marine paint and a vinyl sheet that could be slapped on the stern, covering the sloop's original name with a new one. He also bought a cell phone at a Verizon store and registered it in his name. Yesterday he used it for a few farewell calls to those he trusted. He told Juan he was leaving and unsure when or if he'd return to Florida. Juan didn't question his decision, aware of Christian's problems, the police visits to the farm and the harassing reporters. Last year Christian had set up a lifetime trust for his horses. Monthly funds were wired into Juan's bank account to cover the farm expenses in case Christian died or disappeared. Although he'd miss his horses, he trusted Juan with their care and wasn't worried.

His second call had been more difficult. "Hey, Grandma, I'm letting you know I've transferred ownership of the trailer on Okeechobee into your name. My lawyer will contact—"

"You're going," she said, stopping him in mid-sentence. "Going and not coming back."

"I have to, Grandma."

"Oh, Crissy, I've dreaded this day. We never talked about it, but I've seen your troubles in the newspapers and knew this day was coming."

"Those troubles are my own making. I called to say goodbye and that I love you and Grandpa."

"And we love you too and will miss you terribly. But Crissy, you should call your mother. I realize you haven't gotten along since your arrest last year, but she deserves to know you're leaving."

"Grandma, I can handle her yelling and crying fits, but I don't trust her. If she learns I'm going, she's likely to call the cops or have me committed to a nut house, claiming it's for my own good. She's threatened this stuff before. Tell her for me that I love her and Frank." He ended the call with moist eyes

He had wanted to phone Trish and say goodbye but breaking up with a woman could have an adverse effect. His scar from a bullet wound was the result of ending a relationship. He didn't believe Trish would be that vindictive, but she was a reporter and could blow his cover. Why take the chance? Eventually he'd contact her.

Everything on his to-do list was done except one. He had waited for Secretary Sanders's assassins to show up. With the clock ticking, it wouldn't be long. They were under pressure to kill him before he learned about the secretary of Interior and his crimes. He also considered the killers' mental state. Murdering for a living requires confidence and a bit of arrogance. Christian should know. At the farm they had screwed up the first attempt on his life, which had to have antagonized them. Anger and haste might make them careless. An hour earlier, it had.

To prevent an ambush, a person has to know it exists. When the men sneaked aboard his sloop, Christian got the drop on them. He normally would have killed them with as little thought as squashing a bug. They had, after all, come to murder him. Instead, he refrained so Secretary Sanders would get the message; I'm on to you and will expose the files if you don't back off from me and my friends and put an end to the wolf slaughter.

He figured his threat would most likely be ignored. Exposure for fraud was nothing compared to murder, and Sanders had gone there. Credibility was also an issue. Who would be believed, the secretary of the Interior or a blackmailing terrorist? Still, he had ulterior motives for releasing Vern and his men in the bay with a long swim to shore, and it had nothing to do with his admiration for veterans.

He stopped dwelling and focused on the here and now. He applied the vinyl sheet to the stern, covering the boat's old name, and changed the registration numbers on the bow. *Hank's Dream* was renamed *The Avenger* and had a new identity.

He retrieved the cell phone off the galley counter. "I know exactly where you're going." He hopped back into the motorboat and located a small medical kit that held minimal supplies for emergencies. He slid the phone between several packets of bandages and returned the kit to the covey. Anyone using his cell GPS to find him would think he was on the motorboat in Sarasota. He tossed out the boat anchor, stepped back onto his sloop, and started the diesel engine. *The Avenger* motored south to the end of Longboat Key and turned west at New Pass, which opened into the Gulf of Mexico.

A few miles out in the Gulf, he hoisted the sails for maximum speed. The GPS had been disconnected, so he used maps and the compass to set a southwestern course. With a cool breeze on his face, the bright stars above, and the surging sloop underfoot, he felt truly free. His thoughts drifted to Vince and how he compared life to a poker game that required more than luck to win. A player had to know when to hold, fold, or take another card. Christian was deep into the game now, officially on the run. He wondered how long his freedom would last.

Over his shoulder he looked at the dark coastline and the lit high-rises of Sarasota. His exhilaration of the night faded to melancholy with dawn's approach and the last glimpse of home.

* * *

Vern clung to an orange life vest in the bay and methodically kicked his legs, swimming toward a dim light on shore. His two men, Brian and Larry, followed several yards behind him.

"Looks like another half mile," Brian said to Larry.

"Do you think he was telling the truth about the sharks?"

"Who knows? He might've been trying to scare us."

"It worked. I can't wait to get the heck out of this water."

They knew better than to include Vern in their gibberish. Despite the frigid water, Vern burned with anger. One wrong word and he was capable of drowning the two men for the tonight's botched mission. Brian's job had been to learn Roberts's habits and weaknesses. Prior to the attempt, he'd informed Vern that Roberts was a sitting duck on his boat and an easy target. Larry was supposedly the lookout, but never considered an attack from the water. Vern was in charge of the operation, so he was equally to blame for underestimating Roberts. He glanced over his shoulder and growled, "Will you two idiots shut the fuck up!"

An hour ago, Roberts had once again outmaneuvered and humiliated Vern. Instead of using a horse for his escape, Roberts slipped off his sailboat and surprised them at gunpoint. Clinging to the life preserver, Vern had watched Roberts disappear into the dark.

The sound of the outboard conveyed that Roberts trekked west back toward Longboat Key and his sailboat.

Vern gritted his chattering teeth and vowed to shoot the punk in the morning. He no longer cared about making his death appear accidental or if a murder investigation would be trouble for Sanders. Besides the embarrassment, Vern's unsuccessful dealings with Roberts had damaged his reputation and livelihood.

Vern sensed that his two men were thankful that Roberts had spared them, despite the miserable swim through possibly shark-infested waters. Vern wasn't grateful, but puzzled. Throughout his life, he'd judged men, predicting their motives and capabilities for battle. By all appearances, Roberts didn't seem like a threat, just a lanky, smartass sailor. No wonder Brian had misjudged him. Finally coming face to face with him in the dim sailboat lights, Vern had seen Roberts's hard blue eyes, unflinching when need be. The boy was dangerous. No doubt he was the terrorist Captain Nemo with a head count that surpassed Vern's. Roberts had no problem killing, so why let Vern and his men go?

Twenty yards from shore, Vern reached shallow water and was able to stand. He and his men trudged through the grass beds of broken clam shells to a seawall. They scaled the wall and walked through what seemed like a park of banyan and oak trees to the lights on an old Spanish-style home. Before ascending the steps to the door, they were hit with a flashlight beam.

"Who goes there?" called out a man in a security guard uniform.

Vern stepped to him. "We had boat trouble and had to swim to shore. Where are we?"

The guard looked at their dripping clothes. "That's too bad. You're at the John Ringling mansion. Do you want me to call the Coast Guard? They'll help you retrieve your boat."

"Right now I'd prefer you call us a cab. The water was freezing, and I could use a hot shower," said Vern. "We'll deal with the boat in the morning."

The guard made the call and led them past an extensive rose garden and up the long drive of trees and statues. Lumbering to the exit, they found the cab waiting at an iron gate on Bayshore Road. Forgoing a hot shower at the hotel, Vern instructed the cabbie to drive to the marina where Brian had rented the motorboat and they'd left their car.

Brian drove the car to their hotel near the Sarasota-Bradenton airport. Vern, in the passenger seat, had refrained from speaking to them since the swim, but in the hotel parking lot, he stepped from the car and said, "Don't get comfortable. At daybreak we're going back to his sailboat so I can shoot that bastard."

Brian reluctantly spoke up. "But, sir, Roberts said he'd expose the files and secretary if he dies."

"I don't give a shit. This is no longer business. It's personal."

At dawn Vern and his two men drove out to Longboat Key. They pulled over at a park that his men had used to maintain surveillance on Roberts's sailboat. Vern opened the car trunk and removed a rifle with a scope. In case they happened upon early-rising beach strollers, he wrapped the weapon in a towel. They walked down a sandy path through a mangrove forest that led to the bayside of the key. On a small dock that jetted out into the water, they stared across the bay. In the distance their rented motorboat was anchored off the channel, but the sailboat was nowhere in sight.

"He's gone," said Brian.

"But not for long," said Vern. "That boy will come looking for me." He turned on his heel and marched back to the car.

* * *

On Sunday morning Steve carried his laptop and Karen's bag of personal belonging and walked down the hallway. Alongside him a hospital attendant pushed Karen's wheelchair toward the exit. Frankie, one of Christian's guys, strolled several paces ahead of them, looking like a large bouncer suspiciously eying everyone in their path.

"I don't need this wheelchair," Karen complained to the attendant. "I can walk and feel fine."

"Hospital policy, ma'am," the attendant responded.

Steve smiled at his wife, glad she was returning to her old self. The group reached the outside, and Mitch, the other bodyguard, was waiting on the curb next to a black car that already held their luggage. He opened the car door and ushered Steve and Karen into the back seat. Frankie drove with Mitch in the passenger seat. The car sped away toward the airport.

"Steve, we are stopping at the house for our wedding photos." Karen said.

"We've already discussed it, and I said no. Christian wants us to go straight from the hospital to the airport."

"But those pictures are irreplaceable. I'd feel better if they were with me."

"The real estate agent is having everything put in storage before she rents out the house. You'll have them when you come home."

She fretted. "I should've remembered them when you and Mitch packed our clothes."

Mitch turned in the seat. "Steve, it's no big deal. The house is on our way, and it'll only take a minute to stop for pictures. Whatta ya say, Frankie?"

Frankie shrugged. "Okay by me, but it's your call."

"Yeah, let's do it," said Mitch. "Besides, we've got time. The nice thing about private jets, they wait for you."

"Thank you, guys," Karen said. "They're in the living room under the coffee table, so it won't take me long to grab them."

"You ain't leavin' this car," said Frankie. "Mitch can get 'em for ya."

Steve crossed his arms and stared out the window, annoyed that he had been outvoted, three to one. There was no sense arguing about the change in plans. Karen had the guys wrapped around her finger.

The car pulled up to the house, and Mitch and Frankie scanned the neighborhood and parked cars. "Looks all clear," Mitch said and climbed out. "I'll be back in a sec." He hustled up the walkway and unlocked the front door. As he stepped inside, a thunderous explosion ripped through the house. The blast sent him and the door flying ten feet backwards into the yard.

"My god!" Karen screamed. Flames bellowed out the doorway and windows.

Steve flung open the car door, intending to help Mitch.

"Stay in this goddamn car!" Frankie yelled. "I'll check him." The big guy pulled a 9 mm Glock from his shoulder holster, jumped out, and jogged to his partner. Kneeling over Mitch, he felt his neck for a pulse. He rose and looked around before hustling back to them.

"Is he all right? Is he, Frankie?" Karen cried.

Steve yanked out his cell phone to call 911.

"Put the fucking phone away," Frankie snapped, getting into the driver's seat.

"But…but I need to call an ambulance," Steve sputtered.

"Too late for that. He's gone." Frankie floored the gas pedal, and the car screeched away from the scene and raced to the airport.

"Oh, my god, he's dead?" Karen wailed.

Steve leaned forward in the seat to speak to Frankie. "I should at least call the fire department and police."

"A neighbor will do it. You make that call, and the bomber will know sooner rather than later that you survived. Better you're on the plane and outta here beforehand."

With her face in her hands, Karen moaned, "This is my fault. I send him in there. I should've listened to you, Steve."

Steve agreed but refrained from an I-told-you-so. He placed his arm around her. "It's not your fault. None of us could've known that would happen."

She lifted her head and stared at him with swollen red eyes. "Christian knew. He knew. He said go straight to the airport. Why didn't I listen?"

"Karen, you ain't to blame," said Frankie. "In our line of work Mitch and me knew the risks and that mistakes have consequences. Mitch died doin' the job."

Steve clutched his crying wife and stroked her head as the car moved down the freeway. His mind shifted from the tragic loss of Mitch to the men who wanted to kill him and Karen. He was now firmly aligned with Christian. He'd get those bastards. Obsessed with payback, Steve had yet to consider the loss of his home and everything he owned. He stared at the back of Frankie's thick neck and broad shoulders. The man was built like a bulldozer and apparently had the same amount of feelings. His buddy had died, but Frankie hadn't shown any emotion, not shedding one tear.

The threesome arrived at Reagan National Airport and drove onto the tarmac to the small jet.

"Get her aboard," Frankie said to Steve. "I'll deal with the car and bags."

Steve helped Karen up the few steps into the jet and got her settled in a back seat. She was still inconsolable over Mitch's death. Steve walked up the small aisle into the cockpit and told the pilot to put in a flight plan for Cancun, Mexico.

Frankie stood between the black car and small jet as Karen and Steve disappeared into the plane. One of the pilots approached him and asked about luggage.

Frankie opened the car trunk. "Everything goes except that one." He pointed at Mitch's black carryon and felt the knot in his stomach. The pilot loaded their gear in a storage compartment near the tail of the jet. When closing the car trunk on his friend's belongings, Frankie sighed. It seemed like shutting the lid on a coffin.

A man from the rental agency jogged over to collect the car. Frankie handed him the keys and said, "There's a bag in the trunk. Hold on to it. Someone will pick it up." After the car pulled away, Frankie pulled his cell phone from his jacket pocket. He had time for one last call before leaving the US.

"Hey, boss," he said to Sal. "We're fixin' to leave in a minute."

"You got the money that Roberts wired you?"

"Yeah, all set, but there's been a big snag. Mitch is dead."

"How the fuck did that happen?" Sal asked.

"Explosion. We stopped by the couple's house to grab some photos. The front door was rigged. Mitch opened it and was killed instantly."

"You sure it was intentional?"

"Damn sure. I know a professional job when I see it, but the cops will probably write it up as a gas leak."

"What about the couple? Anyone hurt?"

"No, me and them was in the car. It happened about a half hour ago."

"What a fucking shame. Mitch was a good guy," Sal said with a sigh. "All right, I'll contact his people, and they'll handle things on that end. Once you get where you're going and settled, I'll send another man to replace Mitch. In the meantime, don't let the Kid's friends out of your sight."

"Goes without sayin'. You gonna contact Roberts about this?"

"He's on the lam and can't be reached, but imagine I'll hear from him before long."

"The Florida boy's got some serious enemies," said Frankie.

"Yeah, but I know the Kid. When he learns about this, he'll go ballistic. Those sons of bitches better run for cover."

"Where's that leave us?"

"Don't worry. We'll also be taking heads."

CHAPTER NINETEEN

Agent Wheeler left work after a long, frustrating day and drove home. Standing before his closet, he placed his hand on his hips and gazed at an equally frustrating wardrobe. No one could accuse him of being a clotheshorse. Shopping for his clothes was one of the few things his wife had done for him before their divorce. He pushed aside several suits for work and retrieved a blue windbreaker with FBI in yellow lettering on the back. The lack of warmer attire was the result of living too long in Miami. He placed the jacket and a light sweater into his bag and considered going out to buy a heavy coat and long johns, but doubted that any store in town carried them.

His phone rang in the kitchen. Picking it up, he glanced at the caller ID. "Two calls in a week. I think you do miss me, Ralph."

Ralph ignored the jest and said seriously, "I'm calling about Christian Roberts."

"Speaking of, I was just packing for a trip to Alaska. Nemo put four hunters in the hospital up there, but the Sarasota agents spotted Christian on his boat the day of the shooting. He either hired someone to do it or it's a copycat."

"Forget Alaska, Dave. I've got the ammunition to blow Roberts out of the water. I just spent a few hours with two detectives working a murder case in DC. A woman was strangled in her government office building, and Roberts did it. Eyewitnesses saw him with her before the murder. Surveillance photos show him leaving the crime scene same time as her death, and best of all, his DNA was found in her."

Wheeler eased onto a kitchen stool, not sharing Ralph's enthusiasm. "He said he was in DC., and his car GPS proved he traveled there."

"More evidence to fuel the fire," Ralph said. "The obnoxious prick is going to burn."

"All right, I'll reschedule the Alaskan trip and catch a flight up to Washington."

"No need. We're coming to Florida. These detectives already secured a warrant. It's only a matter of locating Roberts and making the arrest. Do you know where he is?"

"I imagine he's on his boat in Sarasota or at his horse farm in Myakka. You can check his phone GPS. Do you know when they're going to make his arrest?"

"If he's where you say, it could be as soon as tomorrow. I'm coming to identify Roberts and coordinate with the local FBI, US Marshals, and Sarasota police or Manatee sheriff, depending on his location."

"Sounds like overkill," said Dave. "That's a lot of law enforcement for a guy who's never resisted."

"Everyone wants a piece of this SOB, especially me."

"Just keep in mind this guy loves to get under your skin." Last year Ralph had lost his cool when interviewing the aggravating Christian and suggested they step outside and duke it out. Dave prevented the fight and lucky for Ralph because later Dave witnessed Christian in action. Ralph wouldn't have stood a chance.

"Yeah, I know he's a wiseass, but I'll have the last laugh when I throw the joker in a cage."

"We'll see."

The call ended, and Wheeler focused on the murder case. It wasn't an eye opener. Christian had already told Wheeler about it on the sloop, saying the evidence against him would be overwhelming, and he'd be falsely accused of a murder. If Wheeler had acknowledged to Ralph that Christian confided in him, it would have attested to their friendship and added more suspicion to Tucker's witch hunt.

With knowledge of the murder, Wheeler was back to the struggle of scruples. Should he let the arrest, trial, and sentencing play out? Even if Christian hadn't killed the woman, he belonged in jail. Or should Wheeler be objective and search for an alternate killer? If he did, it would further demonstrate that he watched Christian's back.

His thoughts shifted to Christian's arrest. A slew of law enforcement officers would converge on him, possibly as soon as tomorrow. Considering his notorious reputation as Captain Nemo, he was bound to make them nervous. Wheeler turned on his laptop computer, and using his FBI clearance, he searched for the cell tower that was currently connected to Christian's cell phone. The trace showed his phone was no longer on Sarasota Bay, but at a Bradenton marina off US 41, a few miles north of the airport. Christian must've moved his sloop.

Wheeler closed the laptop and pondered his next move. He could drive to Bradenton tonight and take Christian into custody without a fuss, and hold him for questioning in the local jail until the arrest warrant arrived. Christian then wouldn't be subjected to trigger-happy officers.

He slipped into his suit jacket, which covered his shoulder-holstered weapon, and stuffed his badge, wallet, and car keys into his pockets. He grabbed his laptop, hustled out to his car, and started the hundred-mile trip across the state and another hundred miles north up the west coast on I-75.

Three hours later he pulled off the highway at a marina on Bowlee's Creek. He walked to the docks, thinking Christian's large sloop, *Hank's Dream,* should be easy to spot. It wasn't there. Had Christian fueled up his boat and left the marina? Wheeler returned to his car and did another search on the laptop. Using the mapped-out guidance system, he zeroed in on Christian's phone that verified it was still at this marina. Narrowing the location search, he returned to the docks and discovered the phone was somewhere on one of the motorboats in the slips belonging to a boat rental agency.

He laughed. "That squirrelly bastard left his scent to throw off the hunting dogs." Christian had obviously hidden his phone on a boat to fool anyone looking for him. The move suggested he was on the run.

The marina and boat rental company had closed at nine o'clock, and there was no one to question or give permission to board a boat and find the phone. It would have to wait until tomorrow, when he would also track down Christian's sloop and vehicles, but Wheeler was betting one would be missing. Smarter to sail or drive out of the area, since public transportation such as airports, bus and train stations had surveillance and security, making them risky.

He drove to a nearby Ramada Inn and checked in. In his room, he sat down on the bed and called Ralph. "Are you still coming to Florida?"

"Actually the detectives and I just boarded a plane for Tampa, so I can't talk long. Roberts's cell is at a Bradenton marina. We're set for an early morning arrest."

"Recall saying you'll have the last laugh. Don't count on it."

* * *

Secretary Sanders kept up appearances, smiling and working with his staff and fellow cabinet members, but deep down, he boiled. Vern should have contacted him two days ago and confirmed Roberts had been eliminated. Impatient and worried, he had instructed his secretary to do a search on Captain Nemo in the interest of government security. Roberts was a media darling, widely believed to be the terrorist Captain Nemo. His death would surely be splashed across the internet and newspapers.

Sanders tapped his fingers on the desk and stared at the mobile phone. Should he call Vern and ask what the hell was going on? Vern had said he'd make Roberts's death appear like an accidental drowning. Perhaps the corpse had yet to be found in Sarasota Bay, but that still didn't explain Vern's lack of communication. Another possibility was more disturbing. Roberts got the upper hand and killed Vern and his men.

Sanders picked up the phone, but there was a tap on the door and his secretary entered, holding some papers.

"Sir, I found a few recent articles about Captain Nemo. The first is from the Anchorage paper, dated this week." She placed the printouts before him. "The second clipping was in this morning's paper."

"Thank you." He grinned. "That'll be all."

After she left, he quickly scanned the story about the attack on four hunters in Alaska. Captain Nemo was claiming responsibility. If Roberts was really in Alaska, Vern might be tracking him down, which would account for his silence. The job wasn't done.

The second article was more unsettling because of Sanders's involvement. The DC. police had a suspect in the Barbara Davis murder, and it was Christian Roberts, assumed to be Captain Nemo, but he had yet to be apprehended.

"Christ," Sanders muttered. If Roberts was still alive, his arrest would have the police digging into his affairs. They might uncover the files that showed Sanders's fraud and could reveal another possible motive for Davis's murder. He phoned Vern.

Vern answered. "What do you want?"

"What do I want? I want to know if Roberts is dead."

"I told you I'd call when he was. You see me calling?" Vern's sarcasm had replaced his courteous military manner, and he no longer addressed Sanders as sir.

"So he's alive. What happened?"

"The guy's a cat with nine lives. He got away, but I'll get him."

"Vern, he needs to be dead before he learns I'm involved."

Vern chuckled. "Too late, Sanders, he knows. In fact he gave me a message for you. He wants the president to present a plan to Congress that would have researchers make all decisions concerning wildlife, especially wolves. The bill would take that judgment call out of political hands. He also wants us—you and I—to leave him and his friends alone, and if you don't, the files and your name will go public."

"He said that? You spoke to him and did nothing?"

"He was pointing a gun at me."

"Why didn't you call me about his demands?"

"Because our agendas have parted ways," said Vern. "I want the motherfucker dead, so I had my men blow up the house of his accomplices, the Arlington couple. That ends negotiations. He'll be gunning for us, and that's when I'll take him out."

"But what about the files now that you've killed his friends?" Sanders asked. "He might take them public before you get to him."

"That's your problem."

"It's also yours. Today's paper says he's a suspect in the Davis murder. When the police arrest him, he'll run his mouth and also name you. That would put us both in jeopardy."

"It's possible, but I doubt he'll have the law and courts do his dirty work. In his mind prison would be too good for us."

"What makes you think that?"

"He's Captain Nemo, doesn't play by the rules."

* * *

The first day of the Gulf crossing, the seas were relatively calm for winter, the swells two to three feet. Besides manning the sails and checking charts, Christian had little to do. The sloop had a TV, but he favored the outdoors. His only entertainment had been a pod of dolphins that zipped and jumped in front of the bow and the sighting of two large sea turtles. He watched the flying fish leap from the waves and glide for fifty to a hundred feet before splashing down. He'd seen those little fish many times when venturing out in the Gulf but never appreciated their capacity to swim and fly. The planet held many fascinating creatures, but over one million species were under threat of a mass extinction because of mankind. Even the oceans he loved were in trouble with growing amounts of mercury and discarded plastic that created drifts the size of Texas and killed marine life. Every time he turned around, his purpose was reconfirmed. *I've become a bad guy, but for good reasons.*

In the late afternoon, he considered dinner. With the sloop on autopilot, he decided to cook up some fast and easy grub in the galley. It would be another yawner. The monotony ended when he spotted a flock of seagulls up ahead, circling and diving for bait. Beneath the gulls the surface erupted with splashes from large fish. He raced into the cabin and took from the rafters a stout fishing rod with a four-inch silver spoon. He cast out the lure, released a fair amount of line, and set the bail so the spoon dragged beyond the stern. He placed the pole in a holder and adjusted course toward the action of birds and fish. He had the knowledge to catch almost anything that swam, but he had never been a fan of trolling. The mindless sport required no talent, only the brute strength to reel in a fish. Under these circumstances, though, a fresh-caught meal would go well with canned beans.

He sailed into the large school of sardines and quickly spotted their attackers, kingfish. They were the largest member of the mackerel family and great eating when grilled. As soon as the lure reached the school, he heard the clicking and then zing of the reel. Fish on. He snatched the pole out of the holder. The battle was exhilarating but brief. Within ten minutes a yard-long king mackerel lay at his feet, its shiny dark-blue back and yellow-spotted sides glistening in the sun.

He cleaned the fish, fired up the portable grill, and cooked the fillets. The large fish would provide meals for three days, the length of his voyage. Preferring the breezy deck and ocean view to eating in the galley, he took his plate topside in time for the dazzling sunset of gold, orange, and shocking pink framed in lavender clouds.

The next few days were uneventful. He would have liked to call Sal and tell him he'd gotten away clean. He also wondered if the same was true of Steve and Karen. Had his threats convinced Vern and the secretary to leave them alone? Sal was in contact with his man Frankie, and he'd know if they made it to Mexico without incident. Before leaving Sarasota, he and Sal had agreed on no calls. It was too risky. The FBI could be monitoring Sal's calls, and even a burner phone might pinpoint Christian's location. No calls anyway. There were no cell towers in the middle of the Gulf, so Christian's phone had no bars for a call.

The sloop autopilot allowed him to take breaks for sleeping and cleaning up. In the head, he stepped from the shower in the rolling boat and gazed into the mirror at his stubble. It brought back memories of his wife. Prior to their meeting, he shaved daily. Florida was too hot for facial hair, but Allie had loved his five o'clock shadow. She said he looked sexier, so for her he had kept a rugged look. After her death and with no one to please, he went back to a clean face. Today he decided to keep the scruff. His boat had been disguised with a new name and number, and a beard might make him less recognizable ashore.

The quiet days of sailing left him reflecting on all that had happened, all he'd left behind, and what lay ahead. His journey had started with saving wolves. The goal became sidetracked with conspiracy and murder. Like the maligned wolves, he was also on the run for a crime he hadn't committed. The twists, turns, and complications had delayed his success, but he still believed in his cause.

On the third evening he cruised a mile off of the Mexican coast and came upon the bright lights of Cancun on the Yucatan Peninsula. The city confirmed his location and compass reading. The sloop surged southward, past the high-rise hotels that lined the beaches. *Just like home. Another tourist trap,* he thought and moved on, leaving the town in his wake.

With land close by and the abundance of boats in the area, he didn't trust the autopilot so he could not sleep. His boat could run aground or hit another vessel in the dark. The last forty miles of his voyage became a night of coffee drinking to stay alert.

At daybreak he gazed at Cozumel ahead in the distance. The island was roughly five miles off the coast of Playa del Carmen. He turned the sloop into the wind, lowered the sails, and motored closer. He came upon a stationary post out in the water with no sign or number, but it indicated the mouth of a narrow inlet that was shrouded in jungle. Better yet, the barnacles on the post were submerged under water, proof it was high tide. The sloop's deep shaft was less likely to run aground in the inlet.

He slowed the engine to a crawl and turned into the mouth of the inlet. Carefully guiding the boat, he shifted his attention from what lay ahead to the clear bottom below and to the depth gauge. Even with a high tide, the sloop could still get stuck and stranded in a shallow waterway.

The channel was apparently a tidal creek, a bayou. The banks consisted of a mangrove forest with oyster beds attached to their raised roots. The razor-sharp shells would shred human flesh if one attempted to traverse it. After a little while, he began to see signs of civilization. A few breaks in the mangrove revealed some houses, shacks really, with small weather-beaten boats attached to pilings. The dilapidated places appeared uninhabited, but he was in Mexico, home to many poor people. Through the heavy underbrush he caught glimpses of a shell road.

The sloop rounded a bend, and the waterway widened into a circular cove that contained a small port. A spider web of pilings and planks jutted out into the basin and served as docks for a crude fleet of fishing boats. At the far end was a long, open-air warehouse with a crumbling seawall and fractured cement boat ramp. The rundown tin building was obviously where the fisherman unloaded and sold their catch.

When in Sarasota prior to his journey he had used Google Maps and had found the tiny, remote marina tucked into the jungle with sparse, small houses in the area. It was perfect for his needs. He motored into the cove, and heads appeared from below deck on the boats. By the time he crossed the cove to the marina, a small crowd of Mexicans stood on the boats, docks, and shore watching him and his fancy sloop. Pulling up alongside the seawall, he cut the engine. Two men sitting on wooden crates left the warehouse to help him tie up. One man grabbed the bow line and the other took the stern. They fastened the lines to docking cleats.

"Gracias," Christian said and hopped off his boat. His Spanish was limited, so he continued in English. "I'd like to keep my boat here. Who do I talk to?"

The two men frowned. Either they didn't speak English or were baffled that an American would put his big, expensive sailboat there.

A short, stout Mexican wandered up. "That would be me, Señor. I own this marina."

Christian stepped to him. "I'd like to rent a slip. How much?"

The owner eyed the sloop and said, "Fifty US dollars a day."

Christian knew he was being overcharged for a slip at this rundown marina because he obviously appeared to have money. It didn't matter. Sanctuary was far more important. "Tell you what I'll do. I'll give you two hundred a day if you add security. Don't want my boat stripped."

The marine owner grunted. "We might be poor, but we are not thieves."

"Sorry," Christian said, lifting his hands and exposing his palms in surrender. "Didn't mean to offend."

The owner nodded. "You are wise to be cautious. Some marinas would not only strip your boat but take it." On the seawall, he walked the length of the sloop. After surveying the boat, he scratched his head and said, "She is a beauty. For the money, you could keep her at the finest harbor in Mexico."

"I know, but that's the other part of the payment. I don't want the passport hassle. Two hundred a day and no questions asked."

With narrow judging eyes, marina owner stared at Christian, obviously processing the illegal arrangement. He grinned wide.

"Señor, you have come to the right place." He offered a weathered hand. "I'm Jose."

In the warehouse, Jose led Christian into his tiny, cluttered office. Christian paid cash for a week's dock rent. Jose said that besides around-the-clock security his men would swab and polish the deck and scrub the hull at no extra charge.

After the transaction, Jose removed a bottle of tequila from a desk drawer and poured two shots. He offered one to Christian and lifted his glass in a toast. "Welcome to Mexico, Señor Christian."

* * *

In Playa del Carmen, Mexico, Steve sat at the kitchen counter with a view of the pool and the surrounding small jungle. Beyond the backyard on the golf course, two men stood with clubs on the putting green. He turned from the activity in the lavish neighborhood and focused on his laptop, responding to an email from his assistant who was keeping Steve's company up and running. Before leaving the US, Steve had set up internet accounts on the dark web to stay in touch, but the time change between Mexico and DC. had him on a different work schedule.

In the sunken living room, Angel chuckled at the program on the TV. He was the new bodyguard who had arrived yesterday. The Italian appeared to be in his mid-forties with an average build, but his squinty dark eyes gave him the sinister look of a killer, Steve thought despite his name. With Mitch's murder, New York had sent a badass replacement.

At eleven in the morning the two-story house was quiet because Karen and Frankie had left an hour ago to do some food shopping.

Several days earlier Steve, Karen, and Frankie had departed DC and landed in Cancun. Frankie leased an SUV, unsure of the length of their stay. They drove the forty miles south to Playa del Carmen, an upscale little city with well-to-do residents and visitors. They entered the gated neighborhood, and the real estate agent met them at the furnished four-bedroom house with the rent contract and key. Three had settled into a routine, but since arriving Karen seemed closer to Frankie than Steve.

Steve tapped the computer keys, replying to an email when his burner phone buzzed. Only one person had its number. He picked it up and said, "Hey, Christian."

"Steve, jot this down." He conveyed an address as Steve wrote on a note pad. "It's a little joint not far from you. I'll be waiting."

Steve dropped the pen. "You're here? You're in Mexico?"

"See you in a bit, buddy," Christian said, and the phone call ended.

Steve stood, staring at the address for a long moment. He recognized the street, having lived in Playa del Carmen a few years back. The location was in the poorer section of town. "Angel, we need to leave. I'm meeting someone."

"Sure thing, Steve-o," Angel said, rising from the semicircular couch. "Let me just grab my piece and the keys."

By the time Steve scribbled a message for Karen, saying that he was going out and not to worry, the bodyguard was waiting at the front door. They climbed in the second car, a rented silver compact, and Angel drove past manicured homes toward the main road. At the guard station he nodded at the two uniformed men and asked Steve, "So where we off to?"

"Take a right toward town."

"Who ya meetin'?" Angel asked with his Brooklyn accent.

"The man who signs your paychecks."

"The Florida boy," said Angel. "Never met him, but heard some shit."

Steve had noticed that Frankie, Mitch, and now Angel never used Christian's name, but referred to him as the Florida boy. "So what did you hear?" he asked, expecting to learn about one of Christian's terrorist attacks to save wildlife.

"The way Frankie tells it, the boy got pissed off and nearly killed Frankie and the bosses. He took them for a speedboat ride and nearly drove into a big-ass freighter on Tampa Bay. The last second, he spun the wheel, and the freighter cruised past 'em within arm's reach." Angel laughed. "Frankie said he ain't never been so scared in his life, screamin' like a little girl. And that big man don't scare. Yeah, not smart to fuck with the Florida boy. He's crazy."

They drove into an area absent of tourists and pulled up to the restaurant on a street corner. The trashy colorful joint featured a large, open cabana covering tables and potted palms. Despite wearing sunglasses and sporting a slight beard, the blond stood out in the crowd of dark-haired Mexican diners.

Christian acknowledged Steve with a smile. Steve waved and walked to Christian's table. Angel leaned against a post to guard them.

Steve sat down and mockingly said, "You sure picked a fancy restaurant."

"Prefer places off the beaten path. The food is usually authentic and better. This one came highly recommended." He rested his fork on a platter of fish, shrimp, and octopus floating in a clear sauce. "Their ceviche is fantastic. You should try it," he said and took a sip of a margarita.

"Raw fish, no thanks."

"It's not raw. The fish was marinated in lime, and the citrus acid cooked it. You probably also don't eat oysters on the half shell, sushi, or rare steak."

"Those dishes are a health risk."

"Give me a break." Christian laughed.

Steve smiled, realizing the absurdity of preaching to the risk-taker. "So you came to Mexico."

"Things were getting too hot in Florida."

"Washington as well. Have you heard they blew up my house, and Mitch, one of the men you sent, was killed in the explosion?"

Christian's smile vanished and he dropped his napkin on the plate of half-eaten food. "Damn," he muttered and shook his mop of yellow hair. "No, I hadn't heard. I've been on my boat and out of touch for the last several days. You're the first person I've contacted. How'd it happen, Steve?"

A waiter approached for Steve's order, halting the discussion. "Just a margarita," Steve said. The waiter left, and he answered Christian "After Karen was released from the hospital, we stopped by the house on our way to the airport."

"Goddamn it, Steve," he growled. "I told you—"

"I know. I know what you told us." Steve stared down at the table. "It was just a big screwup. Karen wanted our wedding photos at the house, and the guys were okay with stopping to get them. Mitch opened our front door, and an explosion killed him instantly." He lifted his gaze to Christian's. "Karen still hasn't gotten over it. She miserable and blames herself. She barely talks to me, probably because I was against going to the house, but, Christian, I'd never throw that in her face."

Christian breathed in a sigh and said quietly, "She shouldn't feel that she's to blame. Shit happens when you deal with assholes." He looked up. "That happened on Sunday?"

"Yeah, Sunday morning."

"The fuckers," he cursed. "I warned Sanders's men to back off and that if any harm came to me and my friends, I'd take the files public. They had time to make a call and prevent the explosion. That means they're not willing to play ball."

"Are you going to release the files then?"

"Eventually, but the punishment doesn't fit their crimes. And if they're in jail, I can't get at them easily."

CHAPTER TWENTY

Charlie Tucker trudged through knee-deep snow and retrieved the morning paper in the yard. A Canadian front had blown into the little town of Salmon, Idaho, and dumped another foot of snow overnight. He hustled into the foyer, stomped his boots, and hung up his jacket. Strolling into the kitchen, he said to his wife, Liz, "Damn cold out there." He placed the paper on the table. "Freezing my butt off for news that's mostly crap. No credibility these days."

Without turning from the sizzling bacon on the stove, Liz asked, "With this front are you going to work today?"

"Sure I'm going." He scowled "It's my job." He poured a cup of coffee and sat down at the table.

"Last night you said it was rather quiet. The out-of-state hunters were gone, and the weather was so bad no one would be out committing crimes. I thought you might take the day off."

"As soon as I do, there's sure to be a fender-bender." He opened the paper and began reading while waiting for breakfast. "Fools," he grumbled.

"What is it?"

"This damn group, Idaho for Wildlife, is thinking about having another predator hunt. The director says they won't call it a wolf hunt because it brings out the nuts. Man's an idiot if he thinks the animal fanatics will stay away. The protestors will fire up the hunters, and I'm left with keeping the peace. All this trouble over a few dead coyotes. They've wiped out so many wolves here that nobody got one in the last contest."

She set the plates of bacon and eggs on the table and joined him. "Ann's husband is a hunter, and he says these contests are necessary. Wolves are killing all the deer and elk."

"That's horseshit. State figures show roughly seven hundred wolves are in Idaho, but the biologists figure it's less than three hundred. Either way, the deer and elk number in the thousands. There aren't enough wolves to affect the population. And I know Ann's husband. He's a moron who just likes to shoot things."

"Charlie, that's a terrible thing to say. Ann is a good friend."

"Well, I'm fed up. Since Captain Nemo bombed the restaurant, I've done my own research on wolves. Over the last few years, Idaho spent over a million of our tax dollars to take out wolves. Now they want more money. It's an outrage. They could better spend their budget on new vehicles for my department."

She smiled at him. "I didn't realize you care about wolves."

"I don't, but there's something about a wolf howling at night. The sound echoing through the valley was kind of thrilling, like I was back in the wilderness, before houses and roads were built."

"That's so romantic, Charlie."

"Now don't go blabbing about it. People get the wrong idea." He took a bite of toast, and his thoughts returned to the predator hunt. He tapped the article. "If they go through with this contest, the wolf controversy won't just stir up the protesters and hunters, but it could bring back the terrorist. He apparently isn't satisfied with blowing up restaurants and helicopters. He's moved on to shooting some hunters in Alaska."

"Do you really think he'd come back? You flew to Florida and met him."

"I know a car full of assassins didn't faze him. Anyone with balls like his is liable to do anything."

After breakfast Charlie drove to the police station. Two steps inside, and Helen, his secretary blocked his path. "Chief, more news on Christian Roberts," she said and handed him some printouts.

Charlie took off his hat and wearily ran his hand over his balding head. "What's he done now?"

"It's horrible. The story says he's suspected of murdering a woman in Washington, DC."

"DC? What's that got to do with wolves?" he said, glancing at the paper.

"Nothing. That proves he's innocent."

He grinned. "Helen, you have no clue of what he's capable of doing."

"Well, Christian didn't do that, Chief. He's an animal lover and has never hurt a woman," she said with a huff and returned to her desk. Helen was middle-aged, single, and slightly overweight, and she lived with five cats. Upon Charlie's request, she'd dug up every photo, newspaper, and magazine article on the swoon-worthy Mr. Roberts. His secretary now had a crush on the terrorist.

Charlie wandered into his office, fixed a cup of coffee, and sat down at his desk to give the printout his full attention. After reading it, he held his chin in contemplation. Helen could be right. Murdering a woman seemed out of character. He'd pegged Roberts as an intelligent young guy, but mixed up. Charlie never saw a sadistic side or the hint of a woman abuser.

He picked up the phone to feel out Wheeler, the man who knew Roberts best. "Chief Tucker here. Made any progress on Nemo?"

"I'm flying to Alaska next week," said Agent Wheeler. "Captain Nemo has taken credit for shooting and wounding four hunters. I want to see what the agents up there have uncovered."

"I heard about that, but what about this woman's murder in DC? Roberts is a suspect."

"That's a local crime, and the Washington police are handling it. They've already secured an arrest warrant for Roberts."

"So you're not getting mixed up in the case, even though it concerns him?"

"The murder, by all accounts, is neither a terrorist attack or related to Captain Nemo. The case falls under local jurisdiction, and the district department is in charge. Right now there's no need for an FBI investigation."

"But Roberts is Captain Nemo, so this murder deserves your full attention."

"May I remind you, Chief Tucker, there's no solid evidence connecting Christian Roberts to Captain Nemo."

"That's bull crap, Wheeler. You forget I've met the fella. We both know he's the terrorist."

"It's your opinion, not fact," Wheeler snapped. "And your presumptions have proven to be misguided."

Charlie lifted an eyebrow, detecting Wheeler's hostility. Apparently, he was still miffed over their last phone call, when Charlie had suggested that Roberts might be bribing or blackmailing the agent, not buying that their friendship was based on mutual respect. Something was fishy. "So you're not getting involved with the murder?"

"The FBI's only role is assisting the police with Roberts's arrest. I drove to Sarasota to apprehend him, but he and his sailboat were gone. It appears he left town."

"You went alone to make this arrest?"

"Christian knows me and wouldn't give me any trouble. If I took him into custody it would have been safer for everyone involved."

"You mean safer for your boy, not having to face all those lawmen guns," said Charlie. "Wheeler, this raises more questions about your relationship with him. With no witnesses around, you might've found him and warned him about the warrant. Could be why he took off out of the blue."

"Chief Tucker, I am tired of your unfounded accusations. When I have the proof that Christian Roberts is Captain Nemo, he'll be charged. I'm aware you contacted my old partner to dig up dirt that I'm in cahoots with Roberts. You're dragging my reputation through the mud with your imagined scandal. It better stop." Before Charlie could respond, Wheeler hung up.

"No one hangs up on me," he scoffed and stomped around his office for several minutes. Finally calm enough for another call, he sat down and looked up a number in his address book.

A woman answered. "Senator Riley's office."

"This here's Chief Tucker in Salmon, Idaho. Is John busy? I need to talk to him."

She said she'd check.

"Hello, Charlie," said the senator. "Luckily you caught me between meetings. What can I do for you?"

"I had you talk the FBI chief of staff into having Agent Wheeler take over the Captain Nemo case, but I fear I've made a mistake." He laid out his suspicions. Wheeler and Christian Roberts, alleged to be Captain Nemo, had both freely admitted they were friends, which was not the typical association between an agent and his suspect. They had even spent time on Roberts's sailboat. And the latest, Wheeler would not take part in a DC murder case, even though the evidence implicated Roberts. Charlie believed that Roberts was paying Wheeler off or had something on him.

"John, I've been a lawman all my adult life and can smell a rat," said Charlie. "I can't put my finger on it, but something's going on between those two. Roberts is a murderer and belongs behind bars, and Wheeler isn't helping to put him away."

"That is troubling, especially since Captain Nemo is on the FBI's Top Ten Most Wanted list. Sailing together does seem unscrupulous. And you say Agent Wheeler repudiated the agency from the murder case?"

"He said the FBI would assist with the arrest, but otherwise, it's not getting involved. That's another thing. Wheeler went to arrest Roberts by himself, no partner, backup, or US Marshals. It's unheard of when confronting a suspected felon. Then Roberts vanished before the troops showed up. That makes me wonder if Wheeler gave him a heads-up."

"All right, Charlie, I'll give Quantico a call and ask them to look into it."

* * *

Christian finished his lunch with Steve, but with so many people within earshot, they didn't discuss Captain Nemo or future plans for Sanders, Vern, and his men. "I was going back to my boat and catch some shut-eye. I'm still whipped from this trip," he said, rising from the table, "but in light of Sunday, we need a private chat at the house to get things rolling."

"Christian, I'd appreciate it if you would also talk to Karen. She likes you and will listen. Maybe you can get her out of her slump."

"No problem," he said and removed his wallet from a back pocket of his cutoff jeans. "Hold up for a minute. I need to tell my ride I don't need him." He dropped cash on the table for lunch and walked to Jose, still eating on a picnic bench. The marina owner had given Christian a lift in his old pickup. Christian told Jose he was heading out and was unsure if he'd return to his boat tonight.

"Don't worry, Señor Christian," said Jose. "My warehouse workers will guard her like she's my baby."

Christian smiled. Universally boaters shared a common bond for their vessels. He and Steve left the restaurant, and his bodyguard stood near the silver car on the street.

"Christian, this is Angel," said Steve. "He took over for Mitch."

"It's an honor to meet you, Mr. Roberts," Angel said and shook Christian's hand.

"Angel was telling me about your hairy boat ride with Frankie," Steve said, grinning. "He said you nearly crashed into a freighter."

"I was making a point," said Christian.

Steve lifted his eyebrows. "Okay then, let's get to the house."

They piled into the car and soon drove through the gates into a persnickety neighborhood, the houses rivaling those on the wealthy Keys off Sarasota. At the house, they climbed out of the car, and Steve and Angel walked through a courtyard toward the front door. Christian hung back momentarily, staring up into a tree at an olive-green bird that resembled a large pigeon. The tropical Yucatan held a variety of creatures he had never seen. Fascinated, he watched the bird for a minute before walking to the house.

When Christian stepped inside, Steve announced, "Karen, I have a surprise for you."

"Oh my, Christian," she exclaimed in the kitchen. She rushed to the foyer and hugged him. "I'm so sorry about Mitch," she said, tearing up. "I wanted my stupid wedding pictures, and it got him killed."

He embraced her and kissed her forehead. "Hush now," he whispered. "I'm the one who should apologize. I got you involved in this mess, but Karen, let's put the blame where it belongs. Sanders's men did these terrible things, not you or me." He lifted her chin and stared into her eyes. "I know how you feel. Been there. Got so consumed in guilt and grief I couldn't breathe. I learned that living with regret is letting the past cripple the present. You have to put the shit behind you, take back your life, and move on."

She nodded and wiped away her tears. "I'm so glad you're here."

Frankie strolled to him and said, "Chris, how you doin'?"

When it came to the mob guys, Christian knew that 'how you doing' was a greeting, not a question. Frankie didn't give a shit how Christian was doing. "Good seeing you again, Frankie." He offered his hand, but the big Italian pushed it aside and gave him a bear hug.

After squishing Christian, Frankie smiled. "Yeah, you too."

Frankie had been one of Vince's regular guys, so Christian spent time with him, but after Vince died, Frankie left Florida and returned to New York. He occasionally worked for Sal, like now. The group moved poolside and over drinks, the small talk turned to business.

"Christian, have you been following the news on the Internet?" Steve asked.

"Haven't bothered."

"You're making headlines. The DC police are accusing you of the Barbara Davis murder. They have a warrant for your arrest."

"Knew that was coming," said Christian. "Partly why I'm here. It's kinda a paradox. With all the crap I've done, I'm being charged for something I didn't do."

"There's more," Steve went on. "Captain Nemo is claiming responsibility for shooting some hunters at an Alaskan lodge."

"Alaska?" Christian frowned in confusion. "I didn't do that either. Hell, never even been there." He suddenly recalled his conversation with Bill when he had expressed his disgust that Congress had removed protection for wolves and bears in Alaska. And the state's plan to kill those animals in the wildlife refuges so hunters had more caribou. Bill mentioned he might visit the state. The crazy little guy must've taken up Christian's cause. "How many died?"

"None, but four were wounded. If you didn't do it, who did?"

"I've got an admirer who probably did it."

"So you're getting falsely accused," said Frankie. "But I wanna know what you *are* gonna to do about those bastards who killed Mitch. I spoke to Sal, and we want in. I'll take 'em out."

"I'm sure you would," said Christian, "but they'll be dealt with in good time and on my terms."

"No disrespect, Chris," said Frankie. "You might've dug up these worms, but when they murdered one of our guys, they became Sal's and my concern. A tap to the head and it's done."

Angel nodded, concurring.

Steve swirled the ice in his glass. "I agree with Frankie. Those assholes killed my friend, Felix and my dog. They put my wife in the hospital and blew up my house. The sooner they're dead, the safer Karen and I will feel."

Christian glanced at the three men who wanted to rush in and get satisfaction. He looked to Karen. "What do you think?"

"Of course I want them gone, but I trust you." She turned to Steve and Frankie. "Let Christian handle it."

Frankie released a growl and stood. "The Florida Boy has brains and guts, but I've got experience, been at this longer. This bullshit needs to be handled now."

Christian leaned back, crossed his arms, and stared up at the looming, angry mobster who called him the *Florida Boy*. When Vince was alive and took Christian under his wing, the guys had called him *Vince's boy*. As Christian's reputation grew, the *boy* term was used with fondness and respect. Frankie, however, was demeaning him, but confronting and arguing with the big man was counterproductive.

"Frankie, you mentioned bullshit," Christian said with a smile. "That reminds me of a joke a rancher told me. Two bulls, one young, one old, stood on a hill and gazed down at a herd of cows. The young bull says, 'let's run down there and screw one of those cows.' The old bull says, 'let's walk down and screw all of them.'" Everyone grinned.

Christian stood. "Now I'm a cracker, born and raised in Florida, and you all are from Washington and New York. All my life I've heard Northerners bitch about us slow-moving, slow-talking Southerners, preaching, 'This is how we do it up North.' Let me enlighten ya, slow doesn't mean stupid or less motivated."

Christian faced the small group. "I realize y'all have a dog in this fight, but I wanna handle this like the old bull. Take my time and screw all of them, even the ones behind the scene. Yeah, I dug up these worms. That makes it my fishing trip, hooking every worm so none wiggle away. It's not up for debate."

They glanced at one another. Frankie said, "Okay, Chris. We'll do it your way."

* * *

In DC Trish stood before the police precinct. She fluffed up her hair and straightened her skirt before pushing through the door. "I'm Trish Stevenson with *The Washington Post*," she said to the officer at the lobby desk. "I have an appointment with Detective Graham concerning the Barbara Davis murder." The officer picked up the phone to summon Graham. Several minutes later the detective arrived. Wearing a shirt and tie, the black man appeared to be in his early forties with a clean-cut look. He greeted her with a smile and open hand.

"Thank you for coming, Miss Stevenson," he said, shaking her hand.

"It's a two-way street. I'm hoping you'll update me on this murder. You've secured a warrant for Christian Roberts's arrest for murdering Barbara Davis. Are you any closer to catching him?"

"We learned he left Sarasota on his sailboat, but it shouldn't be long before he's apprehended. Those boats aren't exactly fast."

Trish smiled. "You don't know him. He's a very good sailor. I also don't believe he's guilty of killing that woman."

"Innocent men don't run, but I asked you here because you do know him. Let's go upstairs and talk."

They walked toward the elevator, and she said, "A reporter has the right to protect a source, so I'm not sure how much I'll tell you."

Graham shrugged with a grin. "I doubt a boyfriend qualifies as a source."

"I've interviewed Christian Roberts about his possible ties to Captain Nemo, but we are only acquaintances."

"Do you often sleep with your acquaintances?" he asked as they stepped into an elevator. "You give me any information that you don't think steps on your constitutional rights."

Trish felt like doing an about-face and running, but her reporter's curiosity won out. "What makes you think I slept with Christian?" she asked when they entered a closed interrogation room. She sat down at a small table that held a case file folder.

He stepped to a video camera in the corner. "Do you mind?"

"Go ahead," she said, despite the consequence that her statement could make her a witness and land her in court.

Graham turned on the camera record and turned back to Trish. "To answer your question," he said. "Captain Nemo contacts you to publicize his terrorist attacks, and it is common knowledge that you and Roberts are tight." He sat down and opened the file. "The FBI keeps track of him, and according to them, Roberts phones you often, and the GPS in his Porsche shows his travels. The weekend of the Davis murder, he was in DC and stayed at your apartment. I don't have proof you slept with him, but I imagine that good-looking guy didn't sleep on your couch."

Trish rolled her eyes. No sense denying the obvious. "Fine, Christian and I have a relationship, and he was with me that weekend, but he didn't kill anyone."

"Miss Stevenson, before you lie and give him an alibi, let me warn you, the evidence against him is substantial. Witnesses, surveillance photos, and DNA prove he was with Davis Friday night. He picked her up at work, took her to a bar where they drank until midnight, and then they went back to her office where she was murdered. At the time of her death he was with her."

Trish recalled that Christian had left her Friday afternoon and didn't return to her apartment until four in the morning. Could he have done it? "If you have that evidence, why bother questioning me?"

"I'm a stickler for motive. Was there a reason he killed her, or is he just a psychopath?"

"Christian isn't a lunatic," she snapped. "He's a very sweet, considerate man."

Graham smiled. "It's obvious you care for him, but consider, he is a suspected terrorist who has killed a lot of people. But let's move on to his possible reasons. Before the murder, had you ever heard of Barbara Davis? Did Christian ever mention her name?"

"No."

"For now we'll say it was a chance meeting. But it is puzzling. Why leave a beautiful girl like you at home and pick up an older, less attractive woman? Did you have a disagreement with him?"

"We were getting along fine."

"All right, let's go back. Was there a reason he came to DC besides to see you?"

Trish knew she should shut up, but she also wanted answers. "I told him about a source who claimed her friend, a government analyst, was murdered because he discovered the misappropriation of congressional funds in a wolf study. The analyst died of a drug overdose, and his death was ruled a suicide. There was no proof of a murder, so I didn't write up the story, but Christian took an interest and wanted to talk to her. Before you ask, I'm not revealing any names."

"This government analyst, any chance his name was Felix Alveraz?"

Trish's mouth parted, alarmed. She finally summoned an answer. "I don't remember."

"I'm sure that information is in your emails and notes, and your editor probably also has it."

She grew flustered and blurted out, "What does the analyst have to do with the Davis murder?"

"A lot," Graham said, smiling. "So happens I handled the Alveraz case, clearly a suicide, but in the investigation, I interviewed his boss, Barbara Davis, to confirm signs of depression. That connects the dots and proves Roberts's motive. Captain Nemo's current cause is saving wolves. He wanted Davis's computer files about that wolf study and killed her to get them. Thank you, Miss Stevenson. You'll be getting a subpoena to appear in court."

Trish jumped out of the chair. "Detective Graham, your theory on a motive is different from mine. My source was correct. Her analyst friend was murdered to conceal government fraud, and Barbara Davis was silenced for the same reason. That's what I'll say in court."

"You're very loyal to Christian Roberts. It's a shame he's not as faithful to you. While you were waiting for him to return, he was having sex with Barbara Davis. The DNA test results confirm his semen inside her."

Trish's eyes watered and she felt the flush in her cheeks. Without another word, she rushed out of the interview room and exited the precinct, managing to hold herself together until inside her car. Lowering her head onto the steering wheel, she broke down and cried. She regretted going there, providing the police with a motive for the murder, but more so, she was upset with Christian. He had betrayed her.

CHAPTER TWENTY-ONE

Sal drove his black Caddy up US 41 past the numbered streets that led to downtown Sarasota. At Sixth he turned left toward the bay and pulled up to the Hyatt House entrance. He climbed out and the valet greeted him. "Good afternoon, Mr. Lamatto."

"Yeah, nice day," Sal said, handing over his car keys "Beats the fucking snow up North." He strolled into the lobby, like he owned the place, and the desk clerks acknowledged him the same way. "How ya doin', girls?" He smiled and rounded a corner to the bar. Settling on a bar stool, he gazed at the docked boats in the small inlet. Most the bar patrons were middle-aged men in tourist garb, probably taking a break from their wives and kids at the pool. Sal was the only one wearing a suit, though one was not required. T shirts and shorts were for lowlifes. Despite the busy lounge, the bartender immediately came over.

"Bourbon, Mr. Lamatto?" he asked.

"Sure, Mike." Sal quickly glanced at the teeming restaurant across the room. "And bring me a menu. I'm havin' lunch here." He visited the Hyatt several times a week, the reason everyone knew him. The food and atmosphere were decent, but Sal mainly came because of his understanding with the food and beverage manager, also a New Yorker. Anyone who wanted to reach Sal yet stay anonymous contacted him at the hotel. The feds could wiretap Sal's phones, but few judges were willing to sign a warrant for every phone in the Hyatt.

He sipped his drink, waited for his shrimp linguini to arrive, and reflected on his talk with Wheeler. The FBI agent had shown up at his condo, unexpected, several days ago. Sal had retired from illegal mob operations, so before Wheeler opened his mouth, Sal figured the unannounced visit concerned the Kid. Where was Christian?

At the time, Sal claimed ignorance, and it was true. Christian had taken off on his boat, but never said where he was going. In the end Sal benefited from the exchange with Wheeler, learning that Christian was wanted for the DC murder, but he'd slipped away before the cops nabbed him. "That boy's on the water," he had told Wheeler. "Good fuckin' luck catchin' him."

Sal had arranged for Angel to replace Mitch, so he knew that Frankie and Christian's friends, the Arlington couple, were holed up in Playa del Carmen, Mexico. Yesterday Frankie called the Hyatt and relayed that the Florida boy had landed there. No shocker. Christian wouldn't disappear and leave a job undone. He had scores to settle, and his hacker buddy in Mexico could help.

Sal's lunch arrived, and he dug into the noodles and shrimp smattered with a creamy white sauce. He ignored a tourist, a scrawny guy in a loud floral shirt, who took up the stool next to him.

"That looks good," commented the tourist.

"Yeah, it is," Sal said and shoved another forkful into his mouth.

"You certainly like to gorge. It's no wonder you're fat."

The insult jolted Sal in mid-chew. "Who the fuck…" he snarled, turning to the guy and seeing the hit man. He managed to swallow the food. "What are you doing here?"

"I'm looking for him," said Bill.

With the loss of appetite, Sal pushed his food aside. Looks were deceiving, and the bug-eyed twerp was one of the most dangerous men in the country. Even the mob was scared of him. Bill was also totally out about his sexual preference, probably never saw a closet, much less hid in one. He'd caught a whiff of the Kid and became infatuated, so the *him* was Christian.

"He ain't here." Sal said and emptied his drink with one gulp.

"No shit, fat man. Where is he?" Bill asked while simultaneously hailing the barkeep. With a ghoulish grin, he ordered a vodka and tonic.

"He's gone into hiding, took off on his boat because he's wanted for a murder in DC. A politician and his henchmen are also after his head."

Bill closed his eyes and muttered, "Idyllic picturing that creature on the run."

The bartender set Bill's cocktail on the bar and asked if he'd like to charge it to his room.

"No, I'll pay cash. Bring my friend here a refill. He looks like he needs it and put his lunch on my tab."

"Why you lookin' for Christian?" Sal asked. "He paid you off, right?"

"We're good. This has nothing to do with business. The young man affects me like catnip, and I like to keep track of him. Now where did he go? And, Sal, don't give me crap or play stupid."

"Mexico, he's in Playa del Carmen, Mexico."

"I knew I could count on you." He looked at Sal's barely touched meal. "Are you finished?"

"I am now."

Bill paid the bartender and rose from his stool. "Let's take our drinks up to my room where it's quiet. I want to hear about Christian's problems and this politician who's giving him grief."

* * *

"Christ, here we go again." Russ Manning, head of the National Gun Association, bristled in his lavish Texas office with trophy animal heads on the walls. Alongside a full-sized mounted grizzly, the TV displayed the breaking news. Yesterday evening another mass shooting had erupted at a mall. A nut with an AR-15 semi-automatic had mowed down a dozen shoppers. While the event was unfortunate, Russ was more concerned about the resulting media frenzy. Before the bodies were cold, the opportunists, politicians, and Hollywood would line up in front of the liberal press and preach about gun control and stamping out the Second Amendment. Those same showboats had armed bodyguards protecting their backs. Hypocrites!

Russ and his organization would take up the old standby: Guns don't kill people, people kill people. They framed the problem as a lack of security and loopholes in the background checks. Too many felons and dangerous retards could purchase guns without repercussions. Also, forcing law-abiding citizens to surrender their weapons wouldn't stop the shootings, when degenerates who rape, rob, and murder, aren't going to comply with a gun-control law. Unarmed citizens only helped criminals. Chicago was an example.

On TV an FBI agent stepped before the cameras and microphones to make a statement. "Come on, come on," Russ said, hoping he'd announce that the shooter was an illegal alien or a fanatic with ties to ISIS or another terrorist group. The NGA would not face the heat when press coverage shifted from gun control to securing US borders or more military aid to wipe out terrorists. The agenda could then be pushed that citizens had the right to protect themselves. Gun sales and NGA membership would skyrocket.

To Russ's disappointment, the agent said the shooter had been identified but his motive for the killings was yet unknown. The investigation was ongoing.

A tap on his office door, and his secretary stuck her head inside. "Phone call, Mr. Manning," she said.

"I said no calls. I'll address the press when more is learned about this shooting."

"It's not a reporter. Secretary Sanders is on the line and says it's urgent. I thought you might want to take his call."

Not really, he thought. The needy, stupid man was becoming annoying. "All right, put him through." With a sigh, Russ picked up the phone. "What's up, Jim?"

"I have big problems."

"Don't you watch the news? I've got my own troubles. With this shooting, my organization will be catching flak from the media, and our lobbyists will be forced to shell out more money so the politicians stick with us."

"If you don't help me, you'll face more than bad publicity. This issue can put us in jail."

"All right, what is it? But make it quick."

"Captain Nemo, he opened the files and knows who I am and what I did. He's threatening blackmail if I don't pressure the president into reversing the policies to save wolves."

"I thought Vern took care of him."

"He didn't. For the second time, he underestimated that Christian Roberts and failed. Roberts even held Vern at gunpoint and gave him the ultimatum. Your guy is rubbish."

"Vern has never disappointed me. Perhaps he met his match. I'll send in someone else to deal with Roberts. Where is he?"

"No one knows," said Sanders. "He left Florida on his sailboat and disappeared. He's wanted for murder in DC, so there's a good chance he left the country. If the police catch him before we do, the lid will come off. He'll name everyone connected to those files and the payoffs. The FBI will get involved. This mess started with the NGA wanting wolves wiped out so there'd be more game for hunters. Now it's gotten out of control."

"Don't forget you were well paid for your services. It's you who got sloppy with those files."

"Fine. I'm not going into the blame game. The fact is, Roberts can bring us all down."

"All right, Jim, calm down. I'll handle it."

After hanging up, Russ leaned back in the large leather desk chair and considered that Secretary Sanders tended to be excitable and prone to exaggeration. This time he could be correct. Christian Roberts, alias Captain Nemo, presented a serious concern. He dug into his pocket and grasped a small gold key on his key ring.

Unlocking the bottom drawer of his desk, he took out his address book and called Vern.

"I just spoke to Sanders."

"Yes, sir," said Vern. "I'm sure he explained the situation and wasn't pleased."

"To say the least. How do you intend to find Roberts, or have you given up?"

"No, sir, but I don't plan to look for him. He's got an axe to grind. We blew up his friend's house and killed one of his men. He'll come looking for me."

"Okay, Vern, but I told Sanders I'd send in additional help, a British guy, goes by Hagan. He's an international assassin, very professional and deadly. He'll contact you, and I expect your cooperation."

"Sir, I don't think it's necessary. I'll get Roberts, but if it makes you and Sanders happy, my team and I will play along."

"The more the merrier, right?" he said and hung up.

Russ glanced at his watch. It was eleven at night London time, still early enough for a call. He flipped through his address book and dialed Martin Hagan.

A wealthy oilman friend had pointed out Martin at a gun convention and said the lean, stylish man with salt-and-pepper hair was a former British spy. If Russ needed anything illicit done, Martin was the go-to man, having connections with retired KGB agents, Brits, French, and Arab operatives who handled problems worldwide. Russ was introduced to Martin, and they stayed in touch. Martin even visited Russ's ranch for a dove shoot one year.

Russ had never needed Martin's services, because Vern had done a satisfactory job, up until now, but with two failed attempts, the ex-military man appeared to be in over his head. It was time to bring in a heavy hitter, especially if Roberts had fled the country. Martin's global connections would find him.

The phone rang numerous times, and Russ nearly hung up before Martin, slightly out of breath, said, "Hello."

"Martin, this is Russ Manning in Texas. I hope I'm not disturbing you?"

"I was actually entertaining a lady friend," he said in a British accent.

"I'm sorry. I'll call you back in the morning."

"No, I shan't be a minute. Hold on."

Russ heard voices in the background and Martin saying, "Yes, dear, we'll do this again." A door slammed shut, and Martin came back on the phone. "So, Russ, what can I do for you?"

"I need to hire you for a job. Have you ever heard of Captain Nemo, the terrorist?"

"America's notorious lone wolf who commits crimes for wildlife," Martin said. "The young man is well respected in my circles."

"His real name is Christian Roberts."

"I saw the chap on the telly last year when he was suspected of poisoning diners in a London restaurant."

"Well, this chap is currently blackmailing one of my political sources. Eventually this trouble will lead to my organization. My man has been unsuccessful in getting rid of him. To make matters more difficult, Roberts left the US on a sailboat and is probably hiding out in the Caribbean, Mexico, or Central America."

"There's no place he can go where he can't be found. But Captain Nemo is not your typical target. Because he's a resourceful, proficient killer and a bigger risk, the cost of the task will be considerable."

"How much?"

"Three million," said Martin. "Once the funds are wired into my account, your troubles will vanish."

"That's a lot of money, but it's got to be done. What's the number of your account?"

* * *

In Playa del Carmen, the morning light broke through the dense tree canopy and invaded the upstairs window. With the smell of brewed coffee, Christian stirred in the bed despite dosing for only a few hours. He and Steve had stayed up all night while Karen and the two bodyguards slept. Steve did an online search on Secretary Sanders and hacked into his hidden bank account. The information would reveal those he paid such as Vern and the deposits of who paid the secretary. Christian wanted the names of all the players, along with their weaknesses and pressure points. At dawn they called it quits. Steve had said finishing the job might take upwards of two weeks.

Christian slipped on his cutoffs and descended the stairs barefoot and shirtless. Rounding a corner, he saw Karen in the kitchen. Frankie sat at the counter eating breakfast. Angel stood in the living room and held a cup of coffee. They all were watching the news coverage on TV.

"Eighteen years old," Karen said. "How could he have gotten so screwed up to shoot those poor people?"

"They should hang the bastard in a town square," said Angel. "Let him squirm, gag, and piss himself for all to see. That would deter shootings like this."

"When I was kid everyone had a gun," said Frankie, "but there were never mass shootings. The Internet is the blame, every kid glued to a screen. They don't relate face to face and got no compassion for others. And the parents now days don't have the know-how to raise their brats, too afraid to give 'em a crack on the ass."

Christian listened on the staircase and found it amusing that two gangsters were outraged over the shooting. He rounded the corner and meandered into the kitchen. "Mornin'."

Karen looked up with a smile. "Christian, I didn't hear you come down. You're as quiet as a cat."

Christian smiled. "My wife used to say that."

"I thought you'd sleep in, since you and Steve worked all night."

"Don't sleep well when the sun's up." said Christian, "And Steve did all the work. I was only there for moral support. Your husband is a wiz on a computer."

"We won't see the wiz until noon." Karen removed a cup from the cabinet. "Would you like some coffee and breakfast?"

"Yeah, join us, Chris," said Frankie. "We're watchin' this shit on TV. An asshole shot a bunch of people in a mall."

"Caught it last night on the Internet, but I live in a glass house and can't comment." Everyone turned and stared at him. "Hold off on the coffee," he said and opened the sliding door. He walked to the pool and dove in. For a half hour he vigorously swam laps. Water made him focus and eased the tension in his body and mind, which was probably the reason he was addicted to the sea.

He hoisted himself out of the pool and saw Frankie sitting nearby in a lawn chair under a shade tree. Frankie held up a towel. "I brought your coffee."

"Thanks," Christian said. He shook the droplets from his mop and dried his face with the towel. He pulled a chair over, sat down next to Frankie, and picked up his coffee cup from a side table.

"I was watching you," Frankie said. "You're damn fast, move like a bullet in that pool."

"Don't swim as much as I use to."

"So, where we at? Did Steve uncover anything useful about those guys?"

"We learned a lot about Sanders, but it'll take more time to hack into the lives of the others."

"He needs to hurry up so we can blow those bastards away."

Christian took a sip of coffee and glanced at Frankie. The guy had the body and mindset of a bull, charging ahead without thinking, despite agreeing yesterday that Christian would run things. "No worries, Frankie. These guys will be handled."

"So you stayin' with us till Steve's done?"

"Nope, heading back to my boat. I'm less likely to be noticed there. Also don't like being cooped up in a house."

"I wish you'd reconsider for Karen's sake. When you showed up, it was the first time that poor girl smiled. Of course maybe you don't like the company."

"The company is fine. I've always been a loner. Never had the need for buddies or have a girl attached to my arm. My wife was the only one I ever lived with, but she knew to give me space. I'm just happier, more relaxed by myself."

Frankie grinned. "Yeah, the crew pegged you as an oddball, but the boss sure loved ya. Vince spoke like you was his son."

"I miss still him."

They returned to the house, and Karen served Christian scrambled eggs and sausage wrapped in a warm burrito with salsa and a side of sliced mangos. Her mood was cheery until she learned he was returning to his boat. "Please don't go."

"Karen, my face has been plastered all over the media," Christian said. He nodded toward a man who had entered the backyard and was removing leaves from the pool with a net. "Even in Mexico, that pool guy, the gardener, maid, or even a nosy neighbor might recognize me here. If that happens, you all could be charged with hiding a fugitive."

"What makes you think you're safe on your sailboat?"

"I'm not, but I'm paying the marina owner to keep me and my boat anonymous. Makes the odds a little better there."

After breakfast, Christian gave Karen a farewell hug and said, "Steve has my number. Tell him to call when the research is done." He walked out the door with Angel, who was giving him a ride to his boat.

For the next several days Christian resided on his sloop and became friends with the local fishermen in the cove. He worked on their boats repairing the diesel and outboards motors and began a project restoring an old man's weathered little vessel. With the boat in dry dock on blocks, he replaced the rotted planks and sanded the hull in preparation for a fresh coat of paint.

At sundown the small fishing fleet returned to the cove, and Christian helped the men unload and ice down their catch. The fishermen showed their gratitude by bringing him tasty Mexican dishes made by their wives. The labor wasn't charity. Working outdoors he was happier and suffered fewer bouts with depression.

In the late afternoon he sat on the corroded seawall with his feet hanging above the clear water. Jose's three young daughters were alongside him. He pointed out the black-and-white striped sheepshead and brownish-red mangrove snappers that darted over the sandy bottom and oyster beds.

Jose wandered up. "My chicas are growing very fond of you."

Christian smiled. "They're great kids."

Jose said something in Spanish to the girls, and they scurried toward home. "Time for their bath and bed," he translated. "They have school tomorrow." He took up their seat next to Christian. "You are unlike any American we have known. You work hard, helping everyone here, but..." He gave a nod toward the sloop, "you have money. The wealthy usually have people working for them. You are a mystery to us, Señor Christian."

Christian chuckled. "No mystery. I used to own a boat-rental business and got the know-how to fix boats. It's nice getting back to basics."

"And now what do you do?"

"I try to save endangered wildlife."

"That is worthy work. The fish are disappearing, along with the jungle and its wild animals. Parrots I saw when young are gone. I worry for my children and their children. What kind of world are we leaving them? But why do you hide here and avoid the passport officials?"

"My methods aren't exactly legal."

"Ahhh," Jose turned to look at him. "You seem like a good man, honest and generous, but there are storm clouds in your eyes. You are deadly, yes?"

Christian stared down at the water, hesitating to answer. He sensed Jose could be trusted and came clean. "Yes."

"Perhaps you are the dark angel that God has sent to help us."

Perplexed, Christian asked, "What do you mean?"

"There is a very bad hombre here. He exports elephant tusks, rhino horns, and tiger bones to Asia and buys and sells rare animals. His crimes might be of interest to you."

"I'm interested, but what's this dark angel stuff?"

Jose breathed deeply. "This man also sells drugs and armas, weapons, but it is said he also deals with human trafficking. My wife's friend, her daughter disappeared, and we believe his men took her."

"If everyone knows, how does he get away with it?"

"Dinero, he pays off the policia. Even in your country, he was arrested, but the sustantivo, the judge, let him go. Perhaps you are the angel, our savior to rid us of this man."

Christian leaned back on his palms and considered. He had time on his hands and eliminating the bad hombre sounded worthwhile. *Who am I kidding? To save one elephant, I'd kill this jerk.* "Sure, Jose, I'll get rid of this badass, but the biggest problem is getting close to him."

"Mañana, you shall come to my house for dinner and meet my brother-in-law, Manuel. He is a bartender at a fancy club on the water, and this hombre lives in a big house nearby and comes to the club to eat and drink. Manuel knows how to get close to him."

The following evening Christian climbed into Jose's truck, and they drove a short distance down the shell-covered road. At a small white house, Jose pulled into the driveway and pointed to a dark blue Chevy. "Manuel is already here."

As soon as Christian stepped from the truck, the front door swung open and the three little girls burst out yelling, "Señor Christian, Christian." They circled him and hugged his jeans.

Christian laughed and playfully rubbed their long black hair. "Okay, okay, I'm here."

"You see, children love you," said Jose. "You should be a father."

"Maybe someday, if I'm lucky." Christian's mood darkened, recalling the night when he and his wife decided to have a baby, and their lovemaking lasted until dawn. The next day she was murdered. He coerced a smile. "Come on, girls, let's go in." They grabbed his hands and tugged him inside.

A good-looking man with a mustache introduced himself in perfect English as Manuel. He handed Christian a fruit-filled yellow drink. "I hope you like sangria. It's my own concoction."

Christian took a sip and scowled. "Wow! This baby is strong. There's more than white wine in it."

Jose chuckled. "Three of Manuel's drinks and you will pass out on my floor."

Christian meet Jose's wife and the group soon gathered around a table and ate enchiladas. With the children present, the talk was innocuous. Christian couldn't contain a grin. These people had opened up their home and hearts to him. For a brief time, he felt normal and missed it. The spell was broken when the kids went to bed and he, Jose, and Manuel stepped onto the porch to discuss business. Christian stared out at the surrounding mangrove forest and listened to the men.

"I will help you, Christian, because my sister wishes it," Manuel said. "The drugs, guns, and animals are not that important, but people live here in fear of being taken. Jose believes you are the kind of man to end this."

Christian turned from the view and looked at Manuel. "Yeah, I'm that kind."

Manuel took a breath. "Getting to Mr. Lopez will not be easy. His home is heavily guarded, and the place of his operation is unknown."

"Just get me one minute alone with Mr. Lopez," said Christian, "and I'll take out your rat."

CHAPTER TWENTY-TWO

Christian stood in his sloop galley and washed dishes. Two days earlier he had meet Manuel and followed up with an online search on the bad guy, Roberto Lopez. Only one article appeared, with information about Lopez's arrest in Texas for trafficking pangolins, little endangered anteaters. The judge had thrown out the case because of a mishandled arrest. It wasn't much, but enough proof for Christian that Lopez had to go. Christian now waited for a window where he'd be alone with the guy.

He stowed the dishes and took out a broom to sweep the wooden floors. He wasn't a cleaning freak, but untidiness was amplified in small quarters. He heard Jose calling from the seawall outside.

"Señor Christian!" Jose yelled.

Christian hustled topside. "He called?"

"Si, Manuel says Lopez is at the bar now."

"Give me five minutes." Christian raced below, stripping out of his thread-worn T shirt and cutoffs. After a fast shower, he trimmed his face stubble, splashed on cologne, and dressed in a black silk shirt and tan Dockers. Transforming from a pot-scrubbing boat dweller into a jet-setter befitting a wealthy club visitor, he slipped on a Rolex watch, sunglasses, and tucked his .38 revolver into his front waistband, and covered the weapon with his loose shirt. He emerged on the deck and said, "Ready. Let's go."

"Wow! You look really nice," Jose said.

"Gotta play the part."

They hurried to the truck, and Jose drove into town. He pulled off on the coastal roadside in front of a hotel that was a city block from the swanky beach club and its resident estates. Christian climbed out, and the truck drove away. He walked through the hotel, past its rooms and onto the beach. Wandering down the Gulf shoreline, he took in the waterfront mansions until he reached the club. He entered the lush grounds and spotted a security guard. Instead of avoiding him, he walked directly to the guard. "Say, how late do they serve dinner?" he asked, acting like a guest who had meandered in after a stroll on the beach.

"Ten o'clock, Señor," answered the guard.

"Thanks." Christian smiled and took the steps up to the luxurious resort's bar and restaurant. In the bar he made eye contact with Manuel, who shifted his gaze toward two well-to-do Mexican men seated at the far end.

Christian recognized Lopez from the picture taken during his arrest, although now the man had longer hair and a beard. Christian strolled up and sat down next to Lopez.

Manuel stepped to Christian. "What would you care for, Señor?"

"Heard the sangria is pretty good."

"The best," Manuel said, and left to fix his drink.

Christian listened to the men who conversed in Spanish. When they paused, he took the opportunity to break in. "Excuse me, but do y'all speak English?"

Lopez looked him up and down, and Christian apparently met with his approval. "How can I assist an American?"

"My girl and I have been lying on the beach. The waves are too tame for surfing. You guys look like locals and probably could suggest a must-see."

"Most tourists enjoy the Tulum ruins of the Mayans."

"We plan to visit them, but I was hoping for something a little more adventurous."

"A cave tour or swimming in the cenotes might be to your liking. My sons love the cave at Kantun Chi. I'm taking my family there Sunday."

"That's exactly what I wanted to hear. Thanks, I'll check it out." Christian said. The men finished their drinks and left the bar as Manuel served Christian his drink.

"The one you spoke to is Lopez," said Manuel. "His house is close, and he often walks here. You could follow him."

"No good; too many eyes on the situation, but it's okay. I have another plan." He drank half his drink and walked through the lobby to the outside. A valet secured him a cab, and he told the driver, "Take me to a place that sells motorcycles." *Time I got my own transportation.*

Christian was soon zipping through city traffic on a new 350 Honda purchased with cash and his fake ID. He disliked relying on others to get around, and further, didn't want their vehicles associated with him and his crimes, like the one coming Sunday.

On Saturday he drove his bike to the Kantun Chi Cenotes and Caves and played sightseer. He walked the garden paths to the cenotes, sinkholes filled with pristine water that were partially covered with overhanging jungle cliffs. He then joined a group for the cave tour. Outfitted with a helmet and life preserver, he followed the guide and visitors down a ladder into the watery underground. Following the passage lights, he trudged through ankle- and knee-deep clear-flowing water. At other times he swam across a large grotto with hanging stalactites and then was forced to his hands and knees to crawl through a small, low cavity. He had come to scope out the place for a serious mission, but was having fun with the experience.

The next day before dawn, he returned to Kantun Chi and hid his motorcycle off the road in the jungle. Armed with a waterproof flashlight, a wire cutter, and his dive knife strapped to his leg, he crept onto the premises and entered the vertical shaft of the cave exit. In a large, dark chamber, he turned on the flashlight and walked around the impressive columns of stalagmite. Crawling through the narrow passageway, he entered the expansive pool-filled grotto. On Saturday he'd noticed several cave offshoots and now chose to hide in one.

Several hours later, the cave lights came on and visitors began to arrive in the cavern. Christian peered out from behind a boulder, waiting for Lopez. An hour later, the man showed up with two pre-teenage boys and a wife, but no bodyguards. Christian had counted on the lack of a security attachment. The family bobbed across the pool to the tight cavity that led to the cave exit. The boys, being boys, were impatient and went through the opening first, followed by the wife. *Perfect,* Christian thought. He cut the electrical wire to the lights and heard the panicked screams of people caught in pitch black. He slipped into the water and surfaced behind Lopez. Clutching Lopez's chin and jerking back his head, Christian pressed his knife to the man's throat. "Struggle or scream, you'll die," Christian whispered into the man's ear.

Feeling the sharp blade at his throat, Lopez yielded. "What do you want?" he asked, petrified.

"Justice."

"Wait! I'll tell you where they are. Just don't hurt me."

"Where who are?" Christian asked.

"The children, the school bus of children. They're still alive and haven't been harmed."

Still alive? Christian realized Lopez was talking about the human trafficking but if the intent was prostitution, why would he kill the kids? "Tell me your plans for these kids, and I'll let you go."

"I can tell you're an American and understand business. A few missing Mexican kids shouldn't matter to you."

Christian forced the knife into Lopez's neck, breaking skin and drawing blood. "But it does. Answer my question."

"Their body parts, I planned to sell them on the black market."

Christian was rarely horrified, so it took a few seconds to grasp the unthinkable. The monster was kidnapping and murdering children for their organs. "Where are they?" he growled.

"North of here, in the old tin mines. You'll find them there," Lopez said. "Now you said you'd let me go."

"I lied," Christian said and sliced the artery in Lopez's throat. Within a minute the man bled out and went limp in Christian's arms.

Towing the corpse, he swam to a far corner in the chamber where Lopez's body wouldn't be discovered for hours. He concealed the knife in his pants and put on the man's life preserver and helmet, hiding his blond hair. He swam out of the grotto toward the cave entrance, traveling to the alarmed voices. In darkness, he felt his way through the cave and past several clusters of frightened people. A guide appeared with a flashlight and directed everyone to follow him. Christian blended in and tagged along with the group until outside.

Some people were slightly injured with head bumps, scraped knees, and stubbed toes suffered while fumbling around in the dark. The Kantun Chi employees had their hands full with hysterical visitors. In the chaos, Christian wandered up a path and into the woods. He removed the helmet and life preserver, wiping off his prints with his shirttail. He buried the cave gear under dirt and leaves, found his motorcycle, and drove away.

Christian pulled into the marina before noon and parked his bike near the warehouse. He swept the long strands of hair from his eyes, and took a deep breath to shake off his anxiety.

Jose left his office and approached. "It is done?"

"Nearly," Christian said. "He's dead, but you need to make a call." He fetched his disposable phone from the sloop so the call couldn't be traced. Handing it to Jose, he relayed who he should phone and what to say.

Jose made the short, anonymous call to the police. In Spanish he gave them the location of the kidnapped children on the school bus and that Roberto Lopez was responsible, planning to kill the kids and sell their body parts on the black market. He ended the call with a disgusted head shake. "The police will not try hard to find Lopez's killer. They are also parents and will think the man deserved to die."

Christian nodded and thought, *One less bad hombre in the world.*

* * *

Sitting at the dining room table, Steve closed his laptop in the late afternoon. "I believe I've gone as far as I can go," he said to Karen. He straightened the stack of papers that contained handwritten notes, printouts, and photos.

"Good, you can go with me tomorrow and pick up our new baby," she said. "I know you'll love him." She and Frankie had made several visits to the local pound and found a flea-bitten, matted mutt that was small, white, and part poodle. Wanting to replace Coconut, she had filled out the adoption papers, but the dog needed shots, neutering, and grooming before its release on Monday.

"I just hope the little guy is housebroken." Steve rose. "I'd better call Christian and let him know where I am."

"He's probably bored, sitting around on his boat. Why don't you invite him to dinner, and you can discuss your findings?"

"Good idea." In the kitchen he retrieved his cell phone and glanced at the two bodyguards outside. "Christian wouldn't be the only one fed up with sitting around. Angel would be happy to go get him." Steve dialed the number.

"I'm assuming you're finished," said Christian.

"Not quite. I found a lot, but I've hit a dead end. Why don't you come to dinner tonight, and we'll discuss it. Angel has been to the marina and can give you a lift. Um, did I mention we're having steaks?"

"After fish and Mexican food, I'm ready for a steak."

"You got it, and I know you want yours rare."

As they waited for Angel to return with Christian, Steve fired up the grill, seasoned the steaks, and mixed up a batch of margaritas. Karen prepared a salad, and Frankie cooked an Italian side dish. Oddly the strange mix of people functioned like a family. Christian, of course, was the star who guided them. They looked forward to seeing him.

The front door opened and Angel and Christian strolled in. "There he is," Frankie announced with a booming voice and big grin. "So what ya been up to?"

"Not much, just a laidback Sunday," Christian said and took a margarita from Steve. "Thanks, I needed this." He pulled Steve aside. "After we eat, you and I can discuss what you've uncovered." He glanced at Angel. "We'll do it upstairs. No sense involving the others."

"Okay," Steve agreed but wondered why all the secrecy. Then again, that was Christian, overly cautious and a man of mystery.

Over drinks and dinner, Karen talked about their new dog, and Christian mentioned he was fixing some old fisherman's boat. Frankie said he'd contacted Sal and let him know that Christian was here.

Afterwards Steve took his laptop and paperwork up to his bedroom with Christian. "Is there a problem?" he asked after closing the door. "You don't want the guys to know what's going on?"

"That's right." Christian sat down on the bed. "I don't know Angel, and Frankie thinks I lack know-how. If he disagrees with my plans, he might take matters into his own hands. He could screw things up."

"But you trust me."

"Sorry, Steve, but it's more a matter of need. You can go where I can't on the Internet."

Steve realized Christian had an unusual outlook, like he was playing a game. He studied each player, considered their motive and possible threat before making his move, which was probably why he sat on Steve's bed instead of a prison bunk.

"Okay, let's get started." Steve showed Christian the papers. He had gathered every bit of information on Sanders. His bio, habits, contacts, and movement were easily accessible. His overseas bank account revealed his payoffs. Sanders's hired assassin, Vern, was among the names and Vern's information—address, phone number, contacts, credit cards and bank account—were also available. Steve said, "I'm surprised that an ex-CIA op wasn't more careful and could be hacked."

"That's not sloppiness. He's using the same bait I did and hopes to lure me in." Christian studied the photos of the men suspected of working for Vern. He tapped two pictures. "I know these two, this guy and Brian. They were with Vern when they tried to do me in on the bay. These other three work for Vern?"

"I'm pretty sure. They don't have regular jobs, and all five served under Vern in the military, and he pays them well. They seem tough."

"They remind me of some bullies I knew in school." Christian chuckled. "Ya think it's over when you're grown up, but I'm still getting hassled by assholes."

"You were bullied? That's hard to believe."

"I was a pretty skinny kid and didn't make friends easily and then puberty hit. The girls started liking me, and that created problems with the jocks, but it taught me to fight back. What else you got?"

"I discovered who made deposits into Sanders's account. The Sahara Hunting Club gave him fifty grand, but the biggest contributor was the National Gun Association under Russ Manning. Unfortunately that's where I hit a brick wall. His computer is protected, a firewall."

"I have to get into that computer and find if Manning is paying off other politicians."

"Maybe there is no one else. Saunders might've acted alone and committed the murders and attempts on our lives. With what I've uncovered, we can nail him."

Christian leaned back on a pillow and gazed at the ceiling. "Remember when we first met? We had two different agendas. You wanted your friend's killer to be found and punished. I wanted to learn who was responsible for the wolf slaughter and stop it. Turned out we wanted the same guilty party. Saunders is one rotten link in a corrupt chain. I haven't reached my goal. To do it means exposing everyone responsible for the wolf killing. If I have to break into Manning's office, and install another RAT, I'll do it."

"Killing Manning might be easier," Steve joked.

"I would if it saved the wolves. Problem is the NGA would only replace him. I need to bring down the whole organization."

"Do it, and you'll be taking a stand for gun control. That would be great, considering the recent mass shooting."

Christian sat up with the subject. "Steve, I realize you're from the DC and have liberal ideas on gun control. But I live in Central Florida that's mostly conservative, and we support the Second Amendment, glad the NGA protects my gun rights, but the organization stepped over the line. When they promoted wolf killing for greed, they lost me. My plan is to follow their money. I guarantee that Sanders and his men didn't act alone. There were others with powerful backing."

"All right, Christian, I'm with you. We'll bring them all down." Steve stood, paced the room, and then stopped short. "There's another way to retrieve the information on Manning's computer that's easier than physically breaking into his office. I could create a virus and email it to him in an attachment. Once he opens it, it works like a RAT, and I'm in. The trouble is most people know not to open attachments from unknown sources."

Christian pulled up a knee and rested his chin on it. "So the sender should be a person Manning knows and trusts, maybe a celebrity or trophy hunter."

"Yeah, that would work. I could take his name and create a fake email account."

Christian smiled. "I know just the guy. The jerk has pissed me off with his online posts of threatened wildlife he's shot. I thought about adding him to Nemo's hit list, but he's small potatoes."

"Okay, sounds good. So while my head is buried in a computer, what are you going to do?"

"You've given me enough information to act on. I'm heading to Washington and take care of the pricks who tried to kill us."

* * *

Sal strolled into the Hyatt lobby on Tuesday, anticipating a casual lunch and cocktail. As he neared the front desk, a clerk hailed him. "Mr. Lamatto, Mr. Abraham would like to speak to you." Sal stepped to the counter while the clerk placed a call. She hung up, smiling. "He'll be here shortly."

While waiting for the food and beverage manager, Sal took a couple of hundred-dollar bills from his wallet and placed them in his pants pocket. That was the drill when Abraham received an important message for Sal. It was about time. He hadn't heard from Frankie or Christian in a while.

Abraham appeared from a hallway. Approaching, he said, "Sal, it's good to see you."

"Yeah, you too," he said. As they shook hands, Sal slipped Abraham the bills.

"Allow me to escort you to a table," said Abraham. "I believe there's one overlooking the water or would you prefer the lounge?"

"The bar is good." Sal said, walking through the lobby. In the lounge they exchanged brief niceties, followed by a second handshake that contained a note. The manager left, and Sal sat down. After ordering a drink, he unfolded the slip of paper that said, "Cancun tomorrow, C." Sal was still reflecting on the message when the bartender served him his drink.

"Would you like to see a menu?"

"Not today, Mike; looks like I'm skipping lunch."

The gist of the note was clear. The Kid finally had a plan of action.

CHAPTER TWENTY-THREE

At the Cancun airport, the small silver car pulled up to Departures, and Christian climbed out of the passenger seat. Slinging a black knapsack over his shoulder, he gathered his jacket and carryon from the backseat. He bent down and made eye contact with the driver. "Thanks for the lift, Angel."

"Hope all goes well in DC."

Christian's smile evaporated. "How'd you know I was going there?"

"I overheard Steve telling Karen."

"Oh," Christian said with a slight nod. As the car drove away, he walked toward airport doors, not pleased that Steve's household knew his destination. The concern was minor compared to the ones ahead. With the Nemo attacks, his mug had been publicized throughout the media outlets, and he was foolishly returning to a city where the cops and a murder warrant awaited him. Plus Vern and his men were there, hoping Christian would show up so they could do him in. *I've lost my mind. Be so much smarter to sail off into the Gulf and forget this bullshit.*

To help mask his looks, he still sported a beard, and with no time for trims, his hair was nearly shoulder length and drawn back into a ponytail. He entered the terminal wearing sunglasses, a black T-shirt, and faded jeans, appearing like a beach bum returning to the States after a Mexican vacation. At Security, he handed an agent his fake passport that identified him as Jeff Rhodes. He then wandered through the crowded building past large open stores selling liquor, perfume, clothing, and jewelry, duty-free stuff for tourists to take home. He reached the gates where a spacious window displayed a runway and the parked jets. At the end of the building he went outside and walked to the waiting eight-seat Lear. Stepping aboard the small jet, he said to the pilot, "Going to DC."

"DC?" thundered a voice from the back of the plane. "Are you nuts?"

Christian smiled at Sal. "I was wondering the same thing." He moved down the narrow aisle and gave the big man a hug.

Sal stepped back with a frown. "Damn, Kid, you look like crap. With that beard you could pass for Tom Hanks in *Castaway*."

"Always the movie references with you and Vince."

"It's called fucking retirement."

They settled in the seats facing each other, and the jet engine fired up. Sal glanced out the window. "I always wanted to visit Cancun."

"Now you have."

"You're an asshole," Sal grumbled. "Flying over a city don't count."

"How are things in Sarasota?"

"The goddamn traffic gets worse every year. The highways look like parking lots."

The jet taxied to the runway and took off. They were soon flying over the Gulf of Mexico.

Sal swirled the bourbon in his rocks glass and asked, "So what are we doin'?"

"I'll tell you what you're doing." Christian dug in the tote bag and removed photos and paperwork on Vern's five men. He pointed out three. "These guys planted the explosive in DC that killed Mitch. The other two were with Vern when they came after me on my boat."

"I take it you want me to handle 'em?"

"I'd appreciate it." Christian left his seat and fetched a Coke from a small refrigerator. Sitting back down, he popped the can. "I am concerned about Frankie. He wanted in and might have issues when he's not part of it."

"Don't worry about Frankie. He'll be okay as long as someone pulls the trigger and those fuckers pay for Mitch's murder." Sal scrutinized the papers. "So I eliminate the flunkies, but what about their boss, this Vern, and the politician?"

"Vern and Sanders are mine," Christian said and took a sip of soda.

"There's no harm in having help."

"Shooting them is too fast and painless. They tried to kill me twice, Sal, and deserve to agonize a bit. I'd also hope to accomplish another objective. I'm blamed for a murder that Vern committed, and wolves have been demonized so the secretary of the Interior can fulfill his agenda and have them killed. We've both been unfairly targeted. I'd like to clear that up."

* * *

Secretary Sanders looked out his study window at the two men posted on his front porch. Vern, erect and clasping his hands, stood beside him. "You really think he'd come after me at home?"

"I would if I were him. You're nearly untouchable at work."

"What about a guard for my wife?"

"She's fine," said Vern. "Roberts kills to make a political statement to promote causes. Your death would shed media light on how you screwed the wolves. Besides, Roberts's profile suggests he likes women. He'd never hurt one."

"The DC police obviously haven't read that profile. They believe he killed Barbara." Sanders stepped to the small bar and mixed a cocktail. "His arrest is another worry that leads me to ask if you've heard from Russ's man."

"We've been in touch with the Limey. Apparently, he has an informant, a friend of Roberts, who said he's been hiding out on his boat near Cancun. The Brit had planned to fly over, but he just learned that Roberts left Mexico and is supposedly heading here. We're to sit tight until he catches up with Roberts, and it's over."

"It's amazing how that Florida hick continues to evade you so-called professionals."

"The hick has had a run of luck, but if I see him, his time is up. I'll terminate him, and the Limey can eat the job."

"I don't care who kills him, so long as it's soon. I'm a nervous wreck, and my house looks like a fortress. I've had to tell my wife I've received threatening emails, to explain why your men are here. She's not happy with the intrusion." He heard heels on the stairs and put a finger to his lips.

Amber sashayed into the den in a short black cocktail dress. He frowned because the hem barely covered her crotch, but said evenly, "Are you going somewhere, dear?"

"Jimmy, I told you last week about the charity event at the Ritz. We're trying to save elephants. I asked you to go, but of course you're always too busy." She glanced at Vern and said with disdain, "Hello, Vern."

"Mrs. Sanders," Vern replied.

Sanders said to her, "I'm sorry, I must've forgotten. I thought you gave up on these socials—they're all old people, and you don't fit in."

"It's better than sitting around and being ignored."

"Amber, I promise when the police catch the one responsible for those emails, we'll go on a nice trip."

"I've heard that before," she griped. "It'll be nice when your new buddies are gone and I have some privacy."

"Vern and his men are protecting me."

"Whatever," she said. The black Town car pulled up outside. "There's my ride." She gathered her purse and coat. "I shouldn't be late. Old farts are in bed by ten."

* * *

The private jet landed at Reagan National, and Sal parted ways with Christian who headed to a car rental agency. Sal walked to the exit where his two-man crew from New York would pick him up.

During the flight the Kid had said he wanted Vern and Sanders to sweat and suffer, but hadn't revealed how he'd deal with them. Would he kill them expose them, so they'd face prison? But that was normal. Christian rarely divulged his plans. Sal generally learned about his exploits after the fact.

Bundled up in a heavy coat, Sal left the private-jet terminal and found Anthony and Tony outside in a spacious dark sedan. "Damn, fucking cold here," he said. "I'm missin' Florida already."

"Good seein' ya, boss," said Anthony, the driver, as Sal climbed in.

"I hope you boys located a decent restaurant and hotel in this fucking city," said Sal. "I've been on a goddamn plane all day, flyin' back and forth across the Gulf to pick up the Kid and then up here. I'm ready for some good Italian food and a bed. Tomorrow we'll be busy."

The car pulled away from the terminal, and Anthony said, "We half expected the Florida boy to be with ya."

"He ain't a team player; likes to work alone."

The next day over a leisurely breakfast, Sal discussed the operation with Tony and Anthony. Christian and his hacking buddy had been extremely thorough, providing photos of Vern's men; their addresses; the places where they frequently ate, glancing at their credit card statements; and even the GPS tracking numbers for their cars. The Kid and his computer buddy were making the task easy.

Sal proposed a brief surveillance on the targets. At the first opportunity, take them out, nothing fancy, just a head shot. He intended to hit all five in a single day. In the *Godfather* movies, the strategy of killing all the enemies at once appeared to be done to make a point: don't screw with the godfather, but in reality, it was smart. With little time between shootings, the targets didn't learn of the other murders, so they couldn't prepare a defense or go into hiding.

Sal was too old and out of shape to engage actively but he would drive the rented panel van with its stolen tag to each location. His younger men could do the dirty work.

On the jet Christian had said Vern's men were hard-core professionals who operated like a military unit. Sal saw the military aspect as a disadvantage. His mob boys thought on their feet and used their instincts; no one instructed them. Since teens, they'd gained plenty of skill and practice. Failure was not an option, and in this case, they had the element of surprise. Vern's men might expect Christian, but not his backups.

"Hit men going after hit men," Sal had said to Christian. "It reminds me of the drug wars and the good ol' days. Vince would've loved it."

At noon Sal and his two men met again in the hotel parking lot. They wore the uniform garb of blue-collar workers. Daylight killing demanded the masquerade. Sal drove to the first target, a Henry Slater, who lived in a condo. Anthony entered the building and took the service elevator to his door. He knocked, claiming to be a cable man.

Slater had apparently just left the shower and wore a towel around his waist. He opened the door and said, "I don't have any cable problems."

"But you got problems," Anthony said and aimed his silencer.

The second residence was a house in a quiet neighborhood. Sal parked the van a few houses up the street, and his men prepared to get out and do the deed.

Sal saw the front door open. "Hold up," he said, and watched the target leave the house and walk to his car.

"I can take him now," said Anthony.

Sal looked around at the neighborhood, "Too many damn witnesses peeking out windows. Let's follow the dipshit." He started the engine and trailed the man's car. The move proved lucky. The man pulled to the curb on an empty street corner and appeared to be waiting for someone. Soon another guy, also on the hit list, showed up. After he climbed into the passenger seat, Anthony strolled up and tapped on the window. He took out both men with a shot to their heads. Tony shoved aside the driver's body, slipped into the car, and drove up the nearby alley. Anthony and Tony tossed the corpses inside a Dumpster so they wouldn't be discovered soon.

Toward evening, the last two targets weren't at home. Sal used the GPS in their cars to find them, and then called Christian. "Three down, but the other two guys are at Sanders's home, most likely pulling guard duty. A rifle could do the job, but it'd call attention."

"No, leave them," said Christian. "Tonight I'm making my move, and it should draw them out for you."

"Okay, we'll stake out the place and wait till they leave."

"After midnight things should start popping."

"Trouble is, by then they'll know their buddies are missing and something's up. Kid, you'd better grow eyes in the back of your head and don't be fucking reckless."

* * *

Christian had left Sal at the airport and located the car-rental agency. He'd upgraded to the agency's best ride and arrived at the Ritz-Carlton in a dark-blue Corvette. He checked in using his alias, Jeff Rhodes, and went up to his top-floor suite with a great view of the Capital. He had a quiet evening, ordered room serves, and watched a movie.

Early the next morning, he showered, shaved off the beard, and hit the streets of DC. The Yucatan, like Florida, had been warm and sunny, but the weather in Washington was nippy with dreary skies. He was glad he'd brought a jacket. First on his to-do list was finding a salon, preferring female hairdressers to barbers. An hour later his hair had been trimmed and layered collar-length. His next move was to seek out the high-end clothing stores. After a late lunch, he returned to the Ritz with shopping bags, ready for tonight.

At evening's approach, he stepped out of the hotel elevator a new man. The grubby sailor was gone. In a pricy gray suit and pale-blue tie, he strolled through the lobby to the convention room. He entered a gala sponsored by a conservation group that was raising funds to save African elephants. At the podium a man stated, "Every thirty minutes poachers kill an elephant, and within the next decade wild elephants will be extinct like the white rhino."

Listening to the speaker's assertions, Christian felt disgust about the elephant slaughter. *After the wolves, maybe Nemo needs to focus on Africa.* He stood near the doorway and scanned the faces in the large room. He felt like the cliché, a wolf in sheep's clothing, searching for his quarry. Instead of joining a table, he wandered to the cash bar and ordered a Chardonnay.

The woman, his age with long copper hair and wearing a short black dress, leaned against the bar several paces down. She glanced his way, sized him up with her eyes, and made the first move. "You like white wine, too," she said.

"I do," he said, smiling with his fib. He'd never been a wine enthusiast. She returned a red lipstick grin. Through computer hacking, Steve had uncovered Mrs. Sanders's RSVP to this event, saying she'd attend alone. Christian had seen her photo, but in person she was far more attractive.

"I take it you also care about elephants."

"I'm an advocate for all wildlife that's threatened." Sidestepping to be next to her, he reflected on his mentor's advice. Vince had said he should use his assets to accomplish his goals. Initially Christian had resisted, feeling like a jerk for using his charm and looks to seduce women. He finally realized the causes outweighed his principles. "So do you enjoy these events?"

"I hate them, but I want to help the animals."

He looked over his shoulder at the gathering. "They do seem rather stuffy. Most of those people are probably here for appearances and to prove they have a heart."

She giggled. "I agree." She extended her hand. "I'm Amber."

"Christian," he said with a gentle handshake. He noticed that her drink was nearly gone. "Allow me to buy you another wine."

She nodded shyly. "Thank you."

He lifted her glass, hailing the bartender for a refill and asked her, "Amber, why come here when you could simply mail in a donation?"

For a moment she chewed a nail. "You mentioned appearances. I started going to these things to show that my husband and I support wildlife. You see, he's the secretary of Interior. Now I go to get out of the house." She looked up, embarrassed. "Don't get me wrong, I love animals and want them protected."

Christian drew back with a scowl. "Really? You're James Sanders's wife?"

"You know him?" she asked, a little astonished.

"I know of him, but we've never met."

"You're probably surprised with our age difference."

"That's not it. You said you cared about animals and conservation, but you're married to a man who's done a lot of harm to wildlife."

"What are you talking about?"

"Forgive me. It's not polite to talk politics or criticize one's husband."

"No, tell me."

Christian did. He talked about the wolf crisis benefiting hunters, the proposed grizzly hunts outside Yellowstone, and her husband's agenda for the expansion of oil drilling off every US coastline and in wildlife refuges, national parks, and monuments, all of which could affect the survival of many species. "Your husband and the US Wildlife Department are cozying up to trophy hunters and plan to overturn the ban on importing African trophies. That would encourage elephant hunting, so it's rather ironic that you're here to save them."

"Christian, are you sure about all that?"

"It's on the Internet and in the media." He glanced at her, realizing while beautiful, she was a bit dim. He'd also gathered over the last hour that she was lonely and unhappily married. The wine had fueled her emotions, and he watched her change from disillusioned to angry. The research on the former waitress was on target.

She lowered her head and mumbled, "I thought I was doing something, something important. Turns out I've done nothing. I'm just a trophy like those poor animals."

The event wrapped up, and the crowd began to file out of the ballroom. Christian placed his arm around Amber's shoulder and gazed into her moist eyes. "I'm sorry," he whispered and kissed her forehead. "I didn't mean to upset you."

"It's not your fault. I'm angry with Jimmy for lying to me." She straightened and turned to him. "I don't want to see that prick tonight."

"You don't have to."

* * *

In his home study off the foyer Sanders worked on memos, making notes for his secretary to prepare at the office. Vern had left earlier, but his two men remained as sentinels. Sanders stopped writing and glanced at his watch. It was after midnight. Amber should have been home. Had she slipped in without knocking, too irritated to say goodnight?

Lately she'd been glum, complaining about him and their marriage. She claimed to be unfulfilled, isolated, and neglected, and that he didn't care. True, he ignored her fuming, but he had more important concerns, such as Christian Roberts, alias Captain Nemo. The terrorist had threatened to expose the files and crimes that would destroy Sanders's career and life, and the danger had escalated. Vern had botched several attempts to silence Roberts, who would now seek revenge. The man was no stranger to murder. Sanders's fear of prison had become a fear of dying.

He shuddered and gulped down the last of his cocktail. His thoughts returned to Amber. When the threats were over and Roberts was dead, Sanders would make it up to her. After all, she lived among the elites in a large, expensive home and had money to burn. Instead of bitterness, she should feel fortunate that she wasn't still slinging hash to truck drivers. Her grievances could wait.

At one in the morning he grew tired and decided to call it a night. He walked upstairs to their bedroom with sex on his mind. Fornication had become another of Amber's gripes. She claimed that sex with him was too brief, infrequent, and one-sided. He opened the bedroom door and was shaken to discover an empty bed. He hurried down the hall and flung open the other bedroom doors. He then searched the rest of the house. She wasn't there. In his office he called her cell phone but got voice mail. "Amber, pick up." He texted her and still no response.

Panicked, he threw open the front door and shrieked to Vern's men. "Have you seen my wife? Did she come home?"

"No, sir," one answered. "We figured she'd made arrangements and spent the night in town."

Sanders covered his mouth in thought. That was possible. A few months earlier she had gone on strike and refused to give him oral sex. Not coming home might be another protest to punish him for neglecting her. "She was going to the Ritz-Carlton. I'll call there and see if she checked in."

He hustled back inside and called the hotel. A desk clerk informed him that no Amber Sanders or Mrs. James Sanders was registered. He hung up. His worst fears loomed. Maybe Captain Nemo had kidnapped and killed her.

* * *

Vern woke to the buzzing of his cell phone on the nightstand near his bed. He turned on a light and glanced at the alarm clock. Seeing Sanders was on the caller ID, he growled into the phone. "This better be damn important, Sanders. It's going on two in the morning."

Sanders's hysterical prattle was barely lucid. "Amber's missing. She didn't…didn't come home tonight. I…I checked the Ritz, and she's not there. You said my wife would be fine…fine, and now she's gone. Christian Roberts did this. He killed her to get even with me."

"Goddamn it, calm down." Vern sat up and swung his legs off the bed. "You're jumping to conclusions. Has she ever stayed out before?"

"Never, and if she did, she'd call. I know she'd call me, if only to rub it in my face. Something has happened to her."

"All right," Vern said with a deep sigh. "I'll drive over to the Ritz and see if I can find her." He heard Sanders speaking to someone else.

"Wait a minute," said Sanders. "One of your men is here and wants to talk to you."

Brian came on the line. "Sir, we might have another problem. The night shift should've been here two hours ago to relieve us, but they never showed up. I've tried phoning them, but got no answer. I planned to call you, but then Sanders's dilemma with his wife came up."

"Okay," said Vern. "Keep trying to reach them. I'll be right there after I swing by the Ritz and check on the wife."

Vern quickly dressed, hopped into his SUV, and drove to the Ritz. He parked in front of the hotel and entered the lobby. With authority and the flash of a federal badge, he told the desk clerk he needed to speak to security. He soon stood in a backroom with numerous monitoring screens. Alongside him was Phillips, the head of night security, and his two guards. They watched the screens that held the footage obtained from surveillance cameras throughout the building.

"Pull up tonight's convention," Vern said. Four screens showed a view of the ballroom and seated guests. As the cameras panned the space, he searched for Mrs. Sanders. "Son of a bitch," he cursed when he saw her at the bar, but not alone. Next to her was Christian Roberts, decked out in a suit and looking like a million bucks. "Focus on the two at the bar." Roberts and Amber shook hands and seemed only to talk.

"Fast forward to the end of the event," Vern said. The crowd rose and slowly moved out of the room, but Roberts and Amber remained at the bar while the staff cleared the tables. Over the course of the evening, they apparently had become very friendly, leaning against one another.

When Roberts kissed Amber's forehead, one of the guards commented, "I bet he gets laid."

Vern watched the couple leave the ballroom arm-in-arm. "Give me a view of the hallway. I need to know where they went."

The hallway video proved Mrs. Sanders wasn't abducted. She was actually the aggressor. She pulled Roberts into a doorway indent, pinned him against the wall, and kissed him. The guard enlarged the image to scrutinize details. Spellbound, Vern and the guards watched as the kissing and groping escalated to clothes fumbling. Roberts lifted her up, and she clutched his neck and wrapped her legs around his waist. The copulation wasn't tame but hard-driving sex, as if the pair had been starved.

A guard chuckled. "I can't believe he's humping her in public. They couldn't even wait to get a room."

Roberts eventually released her with a tender kiss. Vern thought the show was over, but Mrs. Sanders obviously hadn't finished with her new lover.

Roberts tossed back his head and closed his eyes in submission as she chewed his neck and fondled him into a second arousal. He turned her toward the wall and penetrated from behind, so focused that he didn't stop even when a two-man cleaning crew walked past them.

"Damn!" said a guard. "That boy is an animal." The men were enjoying the performance.

Vern, however, had seen enough. "Fast forward this shit." The lengthy sex scene finally ended. Holding hands, the couple walked through the lobby to the hotel entrance. An outside surveillance camera showed Roberts giving the valet a ticket, and soon a dark blue Corvette pulled up to the doors. He and the girl got into the car and drove away.

"I need the hallway and outside footage on a thumb drive," said Vern to Phillips.

"I can download it to a disc," said Phillips.

"That'll work. Also print out a picture of that blond guy and show it to the staff. His name is Christian Roberts, but he might have checked in here under an alias. Call me if he returns to the hotel."

"What about the woman?"

"Forget you ever saw her." Vern knew the media would love to learn that the secretary of the Interior's wife had screwed the terrorist Captain Nemo. Waiting for the sexual encounter to be downloaded, he called Brian. "Did our men show up?"

"No, sir," said Brian, "and Sanders is freaking out. I had to stop him from calling the police."

"Tell that goddamn idiot I found out what happened to her, and she's okay. I'll be there shortly."

At four in the morning Vern drove up to Sanders's home, and the secretary rushed out before the SUV rolled to a stop. He looked inside the vehicle. "Where is she?" Sanders yelled. "They said you found her."

Vern eased out of the driver's seat. "I said I found out what happened to her. You were right about one thing. She's with Roberts. This should explain a few things." He handed the disc to Sanders.

Sanders stared at the disk with a puzzled expression. "What's this?"

"It's footage from the hotel. I suggest you fix a stiff drink and sit down before you watch it." He disliked the whiny little politician, but giving him the disc was cruel, even for Vern.

"But he might hurt her."

"As I said, he's not the type. Once I locate my missing men, we'll find her. That is if you still want her back."

Sanders looked at him strangely and walked back inside.

Brian stepped to Vern. "Roberts got his hands on the wife?"

Vern lifted an eyebrow. "His hands and dick, the disc shows them screwing for nearly an hour."

Brian glanced toward the inside of the house. "Sir, the secretary was going crazy, but that will blow his mind."

"I believe that was Roberts's intention. This is Sanders's own damn fault, marrying a girl half his age. Then she's out by herself, drinks too much, and a hot young stud sweeps her off her feet. Unsurprising she fucked him and left in his car." Vern wearily rubbed his forehead. "I can't deal with him now. We need to find our three men. Roberts is likely responsible for their disappearance, but the hotel surveillance shows he was at the Ritz all night. Proves he's not acting alone. I'll stay here and guard Sanders while you and Larry search for our men. Just be damn careful, Brian. Roberts has mob friends."

CHAPTER TWENTY-FOUR

In an all-night diner Christian sat in a window booth across from Amber. He lowered his coffee mug and asked, "You feel better now?"

She grinned and pushed the half-eaten plate of pancakes aside. "Much. I should've known not to drink on an empty stomach." She gazed down at the table and said quietly, "Thank you, Christian, for telling me everything about Jimmy. I still can't believe he had Vern murder those people."

"I hadn't planned to tell you, but when it all comes out, you shouldn't be blindsided. What are you going to do?"

"Go home. My family lives in Illinois. I'll file for divorce. Just so you know, it has nothing to do with you or what I learned tonight. I've been down in the dumps and fed up with my marriage for a while. With a good lawyer, maybe I'll get Jimmy's house." Her mood lightened. "It's a big house, and I could use a roommate. Any chance you're available?"

"Tempting, but you don't want me. I'm nothing but trouble."

"Because you're Captain Nemo?" she said, smiling. "Christian, I'm not the brightest bulb on the chandelier, but I can put two and two together. For hours you talked about saving animals, especially wolves, and then it clicked. I recognized you. Bored housewives read the tabloids."

"I'm only suspected of being him."

She chuckled. "You're him, but I don't care. You're as cute as Christmas, very sweet, and an incredible lover. That's good enough for me."

"Amber, you deserve a nice guy."

"Guess that's a no."

He reached into a back pocket for his wallet. "You need money?"

She lifted a small black purse. "I've got credit cards. They should be good for a few days before Jimmy cancels them."

They wandered out of the diner and climbed into the Vette. Christian drove Amber to the airport, where she could catch an early flight to Illinois. Initially she'd wanted to take a taxi back to the house, pack a bag, and tell her husband off. Christian convinced her just to leave. She could give him grief over the phone. By then Sanders and his henchmen might have learned she was with Christian. Confronting him face to face was dangerous.

At the Departures terminal, she leaned into the car window and kissed him goodbye. "Christian, I'll remember you as long as I live."

"Better if you forget me."

"Impossible." She laughed. "No woman could sleep with you and forget it."

* * *

Vern stood on the front porch and stared down the dark driveway. He preferred the chilly weather rather than being around the meltdown when Sanders watched his little wife jump Christian Roberts's bones. The disc attested to the lengths Roberts would go for payback. Sanders not only faced political ruin and prison, but also his personal life was devastated.

Vern fidgeting, thinking about what Roberts had in store for him. His phone rang, and he saw the call was from the Ritz. "Vern speaking."

"Mr. Vern, this is Phillips with Ritz security. I made some inquiries about the blond guy. Christian Roberts is not a registered guest, but I showed his picture to the girls at the desk. One of them said he looked different, had a beard and long hair when he checked in, but it was definitely the same guy. He used an alias, registered under Jeff Rhodes. He has a top floor suite, the best in the hotel. I also questioned the valet. He noticed his Corvette has a rental decal. I was fixing to call you with this information when he came in. He strolled right past me in the lobby and took the elevator up to his room."

"Did he have the woman or anyone else with him?"

"No, he was alone, but he looked a little whipped, tie and jacket off and messed-up hair. After being with that woman, he's headed for bed," Phillips said. "He shouldn't be any trouble if my men and I roust him. If he really is Christian Roberts and used a fake ID and credit card when registering, we can hold him in my office until you and the authorities get here."

"No, don't call the police or bother him. I'll handle it. Just keep me posted if he leaves again."

* * *

In the study Sanders fell into his desk chair and stared in a daze after watching the disc of Amber and Christian Roberts in the hotel hallway. Most husbands would be cursing, outraged that this bad boy, bad beyond the cliché, had seduced his young, gullible wife. Even more upsetting was Amber's passion for Roberts, something she'd never displayed during their marriage. Instead of anger, Sanders was in shock, as if a building had collapsed on him. He tried to analyze his missteps. *I should have addressed her needs and gone to those events. I should've done better in the bedroom.* He ran his hand through his hair. His biggest mistake was going after Captain Nemo.

The phone on his desk rang, but distressed, he didn't look at the caller ID or answer it. After several rings, he picked up the receiver. "Yes?"

"It's me, Jimmy," said Amber.

He leaned forward. "Amber, Amber, are you all right?"

"I'm fine."

"Tell me where you are, and I'll come get you."

"I don't think so, Jimmy. I'm leaving you."

"Amber, listen to me. That man you were with at the Ritz, he's a terrorist, a killer. He obviously manipulated you with his lies."

"So you know I was with Christian. He didn't manipulate me. You did. You had me believing you cared about wildlife, and behind my back, you were destroying it. And the murders, Jimmy, how could you have Vern kill those people?"

"That's not true. I had nothing to do with those murders."

"Jimmy, most people would ask what murders, but you know about them. That proves you're guilty and a liar. You deserve whatever Captain Nemo does to you." The line went dead. He slowly hung up the phone.

Vern rushed into the room. "I found him. Roberts is staying at the Ritz. As soon as my men get back, we'll go after the son of a bitch."

Sanders glanced up and said quietly, "Amber called. She's leaving me."

"Sanders, did you hear what I said? I'm going after Roberts."

Sanders couldn't focus on Vern's chatter. His mind was beginning to fathom that everything he had worked for and cared about was gone.

Vern shook his head at Sanders. The man was incoherent. Vern's cell rang, and it was Brian. Vern stepped back outside to take the call. "Did you find them?"

"I'm in Henry's condo. He's dead, sir, shot in the head at close range. It's a professional hit."

"Jesus Christ! Have you checked on the others?"

"We plan to head their way next, but what about Henry?"

"Just get out of there before someone spots you and you're implicated. Call me when you learn something." Vern suddenly heard two muffled shots that sounded like they came through a silencer, followed by two thuds hitting the floor. "Brian, Brian, are you there? Brian, answer me!"

A deep voice came on the line. "Afraid your boy is indisposed, along with the rest of your guys."

"Who's this?"

"The Captain sends his regards."

* * *

Christian pulled up to the Ritz after dropping Amber at the airport and handed the car keys to the parking valet. With his tie hanging loose around his neck, he pushed the hair out of his eyes and felt the head pounding from a slight hangover, the reason he didn't drink wine. He walked through the lobby to the elevator. In his room the curtains were ajar, and he gazed out at the dawn that highlighted the surrounding white monuments. Watching the sunrise had become a habit, wondering if every morning was his last.

He turned away toward the big soft bed. A few hours of sleep tempted him, but he had too much to do and too little time. He had to be in and out of Washington before someone besides Amber recognized him, and he was arrested.

He popped some Advil for the headache and jumped into the shower. When he emerged from the bathroom, he noticed Sal had left a text message that said only, "Done, and he knows." The meaning was clear. Vern knew his five men were history.

When it came to taking out the trash, Sal's guys were fast and efficient. Christian had learned so from personal experience. A few years back, a corrupt horse trainer and some cutthroat Arabs kidnapped Christian over a horse deal and planned to kill him in the Everglades. As they were about to slice Christian's throat, Sal and his crew came to his rescue. The kidnappers were never seen again.

Christian figured Sanders was probably devastated about his wife. Vern was likely freaking out over his dead men. Christian had them where he wanted, like a cat toying with a cornered mouse. Time for the next step and instigate more panic. He called Vern's cell phone.

* * *

"Damn, damn," Vern muttered after the anonymous voice informed him that his men were gone. He paced back and forth on Sanders's front porch as the sun came up. He rarely hesitated when making a decision, but Roberts had him flustered. On the sailboat, Roberts had warned he'd destroy Vern and Sanders. Now he was making good on the threat.

Vern's first instinct was to drive to the Ritz and blow the bastard to hell. That move, however, would be stupid. Killing Roberts at a prominent hotel in broad daylight was asking for prison. Even if Vern got away with it, he realized three hotel security guards knew he was looking at Roberts, and they would become witnesses, making Vern the prime suspect.

In addition if Vern left Sanders defenseless and the secretary was murdered, it could have repercussions. Russ Manning and others might take their business elsewhere.

His cell rang, but the caller ID didn't display a name. "Yeah?"

"How ya doin', Vern?"

"Who is this?" Vern asked.

"Your Florida buddy, say, how was that swim?"

"Roberts, is that you?"

"Yours truly," said Roberts. "I was thinkin' about now you're feelin' a little lonely."

"I'm going to get you, Roberts. I'm going to torture you for hours, tear your fucking nuts off. I'm going—"

"Hey, hey, settle down, Vern. I realize you're upset, but you should stop with the threats. They can have consequences."

Phone clicked, and Vern heard sounds of whistling wind and slosh of waves. "All right, you little shit," said his own voice on a recording. "What are you going to do with us?"

"Well, Vern, I'm not too happy with you," said Roberts's voice. "To cover up the misappropriation of funds in the government files, you killed that poor analyst in DC, made it look like an overdose. You then used a van to mow down my friend, Karen when she and her husband got wind of the files. And you've come after me twice. What I don't understand is why you strangled Barbara Davis? She told you that the analyst discovered the file and that got him killed. The woman was on your side."

Vern recognized the conversation that had taken place on Sarasota Bay aboard Roberts's sailboat. With dread, he listened to his response. "She fucked you, compromising her side and couldn't be trusted anymore. She was also careless, letting you get access to her computer. But what I did to her and the others is nothing compared to my plans for you."

Vern heard another click, ending of the recording, and Roberts came back on the line. "See, those threats have gotten you into a heap of trouble."

"You…you taped me on the boat."

"Actually it's a video, but it was dark, so the motion-sensing camera didn't pick up the best images. Although, your white hair does stands out."

"You can't use that in court."

"Maybe, maybe not, but when the cops hear you confess to the Davis murder, I believe the heat will shift from me to you."

"You son of a bitch," Vern growled.

"Yeah, you too, Have a nice day."

Vern collapsed into a porch rocker, huffing with anxiety. Again Roberts had outplayed him. For several minutes he couldn't think or move. He then realized he had one last hand to play. Something Roberts would never expect. He pulled out the phone and looked up Hagen's number, the Englishman hired to kill Roberts.

"I'm calling about Christian Roberts," said Vern. "Your informant was right. He's in DC. How soon can you get here?"

"I'm already here, chap, arrived yesterday." said Hagen. "He took a private jet from Cancun and landed in the Washington two days ago, but then his trail went cold."

"I know exactly where Roberts is," said Vern. "He's staying at the Ritz in a top floor suite, registered under Jeff Rhodes. A security guard is watching his movement and keeping me informed. He's also rented a dark-blue Corvette."

"Thank you, old boy. You're a big help. I'll go straight away to the Ritz and deal with him."

"Do me a favor. He's got a video recording I need."

"No problem. I'll be happy to retrieve it for you."

* * *

After Christian called Vern, he was feeling good. His plans were coming together so he took his time getting ready. He shaved and dressed in casual jeans and shirt and put on a black leather jacket. He stuffed his paperwork in a tote bag, slipped on his sunglasses, and meandered downstairs for his ride. He hopped into the Corvette and drove into the city traffic. He had requested the car as part of his guise, portraying a distinguished, rich guy, but after driving the Vette, he was falling in love. At a street light he tapped the gas, and the car responded like a dragster. He loved his new Porsche, but the Vette's sleek design and its sturdy fiberglass chassis gripped the road. The rumbling thunder of its engine screamed of power.

He had always been a water worshiper and invested every dime in surfboards, boats, fishing gear, and dive equipment. For years he had tooled around in a little rusted pickup and that was fine, never having the interest or money for cars. *Maybe if I'm not in jail or dead when this is over, I'll get one of these babies. I can afford two cars.* He realized the absurdity of considering such things in the middle of a treacherous operation.

In the busy downtown he arrived at the park that covered roughly a city block, and parallel-parked on the street across from *The Washington Post*. Massaging his jaw, he stared at the building and wondered if Trish was upset with him. He had promised to stay in touch but hadn't spoken to her in weeks. As a reporter, she surely knew he was wanted for murder and was hiding out on his sloop, making contact difficult.

Normally a good judge of character, he usually could sense a woman's feelings, but he wasn't a mind reader. Through the shirt he touched the scar below his ribs, a reminder of when he failed to predict a woman's anger. Trish wouldn't shoot him, but she had other means of destroying his life. He shuddered in the car seat. *I'm getting way too paranoid.* On the disposable phone, he dialed her number.

"Trish Stevenson," she said.

"Hey, it's me." There was a long silence. Not a good sign.

She finally said, "Christian, what a surprise. I thought I'd never hear from you again."

"I've been a little occupied."

"I've heard you're on the run to avoid a murder charge. It seems you're always in trouble. What do you want?"

Her icy tone made him leery, and his instincts screamed "Hang up and get out of here." Instead he shook them off and said, "I'm in DC, down in the park, and I'd like to give you something. It's important."

Another long pause ensued. "Fine. I'll be there in a minute."

He stepped out of the car and leaned against the fender. Their brief conversation conveyed she wasn't happy with him, but was she angry enough to call the cops and turn him in? Meeting up with her could be huge mistake number two.

Ten minutes passed, more than enough time for her to come down and see him. Maybe a call to the police was holding her up. Planning to get the hell out there, he opened the car door and climbed halfway in before noticing her in front of the building. He got out of the car and waved. She saw him but didn't reciprocate and wave back. He sucked in a deep breath.

After crossing the street and approaching, she scolded, "You were getting ready to leave, weren't you, Christian."

He stuffed his hands into the jean pockets. "Well, yeah, was thinking you weren't coming because you're obviously pissed at me."

Her eyes became slits. "That's not it, you bastard. You didn't trust me, and thought I was turning you into the police."

"That also crossed my mind," he said with a shrug. "Spend a day in my skin, and bad vibes bring out the red flags."

"Oh, you poor thing," she sniped. "You've created your own problems, but get it straight. I'm a journalist and you're my source. I'd never call the police."

"Okay, Trish, I'm sorry, but why are you so damn mad at me?"

"What did you want to give me?"

He removed the tote bag from the car. "Remember Karen, the woman who believed her analyst friend was murdered because he uncovered the fraudulent wolf-study files? I've got proof in here she was right. Trish, it's a huge government scandal."

Trish chuckled and shook her head. "Silly, me. I thought you were here to give me a ring. I should've known you'd never commit."

"Oh, didn't think of that." He lowered his head and chewed his lip. He finally asked, "If I had a ring, would you take it, Trish?"

"Probably not. We obviously have trust issues. So you have proof the analyst was murdered. Funny, I've also learned a few things about the analyst, like his boss was Barbara Davis, the woman you're accused of strangling."

"You know I didn't do it. I got proof in this bag."

"I never believed you killed her, but you did sleep with her. How could you, Christian? How could you screw her and then right after, you had the nerve to crawl into my bed?"

He looked upward, finally understanding her anger. "Let me explain." He reached out to take her hand.

"Don't touch me!" she said, jerking away. Her eyes watered. "We're done, Christian. I'm not interested in your explanation or bag of evidence." She swallowed, staring at him. "The next time I see you will probably be at your trial when I'll have to testify about your whereabouts that weekend. And I won't commit perjury for you."

"I don't want you to lie for me," he said quietly, staring at the curb. "Being with Barbara meant nothing. It was business. It was the only way I could get at her computer and expose the crimes against wolves."

"First sharks, now it's the goddamn wolves," she said. Tears streamed down her cheeks. "You care more about those animals than us or me."

"I never misled you, Trish. These causes are more important than my life. You should know that by now."

"I only know I loved you, Christian, and you broke my heart." She abruptly turned, ran across the street, and disappeared inside the brick building.

"Shit." He felt sick about hurting Trish. From the start she had stuck by him, but when it came to their relationship, he had warned her of his priorities. *Fucking causes,* he thought. He opened the car door and threw the tote bag on the passenger seat. Slamming the car door, he wandered into the park and sat down on a bench. With clasped hands, he tapped his thumbs against his chin and watched a mother and her two little kids run around the trees. He had wanted the same thing, a real life with a wife and kids, and he had delusions it could work with Trish. The pipe dream was now gone.

* * *

Agent Ralph McKenna sat in his white Toyota Camry on the street and read a newspaper. His private stakeout had become a daily ritual since Christian Roberts vanished several weeks earlier. Ralph and other law enforcement officers had searched for him, but by the time they had discovered his sloop was missing from Sarasota, Roberts had a minimum two-day head start. The Coast Guard pursuit with planes, helicopters, and ships had proved futile. Without knowledge of Roberts's destination, even satellites and drones were useless. The Gulf of Mexico, Caribbean Sea, and Atlantic were too vast to pinpoint a single sailboat. Ralph had flown to Florida in high spirits, anticipating Roberts's arrest, but returned to D.C, miffed.

The hunt for Roberts had gone digital. Most of Ralph's counterparts hoped Roberts would slip up and use a credit card or that he'd be spotted by a witness or surveillance camera. They figured Roberts would eventually turn up. Ralph was the only agent still actively pursuing him; the job had become an obsession. He felt indifferent toward other felons, but he detested Christian. Every past encounter, whether an interrogation or serving a search warrant, Roberts had a knack for undercutting Ralph's authority and making him look stupid. Most recently was his last trip to Florida.

Ralph had one lead, Roberts's girlfriend, a reporter at *The Washington Post,* so his off-duty hours, he followed Trish Stevenson in case Roberts contacted her. That morning he had trailed Stevenson from her apartment to her job and parked a half block down the street from the *Post* with a clear view of the front door. Glancing at his watch, he still had an hour before driving to the FBI field office to work on another case. With no time for breakfast, his stomach groaned, and he eyed the vending trucks lined up on the street. He left his car and walked the length of the park toward them, the aroma of cooked food growing stronger. The eight curbside trucks offered a variety of meals, but he settled on scrambled eggs, sausage, and hash browns. Holding the Styrofoam plate of food and cup of coffee, he started back to eat in his car, but instead of taking the sidewalk, he walked through the park to enjoy the scenery.

CHAPTER TWENTY-FIVE

At Sanders's home, Vern had informed the British assassin that Christian Roberts was at the Ritz-Carlton. Once Hagen took out Roberts, Vern could abandon the despondent secretary and get on with his life. First on his list was recovering the bodies of his dead men and arranging for their funerals. He stepped into the house to tell Sanders the latest news. Perhaps it would snap him out of the distress of losing his wife. Amazed that the pathetic man had risen so high in politics, he thought, *No wonder the country's in trouble.*

Vern walked into the den. Sanders hadn't budged. He still sat at his desk and stared in a stupor. "I just spoke to Russ Manning's guy," Vern said. "He's on his way to the Ritz to take out Roberts. That boy will pay for screwing your wife. Saunders, did you hear me?"

At first, Sanders had no reaction. He finally looked up and said quietly, "I'm tired. I think I'll lie down. When the housekeeper comes tell her she has the day off." Wearily he rose from the chair, appearing like he'd aged a decade overnight.

"Probably a good idea," said Vern. "I'll be in the kitchen having coffee if you need me."

Sanders trudged past and slowly ascended the stairs to his bedroom.

Vern entered the kitchen, and from an assortment of coffee he chose the one with the most caffeine. He placed it in the fancy machine, and his phone chimed.

"This is Phillips again, with Ritz security. I'm calling about your young guy, Christian Roberts. One of my men spotted him out front. A valet brought his car around, and he took off. I thought you'd like to know."

"Yeah, thanks." Vern disconnected and looked up Hagen's cell number to tell him Roberts was on the move. Before he pressed the numbers, he heard a loud bang upstairs that echoed throughout the house. Familiar with gunfire, he pulled his Glock from the shoulder holster and hustled to the staircase. His first thought was that Roberts's men had broken in and shot Sanders. He cautiously crept up the stairs with his arm extended, pointing the weapon with a finger on the trigger. At Sanders's bedroom, he kicked open the door and stepped into the room. The secretary was sprawled on the bloody bed sheets, the back of his head blown off, and his hand gripping a snub-nosed revolver. The room was undisturbed, windows locked, with no sign of a break-in or intruder.

"Jesus," Vern said and holstered his weapon. It was clearly a suicide, not unexpected, given his mood. Roberts had brought Sanders down without touching him.

The housekeeper would arrive soon, and Vern decided to let her find the body and deal with the police. His guard duty was over. Free to leave and act, he changed his mind about telling the Englishman that Roberts had left the Ritz. Vern wanted to take credit for killing the infamous Captain Nemo. Revenge further fueled his objective. Roberts had damaged Vern's reputation, turned his life upside down, and murdered his five men. He also hoped to restore Russ Manning's confidence in him. Lastly, he hated Roberts for outmaneuvering him at every turn. *Time to nail that Florida bastard.*

He hustled downstairs to Sanders's computer and did a search on car rental agencies that were close to the airport and carried Corvettes in their inventory. He found one and called it. "This is Detective Jones with the DC police," Vern said. "This is urgent. You recently rented out a dark-blue Corvette to Jeff Rhodes. That car would have a monitoring chip in case of theft. I need to know where the car is now."

"Of course, detective. I'll look it up," the agent said and a minute later he was back on the line. "According to the rental agreement, Mr. Rhodes took the car two days ago, and I remember him, tall, young, and blond. He struck me as a daredevil, and I had wondered if the car would come back in one piece."

"That's the guy."

After the agent relayed the data for the car's present location, Vern hustled out of the house and hopped into his SUV.

* * *

On the park bench Christian shook off the distress of losing Trish, deciding to deal with the guilt later. He shifted his focus and concentrated on his next step. With Trish unwilling to break the story about Sanders's and Vern's crimes, he moved to plan B, contacting a person he trusted, who was credible, and could take Christian's bag of evidence to the police and be believed. He pulled out his phone and dialed the number.

"Hey, Dave, it's me."

"Christian?" said Wheeler.

"Afraid so."

"Good god, I can't believe you're calling. Did you know there's a warrant out for your arrest? It's for murdering a woman in DC."

"I'm aware. Told you on the boat that charge was coming, and the evidence against me would be overwhelming."

"It is. I've seen what the police have. Listen. Go to the nearest police station and turn yourself in. Right now you run the risk of being shot down. Everyone is gunning for you,"

"That's nothing new. The reason I called is I have proof I didn't kill the woman and evidence for a slew of other crimes. I'd like to get it to you."

"Wish I could help, but I'm not with the FBI anymore."

"Jesus. How'd that happen?"

"The little chief in Idaho, Tucker, apparently has powerful connections and convinced a senator that you and I were too friendly. Came down from the top, I could either retire early or be fired."

"Damn. I'm sorry, Dave. Why didn't you just tell them the truth? You didn't do anything wrong."

"Screw them. Besides, I was ready to get out. I can now spend time with my daughter and maybe buy that boat. You said you'd teach me to sail."

"Maybe when I'm freer."

"That'll happen only if you do as I say. Where are you?"

"Rather not disclose that info right now."

"Fine, but take my advice. I'm trying to help you. Bring your evidence to the police and give yourself up. That is the best way to handle the situation."

"Already went down that road. Sat in a New York jail because no judge would let Captain Nemo bond out."

"But this is a different situation. You have proof of your innocence."

Christian chuckled. "Ain't different, Dave. Given my tarnished reputation, there's a good chance the cops won't believe me and will reject my evidence. If that happens, we both know how it would play out. I'll sit behind bars for a year while cops fuck around with the investigation and build a case. It would be another stretch in jail waiting for my trial, and then I'd have to gamble with a jury. Appreciate the advice, but no thanks. I'll take my chances on the streets."

"Christian, that route is better than being shot to death. You need—"

He lowered the phone, cutting Wheeler off in mid-sentence when he recognized an approaching man. "Are you shitting me," he muttered to himself and pocketed the phone. The beanpole in the suit ambled closer. The FBI agent was so focused on not spilling his drink or dropping his food that he hadn't spotted Christian.

During Christian's pursuit of saving sharks, he had come to know Ralph. The exchanges weren't friendly. Christian slowly rose from the bench, wondering, *What were the friggin' odds of bumping into this sucker in a DC park?* He considered fleeing, fairly confident he could beat the agent across the park. Once in the Vette, no car could catch him, and he'd be home free, but the agent probably carried a gun. Better to let Ralph come within striking distance, bring him down, disarm him, and escape. Christian lifted an eyebrow with the plausible plan.

Several feet away, Ralph glanced up, and Christian nodded with a smile. Ralph returned a grin, but then did a double take.

"How ya doin', Ralph?"

"Holy shit," Ralph exclaimed as his food items hit the ground, with coffee splattering his pant leg. He pulled back his jacket to grab his weapon.

Christian dove at him, knocked him on his back, and slugged his face, hoping to disable him. It didn't work. Ralph swung back and managed to punch Christian's lip. The fight became a wrestling match as the two men rolled around in the dirt and leaves, trying to subdue each other. Christian finally got behind him and applied a half-nelson, but the wiry agent elbowed his stomach, slipped out of the hold, and broke free.

Ralph scrambled to his feet as Christian rolled to a stand and stepped to him. Ralph raised his fists to defend himself. Boxing was more Christian's speed. He lacked a wrestler's weight and was quick on his feet with a long reach. Christian released several lightning-fast jabs to Ralph's nose. Despite the pounding, Ralph remained persistent and stepped in to retaliate.

As they circled each other with fists up, Christian analyzed his determined opponent. "Ralphie, you wanted to kick my ass in Miami," he taunted. "Here's your chance, boy." An antagonized rival tended to lose concentration and act hastily.

"Yeah, I've been hoping for this," Ralph said, puffing. The obvious reason he hadn't gone for his gun was to prove he could win the fistfight.

"Okay, Ralphie, let's do it."

Sneering, Ralph launched into a series of wild swings but didn't connect. Christian ducked and danced away from the futile attack and popped Ralph's nose, mouth, and eyes. With the relentless hammering, Ralph went on the defensive and raised his arms to protect his face. Christian switched targets and delivered a hard gut blow. Ralph doubled over, clutched his stomach, and staggered, but kept his footing. He looked at Christian with dread and took a wobbly step forward.

Christian shook his head. "Come on, man. Give it up," he said. "My mom's got a bunch of boxing trophies from my school days. You can't win, and I don't enjoy beating the snot out of you."

Ralph's eyes watered and he wiped the dripping blood from his nose and mouth with a hand. "I'm taking you in, Christian," he stammered, out of breath. "You have to pay for your crimes."

"I don't. I just have to live with them."

Several people in the park had moved closer to see the brawl. Ralph must have finally realized he couldn't physically subdue Christian, so he scrambled backwards and pulled his gun. "FBI. Hands up," he shouted, aiming his .45 semi-automatic.

Instead of lifting his hands, Christian placed them on his hips. Ralph was a clown, but Christian also knew the agent was a decent guy and played by the rules. He'd never shoot an unarmed man, especially in front of witnesses. "I'm leaving, Ralph. We'll catch up another day." Christian turned and took a step toward his car.

"Stop! Stop!" Ralph yelled.

Christian ignored him and started to move on.

Ralph fired into the dirt a few feet away. "I mean it, Christian." The gunfire sent the small gathering of observers screaming and running for cover.

Christian wheeled around, furious. "Are you fucking nuts?" he growled. "That goddamn bullet could've ricocheted and hit a kid."

"Well, well that would be your fault for resisting. Now please, Christian, stop and put your hands up," Ralph pleaded. His flushed face was streaked with sweat and blood, and he was so rattled that the weapon shook in his hand. "I don't want to shoot you."

"You'll have to. I'll die before going with you."

"Wheeler always said you were suicidal."

"Yeah, comes with the territory, but I also know you. Don't believe you'd shoot an unarmed man in the back." Christian turned on his heel and walked away.

"I'll wound you. I'll...I'll shoot your leg," Ralph screamed behind him. "Stop, Christian!"

For Christian the discussion was over. Ralph would either let him go or shoot him and risk the consequence of using deadly force. It was a gamble. Christian headed toward the street while Ralph kept yelling.

As Christian passed a large tree, he was blindsided. Someone leaped out from behind and tackled him, knocking him to the ground face first. A heavy body pinned him down, kneed his spine, and forced Christian's arm to his backside. When he struggled to break free, his arm was wrenched further back and up. The excruciating pain caused his eyes to tear, his limb close to snapping or being dislocated. He stopped thrashing. "All right, all right, I give up." Panting, he watched Ralph holster his weapon and rush in to further restrain him.

"I've got handcuffs," Ralph said excitedly. "Hold him until I get them on."

"It looked like you needed help, officer," said his attacker's voice.

"Yes, thanks. I'm FBI," said Ralph. "I should've had my radio with me to call for backup."

Christian felt the steel clamps tighten on his wrists. He still couldn't see his ambusher, but concluded that with the swift, proficient takedown, the man must have had expert training. When the two men hoisted Christian to his feet, he was nose to nose with the big lug who had tackled him. Vern wore sunglasses and a baseball cap to conceal his face and white hair.

"Ralph, don't trust this guy," Christian said emphatically. "He's a kill—" Vern clobbered the side of Christian's head before he could explain. Nearly rendered unconscious, he stumbled but was snatched upright and belted in his stomach. The sledgehammer blows knocked out his wind, and Christian huffed for air and tried to keep his knees from buckling. His head throbbed and reeled from dizziness, and his painful gut had him on the verge of retching. He stood, quaking like a tethered punching bag ready for more abuse.

Grinning, Vern grabbed Christian's jacket front to hold him in place and pulled back to deliver another wallop, but Ralph stepped in. "That's enough. Anymore and he'll have to be carried out."

"Yeah, this scrapper can dish it out but can't take it," Vern said with a chuckle.

The two men gripped Christian's arms to keep him steady and walked him through the park. Christian staggered, still stunned, as Vern explained to Ralph his military career and work with the CIA.

"It's lucky you came along when you did," Ralph said.

"Yeah, this boy was getting the better of you, but when I realized you were in law enforcement and trying to arrest him, I stepped in."

"He's Captain Nemo, the terrorist, and wanted for murder."

"I'll be damned. Maybe I'll get my picture in the papers."

"Actually, there's a substantial reward for him. You're definitely entitled to it."

"That's even better."

They reached Ralph's Camry and shoved Christian into the back seat. He collapsed on his side, his stomach and head still in anguish. He tried to regain his faculties and catch the conversation outside.

"I'll call it in," Ralph said. "A squad car can take him to a precinct. Hop in so I can get your name and info for my report." He rounded the car and sat down behind the wheel.

Vern climbed into the passenger seat.

Christian knew that he and Ralph would never see a precinct. Vern wanted Christian dead, and poor Ralph had become a witness who could ID Vern. Ralph picked up his radio, but Vern wasted no time revealing his gun and true nature.

"Put it down," Vern ordered, pointing the weapon at Ralph.

"What? What is this?" Ralph said and dropped the radio. "Who are you?"

"You should've listened to Roberts and not trusted me," said Vern, "Now slow and easy, hand over your weapon with your left hand."

Ralph removed his handgun from under his jacket and reluctantly handed it to Vern.

"Now I'll need the key to those cuffs." After securing Ralph's weapon and the key, Vern motioned with his gun. "Let's go."

"Where are we going?" Ralph asked, starting the car.

"Just drive." They went several blocks and Vern said, "Up ahead, turn into that alley."

Christian maneuvered quietly to his back. His hands were restrained, but he could still strike out with his feet. Ralph drove into the alley and passed several back doors to stores on the street.

A little way down, Vern ordered Ralph to stop.

In the back seat Christian quietly drew his legs up to his chest, coiling his body like a spring. When the Camry came to a stop, he kicked the back of Vern's head and yelled, "Run, Ralph!" With Vern busy fending off the blows, Ralph leaped out of the car, but not fast enough. Vern managed to get off a shot, and Ralph crumpled on the asphalt.

"You son of a bitch," Vern said and hopped out of the passenger seat to escape Christian's kicking feet. He rounded the car with the apparent intent to finish off Ralph.

Christian sat up and saw that Ralph was gone. He must have limped away and hidden behind the numerous garbage cans and Dumpsters.

"Goddamn it," Vern cursed and shoved a garbage can aside, looking for the agent.

The gunfire had drawn attention. A few doors down a man in an apron stepped out into the alley and yelled at Vern. "What's going on down there?"

Vern stepped to the Camry, threw open the back car door, and grabbed Christian's jacket. Yanking him close, he said, "I've had enough of your shit." With the heel of his gun he cold-cocked Christian.

* * *

Vern stared at Roberts, unconscious on the back seat. He'd love to kill the fucker, but that had to wait. Blood on the alley pavement confirmed he'd wounded the FBI agent. To find him and finish him off, he only needed to follow his blood trail, but first he had to eliminate the witness, the man standing in the doorway. He took a few steps toward the guy, but then two women appeared next the man. The three stared down the alley at Vern holding a gun.

It's becoming a goddamn party, he thought, and climbed back into the Camry. He was out of time to contain the situation; in a few minutes the cops could arrive. He started the engine and threw the car in reverse. Backing out of the alley would prevent the rear plate from being seen. He merged with the city traffic, wondering if his hat and sunglasses were enough of a disguise so the three witnesses couldn't pick him out of a lineup. They were a good distance away, and with any luck, the wounded agent would die before he talked. Odds were fifty-fifty he'd beat this shooting.

As Vern drove, a scheme formed in his mind. He had an hour or two before the police put the case together, identified the agent, and searched for his Camry. Before ditching the car, he needed to stage

Roberts's suicide so he'd be found dead in this car with a bullet in his head and the agent's gun in his hand. The cops would buy it. Terrorists often blew their brains out rather than face capture. Before implementing the plan, he had one loose end, getting the video recording of his murder confessions on the sailboat. Roberts knew where it was, and he still breathed for that reason.

Vern took the George Washington Memorial Parkway to the city outskirts and headed for Roaches Run Reserve, a quiet place with few witnesses so he could deal with his hostage. Roberts's background attested to the fact he wasn't easily intimidated. To get the tape might take torture and time.

Vern repeatedly glanced over his shoulder, checking that Roberts wasn't coming around. At the reserve he drove past the lake and entered Long Bridge Park. Half the park was a former industrial wasteland and remote. He drove down a gravel road surrounded by tall reeds and parked on the edge of the lake. The place was deserted except for some waterfowl. The birds seemed oblivious to the large city beyond and the roar of jets taking off from the nearby airport.

Vern opened the back door, dragged out Roberts's limp body, and dropped him on the muddy grass. Although Vern shook and yelled at him, Roberts remained out cold. Vern straightened and stared at him in frustration. Maybe the blow from the gun grip had been too hard, and Roberts was in a coma.

The loud quacks from two squabbling mallards caught Vern's attention, and he focused on the lake. *A dunking in frigid water might revive this bastard.*

Snatching Roberts up, Vern tossed his lanky body over a shoulder, trudged into the lake, and dropped him in a few feet of water. The startled fowl squawked and took flight. For several moments, he massaged his jaw and stared at Roberts's submerged body, considering whether to save him or let him drown. Roberts's profile indicated he was a sailor, surfer, and scuba diver, the kind unlikely to die from drowning. Not only would the cops question his death, but it also wouldn't fit Vern's intended suicide scenario. He reached down to retrieve his captive but, Roberts jolted upright and sat, choking and coughing.

Vern laughed. "Boy, I was starting to think you were brain dead."

Roberts finally stopped hacking. He shivered and looked up wide-eyed at Vern. His bewildered state didn't last long. His alarmed eyes mellowed when he glanced at his surroundings. Tossing the wet strands of hair from his face, he cleared his throat and asked evenly, "What are we doin', Vern?"

"Where's the video recording of me?"

With a headshake, Roberts chuckled. "Was wondering why I'm still alive. Although once I tell you, I'm a dead man."

"Yeah, but consider how you want to go out. Give me the recording and I'll make it short and sweet. Refuse and it'll be bad. With anyone else cuffed and sitting in a lake, I'd start with waterboarding, but it might take too long with you. And I'm in a hurry." He took out a pocket knife and flicked open the blade. "Maybe I'll make good on my earlier threat and remove your nuts. I imagine they're rather important to a young prick like you."

"I'm not *that* young." He smirked. "But I'll save you the mess. The recording is on an iPad, and it's where you, literally, ran into me at the park. It's in a tote bag on the seat of a blue Vette parked across from *The Washington Post*."

Vern stepped back and studied him. His initial plan was to eliminate Roberts once he learned the location of the recording, but the damn guy was so calm and cool, Vern couldn't tell if he was telling the truth. If the recording wasn't in the car and Roberts was dead, Vern would never find it. "It better be there or—"

"You'll kill me?" Roberts smiled. "Sorry, Vern, but those threats don't work on me. I toy with ending my life all the time. If I croak, my only regret is failing to save the wolves. I really hoped to do that."

Vern had looked forward to Roberts's terror when taking his last breath, but realized the ballsy piss-ant would probably die with a grin. Vern had trained hundreds of men, and Roberts was a rarity, a combination of brains, talent, and raw courage. Vern had enjoyed watching the boy whip the agent's ass. Under different circumstances, Roberts would've been a welcome addition to Vern's team. "Roberts, you've been a fucking headache, but I'll give you this. Your wolves have one less enemy. After Sanders saw you fuck his wife on hotel surveillance, he shot himself."

"Really? He's dead? Kinda wish he'd lived to change those policies against wolves."

"You said you'd destroy him and did. Now get up." Vern reached down and jerked Roberts to his feet.

"Where're we off to?"

"Back to the park for the recording," Vern said. "If it's not there, you won't just die. I'll fuck up that pretty face so bad the coroner will need DNA to ID you." He shoved the back of his cuffed prisoner and walked behind him to the car.

Vern popped the trunk and picked up some rags near the spare tire. He crammed them into Roberts's mouth and with another rag, secured it around his head. He couldn't risk having a voice yelling for help inside the trunk. He next removed the Vette keys from Roberts's jeans. "Get in."

Roberts stepped into the trunk and curled up.

Vern wasn't taking any more chances with this boy's long legs, opening the trunk to a kick in the teeth. He removed his belt and fastened it tightly around Roberts's ankles. He smiled at his bound and muzzled captive. "You never looked better," he said and shut the trunk. After he had the recording, he had no intention of giving Roberts a quick, painless death. Vern was an expert on inflicting pain without leaving a mark. Before the suicidal bullet to the head, Roberts would suffer for killing his men.

He sat down in the Camry and sent a short text message to Russ Manning in Texas that said, "Worries over. I got CR." He started the engine and drove back to DC.

* * *

Russ Manning read Vern's text with pleasure, knowing Christian Roberts was no longer a problem. Getting back to work, he turned to his office computer and read his emails. Most concerned NGA business and were boring messages from faculty, along with a few from legislators and gun companies. He came across a personal email from Tim Nugent, an old rock star and hunter. The guy was a hoot. During the public outrage over the shooting of Cecil, the lion in Africa, Tim had further enraged the bleeding-heart animal lovers and posted a photo online of him and a dead lion he'd shot.

The subject of this latest email was "My next kill." and the contents said, "Russ, Florida bear haven't been hunted in years and should be easy pickings. See the attachment. Hope you'll join me. Tim." Russ opened the attachment.

It contained a Florida newspaper article with a photo of a bear and her cubs. The story was about the controversial bear hunt. Twenty years earlier the Florida black bear had nearly gone extinct from overhunting. They became protected and their numbers increased to 3,000. The Florida Wildlife Commission had a slim majority of pro hunters, and they voted to open bear season again. The decision created public outcry and protests took place in many cities, claiming the bears weren't a nuisance. Tim, being a celebrity, was quoted in the article that he'd be in Florida for the hunt.

Russ knew one of the Florida commissioners who voted in favor of the hunt. She owned thousands of acres in the Everglades where some of the 150 endangered Florida panthers lived. Because of the panthers, she couldn't turn her land into a housing development. The panthers had to go, and she had suggested a panther hunt. The outcome was still pending. Russ found it amusing that a commissioner who was supposed to protect wildlife was doing her utmost to destroy it.

He flipped through his calendar for the hunting date, seeing if he could get away. Tim was right about the bears. They'd grown accustomed to people in the parks and would be easy targets. It would be more slaughter than sport.

* * *

Steve closed the lid of his laptop and leaned back. He was finished. Christian's suggestion of using an email from the washed-up rock star had fooled Russ Manning into opening the attachment. Steve now had access to Manning's computer and learned about the NGA's contacts, memberships, and its bank accounts. Steve compiled a long list of names and proof of the payoffs that went to governors, congressmen, and senators. Even the director of the US Fish and Wildlife Service had received bribes to destroy wildlife. The scandal was enormous.

He had only one job left, and it required only a few taps of the keys to complete the task, but he was waiting to hear from Christian. He found it a paradox that his entire career had been in security, protecting people and companies from hackers, computer viruses, identity theft, and financial fraud, but now he had committed a huge cyber attack. He often wondered about his decision, jumping in with both feet and let the dashing terrorist lead him to where he sat, a felon, hiding out in Mexico.

Karen came down the stairs with her new little dog on her heels. "How's it going?"

"I've gotten everything Christian wanted. I'm just waiting for his call to wrap it up." He glanced up her. "Karen, are we doing the right thing here? I mean I want to bring down those guys, but once I commit this major crime, we might never be able to go home. We'll be on the run like him."

"You're asking if it's the right thing to do. It is. We have one life, one chance to do good and bring about change."

"God, you're starting to sound like Christian."

"I almost died, Steve. That can open your eyes."

"When this is over, where will we go?"

"Home is wherever we make it." She bent down and kissed his cheek. "I'm proud of you."

Frankie walked in from the patio. "Hey, I just heard from Sal. He's back in Sarasota and called from the Hyatt. Vern's men are goners, the same bastards that put Karen in the hospital and killed Mitch."

"Good," Karen said. "The assholes also killed my dog."

"Sal also learned that Sanders shot himself. We can go back to the States soon."

"What about Christian, any word?" Steve asked.

"Not yet. He's taking care of Vern, but I'm sure he's okay."

CHAPTER TWENTY-SIX

Vern drove toward downtown DC in the white Toyota Camry with his hostage, Christian Roberts, gagged and bound in the trunk. He anxiously tapped the steering wheel with his thumbs. Returning to Roberts's rental, the blue Vette at the park was risky, but the car held the video recording of Vern's murder confessions. He had to get it or face a multiple murder charge. A glance at his watch conveyed that two hours had passed since the fistfight between Roberts and the FBI agent and shoving Roberts into the back seat of this car. Several people had witnessed the altercation and Roberts's arrest, but had the police tied the park incident to the alley shooting several blocks away when Vern shot the agent? What if the cops learned the getaway car belonged to the agent and were looking for the Camry and checking plates?

As a precaution, Vern pulled off the highway into a shopping mall. On the fringe of the crowded parking lot, he used his pocket knife to remove the license plate from a car and placed the stolen tag on the Camry. With umpteen white Toyotas, a cop wasn't likely to pull him over without the right tag number. Less apprehensive, he resumed his trek to DC.

He arrived at *The Washington Post* building and saw the Corvette parked exactly where Roberts claimed it would be, but Vern didn't stop. He circled the block, scoping out the area. Busy people hustled down the sidewalks and a few kids and their parents occupied the park square. Everything looked normal. Without a squad car in sight, he breathed a sigh of relief. If the FBI agent had survived his gunshot wound and conveyed the location of his abduction, the police would be swarming the area.

Vern found a parallel parking space about ten cars down from the Vette. With its keys in hand, he strolled up the street. Across from the sports car on the sidewalk, a scrawny guy sat on a bench, engrossed in a newspaper. He didn't appear to be an undercover cop or FBI agent, so Vern ignored him and approached the Vette. Through the passenger window he saw the tote bag on the car seat and hit the unlock button on the key ring. After the car lights blinked and the door clicked, he reached for the handle to retrieve the bag.

"You must be Vern." The man had left the bench and stood behind Vern.

Vern jumped and stepped back, alarmed that a stranger knew him. "Who the fuck are you?"

The man chuckled. "Sorry, ol' boy, I didn't mean to startle you," he said with an English accent. "I'm Hagan, Mr. Manning's associate, sent to dispatch Mr. Roberts. We've spoken on the phone. I make a habit of identifying the colleagues on an assignment so I knew you from your photo."

Vern's tense body relaxed when he recognized the guy's voice, but he lifted an eyebrow, seeing him. The Brit was supposedly a bad-ass hit man, but this odd-looking little guy hardly fit the part. "You're not what I expected."

"Exactly. I'm successful because I don't look like a threat, and people drop their guard. But even still, you seem a little jumpy."

"I am. Roberts's guys snuffed out my men, and the cops might be looking for me. So how did you know I was here?"

"We're must have followed the same leads. I learned Roberts left the Ritz in this rental," Hagan said, glancing at the Corvette. "I've been here an hour, waiting for him to return to his car."

"I got him."

"I see." The Englishman sighed. "That explains the no-show. He's dead then?"

"Not yet." Vern opened the car door, removed the tote bag, and rummaged through papers until he held an iPad. "This holds the recording I wanted," he said with a grin. "Now that boy is toast."

Shaking his head, Hagan was obviously not as delighted as Vern. "This creates a problem for me. I've gone through great trouble and expense to find the young chap. If I don't do the job, I'll have to forfeit my fee."

Vern chuckled. "Guess you do have a problem, then."

"Perhaps we can come to an arrangement. How much are you being paid for the contract?"

Vern reflected that his bankroll, Secretary Sanders, was dead, and Russ hadn't hired him for the hit. He'd likely receive nothing for killing Roberts. "It's not about money. I lost five good men because of Roberts."

"Ah, revenge. It's sweet, but currency is more practical. I can give you both. I will pay you one million dollars for the young man. That still leaves me with a tidy profit for my efforts, and I'll guarantee he'll pay dearly for your men. We can settle this with one phone call." He took out his cell phone, anticipating that Vern would go for the deal.

Vern stared into the distance in thought. He wanted the satisfaction of killing Roberts, but realistically, the short-lived pleasure wasn't worth a cool million, especially since Roberts would die anyway. "Okay, you can do the deed, but I want to see the lights go out in his eyes."

Hagan laughed. "You really do hate the poor bloke. But sure, you can watch." Punching keys on his phone, he electronically transferred the funds into Vern's account. After Vern verified the deposit on his phone, he asked, "So where is this famous terrorist, Mr. Roberts?"

"He's up the street in a car trunk, hogtied and muzzled. Here are the keys for the car and cuffs," Vern said, handing them over. "It's a late-model white Toyota Camry."

"A white Camry?" Hagan said with a frown. "I keep abreast of the police chatter when working a city. I heard such a car was involved in a shooting, not far from here. Any correlation?"

"That was me. To get Roberts I had to kill an FBI agent and take his car, but no worries. I switched the tag on the car."

"Very natty work, sir," the Englishman said with disgust. "The agent didn't die but is in critical condition. If he talks, the police will learn you have his car, and the car's guidance system will lead here to you."

"Shit," Vern said. The agent could also reveal where he'd been abducted. Walking across the park to his SUV had become chancy. "Just make sure you kill that fucker." He clutched the tote bag, slid into the Corvette, and sped off.

* * *

Here I go again, another Hitchcockian dilemma, Christian thought while he lay in the dark trunk of the moving car and anticipated his death. He wasn't fearful, not because he was crazy or suicidal; he just figured the journey and struggle was over. Closing his eyes, he pictured a reef of circling sharks. Despite his many wrongs, he'd accomplished some good. His reflection shifted to the wolves. *Yeah, but I ain't done.* He drew in a breath and thought with wavering optimism, *I've been here before, and things usually worked out okay.*

He listened to the road noise as car drove back to DC. Unconscious on the trip to the lake, he wasn't sure where he'd been, but he'd seen the city buildings and the eastern light on the horizon that suggested late morning. He estimated he had less than an hour before Vern arrived at the downtown park. Once in possession of the recording, Vern wouldn't make a second trip out of the city and would most likely kill Christian in a back alley, like poor Ralph. With limited options and time running out, escaping his predicament was iffy.

Fortunately his long frame, legs, and arms were an advantage. Bending his spine, he pulled his legs to his backside so his handcuffed hands could reach the belt around his ankles. The maneuver wasn't easy in the confining space, but he managed to unfasten the buckle and free his legs. When the trunk opened, he now could kick Vern's face, jump out, and make a run for it. *Shit, before going ten feet, I'll probably get shot. Gonna need a huge stroke of luck.*

The car slowed and stopped. He heard no sound of nearby traffic. A few minutes later the journey resumed. They were again on a freeway. Christian went to work on his next task and rubbed his face against the trunk sides to loosen the rags tied around his head and in his mouth. Without the gag, he could call to people near the car. Vern had fastened the cloth securely, and its removal proved difficult.

The Camry no longer sped down a highway, but moved about thirty miles an hour, stopping and going for traffic lights. They were back in the city. Fifteen minutes later the car slowed, halted, and maneuvered backwards into an apparent parking space. "Damn," Christian muttered, certain he'd reached the park. The motor stopped and he heard the car door open and shut. Vern had left to get the recording.

Christian coiled his body so he could lash out with his feet. He considered Vern's height and where his head would be when the trunk popped opened. Nervously he waited. In hopeless and tense fixes, he became less edgy when he thought about his wife who put him on his path to save wildlife. The day she died he had wanted to join her. With that possibility looming, peace replaced his anxiety.

A half hour passed, more than enough time for Vern to take the tote bag from the Vette and return. Had something happened to him? Maybe he was arrested. The prospect was dashed when he heard footsteps approach the trunk and the jingle of car keys. Odd that Vern would open the trunk on a busy street and risk witnesses seeing his hostage. The trunk lock clicked, and as light flooded in, Christian struck out with his feet, but failed to hit the target.

"Whoa," yelled a man, jumping back as Christian's shoe nearly clipped his forehead. "You're like a damn Jack in a box." Peering into the trunk, he smiled. His short stature had saved him from a head blow.

Christian couldn't believe his eyes and garbled into the gag, trying to speak to Bill.

"Hold on, hold on," Bill said. "Turn over so I can unlock those cuffs. You sure got yourself in a hell of a mess."

With his hands free, Christian climbed out and ripped the gag out of his mouth. He hugged Bill and said, "God, I'm glad to see you." During the squeeze, Bill got in a peck on the cheek.

They pulled apart, and the ugly little guy rocked on his heels, grinning. "Kissing you made all my trouble worthwhile."

Christian laughed and cupped Bill's cheeks. "Shit, man, you deserve one from me," he said and kissed Bill's forehead. "I thought for sure I was a goner. So how in the world did you know I was in DC much less in this trunk?"

"You can thank your fat friend, Sal. He told me you were here," Bill said. "You had us worried, and we decided one of us should watch over you. From my experience even the best laid plans hit snags."

"Ain't that the truth," Christian said with a sigh. Who could've predicted he'd bump into Ralph, an FBI agent who knew him, and Christian couldn't have foreseen Sanders's suicide, which freed Vern to track him down. "You obviously weren't around when Vern grabbed me."

"Sorry about that. I came late to the party. I monitor a hit list, and your name showed up. I notified the London contractor that I'd take the job. Then Sal called and said you left Mexico for DC. I lost track of you after the airport, but then Vern informed me of your hotel and the car rental." He laughed. "He thought I was the Brit out to do you in. I've got a pretty good accent. If Vern only knew how I felt, I doubt he'd been so helpful."

"How'd you find Vern and get him to turn me over to you?"

"I tracked down your Corvette and was waiting here for you when Vern walked up. He said he had you locked in a car truck. I had to pay him a million bucks for you."

"Guess I'm back to owing you money. Where's Vern now?"

"He mumbled something about having the recording, and he left in your car."

Christian scoffed. "He's an idiot. As if I didn't make copies of that recording. Looks like I'll have to deal with him later."

"Yes, much later. Right now we need to distance ourselves from this stolen Toyota. The cops might be looking for it."

They started down the sidewalk, and Christian said, "Yeah, I'm concerned about the owner of the Toyota."

"The FBI agent?" said Bill. "He's in pretty bad shape."

Christian stopped walking. "But Ralph is alive? Jesus, that's a relief."

"Christian, you keep a strange mix of friends, criminals, and lawmen. That's not healthy, dear. How about we have a drink, and I'll enlighten you?"

"Sounds good, but first I'd like to go to my hotel and get out of these wet clothes. Vern dunked me in a lake."

"When we're in your room, you could forget the million and repay me in other ways."

"Man, you're relentless." Christian chuckled, half astonished, half amused. "You know my answer."

"Damn." Bill sighed. He glanced up and halfheartedly asked, "Can I at least see you shirtless, Christian?"

Christian slung his arm over the little guy's shoulder and smiled. "Let's go, buddy."

* * *

At 5:30 in the afternoon Charlie Tucker left the Salmon police station and drove home. An unfamiliar black sports car was parked in front of his house. His eyes narrowed with suspicion when he pulled into his driveway and got out of his Jeep. No one in Salmon owned a fancy Tesla. To spend that much on a car, its owner had to be a green-energy, climate-change nut. Strolling to his house, he wondered what the out-of-towner wanted.

He stepped inside the foyer and called. "Liz, whose car is out front?"

His wife rushed to him. "Oh, Charlie, it belongs to a nice young man. He's in the living room, waiting for you. His organization helps wolves, and he needs protest permits in case the town has another predator hunt."

"Why in the hell did he come to my house?" Charlie grumbled, hanging up his hat, jacket, and gun belt on the wall hooks. "You should have sent him to the station." He rounded the corner with Liz on his heels and stopped short. Christian Roberts sat on the living room couch with a drink in his hand.

Christian placed the glass on the coffee table and slowly rose. "Chief Tucker, I hope I'm not catchin' you at a bad time. I promise this won't take long, and I'll be out of your hair."

Stunned, Charlie's mind raced, and he couldn't speak or move. A terrorist, a killer was before him, but with his weapon in the foyer, out of reach, he couldn't protect his scatterbrained wife or arrest Roberts. Before he could react, Liz stepped to the coffee table.

"Christian, don't worry," she said. "Charlie has plenty of time. Dinner won't be ready for an hour." She picked the empty glass. "Would you like more tea?"

"Yes, ma'am," Christian said. "You make great sweet tea, just like back home."

Charlie quickly got the gist of things. Besides being female eye candy, Roberts was behaving like a sweet Southern boy, and Charlie's naïve wife had fallen under his spell, blind to any danger. "Yeah, get him another drink," he said gruffly, never taking his glare off Roberts. "And I'll take coffee." Brewing a pot would keep her in the kitchen. When she left the room, he growled low, "Goddamn it, what the devil are you doing here?"

"Calm down, Charlie. I just wanna talk."

"Talk? I should arrest you for murdering that woman in DC."

"I didn't kill her and have proof. It's one of the things I'd like to discuss."

"Why come to me? You should be talking to your friend, Wheeler."

"Yeah, about Wheeler," he said, sitting back down on the couch. "You've had a gut feeling that something went on between Dave and me, and you were right. So here it is. We were on Miami Beach one night when Dave spotted a really bad dude, suspected of raping and murdering several women. He took off after the guy. I tagged along a little ways behind to watch his back. God, it happened so fast. The guy got the drop on Dave, took his gun, and shot Dave in the shoulder. I showed up and knocked the crap out of the bastard before he could fire another round and finish Dave off. End of story."

Charlie eased into a stuffed chair opposite the couch and searched Roberts's blue eyes. His steady stare and unflinching body language suggested he spoke the truth. "I read about that shooting when I checked Wheeler's background, but the report didn't mention you."

"Guess Dave thought I had enough problems and left me out of it. We both did each other favors that night, but since then, he's never done anything for me, and I've never asked. And before you go there, I jumped in and saved Dave because I liked him. Still do."

"Why didn't Wheeler tell me?"

"Maybe he figured it was none of your business. Besides, how'd that look, a suspected terrorist helping an FBI agent? Anyway, it's because of Dave that I'm here. Your connections got him promoted and booted out of the FBI. The high-ups must listen to you, and I need your help."

Charlie chuckled at the absurd. "Instead of helping, I should throw you in jail."

"That's still a possibility," Christian said with a smile, "but before you do, let me explain a few things."

"Okay, you've got an hour." He was more relaxed with his outlandish guest. He could see that Roberts wasn't here to cause trouble. At their previous meeting, Charlie had left Florida angry, having nothing to show for his trip, but his years in law enforcement had sharpened his instincts. The young man wasn't sadistic or deranged and was only a danger when his life or wildlife was threatened. Charlie could deal with that.

Liz came back with iced tea and hot coffee. "Can I get you boys anything else?"

"No, we're fine," said Charlie. "We need to discuss business now." It was her cue to leave. Before she withdrew, Christian thanked her.

Christian then took out his cell phone, and said, "I'd first like to clear up that woman's murder. The video on my phone will prove I'm not guilty of the crime. It was recorded on my sloop after those men came aboard and tried to kill me. You kinda met them. They're the same ones who shot up your rental car on my farm. Vern, the white-haired dude in the video, also recently shot an FBI agent in DC." He tapped keys and handed the phone to Charlie.

Charlie leaned back and watched. When the video was over, he was astonished. "You should've given this recording to the FBI or DC police right away."

"Charlie, that's a little tricky for me. I'm supposedly Captain Nemo and not exactly in good standing with the law. I doubt the cops would believe my evidence or me. I thought about going to the press, but the rest of my information is political. The media nowadays has become too slanted, and some tend to ignore or manipulate the facts to fit their agenda. That's why I've come to you. I'm hoping you'll expose everything I've uncovered."

"Why me? I'm a police chief in a little town in the boonies."

"True, but you're perfect to handle this. Important officials in both parties respect you, know you're honest. They'll take these findings seriously. You're also a stubborn SOB who latches onto a case and doesn't let go." With a chuckle and a shrug, he said, "I should know. Regardless, you're the type of man who will right a wrong, no matter the consequence or what it takes. And lastly—" He stood and gazed out the window at forests and mountains. "With your reputation, you could live anywhere, but you chose to be here, on the edge of the wilderness. That makes me think you care about the environment and its wildlife. You're not a wolf lover, but also not a hater. With no bias and loads of credibility, you're the one to reveal this evidence. Don't necessarily like you, Charlie, but I trust you."

Charlie took a sip of coffee, mulling over Roberts's proposal. For months he'd spent time and energy to build a case and lock up the young guy who sat before him. Charlie huffed with the ludicrous notion of helping Christian. "I don't like you either, especially knowing you're the fanatic who blew up the restaurant in my town. But you got me curious. I'll look at your stuff and try to keep an open mind."

"That's all I ask." Christian removed a stack of papers from a satchel. For an hour he explained the government file, with misappropriated funds that led to the cover up and motive for several murders, including the DC woman. The bank statements showed the payoffs to kill wolves so the hunting and gun clubs could have more game.

Charlie was astonished with the conspiracy that Christian unraveled. He had the names and evidence to support his findings. "If this comes out, some big heads are going to roll."

"One already has. The secretary of the Interior committed suicide." Christian clutched his jaw in thought. "I just want this bullshit to stop, Charlie. Politicians shouldn't be able to wipe out a species for lobby payoffs."

Charlie looked down at the paperwork. "I imagine the congressmen will be tripping over each other, passing a bill that protects wildlife. And it'll be suicide for the president if he doesn't sign it into law."

"That's my hope."

Liz came back into the living room. "Charlie, dinner is ready." She smiled at Christian. "Would you like to join us? I fixed meatloaf, and we have plenty."

"Thank you, ma'am, but I need to get," Christian said, rising. "Your husband was already kind enough to give me an hour of his time."

"No, stay," said Charlie. "Have dinner with us."

Christian shrugged. "I do love meatloaf."

When they sat down at the table and began to eat, Liz opened the door to Christian's passion. "I don't understand why you'd want to protect wolves," she said.

Christian launched into his reasons, explaining how wolves balance the environment. By reducing the coyote population, wolves benefitted every creature, from mice to fox to eagles.

"That is interesting, but the wolves kill the deer," said Liz. "People in this town don't like that."

"Yes, ma'am, but too many deer isn't necessarily a good thing. It's bad for an ecosystem and the deer themselves," said Christian. He then talked about the harm of overgrazing, and the wolves weeding out the sick and old deer, which prevented starvation in winter.

Liz batted her eyes and grinned. "You certainly are well informed, but I know hunters who would disagree. They hate the wolves."

"I'm sure they do," Christian said with a nod. "Without deer covering the hills, they probably have to hunt a little harder, but let's consider other people. Tourists visit your national parks, and at the top of their list of animals to see is the wolf. Having wolves in your state is a benefit to the local restaurants, shops, hotels, car rentals and so on. Hunters and trappers get a few hundred dollars for a wolf pelt, yet that single wolf alive puts thousands of dollars in the taxpayers's pockets. It's not logical that your state officials ignore the resident needs and side with the hunters." He glanced at Charlie and said, "Unless they're being paid off."

Charlie ate quietly and listened to Christian talk about wolves. His convictions were persuasive. After dinner, Christian thanked Liz for the home-cooked meal, and Charlie accompanied him to the door. "Christian, I'm going to do my damnedest to bring justice to the scoundrels and expose their crimes," he said in the doorway, "Son, I believe you've saved your wolves."

* * *

In his office Russ Manning sat at his desk and held his aching head. The headache was getting worse after ending a call with the National Gun Association's chief lawyer. The news wasn't good. The government fraud and payoffs had been revealed, and at the heart of the scandal was the NGA. The lawyer warned Russ to expect search warrants for the organization's business transactions.

Even more alarming, the NGA members were deserting the organization in large numbers. Russ's office was flooded with their calls, emails, and letters, saying they were appalled and outraged that the NGA had moved beyond its purpose to protect gun rights and was trying to exterminate wolves to artificially inflate the deer herds. Only the hard-core trophy hunters still backed the NGA and its decision. Hunting clubs were also under fire for contributing to the payoffs.

Russ couldn't believe that a loud-mouthed little police chief from Idaho could rock his huge organization. Although, the real foe was Christian Roberts. When asked where the documents came from, the chief flatly said that to protect the wolves, Captain Nemo had uncovered the scandal. Russ was unable to contact Vern to find out if he'd killed Roberts. Martin Hagan in London said that as far as he knew, the terrorist was dead, yet Russ remained skeptical. No body had been discovered. It didn't matter now. The scheme had been revealed.

Russ's lawyers argued that the documents had been obtained illegally through computer hacking, but the investigators bought Captain Nemo's evidence, verified it and followed up with warrants. Russ's accomplice, the secretary of the Interior and his suicide further contributed to the buzz. The apparent motive was that Sanders feared exposure for his wrongdoing and prison. The fact that his wife had left him was barely a consideration.

Russ breathed deeply, resolved that he and the NGA would have to ride out the storm. The organization had the lawyers and finances to drag the case out for ten years. People would eventually forget, and in the end, the NGA might have to pay a large fine. The NGA was too big and wealthy to be destroyed.

Hearing a knock on his door, he lifted his head and his secretary stepped into his office. "Mr. Manning, there's a problem. I've received two calls this morning, one from an ad agency and another from a lodge. They say our checks to them bounced because of insufficient funds. I was going to call the bank, but thought maybe you should handle it."

"That's impossible." Russ snatched up the phone and called the bank. "This is Russ Manning, director of the NGA. I want to speak to your manager."

A man soon was on the line. "Yes, Mr. Manning, how can I help you today?"

"My secretary just informed me that two of our checks bounced. We have millions in that account, so how's that possible?"

"Hold on, Mr. Manning, while I check into it."

Ten minutes later the bank manager was back on the line. "Yes, Mr. Manning, according to our records, that account has been drained. Normally we'd transfer funds from the other NGA accounts, but their funds are also gone. The withdrawals were done electronically last night."

Russ jumped to his feet and yelled into the phone, "We didn't do that!"

"It seems legitimate, sir. The correct account numbers and passwords were used. Are you sure someone else in your organization didn't reallocate the funds?"

"It can't be done without my authorization. Where did the money go?"

"Oh, this could be a problem. The money was transferred into a Grand Cayman bank. Unfortunately those institutions don't conform to international banking laws. If you'd like to report the theft, the FBI will have to investigate, but finding and arresting the perpetrator might prove difficult. Those accounts are untraceable."

Russ hung up the phone on the verge of a panic attack. He gripped the desk and gasped for air before collapsing in the chair. The FBI wasn't needed. The culprit was Captain Nemo. By stealing the NGA funds, Roberts had jerked the teeth out of Russ's organization for slaughtering his wolves.

CHAPTER TWENTY-SEVEN

After his visit to Idaho, Christian returned to Mexico and hunkered down on his boat for the publicity tidal wave that Chief Tucker would unleash. It didn't take long. Within a week the story dominated the media. Charlie exposed the government fraud, the stealing of funds intended for the preservation of wolves, the payoffs, and the murders in the cover-up. The evidence further explained why the Secretary of the Interior James Sanders chose to commit suicide rather than face humiliation and prison.

The attorney general opened an investigation, and a Congressional committee was formed to explore the wrongdoing. The NGA emails, texts, and bank statements revealed an impressive list of politicians and agency heads who also received payoffs. As the investigators dug deeper, an even bigger scandal came to light. Hush money from oil, mining, and lumber companies had also been shoveled to the politicians and agencies. Under the Endangered Species Act, endangered animals and their habitat fall under federal protection. Remove the animals and protection, and a state can open the doors to drilling, mining, and logging in wildlife refuges, public lands, monuments, and parks.

Christian had started out to save wolves and disclose the hunters' greed for more game, but wolves were like canaries in the coal mine. Their deaths were a warning of the widespread corruption seeping into government at all levels. The heads were willing to sacrifice wildlife for money from big business. The investigation further divulged that some politicians owned land that couldn't be developed because of the endangered wildlife. Their move to wipe out the animals showed a clear conflict of interest. The sellout didn't stop on land. The corruption involved the oceans and the Gulf, where oil drilling was proposed off every US coastline, putting fragile sea life in jeopardy.

When the full scope of the scandal made headlines, the country rose up in a united front. Citizens from all backgrounds and parties were infuriated that their wild lands and animals were at risk, being sold off secretly to the highest bidders. Millions signed petitions, and protests broke out in every major city. The uproar motivated several congressmen to submit a bill that safeguarded wildlife. The ability to remove an animal from the Endangered Species List was given solely to researchers and scientists, taking that decision away from politicians and potentially crooked government agencies. State officials also felt the heat. The grizzly hunts outside of Yellowstone were immediately halted. Wolf killing was suspended. Even Christian was surprised. His cause and outcry to save wolves had started as a ripple and turned into a tsunami.

Chief Tucker faced a barrage of press interviews. When questioned where the scandal information came from, he had given credit to Captain Nemo. The revelation made Christian the most sought-after man on the planet. The media wanted him and his story.

Charlie also contacted the Washington police and turned over the boat video of Vern's confession. Vern worked for the secretary of the Interior and killed Barbara Davis and the analyst to cover up the fraud. Ralph, the FBI agent, further identified Vern as the man who shot him in the alley. With mounting evidence, the detectives reopened the Davis case. Vern's fingerprints had been found on an outside door to the government building, but they'd been dismissed because Christian was the prime suspect. The fingerprints then became relevant. A security guard, fearing implication, came clean. On the night of the Davis murder, Vern had paid him to get in a side door of the building, and then had him erase the video on the in-house surveillance cameras. The warrant for Christian's arrest was lifted, and the manhunt shifted to Vern.

Christian was also looking for Vern. He asked Sal and Bill to put out feelers in the underworld, and enlisted Steve to search the dark web for him. Christian wasn't worried about Vern. The guy was running for his life, so settling a score was probably the last thing on his mind. Still, Christian didn't relish glancing over his shoulder someday and seeing the big white-haired jerk. He wanted to wrap things up, end the ordeal, and move on.

The FBI no longer sought Christian for murder, but he was far from off the hook. He was wanted for questioning about the computer hacking that had uncovered the scandal. The online theft of funds from the NGA and hunting clubs was another case. Steve had covered their tracks and was confident that a felony charge would never stick. Despite the assurance, Christian intended to avoid the authorities. His attack on the government for his cause had created numerous adversaries, people who had the power to manufacture trumped-up charges and put him away forever.

For several weeks he kept a low profile on his sloop, socializing daily with Jose and the Mexican fishermen at the little marina. The gang in town occasionally visited, and Steve kept him updated with the Internet news about his wolf cause. Initially Christian was high-fiving and loving it. He had accomplished his goal and saved not only wolves but countless other endangered creatures.

The trouble with Christian, he was his own worst enemy. The exciting rush of plotting, manipulation, and pressure to undertake a cause while remaining free and alive dwindled, replaced with quiet days of soul-searching. When searching, he found demons. Horrific nightmares of killing or being killed tortured his sleep. His daytime hours weren't much better. Some mornings he lacked the energy to rise off his bed, and his appetite declined. Food just wasn't appealing. Depression, like an unwanted visitor, had returned. Homesickness added to his gloom. He missed Florida, his grandparents, and horses, but going home was impossible. Everyone was looking for him, and some days he felt like a paranoid cat in a dark alley, jumping at every sound and shadow.

Today he woke after enduring another restless night and made a decision. To stop the downward spiral, he needed to breathe new air into his life. On the open sea he could relax and not have to deal with anyone. A voyage might get him back on track. It had worked before.

He slipped into a pair of cutoffs and went topside to take in the small cove that had become a temporary home. Most of the boats had left for a day of fishing, but he spotted the old man on his newly refurbished skiff. Christian had spent days patching, sanding, and painting the dilapidated boat to make it look new. He meandered down the rickety docks for a chat. As usual the conversation was mostly one-sided. Christian talked and the old guy with limited English nodded and smiled.

"Later," Christian said to him and rose when Jose's pickup pulled into the lot. He strolled into the marina office and told Jose his plans.

In mid-sip, Jose lowered his coffee cup. "Tomorrow? So soon?" he asked.

"Yeah, it's time I go."

Jose shook his head, "You will be missed, especially by my little chicas. They love you very much."

Christian sighed. "I love them, too. Maybe someday I'll come back. Never know where the wind might take me."

"You must say goodbye to them. Come to my house for dinner tonight."

Christian agreed and returned to his sailboat to dress. In jeans, a loose shirt, and sandals, he drove the motorcycle into Playa del Carmen for more farewells. He entered the swanky neighborhood and pulled into the driveway of Steve's rented house. Lowering the kickstand, he flung the hair from his eyes and wondered if he'd ever see these people again. Others who had helped him along the way had become only memories. A terrorist couldn't afford long-term friendships. It wasn't good for all involved.

He stepped inside and was met with silence. Through the sliding glass doors he saw his companions in the backyard, Steve and Karen swimming in the pool, and Frankie and Angel sitting at a shaded patio table. He opened the glass door and stepped out. "Y'all soaking up the sun?"

"Christian, we weren't expecting you," Karen said with a grin. "You're just in time for lunch."

"Mr. Roberts, take my chair," Angel said, leaping out of his seat. "We're drinking margaritas. Can I fix you one?"

"No thanks, but I'll take a soda." Christian said. He knew that liquor made his depression and PTSD worse. He sat down and petted Karen's new little dog that pawed at his legs.

"We're glad to see you, but surprised," Steve said after climbing out of the pool. "I thought you were afraid of being spotted here."

"Yeah, screw that. Time to leave my puddle hideout," Christian said. He reached up and thanked Angel for the Coke. He took a sip and stared at the dog. "Besides, it doesn't matter anymore. I'm leaving in the morning on the high tide."

For a moment speechless mouths parted.

Steve finally said, "That's, that's kind of sudden, Christian."

"I've never been one for long goodbyes."

"But why are you going?" asked Karen.

Christian smiled. "Just don't do well sitting idle. And Captain Nemo has become a hot ticket item with a large reward. Eventually someone will leak to the cops or press that I'm here. I've also pissed off plenty of people who'd love to get their hands on me. It's better, safer, really, if I keep moving."

"That's probably smart," said Frankie, "but where will you go?"

Christian leaned back and breathed deeply. "When I got married, my wife and I set off on a long cruise through the Caribbean, planning to island hop and kick back in friendly little bars." He looked down with the painful revelation. "She was killed a few weeks into the trip. I've often thought about finishing that voyage. Maybe it'll bring me some peace." Realizing he had disclosed too much, he grinned. "Besides, pull into a port, and women flock to a guy with a big sailboat."

"Give me a break," Frankie said, "As if you need a boat to get women."

"What about Captain Nemo and your animal causes?" Karen asked.

"Nemo needs to retire."

"You can't mean that, Christian," she said.

"Right now I'm done, burnt out, but if I have a change of heart, I can always find another critter to help. But enough about me. What are your plans?"

"It sure as shittin' ain't sitting around on a rocking boat, sweating," said Frankie. "That's not a fat man's idea of fun. These kids don't need me anymore, so I'm off to New York in a day or two. I miss the cool weather, pizza, and attitude."

"Same here," said Angel. "I gotta get back to the old neighborhood and take care of business."

"What about you two?" Christian asked Karen and Steve. "Are you going back to Arlington and rebuild your house?"

Karen looked at Steve and smiled. "Should we tell them?"

Steve hung a towel around his neck. "We spoke to the real estate agent about this place and made an offer. We love Mexico and are staying."

"Congrats," said Christian. "Now I'll know where to find a good hacker."

"Speaking of hacking," said Steve. "There's a little article online about those conservation groups that received the huge anonymous donations. They're putting the NGA's money to good use, buying land for wildlife and setting up research labs. But Christian, this is the cool part. They know you're Captain Nemo and responsible for saving the wolves. They probably also figured you're behind the donated money. A wolf sanctuary is erecting a life-size bronze statue of you with a wolf."

"That's bullshit," Christian grumbled. "I'm a damn criminal, a terrorist. I don't deserve crap."

"You're wrong," said Karen. "You're a hero who fought corruption and avenged wildlife."

"Here, here," said Frankie, lifting his glass in a toast. "To our lone-wolf terrorist; may he have a long, happy life."

Christian rolled his eyes. "Y'all know most statues are erected to dead people?"

After lunch Christian left for the marina to prepare the sloop for the voyage. The water and gas tanks had to be topped off, and his new cell phone needed charging. Sal and Bill were the only ones who had the number and only because they might find Vern. Once Vern was eliminated, Christian intended to toss all communication overboard and cut himself off from the world.

He finished readying the boat and checked his supplies. He patted the hatch deck and said, "Okay, girl, I think we're good to go." Out of habit, he talked to his boats. He entered the cabin to get ready for dinner with Jose's family. Rubbing his mouth and jaw, he thought *One more night, one more obligation, and the show's over.* He put on a pretty good act, concealing from friends his inner torment. But tomorrow was a new day.

He took a shower, shaved off the beard stubble, and put on a silk Tommy Bahama shirt and jeans. His adopted Mexican family had seen only the scruffy boat bum in stained T-shirts and ragged cutoffs. On his last night with them, he wanted to look decent, for a change. Hearing Jose calling him from the seawall, he stepped onto the deck.

Jose's eyes brightened. "Amigo, you amaze me how you change your looks."

"Got a date with three beautiful girls."

"I will be unable to keep them off you. My wife says dinner will be ready in an hour."

"I'll be there."

After Jose left for his truck, Christian went below to the front berth and removed the wooden slats to his hidden boat compartment. Pushing aside his revolver, bank book, and fake passport, he retrieved the paper bag of money and stuffed the bundles of bills into a small tote. Slinging the bag over a shoulder, he went ashore. The small fleet had returned to its slips, but there wasn't a soul in sight. He'd hoped to say *hasta la vista* to the fishermen, but they'd apparently gone for the day.

The sun was setting on the Yucatan horizon when he moseyed to the seafood warehouse and his parked 350 Honda. Removing its key out of a pocket, he had second thoughts about riding the half mile to Jose's house. *Don't need this sucker anymore.* He walked into the office and placed the key on the desk. Jose had mentioned that he'd love to have a motorcycle someday, and the bike would only be in the way on the sloop.

He left the marina and strolled down the shell-covered road with a strong gulf breeze in his face. Through the thick mangrove forest that encroached on both sides of the lane, he smelled the salt and seaweed from the nearby bayou. With a mix of sea, jungle, and good people, the place had been perfect for Christian, and he would have loved to remain. But it wasn't realistic for a man on the run.

Approaching the house, he saw several old cars and trucks parked along the road. More were in a vacant lot next to Jose's little white house. Christian halted, seeing thirty-something people in the front yard. Boards and fish boxes served as tables laden with Mexican dishes, and over them, twinkling lights were strung through the trees.

Jose's eight-year-old daughter caught sight of him and screeched his name. She raced to him and hugged his waist. The crowd turned and cheered. Christian was taken aback. He had expected a quiet dinner, not a party.

"Margaret, what's going on?" Christian asked, stroking her silky black hair.

"Fiesta for you," she said.

Jose hustled to him. "You snuck up on us. We thought we would hear the approach of your motorcycle, but come, come. You are the guest of honor."

"Why?" Christian asked.

Jose grimaced at the question. "You should know. You have helped everyone here, worked on their boats and unloaded their catch, but more important, you rid us of an evil man. You arrived as a stranger, a tall, quiet American, but have become part of us. This is our way of showing we will miss you."

Christian awkwardly massaged his neck. "I don't know what to say."

"There is nothing to say, Christian. Your actions and good heart tell all," Jose pressed his back, and Margaret tugged on his hand, urging him to follow. He recognized the fishermen and assumed the women and children were their families. He'd sworn off drinking, but accepted a goblet of sangria. With handshakes, hugs, and pats on the back, he smiled, but behind the grin was sadness. He'd miss them, too.

The eating, drinking, and laughter ended around midnight. After the guests left, Christian gave Jose the small tote bag.

"What is this?"

"A gift," said Christian.

Jose stared into the bag at the bundles of US currency. His expression turned from curiosity to shock. "Why are you doing this?"

"Two things. You knew I was a wanted man, but instead of turning me in, you protected me. Also I do love your girls. They're probably the closest thing I'll ever have to daughters. There's several hundred thousand in that bag, and I want you to put some of it aside for their college educations."

Tears ran down Jose's cheeks. He trembled and pulled Christian into a bear hug. "Thank you. Thank you, my friend."

Early the next morning Christian and Jose had coffee in the warehouse office, waiting for the nine o'clock high tide. The sloop had a deep shaft, and in a shallow low tide it might get stuck in the bayou when he motored out to the Gulf.

Jose noticed the key on his desk. "What is this?"

"You wanted a bike," said Christian. "Now you've got one."

"You have already done too much."

"Where I'm going, I won't need it. Just be careful on the damn thing."

Jose grinned and stuffed the key into his pocket. "When you first came and said you didn't want your passport checked, I thought about calling the police. Lucky for me I needed the money for your boat slip."

Christian chuckled. "Yeah, I saw the uncertainty in your eyes, but I'm a gambler. I was bettin' on you."

The fishermen began arriving at the marina, but before departing the cove in their boats, they stopped in and again bid Christian good luck on his journey. The last to leave the marina in his boat was the little old man. As usual he didn't say a word, just clasped Christian's hand and gave him a nod.

Christian saw Frankie's black SUV pull into the lot. "Christ, I've already said adios to them," he muttered, watching Karen, Steve, and the two men pile out. He walked out of the warehouse and greeted them. "What's up, guys?"

"Oh, good," said Karen. "You're still here. We were afraid you might've already left."

"Yeah, Karen had me driving like a maniac to get here," said Frankie. "She just had to talk to you once more."

Christian looked at his watch. "Well, you're here just in time. I'm fixin' to go in ten minutes."

Karen embraced him and cried into his T shirt and chest. "Christian, I woke with the most terrible feeling, like I'll never see you again. Please don't go."

Christian lifted her chin and smiled down at her. "Come on now; never is a long time. You'll see me again. If I take up another cause, I'll need Steve's help."

Steve scratched his head. "She's been going on about it, pretty upset and emphatic. You know, female intuition and all. She thinks something bad might happen to you."

Christian took a breath and gazed soberly at each face. He then smiled. "She's right. It's gonna be bad if I don't leave on this tide. My sloop will get hung up on an oyster bed, and I'll be screwed."

Thankfully Jose walked up and saved him from the drama. "Christian, you must go now. If you wait, the next high tide is in twelve hours, and you will navigate in the dark."

Christian kissed Karen's forehead. "Don't worry. I'll be okay. I'll drop you a postcard from the next port." He weathered more handshakes and hugs before climbing aboard the sloop

At the helm he fired up the diesel engine while Jose freed the sailboat's bow and aft lines.

"Y'all take care," Christian called and pulled away from the seawall. Unable to sail in the narrow channel, he motored out of the cove. He glanced back and waved to his friends as the sloop rounded a bend in the bayou, and the mangroves blocked his view of the marina. He turned back, facing the bow, and glimpsed the shimmering Gulf up ahead that enticed him like a lover. He'd soon be where he belonged. His mood brightened. His anguish turned into optimism.

On a high branch a white heron stood overlooking the slow-moving sailboat on the narrow waterway, but the bird squawked and fled into the sky, startled when Christian's sloop exploded and burst into flames.

CHAPTER TWENTY-EIGHT

Dave Wheeler wiped the sweat from his brow and walked into the small Miami restaurant. A blast of the delicious cooled air hit his face as his eyes adjusted from the bright sunlight to the darkened room. Sitting down on a familiar bar stool, he commented to those beside him, "Darned hot out there today."

A guy with a roofing company logo on his shirt replied, "Try working in it. Fucking brutal on them shingles."

"I can imagine." Dave called to the bartender. "Jack, I'll take a beer."

"You got it." Jack filled a cold mug with draft beer and set it on the bar. "Catch any today?"

Dave had often heard the question throughout his career. Had he caught a criminal? Today's inquiry, however, pertained to fish. "Afraid not," he said with a smile. "I get plenty of nibbles, but when I reel in my shrimp, it's gone. I'm not much of a fisherman."

"Pinfish," said the roofer. "They'll wipe you out of bait. If you're on a grass flat, get rid of the weight and use a cork. Also try a smaller hook."

The conversation turned to fishing with the customers adding their two cents. Dave explained he was newly retired and had recently purchased a nineteen-foot runabout that was stored in the boatyard up the street. To keep the socializing comfortable, he didn't mention he'd been an FBI agent. Initially he had missed the challenging Bureau work, but was relieved now to be free of the stress. His daily routine consisted of going out on the water every morning, fishing a little, and come here for lunch to cool off and yap with the bartender and patrons. He also enjoyed spending more time with his daughter and soon-to-be son-in-law. Grandchildren might be on the horizon.

Jack set down Dave's Cuban sandwich and chips and lifted his empty mug. "Refill?"

"Yeah, thanks," Dave said, picking up half the sandwich. He glanced at the muted overhead TV that was always tuned to Fox News. He had started to take a bite when the screen displayed the burnt-out shell of a good-sized boat half sunk alongside mangroves. The caption read, "Christian Roberts, alias Captain Nemo, was killed on his sailboat in Mexico."

Dave lowered the sandwich and rose. "Jack, could you turn that up?"

A photo of Christian appeared on the screen. The newscaster said Roberts's sloop had exploded and the Playa del Carman authorities had yet to determine if the cause was accidental or intentional. Christian Roberts was suspected of being Captain Nemo, well known for his terrorist attacks to save sharks and wolves and also was responsible for uncovering the huge scandal that still gripped Washington, DC.

When the newscast ended, Dave sank back on stool and pushed his plate and beer aside. "Jack, give me a scotch on the rocks." The report was upsetting but no surprise. Christian had played with fire, creating a lot of enemies with his causes, and was bound to get burned. Dave stepped away from the bar to an unoccupied corner and placed a call. "I just saw it on the news."

"I was going to call you," said Ralph.

"Goddamn it, Ralph. He's an American citizen. The FBI should be handling the investigation, not the Mexicans."

"Hold on. We're on it. Several agents flew down, but their early reports aren't promising. The boat was an empty shell by the time they examined it for evidence. Also the explosion happened at high tide, and the outgoing tide washed almost everything out into the

Gulf. Even Roberts's body has yet to be recovered. And they're still unsure if it was murder."

"I can tell you now. It's a homicide. Christian was never careless, and he knew too much about boats for it to be a mishap. Someone planted a bomb and killed him."

"You're probably right, but proving it won't be easy. Roberts had so damn many people after him. Just consider all the politicians he just took down. It's hard to know where to start."

"They haven't found his body. Maybe he wasn't on the boat."

"He was on it. Several witnesses saw him guiding the boat down the bayou right before it blew up. I'm really sorry, Dave. I know you liked him."

"He was my nemeses and deserved to be locked up, but doggone it. I enjoyed his company and admired the son of a bitch. He definitely left his mark."

"I keep thinking about how he saved you and me," said Ralph. "As long as I live, I'll never understand him. Why did he help me escape from Sanders's man?"

"He stepped in because it was the right thing to do. Despite the Nemo façade, he still was a decent guy. Sadly, the lines blurred between right and wrong when his wife was murdered. One sure thing, he was controversial. People either hated or loved him."

"He definitely aggravated me, but I wish now I could've bought him a drink and thanked him."

"Everyone has regrets," said Dave. "Listen, if you learn anything new, I'd appreciate a call." He slipped his phone into a pocket and dwelled on Christian the night he stood on that dark Miami Beach and explained his priorities. If he had kids someday, he didn't want them growing up with oceans depleted of sharks. Saving them was more crucial than his life. He succeeded, but probably knew back then he'd die for his convictions. *I'm going to miss him.*

Several weeks later Dave learned about a memorial service for Christian Roberts that would be held in Sarasota, Florida. His remains were never found, so there would be no funeral. The Mexican authorities closed their investigation, and lacking the evidence, couldn't conclude if Christian died accidentally or was murdered. The FBI divers searched the sandy bottom of the bayou, but came up only with an old .38 revolver. His death was headed for the cold-case files unless someone talked.

On the morning of the service, Dave opened the bedroom closet and removed a dark suit that he hadn't touched since his days as an agent. He brushed off some lint, and it occurred to him that Christian had eluded him, even in death.

He dressed and left Miami for Sarasota. The Roberts family was unsure of the number who might attend, so the service was being held in the park on City Island. He arrived in downtown Sarasota and drove out to the keys. On the Ringling Bridge, he looked north across the bay to City Island and the sailboats anchored offshore. The memorial place fit the man.

On Bird Key he saw cars parked alongside the road and filling the small waterfront park. Scores of people marched on the sidewalk and grass toward City Island. He expected a few hundred mourners, but Christian's notoriety had brought thousands. Some carried flowers or held signs that read, "Thank you, Captain Nemo." They were fans, rather than acquaintances or friends.

Dave drove across the smaller second bridge to St. Armands Key and found it jammed with traffic. Police cars with blinking lights dotted the route to control the congestion. He managed to locate a parking spot on the grassy median across from the Sarasota Yacht Club. The memorial service on City Island was several miles away, but probably already full of cars.

A large NBC media van with a satellite dish zipped past. The press couldn't get enough of Christian, even in death. With a head shake, Dave crossed the road and joined the procession that lined the Australian pines.

In front of him a group of young people wore the same blue T-shirt with the Ocean Conservancy logo on the back. Two of the girls clung to each other's shoulders and wept. Behind him, others displayed Defenders of Wildlife shirts. Christian's memorial service had attracted environmentalists and wildlife lovers from near and far, all there to pay homage to the man.

Dave had walked a block when a long black limo pulled up to the curb and a man called out, "Hey, Wheeler, can I give ya a lift?"

He smiled, seeing Sal's big head and black curls sticking out the car window. "Sure," he said, and climbed in. Besides Sal, six other men were in the limo, all Italian, all in expensive black suits. They were obviously Sal's crew. Only Christian could bring an FBI man and the mob together in harmony.

"Hell of a fucking day, ain't it?" Sal said while the limo continued down the road. "I always figured the Kid would outlive me."

"He died too young," said Dave, "but he chose a destructive path."

"True, but he did a lot a good." Sal glanced out the window at the crowds. "Look at this fucking circus. These people didn't even know him, not like you and me, but they're here crying their eyes out."

"People don't have to know a man to grieve his loss. In their minds, he was a hero."

"That he was. The Florida Boy was one brave fucker," Sal said with melancholy.

Dave turned to another matter. "Do you know who killed him, Sal?"

"It was a boat accident."

"Come on. I'm not with the FBI anymore."

"But you still got their ear."

"I'm asking for personal reasons. I cared about Christian."

"Yeah, and for some crazy reason, the Kid liked you."

"That's why I want the guilty party caught and punished."

Sal took a cigar from his jacket pocket and lit it. "Don't worry about it, Wheeler. Our boy will get justice. I'll guarantee it."

* * *

In the Arizona foothills near the Mexican border, Vern scratched his new beard and propped up his feet on a rickety chair in the one-room hunting cabin. The remote place had a gas generator that ran the refrigerator, but other than that, it had few conveniences. He had the money to hide out comfortably in a foreign country, but despite his beard and dark dyed hair, he'd obviously be an American and stand out in a population. He was safer as a recluse in the US wilderness.

Earlier that day he had driven twenty miles on the back roads to a rundown shopping strip and bought gas for the generator, a few supplies, a six-pack of beer, and the daily paper. On such trips he wore gloves to prevent prints and never left anything behind that might carry his DNA.

He returned to the cabin, popped a beer can, and opened the newspaper. "Assholes, idolizing that punk," he muttered while reading about the massive crowd of twenty thousand at Christian Roberts's memorial service. "They conveniently forgot that little bastard was a killer." The article also said the Mexicans had ended their investigation of the boat explosion, unable to conclude the cause.

He then read that a conservation group had erected a bronze statue of Roberts at a wolf sanctuary. Disgusted, he crumpled the paper and tossed it into a trashcan.

A knock on the door brought Vern swiftly to his feet, afraid the cops had found him. He peeked out the window and then relaxed on seeing Hagan, Russ's little British assassin. He opened the door. "You scared the shit out of me. I didn't hear you drive up."

"Using a hybrid," said the Englishman. "The battery is noiseless."

Vern glanced past him to make sure he was alone and said, "Well, come in."

Hagan stepped inside. "I see you dyed your white hair and grew a beard." He grinned, looking around the shambled tiny cabin. "Nice place," he mocked. "With the million I gave you, I'd a thought you'd have it better."

"It's called lying low, but how did you find me?"

"I had an advantage over the police. They didn't know you'd left DC in Roberts's rented Corvette. I tracked the car to Mississippi, where you dumped it. From there it was only a matter of showing your picture around. A used-car salesman where you bought the truck recognized you. I got the fake name you're using on the credit card. You should have paid cash this morning for your beer."

"All right, you went to all that trouble. What do you want?"

"I'm here about Christian Roberts."

"The son of a bitch is dead. Haven't you heard? If you'd done your job in DC and shot Roberts, he wouldn't have given the incriminating tape to the cops, and I wouldn't be hiding out in this shit hole. He was a gift, tied up and helpless in a car trunk. What happened? Why didn't you kill him?"

"I'd never harm Christian," the guy said without a British accent and pulled a Beretta out from under his jacket. Aiming the weapon at Vern, he said. "You see, I loved Christian very much, but you rigged that bomb on his boat and took him from me."

"Now wait just a damn minute," Vern said, just before being shot in the head.

* * *

Mary Lou, her husband George, and four others bounced around on the backseats of canvas-cover caravan Jeep while it traversed the dried-out African ravines, potholes, and rocks. Their black guide drove slowly, pointing out the wildlife along the way. The landscape was brown, with dead grass and sparse, thorny trees. Mary Lou's face, hair, and clothing were covered with dust, but she didn't care. In Ohio she had saved and planned for their safari trip. Despite the heat, drought, and griping husband, she was enjoying the vacation.

"Look, George, I see some zebras behind those bushes," she exclaimed. "The poor things, what could they possibly be eating?"

"Yeah, yeah," said George. He reached over the driver seat and tapped the guide's shoulder. "Hey, any chance of watching football tonight on TV?"

"No, sir," said the guide. "Only BBC news."

George sat back and complained. "No Bud, no sports, and the air conditioner in our room sucks. And I've got another five days of this shit. Mary Lou, for the money we could be living like kings in Florida."

"We've been to Florida numerous times, and I wanted to see Africa and its wildlife.

"You can see them in a damn zoo."

"Oh, George, that would be terrible if these animals survived only in zoos. Besides, this is a real adventure."

"It's a damn nightmare."

A loud bang came from the engine, and steam shot out from under the hood. The guide cursed in his native tongue and pulled over to the roadside.

"Shit!" George exclaimed. "I'm betting it's the radiator or a hose."

The guide stepped out of the Jeep and lifted the dusty hood. Pushing his hat back, he scratched his head and stared at the steaming engine.

"George, you know about mechanics. Get out and help the man."

"Shit!" George repeated and climbed out. He and the guide looked under the hood and shook their heads.

The guide took out his phone and pressed some keys, which resulted in more headshaking. Dust devils twirled in the road ahead as George climbed into the shaded Jeep and retook his seat. "I was right, cracked radiator, and there's no cell service out here. Thanks for the shitty adventure, Mary Lou."

The guide stood next to the driver's seat and faced his passengers. "I am sorry, ladies and gentlemen, but our vehicle is overheating. I can use water in the cooler to prevent the motor from locking up, but it is not enough to make it back to the lodge. There also is no cell service here, but a small road ahead leads to a village. It is about six miles. I am told this village has Internet, so I can contact the lodge. It will send another vehicle to pick you up." He sat down in the driver's seat, restarted engine, and proceeded down the road.

"There goes dinner," said George.

They traveled a mile and reached the turnoff onto the small road that resembled a dried-up riverbed. The engine bearings were screeching as the guide turned off the ignition. After the engine cooled for a half hour, he added water from the cooler to the radiator and continued toward the village. They had to stop two more times and repeat the process.

George was too angry to speak. He sat huffed up with a frozen frown. Mary Lou, however, remained optimistic. Preferring excitement to the mundane tourist venture, she looked forward to seeing the remote village. The wildlife here also seemed more abundant. While the engine cooled, five elephants had strolled past, and a lioness trotting through the brush.

In the late afternoon they arrived at the village, and just in time. The water had run out a mile back. The guide hurried from the jeep to contact the lodge. Mary Lou remained seated while George and other passengers stepped out to stretch and recover from the bumpy ride. They gathered under a shaded tree and held a communal bitch fest. Mary Lou heard their ranting about being inconvenienced.

She turned away and focused on a dozen or so children who were huddled in a circle on a field. From the center of the circle a soccer ball was tossed into the air. When the children scattered to chase and kick it, she saw the thrower. A lanky white man rose from a half-kneeling position. Looking at her and the jeep through sunglasses, he moved off the field to duck behind a hut. A minute later he appeared on a galloping horse and disappeared into the rough.

She left the Jeep and walked to George and the others. "Did you see him, the man on horseback?"

George frowned. "What are you talking about, Mary Lou?"

Before she could elaborate, the guide returned to the group and announced, "Another vehicle will be here within two hours. The lodge will have your dinner waiting."

Intrigued with the horseman, Mary Lou pulled the guide aside. "I just saw a tall white man on a horse. Who is he?"

"You are mistaken," said the guide. "Except for your group, there are no white men in this village."

"I saw him clearly," Mary Lou insisted. "He was a striking young man with a blond ponytail, and he rode off on a dark-brown horse."

The guide hailed one of the village elders, and they spoke for several minutes in their native language. The elder clapped his hands, did a swooshing signal, and walked away.

"Well?" Mary Lou asked.

"He says you saw a ghost."

"He wasn't a ghost. Ask those children out there. He was playing soccer with them."

The guide sighed. "They would deny it. The villagers do not speak of him, but I have heard tales about a yellow-haired American who travels on a horse and visits the villages in the area."

"But why the secrecy?"

"It is said he pays these people to protect their wildlife and has put a large bounty on the heads of poachers. The rumors also say he burned down a hunting lodge ten miles away and caused the disappearance of a foreign trophy hunter and his two guides who sought lions here. The bodies of the three men were never found."

"My god, that's murder."

"There is no proof of murder or that this American exists, but the game wardens have reported that the elephants, giraffe, and big cats are thriving again. None have been killed because the hunters and poachers stay away. They believe the stories and fear this man."

"I see," Mary Lou said slowly. The guide left her, and she stared out across the tall savanna grass, wondering if she should tell George or anyone else about the elusive horseman who defended the animals. Maybe she had been mistaken. Perhaps he was a ghost.

About The Author

Susan Klaus is an author of award-winning and bestselling fantasies and thrillers. She was listed in Amazon's Top 100 Authors of Mystery/Romance. Tor Books released her fantasy, *Flight of the Golden Harpy*, a Royal Palm Literary Award Winner for Best Science Fiction. The sequel, *Flight of the Golden Harpy II, Waylaid* also won the R.P.L.A for Best Fantasy.

Her first Christian Roberts thriller was *Secretariat Reborn*, released by Oceanview Publishing and won the Silver Presidential Award for Best Adult Florida Fiction.. Its sequel, *Shark Fin Soup*, also won the RPLA for Second Best Unpublished Thriller and the Silver Presidential Award for Best Action/Suspense. So far, *Wolf in the Crosshairs* is a Bronze President Award Winner for Best Thriller and won the International Thrill Writers Contest for Best First Sentence..

Klaus is the president/founder of Sarasota Authors Connection Club, with over 200 members. For nine years, she was the radio host and producer of the Authors Connection Show with 18 million listeners in 48 countries. She has had an extensive career with animals; owner of pet and grooming shops, worked 10 years for a veterinarian, raised and showed Himalayan cats, and breed and raced Thoroughbred horses for 15 years.

She was born in Sarasota, Fl. and resides in Myakka City, Fl. on a 40-acre farm, where she currently raises rodeo bulls.

Website: susanklaus.com

On Facebook: Susan C. Klaus

On Twitter: Klaussue

www.ingramcontent.com/pod-product-compliance
Lightning Source LLC
Chambersburg PA
CBHW030552260626
47157CB00006B/2285